Taken for English

VALLEY OF CHOICE BOOK 3

OLIVIA NEWPORT

Valley of Choice series

Accidentally Amish
In Plain View
Taken for English

Print ISBN 978-1-61626-714-8

eBook Editions:
Adobe Digital Edition (.epub) 978-1-62836-383-8
Kindle and MobiPocket Edition (.prc) 978-1-62836-384-5

All scripture quotations are taken from the King James Version of the Bible.

This book is a work of fiction. Names, characters, places, and incidents are either products of the author's imagination or used fictitiously. Any similarity to actual people, organizations, and/or events is purely coincidental.

Cover design: Müllerhaus Publishing Arts, Inc., www.Mullerhaus.net

Published by Barbour Publishing, Inc., P.O. Box 719, Uhrichsville, Ohio 44683, www.barbourbooks.com

Our mission is to publish and distribute inspirational products offering exceptional value and biblical encouragement to the masses.

ecpa Member of the Evangelical Christian Publishers Association

Printed in the United States of America.

Dedication

For my siblings, because of the host of characters they are and the ones they inspire.

Acknowledgments

Writing is often solitary, but I do not find it lonely. I bump into too many people on the road between idea and book to feel lonely.

The largest portion of this story came into being on Saturday mornings at a local coffee shop, with my friend Erin sitting across the table crafting her own story.

Rachelle shares her favorite books with me. Since she has terrific taste, reading these books propels me toward writing more, writing better, writing swiftly.

My family grounds me in reality while also understanding my need to withdraw to another world.

I was working on this manuscript when *Accidentally Amish*, the first in this series, released and I began to hear from readers. If I started to lag, their enthusiasm thrust me back into the game. I admit I was not quite prepared for this particular experience, but I am thankful for the cause and effect.

One

A siren screamed down the highway. Ruth Beiler turned her head half an inch toward the sound, catching the reflex before curiosity about events outside her family's home could distract her from the solemn occasion before her eyes. In a minute, the congregation would sing another hymn from the *Ausbund* and Ruth would savor every note. No matter how many times she went to an *English* church in Colorado Springs, her heart yearned for the plaintive rhythm of the Amish hymns she had grown up with. Music should have space to think, to reflect, to absorb.

And after the hymn and a prayer would come the moment that had Ruth's heart beating fast today.

Annalise Friesen was presenting herself for baptism. Joining the Amish church. This should be all Rufus needed to formally ask Annalise to marry him. If he did not, Ruth intended to have a firm conversation with her older brother.

Ruth glanced at Rufus seated across the aisle with the men. He was twenty-nine and still clean shaven—unmarried. Anyone outside the community might have thought that the small boy next to Rufus was his son, but Jacob was their littlest brother.

Next to Ruth, her mother shifted slightly in her chair, leaning forward. Normally the Beiler women chose to sit toward the back of the congregation of about sixty people, especially when the faithful gathered in their own home. But this day was different. Eli Beiler sat with bearded men at the front of the assembly on the men's side of the aisle. Rufus sat farther back, with the unmarried men, but he had taken a seat on the aisle where he could see well, with Jacob and Joel next to him. Ruth sat with her mother, Franey, and her sisters Lydia and Sophie toward the front, where they could see well but not seem ostentatious.

Because Annalise was being baptized.

Heaviness pressed against Ruth's efforts to breathe. They would not speak of it, but she was sure her mother would be remembering the same event, the fall baptism service, almost three years ago.

Ruth had knelt before the bishop as Annalise was doing today. And during the prayer preceding the baptism, with all heads bowed and eyes closed, she slipped out.

Just left. Ran. Hid. Rode with an *English* man to a bus stop and moved to Colorado Springs, where she was now a student in the university's school of nursing.

Ruth had briefly considered not being present for Annalise's baptism, but her mother would remember Ruth's baptism day whether Ruth was there or not. This was a day of joy for her dearest friend! Ruth did not want to miss a moment.

Another siren shrieked on the main highway that ran past the Beiler property outside Westcliffe, Colorado. In Colorado Springs, two sirens could mean anything. Emergency medical technicians answering a 911 call. A police car chasing a speeder. Fire trucks on the way to a kitchen grease fire. When she was driving, Ruth got out of the way of the emergency vehicles but otherwise went about her own business.

Among Custer County's thin population, sirens were rare.

Ruth heard the slight rustles behind her. Others had noticed the sirens and looked at each other, wondering.

The bishop began his prayer for the baptismal candidates.

Ruth bowed her head but kept her eyes open and watched Annalise.

Annie's heart pounded.

Not out of doubt. Not out of fear. Not with regret.

Until now she had only imagined what it might be like to truly belong to the community of the Amish. She had lived in Westcliffe for more than a year, worshiping with these families every other Sunday. Nothing in her home off Main Street ran on electricity. She had given her car to Ruth Beiler months ago. Her quilt was almost finished. Jeans and T-shirts had gone to a thrift shop in favor of the Amish dresses she had learned to sew for herself.

But this moment. This would make it all real and true and lasting. Anyone who thought she was just playing house the Amish way might drop their jaws, but Annie was going through with this.

Pressing her lips together, Annie tried to focus on the bishop's prayer. Her German still had a way to go, but she picked out the main themes. Faith. Commitment. Vows.

Annie's scalp itched under her prayer *kapp*. She ignored the sensation. The prayer ended, and she let her eyes rise enough to see what was happening. The bishop moved to the first of the baptismal candidates. Annie was one of four and the only one well out of her teen years. The deacon followed the bishop closely, carrying a wooden bucket of water. Behind him was the bishop's wife.

One by one the candidates answered the baptismal questions and made their vows.

"Do you believe and confess that Jesus Christ is God's Son?

"Do you believe and trust that you are united with a Christian church of the Lord, and do you promise obedience to God and the church?

"Do you renounce the devil, the world, and the lustfulness of your flesh and commit yourself to Christ and His church?

"Do you promise to live by the *Ordnung* of the church and to help administer them according to Christ's Word and teaching, and to abide by the truth you have accepted, thereby to live and thereby to die with help of the Lord?"

When Annie gave her final vow, the bishop's wife removed her head covering. The bishop dipped a cup into the water bucket and poured the water into his hand then poured it on Annie's head three times, in the name of the Father, the Son, and the Holy Ghost.

"Rise," the bishop said, "and be a faithful member of the church."

Annie accepted the hand of the bishop's wife, stood, turned, and grinned at the Beiler family.

A siren blared. The third one.

Rufus Beiler could not take his violet-blue eyes off Annalise.

She was a resolute woman. Whatever she decided to do, she did with her whole self. When she spoke her vows, he believed her. Even her posture had taken on a new demeanor in the weeks of her baptismal instruction. In Amish garments, she no longer looked uncertain about how to move around efficiently and gracefully. Her gray eyes and keen mind absorbed detail after detail about Amish life, and her actions moved from awkward imitation of the patterns she observed to fluid heartfelt expression of inward conviction.

Though she had come to them from the *English* world, Annalise Friesen was one of the truest people Rufus had ever known.

And the only woman he had ever loved.

The final hymn began, its tempo slightly faster as an expression of joy. The words emerged from Rufus's mind without the assistance of the hymnal, and he sang with robust belief.

In the few seconds of silence between the final note of the hymn and the bishop's first words of benediction, Rufus heard the footsteps on the front porch. A form crossed the curtainless wide window and paused.

An *English* form. Rufus did not catch enough of the movement to recognize the visitor. It was someone with the good sense not to burst into an Amish worship service, yet a messenger of urgent news. For no other reason would one of the *English* of Westcliffe approach an Amish worship service in progress.

The bishop's voice faded. The service was over. Rufus's glance bounced between Annalise and the front door.

Annalise. Of course Annalise. He moved toward her even as the congregation pressed around her with their congratulations. Many in the community harbored doubt. Rufus knew that much from overhearing tidbits of conversation not meant for his ears. "You have to be born Amish," they said.

Yet Annalise had made the same promises as the three teenagers who had been born Amish. In God's eyes, there was no distinction.

Rufus was tall enough to look over the heads of most of the gathering and catch Annalise's gray eyes. They brightened, and he knew the smile that raised her lips at that moment was meant for him. A strand of hair fell loose from her braided bun, as it always did. He hoped it always would.

He turned when someone tugged on the elbow of his black jacket.

"It's Tom Reynolds," his brother Joel said. "He says it's urgent. He's waiting on the porch."

Rufus glanced again at Annalise and then maneuvered through the congregation toward the front door. The living room windows were open to the fine September day, but the volume of the interior conversations dropped when he stepped out and closed the door behind him.

"What is it, Tom?" Rufus had counted three sirens.

"One of Karl Kramer's houses just burned."

The air went out of Rufus.

"It's the one you worked on," Tom said. "Your cabinetry. . ."

Rufus nodded. "All right. Thank you for telling me."

"I could take you out there." Tom turned a thumb toward his red pickup truck parked among the buggies.

"It's the Sabbath. And Annalise was just baptized."

The front door opened behind them. Annie stepped out.

"Did I hear my name?"

"Hello, Annie," Tom said. "Congratulations."

"Thank you." She looked from Tom to Rufus. "Why so glum? The sirens?"

"Everything will be fine," Rufus said. "One of Karl's houses burned. But the *English* have insurance for these things."

"Was anyone hurt?" Annie asked.

Tom shook his head. "Not that I've heard. It should have been empty on a Sunday."

"Then what caused the fire?" Annie moved farther out on the porch.

Tom turned his hands palms up. "That will be for the fire department to figure out."

"Custer County runs on a volunteer firefighting force," Annie said. "Do they even have forensics capability?"

"I'm sure they have someone to call in if the cause is not obvious," Tom said. "I wanted to take Rufus out there. Maybe it didn't get his cabinets."

"They are no longer my cabinets," Rufus pointed out. "The *English* will sort out who they belong to when a house is almost finished."

"I think you should go." Annie leaned against the porch's railing and looked back into the house. The transformation of the benches into tables was already under way. "Aren't you at least curious?"

"Of course."

"Then go."

"It's your baptism day, Annalise." Those irresistible eyes sank into her.

"I know," she said. "But even Jesus would take an animal out of a well on the Sabbath. You should go see how bad it is, whether you can help to salvage anything. You might reduce the sense of loss somehow."

She could see him thinking as his head turned toward the barn where the Beiler buggies were parked.

"Let Tom drive you," she said. "You'll be back soon enough. The food will still be here." *I will still be here,* she wanted to say.

Two

Tom's truck jerked to a halt. "We're still four houses away."

Rufus leaned forward and peered through the windshield. "Looks like half the emergency vehicles in the county are here."

"Might as well get out here." Tom killed the ignition.

"Are you sure we should have come? It doesn't look like we'll get any closer. We'll just be in the way."

"You have a vested interest." Tom pulled the latch to open the driver's door.

"No I don't. And it would not matter if I did."

"You may be right about the cabinets," Tom said, "but what about the peace of this community? What's going to happen when Karl Kramer finds out about this?"

Tom had a point. A year ago, the hotheaded construction contractor had no use for an Amish cabinetmaker. Rufus had stayed out of his way long enough to gain Karl's trust. Over the last few months Rufus had nurtured an unlikely relationship that drew the two of them together in a community improvement project, a joint effort between the *English* and the Amish. Karl had even gained a few popularity points and practically insisted that Rufus build the cabinets in the house now hidden by emergency vehicles.

And now this.

"He's out of town," Rufus said. "I don't know how to reach him."

"Somebody will," Tom said. "Let's get out."

They slammed the truck's doors and walked the few yards to where a crowd had assembled.

"We don't know that it's foul play." Rufus wished he had left his black jacket in the car. The warmth of the day and the smoldering remains of the fire made him sweat.

"No, we don't." Tom slid his hands into the pockets of his khaki work pants. "But if it was an accident, that means something went wrong with workmanship somewhere."

They inched through the crowd, for what purpose Rufus was unsure. Smoke filled his nostrils and hung in a wall of gray above the house. The front support of the two-story structure had collapsed, taking half the roof with it. Cinders floated on the breeze.

"The fire must be out." Tom pointed to the largest fire truck. "They're not shooting water."

Whatever was left of the house would be too smoky and water damaged to salvage. Certainly the kitchen cabinets, with their carefully sanded white oak finish, would be reduced to scrap.

Tom reached out and grabbed the shoulder of a passing firefighter. "Bryan, what happened?"

The young man turned toward them and gestured for his companion to pause as well. "Hi, Tom. This is my friend Alan."

"Tom Reynolds." Tom offered a handshake. "This is Rufus Beiler."

"All that's left is the cleanup," Bryan said. "Alan and I are here to make sure the scene is secured and the evidence is not compromised."

"Evidence?" Rufus asked. "So you think it's arson?"

"Too soon to say, but the fire chief doesn't want to take any chances in a situation like this."

Annie suspected women were hugging and congratulating her for the second or third time. Surely she had already received more embraces than there were women present during worship. Though she had a plate of food in front of her on a table in the Beilers' dining room, she hardly got to swallow a bite before someone else was tapping her on the shoulder and smiling broadly. Each time, Annie stood and allowed a pair of arms to fold around her.

"It was perfect to have your baptism here at our home."

With her teeth about to close on a forkful of ham, Annie looked up to see Franey Beiler's eyes brimming. Annie reached for Franey's hand. "I confess I'm glad it was here, too. This is where it all began for me, after all."

Annie had first met the Beilers more than a year ago when she stumbled onto their land in the dark with no idea that Amish had settled in southwestern Colorado.

"Eli and I cannot imagine our lives without you," Franey said. "I'm sure it will be only a matter of time now."

Annie tilted her head and shrugged one shoulder. She hoped Franey was right—that she and Rufus would have their banns read and be married before the end of the year. But she would wait for Rufus to decide. She had chosen to be baptized into the Amish church of her own free will. The next step was for Rufus to take.

Someone asked Franey a question, and she disappeared into the kitchen. Annie smiled at the women around her table—but hoped none of them planned to congratulate her yet again. She wished one of the Beiler girls, Lydia or Sophie, might slide into the empty chair beside her.

Instead a young stranger sat down. An unhappy young stranger with no plate of food.

"Hello. I'm Annalise."

"I know who you are," the girl said. "Everybody knows who you are."

"I suppose on my baptism day, that is true." Annie dabbed her lips with a napkin. "If we've met, I'm sorry that I've forgotten your name."

"We haven't met. I'm Leah Deitwaller. From Pennsylvania."

"Oh, the new family. Welcome."

"You don't have to say that. I don't even want to be here. And I'm not staying."

"You're ready to go home already? Have your parents eaten?"

Leah rolled her eyes. "I mean I don't want to be in Colorado. I'm going home to Pennsylvania."

"Oh." Annie doubted the girl was of age.

"Is it true that you're *English*?"

"Until a couple of hours ago that was true."

"Can you help me find out how much it would cost to take the train to Pennsylvania?"

Annie set her fork down gently and took a moment to straighten her prayer *kapp*. "Shouldn't you have this conversation with your parents?"

"I would pay my own way." Leah slumped and crossed her arms. "I just need a job. I know I'm small, but I'm seventeen—nearly eighteen. I'm old enough."

"What does your mother say about your having a job?"

Leah unfolded her arms and slapped both palms on the table. "Never mind. I just thought you might understand."

"Understand what?"

Leah stood, crossed the dining room, walked through the living room, and went out the front door.

Rufus had been gone a long time. Ruth was scraping and stacking dishes in the kitchen sink when she realized more than two hours had passed since she saw her brother step off the front porch and into Tom Reynolds's truck. Before long, the families with younger children or those who came from a greater distance would hook their horses to their buggies and begin the trek home. Because of the sparsity of families settling around Westcliffe, the church district covered a wide geographic area.

The door from the dining room swung open, and Annalise entered with a tray of dishes.

"You're not supposed to be cleaning up after your own baptism." Ruth took the stack from Annalise and began transferring plates to the sink.

"It's a ruse," Annalise said. "Elijah Capp cornered me."

"Elijah?"

Annalise narrowed her eyes. "Don't act like you don't know what he wants."

"He wants what he always wants."

"You. That's what he wants."

Ruth ran some hot water in the sink. "Perhaps I should not have come here for my internship. It's not even a real internship, just a place to work to see if it's the kind of nursing I want to do."

Annalise put both hands behind her waist and leaned against the counter next to the sink. "Right now all he wants to know is if you are going to the singing tonight."

Ruth glanced up. "Are you and Rufus going?"

"You know what Rufus says. We're too old."

"Where did he go?" Ruth asked. "Why would he leave you on your baptism day?"

"I told him to."

"How *English* of you." Ruth flattened a stray strand of her light brown hair.

Annalise nudged Ruth with one elbow. "There was a fire."

"I heard the sirens."

"Tom thought Rufus should go out there. I trust Tom's judgment about these things."

Ruth rinsed two plates and set them in the dish rack. "Did he say where it was?"

"One of Karl's houses."

Ruth exhaled. "Why does everything in this town seen to involve Karl Kramer?"

"Don't worry about it," Annalise said. "What should I tell Elijah? Better yet, go talk to Elijah yourself."

Ruth moistened her lips. "I don't think that's a good idea."

"If you're going to live in Westcliffe for the whole semester, you can't avoid Elijah."

"I know. Not completely. I'm going to be living in town with you and driving around if I need to. I'll just run into him from time to time." Ruth shook water off her hands and reached for a dish towel.

"Are you sure you don't want to live here at home with your own family?"

Ruth moved her head slowly from side to side. "I would only be flaunting my *English* ways. I can come to church and see my family, but I can't keep a car here. I can't get up from the breakfast table every day to go do something my mother does not want me to do. I can't come here in my scrubs."

Annalise reached for Ruth's hand. "I think your mother has found her peace with your decision not to join the church. She loves you. And she knows how much you love God."

"Still, I can't live here. Thank you for letting me use your spare room."

"Of course."

"I feel nervous that Rufus has been gone so long," Ruth said. "I'm going to go find him."

"What about Elijah?"

Ruth pulled off the apron covering her denim skirt and long-sleeve gray T-shirt. "Please tell him I'm not going to the singing. He has to accept that I can't."

Two fire trucks rumbled past Ruth in her blue Prius as she turned off the main highway and into the new subdivision where Karl

Kramer was building homes. Visually following the trail of smoke to the afflicted house was simple. Ruth parked the Prius and proceeded on foot to where two Custer County sheriff's cars cordoned off the end of an unfinished block.

She spotted Rufus's hat, his height lifting it above the gawkers, and she made her way toward him. He stood with Tom and two men she did not recognize who wore fire-retardant jackets and helmets.

"Ruth, what are you doing here?" Rufus had turned and seen her.

"I was looking for you."

"This is my sister, Ruth," Rufus said to the two young men.

"Bryan," one of them said.

"Alan," the other supplied.

"It's nice to meet you both." Ruth took in the scene beyond them. "Well, I guess the circumstances are not so nice."

Bryan cracked a smile. "Then I hope there will be other circumstances."

A blush rose in Ruth's neck. She felt its warmth as she met her brother's eyes.

"I don't mean to be rude." Bryan's eyes were still on Ruth. "But you are not dressed like the other Amish women I've seen."

Ruth swallowed. "I'm not baptized." She slid her palms down the side of her long skirt.

"So you're. . .not Amish?"

"It's complicated." Ruth looked away.

"Maybe another time, then."

Ruth's gut burned.

Alan raised a red locked box in one hand. "Quit your flirting, Bryan. We need to get this place secured and start collecting evidence."

Bryan nodded. "I'll take the kit."

Alan held the box beyond his grasp. "Don't think you're going in there alone and getting all the credit."

Bryan rolled his eyes. "You're so competitive."

Three

May 1892

Roast beef satiated his taste buds before he conceded the necessity to chew, which Sheriff A.G. Byler did slowly. He swallowed the bite and with deliberation took another. His lunch, though delicious, did not please him nearly as much as the movements of his wife at the other end of the kitchen table.

"Are you going to your office today?" Bess thoughtfully smoothed a length of blue twill flat against the table.

"I've managed to lollygag all morning," A.G. said. "I reckon I'd better check on the state of lawlessness in Baxter County before my afternoon nap."

"Abraham Byler, don't make jokes." Bess picked up a pair of scissors and opened and closed them three times above the fabric. "You've been gone for two weeks, and nobody trusts your deputy if things get heated."

"They knew where to send a telegram in Colorado." Stroking his pointed white beard, Abraham considered whether to indulge in his last bite of mashed potatoes before or after he finished his meat. "If Deputy Combs got in over his head, somebody would have let me know."

"Well, we're back in Arkansas now, and sometimes I think the

Wild West is more civilized than Baxter County." She waved the scissors again.

"You're exaggerating." He pointed at the cloth. "Are you planning to attack that innocent piece of material?"

Bess put the scissors down. "I'm trying to decide if it's enough for a romper for little Ransom. I think I've got some green that would be adorable on the twins."

"We just got home last night." A.G. scooped up the potatoes. "We haven't even been outside in the daylight, and already you're fussing about what to send to Malinda's children."

"I know their sizes now," Bess countered, "and their personalities. You don't really expect I would let that information go to waste. They grow so fast. I have to do this soon."

He nodded and smiled. "Ransom sure did laugh himself half to death playing horsey on my knee."

Bess tilted her head and raised her eyebrows. "You're as smitten as I am."

He felt the light in his own eyes. "You were a beautiful sight with those grandbabies Earl and Pearl in your arms."

"I hope Mack and Malinda find what they're looking for in Colorado, because it sure is a long way from home. I don't like being separated from my daughter. Three babies, and we only just saw them for the first time."

"They're working hard." A.G. scraped his chair back, picked up his plate, and moved to set it in the sink. "At least our boys are not too far away. We won't wait so long for the next visit to Colorado. I promise."

"I'll hold you to that." Bess pointed the scissors at him. "Will you make it to Gassville today?"

"I'll check on the tanyard and swing by the jail here in Mountain Home. Then I suppose I'll ride over to Gassville."

"I ordered some buttons at Denton's Emporium more than a month ago. Will you check on them while you're over that way?"

He dipped his head of wavy white hair. "That I can do."

Bess's face clouded. "Gassville seems to give you plenty of trouble these days."

"Child's play."

"I'm serious, Abraham. I'm anxious what news you'll hear."

"You worry too much."

A.G. caught the back screen door before it had time to slam and walked around the side of the stone bungalow out to the street. On the side of the road, he paused to inhale deeply. His promise not to wait so long to take the train back to Colorado was as much to himself as it was to Bess. He did not intend for his grandchildren to grow up not knowing who he was. They were so little they would not remember this visit when he laid eyes on them for the first time. Colorado was a long way, but it was not the edge of the world.

He exhaled and took the first steps toward the center of Mountain Home.

"Why, Sheriff Byler," a female voice said. "I didn't realize you were back in town."

Abraham smiled at Mrs. Taylor, who hung a damp rug over the railing of her front porch. "Yes, ma'am. First day home."

Mrs. Taylor fanned herself with a church bulletin. "Come Sunday I'm sure the children in your Sunday school class will be glad to see you."

"I hope so. I know I'll be glad to see them."

"Where's your horse?"

"I left him with the boys at the tanyard."

"I'm sure they'll be glad to have you back."

He sauntered toward town, reveling in the comfort of being home among the familiar landscape of northern Arkansas and ready to pit its undulating green beauty against rugged red Colorado at the first challenge. After two terms in the state legislature, the kind people of Baxter County had welcomed him back as sheriff, a post he had filled before. He was as glad to have the job back as they were to have him.

His tanyard was at the edge of town. He employed two young men to keep the hides rotating through the lye mixtures, but periodically he liked to satisfy himself that the work was done properly. An hour later, on his own horse again and just three short blocks from the sheriff's office, A.G. looked up and winced. His hope to get through his first day in peace was headed for a crash.

"You have to do something before someone gets hurt." Twenty-four-year-old Maura Woodley shook her dark curls but managed to keep her forefinger from wagging. He was the sheriff, after all.

"Well, now, Miss Woodley," the sheriff said, "let's suppose you tell me what this is all about. I've been out of town, you know." He patted the neck of his horse as he slid out of the saddle.

"I do know." Maura set her jaw. "I'm sorry not to welcome you back more graciously, but really, you must do something."

Sheriff Byler kept walking, leading the horse, and Maura fell into step beside him.

"I've left my cousin Walter with my cart," she said, glancing over her shoulder. "I can't leave him unsupervised for too long. You know what trouble he gets into."

"Has Walter been stirring things up?"

"No. It's far more serious than that."

Finally he stopped walking and turned to her. Sheriff Abraham Byler was the calmest man Maura Woodley had ever met—sometimes too calm. This situation required firm action. Maura pulled off her white gloves and gripped them both in one fist. The gloves were too small and made her fingers itch, but her mother had paid a dear price for the gloves before her death two years ago. They were hand-stitched lambskin. Maura made a pretense at wearing them because they had been her mother's.

"I don't want Belle to get hurt," she said. "She's my best friend, and I'm afraid she is going to get caught in something dreadful."

"Belle Mooney has always had a level head," the sheriff said.

"Not when it comes to John Twigg."

"Perhaps she sees something in him that you do not."

Maura slapped her gloves against an open palm. "It is more a matter of what she does not see. The man is unstable."

"Now let's not jump to conclusions."

"You know it's true as well as I do."

"Then why have you come all the way from Gassville to tell me?"

His calmness infuriated her at that moment, and she did not speak.

"It's the Dentons again, I imagine," Sheriff said.

"Yes. The Dentons and the Twiggs used to get along so well." Maura slapped her gloves again.

"John was happy working for the Dentons for a long time." Sheriff tied his horse to a post.

"Something went wrong, and his father thought giving John his own store to run was a good idea. It's getting out of hand."

"They might still sort it out." He reached a finger under his beard to scratch his chin.

"John remains an unstable sort."

"Perhaps." Byler lifted his eyes and raised his brow. "Didn't you say you left Walter with your cart?"

"That's right." Maura followed his line of vision and sighed. The thirteen-year-old was coming out of a shop. "Walter."

The boy turned red. "Sorry, Maura."

"What am I going to tell your father? And what have you done with my horse?"

"I tied him up tight. I promise."

"I asked you to stay with him."

Walter kicked a bare toe in the dirt. "I know. Sorry."

Maura turned to the sheriff. "I'd better go see about my horse and cart. My father was quite specific about what he wanted me to bring back from Mountain Home." She scowled at Walter. "Everything had better still be there."

Sheriff Byler touched her elbow. "Now, Miss Woodley, you know we don't have that kind of petty crime in Mountain Home. You say hello to your father for me."

"You can let me out in front of Denton's Emporium," Walter said as Maura drove the cart into the outskirts of Gassville, four miles from Mountain Home.

"I don't believe I'm going to let you loose again." Maura had lost Walter once already today—and had not even known it. She did not intend to fail to deliver him safely to his father now.

Maura scanned the street, looking for a good place to tie up the horse for a few minutes.

A gallop compelled them both to turn their heads. Walter pointed. "Isn't that John Twigg, the crazy man?"

"There's no need for name calling." Maura swallowed her own guilt. Walter was merely voicing what she herself believed. And he was right—it was John Twigg, riding down the middle of the street far too fast.

Twigg pulled his horse to a halt and slid off it in front of Denton's Emporium.

"He looks wild." Walter dropped off the bench of Maura's cart.

"Shh. Stay right where you are." Maura stood next to Walter and gripped his shoulder. As much as she loved Belle Mooney and as much as Belle Mooney loved John Twigg, Maura failed to see the endearing qualities of anyone in his family. They made her more nervous every time she saw them with their beady-eyed looks and harsh laughs.

Twigg calmly tied his horse to a post directly in front of the Denton Emporium then methodically removed a stick from a saddlebag.

"What's he doing?" Walter whispered.

"Shh." Maura did not take her eyes off Twigg.

Twigg pulled an arm back then thrust the stick at the chest of the horse. The beast screamed in protest, raised its forelegs, and pulled against the post.

Shoppers poked their heads out of surrounding shops. Seeing Twigg, they quickly retreated. Twigg laughed. Then he untied the horse, mounted it in the middle of its complaint, and trotted down the street to his own store.

Maura let out her breath.

"It's a message," Walter said, "for the Denton brothers."

The street was silent, and Maura considered herding Walter back into the cart to take him anywhere but where they were. Maura's father finally emerged from the emporium, a package in his arms. "Are you two all right?"

"We're fine, Daddy," Maura said.

"You look more like your mother every day," Woody Woodley said. He turned to Walter. "I told the Dentons you would sweep for them this summer. Your daddy said you needed something to keep you busy this summer."

Walter slumped. "Isn't it enough that I sweep for my own father's shop?"

"I wonder if that's wise," Maura said.

"He'll be fine," Woody said.

Maura glanced down the street. "Speaking of Walter's daddy, where is Uncle Edwin?"

"He's at Crazy Man Twigg's store, isn't he?" Walter was at full alert again. "Selling eggs."

Woody shrugged.

Maura clicked her tongue. "I wish people would not aggravate the situation by selling to Twiggs when they have been selling to the Dentons for years."

Woody moved his head from side to side. "Edwin says John Twigg is offering a better price for eggs and hens. Goose feathers, too."

"Can't he see the Twiggs do that on purpose? They're going to make people take sides. Does Edwin really want to be on the side of John Twigg in this feud?"

"Times are tight. Edwin depends on that egg money. He can't very well sell eggs in his milliner's shop."

"But selling to the Twiggs and then letting Walter work for the Dentons—that could be dangerous."

"He'll be fine," Woody repeated.

Maura held her tongue. "I should get Walter home. I'll be home to start supper soon."

Walter pointed across the street. "Who are those men?"

"They were in the emporium," Woody said. "They look harmless enough."

"Mmm." Maura narrowed the space between her eyes. "One can never be sure. I think I'll go find out."

"Now who needs to be careful?" Walter laughed.

"If they are connected to the Twiggs or the Dentons, I want to know," Maura said. The men were oddly dressed in boxy black trousers and jackets with no collars. Maura pursed her lips while she considered what their garb might mean.

"Now who's looking to get in the middle of that feud?" her father said. "You ought to get yourself properly deputized."

Walter laughed. "Ladies can't be deputized."

Maura put her hands on her hips. "But they can get to the bottom of things."

Four

"Yes, your appointment is confirmed for Friday at 3:00." Ruth tapped her pencil eraser on the desktop as she spoke into the phone. She had checked the computer screen three times. "The doctor will have your test results by then."

Ruth hung up and glanced around the clinic's empty waiting room. From a pocket in her blue scrubs, she took a key and went to unlock the front door. The first appointment of Monday morning was scheduled for fifteen minutes later. Ruth returned to the desk and double-checked that the patient files she had pulled from the drawers were in the correct order for smooth handling as patients arrived.

When she arranged for this semester-long internship, Ruth had hoped for more patient contact. She had worked as a certified nurse assistant for over two years in a nursing home and had enough of her nursing degree behind her to be qualified to draw blood and do simple lab work. So far, though, the clinic manager had kept her on the front desk most of the time. She only worked five or six hours a day. After carrying a full course load and working twenty-five hours a week at the nursing home, the reduced schedule seemed like a vacation.

It was only the second week. Surely things would pick up.

Ruth could have arranged some clinical experience in Colorado Springs, with its multiple large hospital systems and wide-ranging network of medical practices. But she had left Westcliffe because she wanted to return to a place like it someday qualified to provide a basic level of medical care. People in Colorado Springs had plenty of doctors and nurses. Amish communities often were spread out and remote, especially in new settlements like the one in southwestern Colorado. Though she had chosen to leave, unbaptized, and get her GED and enroll in college, Ruth also longed to be among her own people.

She had a hard time thinking of herself as *not* Amish, but even in scrubs and behind a desk looking at a computer monitor, she did not feel *English*, either.

The door opened and Mrs. Weichert came through it.

"Good morning." Ruth picked up Mrs. Weichert's file from the top of the stack. "Is all your information the same?"

Mrs. Weichert laughed. "I've lived in this town my whole life. I've had that store on Main Street for twenty years. Yes, my information is the same."

"Sorry. I have to ask." Ruth stood. "They'll be ready for you in just a minute."

Ruth stepped into the hall behind the desk and set Mrs. Weichert's file in a rack. The clinic manager stuck her head out of her office.

"Why don't you take the patient back?"

"Me?" Ruth's heart sped up.

"Sure. Review her list of meds and get a pulse and blood pressure."

Ruth retrieved the chart and opened the door to the waiting room. "I'll take you back, Mrs. Weichert."

In the exam room, Ruth laid the file open. Mrs. Weichert dropped her purse in a chair and sat on the exam table.

"I guess your people are pretty excited about Annie," Mrs.

Weichert said. "Her baptism and all."

Ruth clicked the point down on her pen. "It's a big step for her."

"I respect her choice, but I sure did like it better when she wore jeans to work in the shop."

"She's gotten used to the clothes," Ruth said. "We don't really let our dresses hold us back."

Mrs. Weichert scanned Ruth from head to toe. "You've made a conversion of your own."

Ruth shrugged. "Scrubs are standard." For a long time Ruth had worn skirts to work at the nursing home. Only recently had she relented and agreed to wear scrubs. She had to admit they were practical and comfortable.

"You look like you know what you're doing."

"I assure you, I do," Ruth said. "Let me start by getting your blood pressure."

Rufus took a thermos of coffee from under the bench of his open-air cart. He stroked Dolly's long nose as the horse stood obediently still in the street. Mrs. Weichert's shop had become a familiar destination for both of them. Rufus hoped the shop would be empty for a few minutes. It was noon on a Monday. Tourist traffic should be nonexistent. It was the locals Rufus wanted to avoid.

Annalise smiled when he stepped through the door, making the bell jangle, and reached under the counter to produce two mugs.

"We seemed to have formed a habit." Rufus unscrewed the top of the thermos and poured.

Annalise wrapped the fingers of both hands around the mug to sip. "Ah. I am glad becoming Amish does not mean I have to give up *kaffi*."

"Tell me," Rufus said as he picked up his own mug, "does having an Amish employee attract more tourists to the shop on the weekends?"

Annalise laughed. "I could have made a study of that if I were keeping better records."

"You might have been tempted to write a software program to analyze the data."

She shook her head. "Nope. There are no software programs in my future. I created and sold two successful companies. It's out of my system for good."

"I suppose the busy season is over now." This would be Annalise's second winter working in Mrs. Weichert's shop of unsorted small antiques, rare books, and an increasing inventory of Amish crafts.

"As long as the weather holds up we'll have traffic." She sipped her coffee. "Winter will be quieter."

"Ike Stutzman is complaining that a lantern has gone missing."

"He probably just misplaced it, or one of his daughters used it and didn't put it back."

Rufus nodded. "Most likely. But he was pitching a fit about it yesterday when I got back from the fire. Suddenly he's worried that an overturned lantern will start a fire in his barn."

"It could."

"Yes, it could. But a lantern that is simply lost is not likely to start a fire, now is it?"

"Did anyone get hold of Karl yet?" Annalise picked up a rag and wiped dust from the counter.

Rufus shook his head. "Tom was going to go by his contractor's trailer this morning and see if his assistant has a number for him."

"I heard he went to see his dying father in Virginia."

Rufus lifted his shoulders in an exaggerated shrug.

"I also heard he went to Montana to look at horses he might want to buy for his ranch."

"I couldn't say."

The shop door jangled again, and Joel Beiler stuck his head in. "We have everything ready to load at the back of Tom's store."

"I'll be right there." Rufus drained his coffee cup as his younger brother let the door close behind him.

"Joel seems to be buckling down," Annalise said.

"He is. I believe he has a knack for farming that I never had. He ordered soil nutrients through Tom's hardware store. I promised to help him get the load home."

"I suppose you should go."

Annalise's gray eyes were clear and unsullied.

"You look happy," he said. "Are you still coming to supper tomorrow?"

She nodded.

"I'll see you there." Rufus took his thermos and stepped into the sunlight, wishing he did not have to wait until tomorrow evening to see Annalise again. He never liked being away from her.

He could do something about that dilemma. She had done her part yesterday. Now it was up to him.

Ruth was out of the clinic by two o'clock and walked the few blocks to Annalise's house off Main Street. She only stayed long enough to grab a sweater and a water bottle.

And her car key.

Annalise had given her the blue Prius a few months ago as part of divesting herself of *English* ways. Ruth had surprised herself how quickly she adjusted to the freedom of going somewhere on a whim. Quick trips. Short errands. Just go and do something and come right back.

It was all very un-Amish, and Ruth was not sure any longer that using a car to be efficient with time meant a person did not value the community.

Ruth shook off the brooding. What she wanted right now was fresh air and room to move. She wanted to be on the trail that the Amish and *English* had created together over the summer. But it was five miles away, behind the property line of her family's home. Thus the car.

Just a few minutes later, she parked the Prius at the top of the trail, locked it, and dropped the key in a pocket of her scrubs. Pockets. Another convenience that did not seem the least bit detrimental. Ruth was not hiding anything, simply storing something valuable.

She took a deep breath and quickened her pace, craving the movement. In Colorado Springs, her work at the nursing home sent her up and down the halls, lifting and pushing and pulling for entire shifts. The clinic in Westcliffe simply was not large enough to be physically demanding, and this left Ruth seeking opportunities to move her entire body.

Ruth walked the trail from one end to the other, about a mile across land that began in meadow and ended in the woods behind the Beiler home. When the house came in view, Ruth turned around. Humming a tune from the *Ausbund*, she eyed the large, flat boulder at the edge of the meadow. She had climbed the footholds of that rock hundreds of time in an Amish dress. She could certainly manage it in scrubs and tennis shoes.

She stopped short when she saw a figure on the trail. He was between her and the rock, between her and the Prius. And he was looking at her.

"Ruth Beiler, right?"

The close-cropped blond hair and goatee looked familiar. "You're the firefighter," she said. "I'm sorry. I've forgotten whether you are Bryan or Alan. Yesterday you looked alike."

"We get that a lot." Bryan grinned. "I've known Alan a long time. People are never sure who is who."

"Is everything all right?" Ruth glanced past him toward her car. "At the house, I mean. Where the fire was."

"Funny you should ask." Bryan moved to close the few yards between them. "As a matter of fact, someone violated the tape this morning."

"Why would anybody do that?"

"Good question. There wasn't much there to steal." Bryan glanced at the boulder. "You ever climb that thing?"

Ruth laughed. "All the time."

"I'll race you up."

She could not resist the dare in his green eyes and sprinted toward the rock. Running without a flapping skirt between her ankles was a rich sensation. She got there first and scrambled up the back side before Bryan found his first toehold. Triumphant, she hefted herself over the top—and found Elijah Capp flattened against the rough surface. At the sight of her, he sat up.

"I'm sorry." Startled, she stumbled slightly. "I didn't see you from down below."

"Looks like you have a shadow." Elijah straightened his hat on his head and tilted it toward Bryan.

Bryan put his hands on his hips. "I don't know why I've never come up here before. The view is beautiful."

"You must be new to Westcliffe." Elijah stood now as well.

Ruth was starting to regret her outing.

"I'm Bryan Nichols." He extended a hand, which Elijah shook.

"Elijah Capp."

"Bryan and I met yesterday." Ruth felt her back teeth start to grind. "He's a firefighter."

"Well then," Elijah said, "I imagine he must be something else as well. Custer County firefighters are volunteer."

Ruth's teeth started to hurt.

"True enough," Bryan said. "I'm a cashier at the grocery store, and I'm about to be late to work."

"I suppose you'll be going, then." Elijah nodded.

"Yes, I suppose I will." Bryan turned to Ruth. "It was good to run into you. I hope I'll see you again."

He squatted and began his descent. As he loped across the meadow, Ruth wondered where he had left his car. She turned to Elijah and forced her jaw to unclench.

"You were rude, Elijah."

"What were you doing with him, Ruth? A man you only met yesterday?"

Ruth stared at Elijah. "I was not doing anything. Not that it is your business."

"I feel toward you as I always have." Elijah crossed his arms behind his back, his voice soft.

Ruth said nothing.

"You were laughing," he said. "Happy."

"I feel the joy of the Lord when I come here. You know that better than anyone."

He stepped closer. "Ruth, is your heart open to someone else?"

Annie remembered the days—years—when she pulled on shorts and expensive tennis shoes and traversed the countryside in strides measured for endurance. In her ankle-length dress and with her hair carefully pinned up, these days she aimed for a brisk power walk. Clear mountain air was irresistible after six hours in a shop almost completely dependent on artificial light. Over recent weeks, Annie had tramped down a path several feet off the highway but running alongside it. She gave her *kapp* one last tug and began swinging her arms as her feet set their pace.

Coming out of the grocery store parking lot, where Main Street met the highway, Annie looked up just in time to lurch to one side out of the path of a white horse pulling an Amish buggy. The animal was not going fast, but he seemed confused. Behind him the buggy jostled and tilted in ways that made Annie nervous.

Doing what she had seen Rufus do so many times, she reached out and slid her fingers through the bridle, pulling to slow the horse's random movement, and reached out to run her hand along his neck. A year ago Annie Friesen would not have known what a horse's neck felt like.

"Whoa there," she said. "What's going on?"

She glanced inside the buggy and saw two little boys. Neither one of them looked older than ten.

"Who is driving your buggy?" Annie tried to place their faces.

She thought she knew everyone in the congregation now, even the children, at least by sight. Except the Deitwallers. These could be Leah's little brothers. They stared at her with huge guilty brown eyes.

"What have you boys done now?" An Amish couple strode across the parking lot with two girls in their wake toting plastic grocery sacks.

Yes, the Deitwallers.

"I'm not sure what happened," Annie said, "but the boys seem to be fine."

"Of course they're fine." Mrs. Deitwaller snapped her fingers and pointed. "Girls, get in."

"What about Leah?" one of the girls asked.

"She knew she was supposed to be back here by now." Eva Deitwaller hoisted herself up to the bench beside her husband, who had the reins in his hands now. "I'm tired of chasing after her."

"Would you like me to help you look for Leah?" Annie offered.

"No need," Leah's mother said. "She wants to be treated like an adult. She can learn to show some adult responsibility the hard way."

"Will she know how to get home?" Annie asked. "I understand you haven't been here long."

"Don't worry about her. You'll discover soon enough that Leah is a dramatic child. Don't believe everything she says. I thought she would be better after we moved, but she's not." Eva met Annie's eye for the first time. "I understand you live in town. That's a strange thing for a baptized Amish woman to do."

Annie held her lips closed. She was not about to explain her relationship with Rufus to a woman she had just met. Annie hoped her days of living in town were numbered, but she could not say so with certainty. Yet.

The Deitwallers pulled out onto the highway, leaving Annie befuddled in the parking lot. She was not a parent, and she had only had one brief conversation with Leah Deitwaller, but to her analytical mind, the data did not add up to the girl's parents being so unconcerned about her welfare.

Five

Rufus sat on the wooden chair in the small office at the back of the Amish furniture store in Colorado Springs. Tom would soon be back from visiting his mother, and Rufus was not sure he would be able to hide the disappointment he felt from his friend during the seventy-five miles of highway between the Springs and Westcliffe.

"I'm sorry, Rufus. I wish the news were better." David, the store owner, rolled his pen between his palms. "I'm going to try some new advertising, but right now sales are slumping. I don't have any custom orders for you."

Rufus gave a small shrug. "Usually you like to have some pieces on the floor to stay ahead of demand."

"I know. But I still have two chests, three end tables, and a bookcase from you."

"I see." Rufus's stomach sank.

"You know I think you do beautiful work," David said. "I just cannot afford to buy anything right now."

Rufus stood. "I hope you will let me know if business picks up."

"You will be the first to know." David scratched under his nose. "If you wanted to make a few pieces to sell strictly on commission,

I could make room on the floor."

Commission. Meaning David would pay Rufus nothing unless and until a piece sold. If David's assessment was accurate, that could take months. "I'll give that some thought."

Rufus walked through the store and out into the sunlight to wait for Tom. When Tom pulled up a few minutes later and Rufus got in the truck, Tom leaned on the steering wheel and looked expectant.

"What's wrong?"

Rufus shook his head. "No new orders. He doesn't know how long it will be."

"You were selling quite a bit over the summer, weren't you?" Tom pulled the truck out of the parking lot and onto a major north–south thoroughfare through Colorado Springs heading south.

"David has given me steady work for nearly a year. It could not last forever."

"Surely it's not over. Just a lull?"

"I hope so." Rufus removed his hat and laid his head back against the headrest.

"I'll keep my eyes open," Tom said. "Maybe I'll hear of something."

"I'd appreciate that. In the meantime, I've got to wipe this gloom off my face. If you knew something was wrong, Annalise is certain to."

Rufus reined in Dolly in front of Annalise's house. The narrow green house showed its century-old age, but at least Annalise had let him pour her a new sidewalk. He no longer worried about her falling on winter ice every time he saw the walk.

She had not spoken the words aloud, even as he spent an entire Saturday repairing the concrete, but he knew she hoped she would not be in this house for another winter. Annalise wanted to be with Rufus before winter turned fierce. Every time he thought about that truth, pain clenched his chest.

He wanted Annalise. That was not the trouble. But the questions were not so easily answered.

Annalise did not have a proper post for tying up a horse, but Rufus had long ago stopped fretting about leaving Dolly untied in front of the house. She would be content to nuzzle the ground whether or not she found anything to munch on. Besides, Rufus was only going as far as the front door. He was there to pick up Annalise and take her to the Beiler home for supper.

She opened the front door with a vivid smile even before he knocked. That happened often. Her ears were programmed to hear Dolly's *clip-clop* half a mile away, Annalise claimed. In Rufus's vocabulary, *program* was not a verb. The Amish did not program anything. But Annalise had spent too many years designing software not to think in the vocabulary of her former business success.

"Ready?" Rufus met her gray eyes and drank in the welcome he saw there.

She pulled the front door closed behind her. "I'd like to make a detour if you're agreeable."

"Of course. Where to?"

She spread her arms wide. "Anywhere. I want you to teach me to drive a buggy."

One corner of Rufus's mouth went up.

"You know I'm ready. I've watched you with the bridle and harness a hundred times. I've listened to the noises you make and how Dolly responds. I know how it works."

Rufus's mother and all of his sisters had learned to drive the buggy. Most Amish women did. Annalise's request was not outlandish.

"You are suggesting that we begin now?" he said.

"Why not? We have time, don't we? I won't ask you to take me on the highway in the first lesson. We can stay on the streets here in town where Dolly won't be tempted to go too fast. And you'll be right there."

Rufus chuckled. "You've thought this through."

"That's what I do when I face a challenge. I analyze and think it through."

"Let's do it, then."

Annalise scooted ahead of him down the walk to greet Dolly before accepting Rufus's help up onto the bench. She did not need his help. Learning to accept it anyway had taken her a long time.

She picked up the reins. "I hold them this way, right?"

He covered her hands with his to adjust her position slightly and felt only confidence in the way her fingers curved and gripped.

"Look for traffic," he said.

Annalise laughed. "I drove a car for twelve years, remember? I have not completely lost my instincts."

"Then let's try a turn at the corner so we can stay off Main Street."

He watched as Annalise sucked in both lips and kept one hand beside her wrist in case he should have to take over the reins. Perhaps they should have begun with a horse-riding lesson so Annalise could feel in her body how the horse would move. He had to admit, though, that she negotiated the first turn surprisingly well.

He chided himself. It should not have surprised him. Annalise excelled at everything she put her hand to. Why should driving a buggy be any different?

She made several right turns to take them in a large square around town, bisecting Main Street twice without turning onto it. Satisfaction took on a glow in her face when she announced she was ready to try some left turns.

"Have they discovered anything more about the fire?" Annalise asked.

Though she was doing well, Rufus remained vigilant. "About what started it, no. I get the feeling they suspect arson."

"But why?"

He shook his head. "There is no clear motive, as the *English* like to say."

"And the cabinets?"

He hesitated to answer. "Well, it turns out they belonged to me after all."

"What do you mean?"

"Because the contractor had not done the final inspection and approval, he had not yet assumed the risk. In the legal sense. That is what they tell me, anyway."

"But that's not fair. The Amish do not carry insurance. Will Karl really be that unfair to you?"

"It's not Karl." He guided her wrist again, even though she did not need the help. "It's a legal point, and an insurance coverage issue."

"So you won't be paid the final portion?"

He shook his head, not wanting to speak his thoughts. It had been a big job, with cabinets in the kitchen, family room, and master bedroom. He had been counting on the final one-third of his fee, due upon final approval.

His family expected him to propose. The Amish way was to quietly have the banns read one Sunday. Even the bishop was expecting to hear from Rufus any day now.

It would all have to wait. *Gottes wille*. God's will.

"Watch out!" Rufus pulled on the reins.

Annie wrenched the reins, her hands entangled with Rufus's. Adrenaline pumped as Dolly halted on swift command and the buggy lurched forward in a moment's delay.

Leah Deitwaller had stepped into the street, her head down, something folded in her apron, oblivious to the danger.

"Something is not right with that girl." Annie made sure Rufus had a tight hold on the reins and slid off the bench. "Leah?"

The girl looked up.

"Are you all right?"

"Of course."

"I hope you made it home safely yesterday." Even as Annie spoke, she doubted. Though Leah's *kapp* was in place, the smudge on the left side was obvious. Dirt crusted the hem of her skirt.

"If you mean that farm where my parents live, no, I have not been there since yesterday morning." Leah cocked her head in an I-dare-you position, chin forward.

Whatever the dare was, Annie was not going to accept it. "We could take you."

"If I wanted to go there, I would."

"I see." Annie had not been a particularly rebellious teenager, but she had had her moments when she preferred that her parents not know where she was.

The bundle in Leah's apron moved, causing Annie to start.

"It's a kitten," Leah said. "I found him yesterday, and I'm going to keep him."

"He'll probably be helpful if your parents get mice in the barn." Annie stepped forward. The kitten looked awfully young.

"He's not a barn cat. He's going to be *my* cat."

More than twenty-four hours had passed since Annie encountered the Deitwallers at the edge of the grocery store parking lot.

"Where did you sleep last night?" Annie asked.

Leah raised her head with a sigh and stared at Annie. "You ask a lot of questions."

"I'm concerned."

"You only joined the church two days ago. I was there. This is not really your business."

"You were the one asking me questions on Sunday. Maybe you need a friend."

"I don't need a friend who believes my parents understand anything about me."

Annie felt Rufus beside her now, his light touch on her back. "I don't really know your parents," Annie said.

"I would not bother, if I were you."

"Then maybe you and I could talk, just the two of us."

"I tried talking to you on Sunday."

"Maybe we should try again."

"Maybe. But not now."

Leah brought the kitten to her cheek, pivoted, and strode toward Main Street. Annie started to go after her, but Rufus grabbed her hand.

"Let her go."

"She's in trouble," Annalise said.

"Clearly." Rufus gripped her hand. "I know you want to help, to fix whatever is wrong, but you might make things worse."

"How could they be worse?" Annalise pulled her hand out of his. "Have you spoken with her parents? I ran into them yesterday. They were not the least bit concerned about the fact that she was missing. Obviously she has not been home."

"She is not a child."

"I beg to differ."

"She looks to me to be at least sixteen."

"Seventeen. She told me yesterday over lunch."

"Same age as Joel, and we consider him grown."

"There's seventeen, and then there's seventeen. I don't think you can compare Leah to Joel."

"She doesn't want your help." Rufus held her hand again, squeezing enough to make sure she knew he had no intention of letting go.

"She reached out to me on Sunday. She's unhappy about her family's move."

"That was her parents' decision. She'll have to sort it out with them."

"They don't care. They just drove off without her yesterday. She needs someone to care about her."

Rufus led Annalise back toward the buggy. "It did not sound as if she is ready for that."

"Maybe because she does not expect it," Annalise countered. "Can't you see that?"

He nodded. "I see plenty. I see your beautiful heart. And I see her resistance."

"Where do you suppose she's been?" Annalise relented and climbed up to the bench.

Rufus released the brake. "My guess is she was used to the run of the farm in Pennsylvania."

"She's miles away from her family's farm now. Where was she? Where did she get that kitten, for instance?"

"Stray cats have kittens all the time, and there are any number of empty structures outlying Westcliffe." He paused. "Or *in* Westcliffe. I wonder where she was yesterday morning when the fire broke out?"

"In church. I talked to her myself."

"No." Rufus slowly picked up the reins as he watched Leah turn out of sight. "You talked to her over a crowded, lengthy meal. Can you be certain she was there during the service?"

Annalise turned sideways in the bench and stared, her jaw going slack. "What are you saying, Rufus?"

"I am not saying anything. I am asking questions. It is one of your favorite activities, is it not?"

"This isn't a game." Annalise crossed her arms. "What possible reason would an Amish teenage girl have for starting a fire in an *English* house?"

"I did not say I had all the answers."

Ruth turned up as well for supper on Tuesday night. Annie spotted her as she walked down the long Beiler driveway. She must have parked the Prius up near the road, under the trees, where she would not flaunt it in her mother's face. With eight-year-old Jacob trailing at her side, Annie moseyed up the drive to meet her friend.

"I didn't know you were coming!" Jacob threw himself against his sister's form.

Annie knew what that little boy hug felt like. She loved it.

"*Mamm* asked me on Sunday to come." Ruth picked up the boy under his shoulders and spun him around. "I came straight from work, after I changed my clothes."

"I love it when the whole family is here." Jacob dashed off to the chicken coop.

"We all feel that way, you know," Ruth said to Annie. "You're one of the family."

Annie flicked her eyes in Ruth's direction. "You know I love your family. Every single one of you."

"But not in exactly the same way." Ruth stuck her tongue in one cheek.

Annie kicked a stone. "No, I suppose not."

"So when will the wedding be?"

"I don't know."

"Haven't you and Rufus talked about it?"

"Not since the summer. We agreed I needed to be baptized before we could be serious. It seemed better to just leave the topic alone for a while."

"And now you're baptized."

"Two whole days." They progressed toward the house.

"And he hasn't said a word?"

Annie shook her head. "It's okay if he needs some time."

"Time? Why would he need time? It's not as if he did not see this coming."

"It's all right, Ruth."

"You could ask him. Couples talk about these things together."

"I don't think so. It's better if I wait."

Ruth reached out with an arm to squeeze Annie's shoulder. "You know you're my sister, whatever happens."

Annie nodded.

"I never thought I would be living with you before Rufus was. He doesn't know what he's missing."

The front door opened, and Sophie stepped out. "Dinner's almost on the table."

Ruth leaned her head in toward Annie's. "Maybe tonight will be the night."

Six

May 1892

Joseph Beiler ran his thumb and forefinger along the brim of his black felt hat on the right side.

"You've been doing that since you were nine years old." Zeke Berkey leaned forward, his jaw thrust toward Joseph and his eyes wide green circles.

Joseph dropped his hand. If anyone knew his old habits, it would be the man who had been his friend for all of his twenty-five years. "I do not know why the bishop sent me on this expedition. He should have let your brother come with you."

"He is too young, and the bishop knows he's a wanderer."

"So are you." Joseph met Zeke's gaze.

Zeke nodded. "That is why you're here. And because you communicate exceptionally well in English."

Joseph looked down the main street of Gassville, Arkansas, then glanced at his and Zeke's horses tied to a post twenty feet away. "Maybe we should not have stopped here. We need land for a new settlement, not a town."

"A town helps." Zeke stood with shoulders back and chest high. "A new settlement needs something to attract settlers. If they know they can get on a train to visit their families in Pennsylvania or Ohio, that will make it easier to settle in Arkansas."

Joseph turned his head both directions to survey the town. "I do not see a depot."

"Must you always be so serious?" Zeke elbowed him. "We will investigate. It may even be fun."

"The bishop gave us a serious mission."

"He did not say we should never smile while we carry out his instructions."

Joseph flashed Zeke a half smirk.

"Now that's better," Zeke said. "We at least need to see what this town has to offer in the way of supplies. And the horses could do with a day or two of rest."

Joseph mightily resisted the urge to finger his hat. After journeying from central Tennessee to north central Arkansas, he could do with a day or two of rest himself.

"Can we afford to sleep in a real bed tonight?" Joseph asked.

Zeke grinned. "I told you to break in that saddle before taking it out on the trail."

"Ridiculing me is not helpful." Joseph reached up with both hands and straightened his hat.

"I will make inquiries about a hotel." Zeke turned to face the store behind them and looked up at its sign. "Denton Emporium. Sounds like a place that should have everything we need. Why don't you have a look around? But do not lose the horses."

"Should we not stay together?" Joseph asked. But he was muttering at Zeke's back.

Joseph sucked in his lips while he looked around to get his bearings. It did not take much to disorient him in new places—another reason the bishop should have sent someone else. The main street was only a few blocks long. Joseph allowed one finger to point from his hip at the businesses he saw as he murmured the words he read on the signs. He glanced at the sun to make sure he had his directions right. Churches, shops, and blacksmiths populated a simple grid of streets, interspersed with stretches of homes. It was not an Amish village, but as far as the *English* went, it did not look too complicated.

Joseph breathed relief.

Across the street a huddle broke up and a young woman emerged, straightened her shoulders, and kicked up road dust.

She was headed straight for Joseph. He turned his head in the direction Zeke had chosen, but his friend had disappeared from sight.

Her dark hair was efficiently bundled under a wide-brimmed purple hat above a lavender calico dress. Joseph could see her dark eyes, though, and whatever she wanted, she meant business. He ran a dry tongue over chapped lips.

"You, sir," she said. "I haven't seen you in town before."

Joseph opened his mouth, but no sound resulted. He had learned his English from doing field work beside *English* men, but he was not accustomed to speaking to *English* women.

"I don't mean to be rude." Now that she had a closer view and could see more than his hat, Maura inspected the oddly dressed young man. "But I must ask you to identify yourself and your business in Gassville."

"I am Joseph Beiler." His violet-blue eyes clouded.

"Byler?" Maura's forehead crinkled. "Are you a relative of the sheriff?"

"Sheriff?" The young man shook his head slowly.

"Yes." Maura pursed her lips. Could this man not answer a simple question? "Have you come to see the sheriff?"

"No, miss. Our people are peaceable."

Maura cocked her head. "If I might ask, what do you mean, 'our people'?"

He gestured to the pocketless black wool coat he was wearing even on a warm day. "The Amish."

"Amish? I thought you gave your name as Byler."

"Yes, Joseph Beiler." He spelled his surname.

"Just a coincidence of name, I suppose." Maura shifted her bag from one hand to the other.

"Perhaps."

"What is that accent I hear in your speech?" Maura asked. "Where are you from?"

"Tennessee."

Maura grunted. "Before that."

"Pennsylvania," he said.

"Before that, then."

"We have been in America since before your Revolutionary War."

"Then you are American, and it was your war, too. And you may as well claim the War of 1812, that horrendous mess between the states, and the whole lot."

"We have nothing to do with war. As I said, we are peaceable."

"Ah yes. So you say. Why do you sound German?"

"Our language is German."

"Mmm." Maura glanced down the street. "What happened to your friend?"

Joseph took a step back. "We are just visiting."

"Is he Amish, too?"

"Yes. Do you not know our people?"

Maura fidgeted with her handbag and extracted the white gloves, which she then clutched in one fist. "I cannot honestly say I have ever heard of the Amish." Though he had found his tongue, this man clearly was nervous, and Maura did not abide nervous people. They always had something to hide.

"Though I find your inquiry of visitors curious even for the *English*," he said, "I will answer your questions. You need only ask."

"You find me impolite." Maura waved her fist and the empty fingers of her gloves fluttered. "Your opinion does not deter me. And I am not English. My people came from Scotland."

He shifted his weight. "I apologize. I used our word for all people who are not of our faith."

Maura toggled her chin from side to side. "So you lump us all together, do you?"

He lifted his shoulders and blinked his eyes at the same time.

"Perhaps we deserve it," she said. "I trust our humble businesses will be able to supply your needs."

"I have no doubt we will be comfortable during our brief visit."

Brief. That was the word she wanted to hear.

"We sometimes get troublemakers." Maura waved her gloves at Joseph again. "I just want you to know that I will not hesitate to fetch Sheriff Byler if I believe there to be trouble on the streets of Gassville."

"You will have no cause on our account," he said. "Byler is an Amish name. Perhaps your sheriff and I have something in common."

Maura laughed. "I'm not sure what your people believe, but I assure you Abraham Byler is a good Christian man. His people came from Tennessee and Mississippi, and he is in church every Sunday. The children in his Sunday school class adore him."

"I only meant to comment on the name," Joseph said. He jutted his chin down the street. "Here comes Zeke."

Joseph hoped this woman had no idea how fast his heart was beating. He had never done more than sell his mother's eggs to an *English* woman who thought keeping layers was too much bother.

"Have you made a friend already?" Zeke asked.

Only Joseph heard the jest in Zeke's tone.

"This is my traveling companion, Ezekiel Berkey," Joseph said. "I am afraid I do not yet know the name of this vigilant resident of Gassville."

She arched her back slightly.

"Perhaps vigilant is too strong," Joseph offered.

Without looking at Joseph, the woman offered a bare hand for Zeke to shake. "I am Maura Woodley. I am pleased to meet you,

Mr. Berkey. Welcome to Gassville."

"And I you." Zeke shook her hand, but his eyes moved to Joseph.

"I will not detain you further." Maura stuffed her gloves back in her bag. "The hotel is not hard to find if you choose to stay. It's just down the street. I'd better get back to my horse and cart."

They watched her leave, the two of them still and somber. She crossed the street and marched down the walkway toward a young mare that matched her hair in color and a cart Joseph had an impulse to repair.

"Vigilant?" Zeke said finally. "Is that not a harsh way to describe someone you just met?"

"It is accurate."

"Did you even go into the emporium?" Zeke asked. "Or did you spend all your time flirting with an *English*?"

Joseph scowled. "I am not flirting with anyone."

"Good. Because Hannah is waiting for you. You know that."

Joseph leaned his head to one side. "Hannah." *Maura.*

"Yes, Hannah. She is *en lieb*. What she sees in you, I will never know, but she is my sister and she wants to marry you."

Joseph knew Hannah believed this to be true. He had not known that she had spoken of it to anyone. When this journey was over, the harvest would come and then the marrying season.

Hannah was sure.

Joseph was not. But he would not tell Zeke.

"I went into a store at the other end of town." Zeke brushed his palms together three times. "It was a dusty place. A man named Twigg runs it."

"What kinds of goods does he carry?"

"I did not stay around long enough to find out. He sounded angry. He was going on about the Denton brothers who run this emporium."

Joseph fingered the brim of his hat. He had not even tried to stop. "Miss Woodley is vigilant because she is fearful of trouble.

Perhaps you have uncovered the source of her fear."

"From what I gather, the Dentons and the Twiggs both have cattle spreads along with their stores." Zeke scratched his clean-shaven chin. "If God has already blessed them so abundantly, what can they have to argue about?"

"Mountain Home is only a few miles," Joseph pointed out. "We could ride there easily."

Zeke looked around. "We are in no hurry. Let's take a room at the hotel here."

Seven

Annie pedaled harder. The five miles between her house in town and the Beiler farm inclined at a deceitfully gradual pace but inclined nevertheless. The mid-September sun was bright but not hot, for which Annie was grateful at the moment.

She was looking for Leah Deitwaller. Three days had passed since Annie encountered Leah's parents. Two days had passed since she and Rufus nearly ran Leah over. And still Leah had not returned home. Annie had heard the news not two hours ago from Beth Stutzman, who was passing on information she had heard from her mother, Edna, who had taken a basket of jams out to the new family earlier in the day. Annie recognized the process of transmission as bordering on gossip, but she had reason to believe the information was accurate. How the Deitwallers could be so unconcerned about their daughter befuddled Annie. Even if Leah were a few months older than she was and technically no longer underage, why would they not be concerned for her safety?

Annie opened her mouth wide and drew in crisp, fall mountain air and then leaned forward to put her weight on one pedal and then the other. She had made this ride enough times in the last year—except during the wintry weather—to know just how much farther her endurance had to carry her before the highway would level out. She breathed in and out, in and out, her athlete's instinct being sure her muscles received sufficient oxygen to perform.

At the edge of the Beiler land, Annie could at last cease pedaling and coast a few yards at a time. If she had to, she would pedal all the way out to the Deitwaller farm, but her intuition told her it would be a waste of time to go that far. Leah was making a point. Not a good point, not a wise point, but a statement to her parents nevertheless. She would not lurk in their backyard.

Obviously Leah had ventured into town, a good ten miles from her parents' home. But Annie doubted she was seeking shelter in town. There simply were not enough empty structures, except new construction. Annie shook off the memory of Rufus's question about Leah's whereabouts on Sunday morning.

Annie slowed alongside a fence and waved at Joel Beiler astride his horse, Brownie, in the middle of his alfalfa field. Joel took the horse to the fence. He pulled a shirtsleeve under the brim of his hat and across his forehead, sopping up perspiration.

"It's a fine day to be outside," Annie said.

Joel nodded. "Outside is where the work is. What brings you out here?"

"I'm looking for someone. Leah Deitwaller."

Joel pointed. "Five miles that way."

"Yes, I know that's where their farm is. I don't think that's where Leah is, though."

Joel gave nothing away in his expression.

"Have you seen her?" Annie sat on her bicycle seat with one foot on the ground and the other on a pedal. "Maybe you thought she was on her way somewhere?"

"Yesterday."

Annie gave a slight gasp. She had not really expected any help from Joel. "Where?"

"Walking through the meadow across the highway."

"Could you tell where she was going?"

Joel stretched his lips into a straight line. "It would just be a guess."

"Then guess! I think she's in trouble, Joel. I'm worried."

He bumped a fist softly against his chin. "She was walking west. Not sure why anyone would go that way, but there is an old mining road."

"Where? Tell me how to find it."

Joel hesitated. "I don't want to hear that you got into trouble, too."

"I'm going to keep looking either way, Joel. Just give me some directions."

He shook his head. "Let me have a few minutes. I left the cart at the south end of the field. I'll go get it."

"I'll meet you there." Annie shifted her weight and put her bicycle in motion.

"Are you sure you know where you're going?" Annie gripped the seat beneath her with both hands.

"Well, if I don't, then it's better I did not send you off on a wild goose chase by yourself."

"But do you?"

"I can't promise Leah is going to be there."

Joel swung as hard a left turn as Annie had ever seen anyone make in a horse and cart. She refused to slide on the bench.

"Fine. Just show me where you saw her yesterday and we'll figure it out from there."

Annie scanned the meadow on both sides of the narrow road that Joel had found. It was barely more than a horse trail, but she could see how in Westcliffe's history it would have been an avenue between the mines and the population. Summer was waning. Around her the meadow already had begun to brown. Leah's dress would be bright—a rich blue and a purple apron if she was wearing the same dress Annie had last seen her in. But where on this meadow could Leah have found shelter? Soon home heating systems would go on at night. Even a dedicated camper would look for a way to keep warm.

"I think we found her." Joel slowed the horse.

Annie swung around to look out the other side of the cart, and there was the patch of blue and purple. Leah sat cross-legged on the ground with her head hanging almost to her lap.

Leah was crying, Annie realized. She put up a hand to signal Joel to stop then carefully exited the cart with no sudden movement. Annie glanced over her shoulder when the creak above the left wheel revealed Joel had left the cart as well. Leah's shoulders rose and fell with her sobs. Annie took one slow step at a time toward the girl. Finally, she was close enough to kneel beside her.

"Leah."

The girl's head snapped up. "What are you doing here? Can't a body have a moment of peace?"

Annie licked her lips. "It doesn't look like peace to me."

"I didn't ask you."

"Leah, let me help you." Behind Annie, Joel followed but kept his distance.

"Tell me how to take a train to Pennsylvania." Leah's eyes dared. "Get me a job in that shop you work in so I can earn train fare. You want to help me? That's what you can do."

Annie sat on the ground and said nothing.

"I suppose you want me to go to my parents." Leah sniffed.

"We could talk about it, at least."

Leah picked up a letter from her lap and waved it. "I walked into town yesterday and went to the post office. I asked if any mail was addressed to me, not to my parents, and I got this."

The letter bore a firm male hand and was written in Pennsylvania Dutch.

"Who is it from?" Annie asked quietly.

"From the only person on earth who really loves me."

"I see." Annie understood now why Leah was so desperate to return to Pennsylvania.

"He wants me to come back. We want to get married."

"You're only seventeen."

Leah rolled her eyes. "You're baptized Amish. You have to know that seventeen and Amish is not like seventeen and *English*."

It was still young, but Annie choked back her words.

"Don't say anything if you're just going to sound like my mother."

"Have you had other letters? Have you showed one to your mother?"

Leah expelled breath. "I tried. She tore it up without even taking it out of the envelope."

"I'm sorry." Annie pulled her knees up under her chin. "What if I asked you to come home with me?"

Leah's eyes widened. "To your house in town?"

Annie nodded. It would be a first step. If she could get Leah sheltered and cared for, perhaps the girl would agree to further conversation.

"It's a trick. Don't think Amish girls don't recognize tricks."

"I never said—"

Leah was on her feet and sprinting toward Brownie and the cart.

"Wait!" Annie called.

Joel sprang into action, too. But Leah had too much of a head start on them. She leaped into the cart and picked up the reins. Brownie responded to the sound she made and the signals of the reins and began a rapid trot.

Rufus looked at the newspaper folded neatly on the coffee shop table he had chosen to occupy. It was just the local Westcliffe paper, in print for over a hundred years. Rufus thought of it like the *Budget*, the Amish newspaper out of Sugarcreek, Ohio, that congregations around the nation read. It was full of news and information that might pique the curiosity of members of the community but would not interest outsiders. Rufus nudged the paper out of his way and set his coffee down.

A shadow crossed the table and Rufus looked up. "Hello, Tom."

"I'm glad you could meet." Tom sat across from Rufus. "How are you for work? I might have a lead for you."

Rufus cleared his throat. "Well, the fire has caused a setback, and you already know David has no orders for me right now."

"This could be steady work over the winter."

"I usually try to build hope chests when construction slows down."

"But you have no orders."

"God will provide."

Tom sipped coffee. "Could God provide by giving you a full-time job?"

"Full-time?"

"For a few months. A friend of mine in Cañon City keeps a carpenter on his staff, but the guy got hurt—on his own time. This is nothing dangerous. But he won't be back to work for four months."

Rufus turned the pages of a mental calendar. "Cañon City is too far. How would I get there and back every day?"

"It's not all in Cañon City. The jobs are spread around the southwest part of the state. He remodels apartment buildings, office complexes, and small hotels. You'd be installing ready-made cabinets. It's all indoors."

Rufus twisted his lips. "I don't know, Tom. I don't see how that could work."

"Granted, it would be a change for you. But my buddy's a good guy. Jeff would pay you well. And he would put you up near each job. The money could get you through the winter."

"Sleep away from home?" Among the *English*? Rufus had built cabinets for many *English* homes. Each one was a work of beauty that brought glory to God. Working as an employee of an *English* had never tempted him, though. He did not want to fall into thinking that any work was beneath him, but the thought of separating from his family—and Annalise—fed his reluctance.

"You could do this in your sleep, Rufus." Tom tilted his head back and drank the last of his coffee. "It's honest work. It's temporary, something to get you through a rough patch."

Annie lurched toward the moving buggy. "Leah!"

Joel was four strides ahead of her and broke into a sprint. If it were not for her dress, Annie could have caught him, even passed him. The rhythms of running track in high school and college still rose from her muscles when called upon, and she felt the adrenaline now. But while Annie had to use her hands to lift her hem out of the dirt, Joel pumped his limbs and ran freely.

Leah did not look back as Annie and Joel chased her up the old rutted road.

Then with a thud, Annie hit the ground. Though she caught herself on her hands, the damage was done in her right ankle. Wincing, she sat up. Even Joel was slowing down. If anything, Leah was driving faster.

Joel finally stopped and turned to look at Annie. She pushed up to her feet and started limping toward him, testing her ankle with each step.

"I'm sorry," Annie said once they were close enough to speak. "I had no idea she would do something like this."

Joel offered an arm to Annie. "How bad is your foot?"

"I used to run races on worse injuries, but that's been a few years." Leaning on his arm, she was able to move at a steady pace, but the irregular terrain made speed challenging. "I hope she won't hurt Brownie."

It was an hour later when they reached the highway and found the horse, still attached to the cart, grazing contentedly.

Leah Deitwaller was nowhere in sight.

Eight

Annie lifted her right ankle while Ruth slid a pillow beneath it and gently pressed an ice pack against the lump. "Thanks for driving me out here."

"I was coming for Sunday dinner with my family anyway." Ruth settled at the end of the couch. "Do you need anything else?"

Annie shook her head. "I can't believe I sprained my ankle chasing a buggy."

"You're lucky it's not broken."

"Lucky?" Annie smiled. "Have you become so *English* as to believe in luck?"

A smile escaped Ruth's lips. "*Gottes wille.* You are blessed that your ankle is not broken."

"It's not really too bad anymore. It's been three days, after all."

"Don't rush the healing. It takes time."

"Yes, Nurse Beiler." Annie pulled an afghan off the back of the sofa and spread it over her lap and legs. "I'm glad Brownie and the buggy were all right, but I'm worried about Leah Deitwaller."

"You can't help someone who doesn't want help," Ruth said.

"Oh, she wants help, all right. She just wants it on her terms."

Ruth checked the position of the ice pack against Annie's

ankle. "It amounts to the same thing."

"I wish I understood what her parents are thinking. Do you think they even know about the young man in Pennsylvania?"

"That's hard to say. Many Amish couples keep their feelings to themselves until they are sure that the way is clear for them to marry."

"But surely Leah would have told her parents why she did not want to move to Colorado. What if they don't know this man? What if he is from another district and they don't know that he would be a perfectly wonderful husband for their daughter?"

Ruth cocked her head.

Annie threw her hands up. "I know, I know. I'm meddling. Trying to solve a problem that is not mine to solve."

"Well," Ruth said, "I'm relieved we don't have to have that conversation again."

"You probably think I am as hardheaded as Leah."

"I didn't say that."

"If I didn't think it would hurt my foot to move that pillow, I would throw it at you."

Ruth laughed. "No more acts of *English* aggression from you. You are a baptized Amish now."

The door between the dining room and kitchen creaked open and eight-year-old Jacob appeared lugging a bag of ice. "We're going to make ice cream in the barn. Rufus says I can turn the crank."

Towering over Jacob, Rufus stood with a pan of cooked mixture.

"I love homemade ice cream." Annie met Rufus's pleased expression.

"You won't chase any runaway horses while I'm in the barn, will you?" Rufus's violet-blue eyes teased a warning.

"I think I've learned that lesson."

She watched as the two brothers—the eldest and youngest of the Beiler children, more than twenty years apart—passed through the room and out the front door.

"They'll be back for salt," Ruth predicted. "Rufus never remembers it."

"I know," Annie said.

"Speaking of Amish couples," Ruth said, "has Rufus said anything about making things official?"

Annie had thought he would move their relationship along a little more quickly now.

"Well?" Ruth prodded. "What's he thinking?"

"I wish I knew."

Rufus sent Jacob back to the house for the salt and carefully poured into the metal canister the mixture his sister Sophie had cooked on the stove. By the time his little brother returned, Rufus had the blade fixed in the vanilla goop and the lid on the canister. Together they lowered the can onto the bolt in the bottom of the wooden barrel and fastened it in place.

Jacob began to crank. What the boy lacked in physical strength he made up for in determination. Rufus decided to let Jacob give the task his best effort and see how long he lasted. Eventually, as the ice cream thickened, Jacob would need help.

The barn was the place where Rufus had first met Annalise—who of course had not known what she was getting herself into by turning up stranded among the Amish with her *English* life in a convoluted mess. He had driven her to town, where she hoped to find a ride to a location that met her expectations for civilization, someplace with a rental car business, or at least a bus station.

Only she had decided to stay overnight at Mo's motel. And then a few nights. And then half the summer.

And then she bought a house in Westcliffe and began coming to church.

Certainly Rufus was never sorry she had been so reluctant to leave. Now she seemed to have long ago given up any thought of returning to live in Colorado Springs.

She was expecting a proposal, and he was no less anxious to offer one than she was to receive it. But Annalise had given up a personal fortune to join the Amish. How could he ask her to marry him while the bottom was falling out of his business?

"Peach," Jacob said.

Rufus roused. "I'm sorry?"

"We should have made peach. It's Annalise's favorite."

"That it is." Rufus smiled. Even his little brother knew Annalise well.

The job Tom's friend offered him was only through the winter. Would it be so bad?

One by one, Ruth's family members wandered out to the barn, where she knew they would take turns cranking the ice cream. By now melted ice would be making a mess. Soon the mixture would go into the freezer so it would be ready after a light supper. Ruth would have gone out as well except that Annalise had dozed off, and Ruth did not want her to wake and find herself alone. Ruth had found her mother's mending basket and put her hands to good use while Annalise softly snored.

When she heard the purr of a motor, Ruth sat erect and looked out the front window. She did not recognize the vehicle, a gray Mitsubishi that looked to be a few years old.

But she recognized the man who emerged from the driver's side and spied the front porch.

Ruth pushed the mending basket aside, glanced at Annalise, and crossed the room before Bryan Nichols could ring the bell. She stepped out on the porch. At the last minute she decided to pull the main door closed before shutting the screen door behind her. Taking the seven steps down to the yard, Ruth looked toward the open barn door. Laughter greeted her ears and she was grateful that, for the moment, her family was absorbed in the simplicity of making ice cream.

Because they certainly would not understand the complexity of a visit from Bryan Nichols any more than Elijah Capp had understood her accidental meeting with Bryan on the trail. She put a finger to her lips and motioned for him to follow her around the far side of the house.

"What are you doing here?" Ruth asked when they were out of sight from the barn.

"I wanted to see where you live." Bryan looked around, puzzled.

"But why?" Her heart pounded. "And I don't actually live here."

"I asked someone, and they said this was the Beiler farm."

"It is." Ruth hid her nervous hands in the folds of her calf-length corduroy skirt. "My family lives here. I just came to spend Sunday with them."

"What's going on, Ruth? Why is it a big deal if I drop by?"

She blew her breath out. "It's complicated."

"I'm a college graduate and a firefighter. I understand complicated things."

"Amish complicated is different." His green eyes made something puddle deep in her gut. "Did you need something?"

"I just wanted to tell you I enjoyed running into you the other day. Maybe we could plan ahead next time and enjoy the trail together. And then I could buy you dinner."

She swallowed with deliberation. Was an *English* man asking her for a date?

The sound of a metal feed pail knocking against the side of the house made Ruth jump, though she had done nothing to feel guilty about.

"*Mamm*!"

"I thought you were in the house." Franey Beiler looked from Ruth to Bryan. "Would you like to introduce your friend?"

"This is Bryan," Ruth said. "Rufus and I met him last week out at the house that burned. He is a firefighter."

"Oh. Thank you for your service." Franey set her empty bucket in a stack of six others. "Would you like to come inside? We are about to have sandwiches and homemade ice cream."

Ruth's eyes widened. Her mother was one of the most hospitable people Ruth had ever known, even toward the *English*. But Bryan inside the house? If he were to repeat his invitation where someone might hear it—well, Ruth did not want to imagine the scene that might follow. Silently pleading, she caught Bryan's eyes and shook her head almost imperceptibly.

Annie woke to the clatter of Beilers claiming their front porch. Franey and Eli. Sophie and Lydia. Joel and Jacob.

She loved every one of them. And she knew they loved her. If Rufus did not ask her to marry him, she still had a spot in the Beiler family for as long as she wanted it. If Franey and Eli knew what was in their son's heart, they would not say.

Gottes wille.

They tumbled into the house, Jacob prancing around his father, who carried the canister of ice cream.

"Can't I just have a taste?" Jacob begged. "Just one spoonful?"

Eli shook his head. "It's too soft. And you don't want to spoil your supper."

Annie sat up and tested her ankle against the floor. Perceiving no objection to bearing weight, she stood and moved cautiously toward the door. Where were Ruth and Rufus?

Ruth stood in the long drive, speaking to someone through a vehicle window. Rufus stood at the base of the front porch steps, his arms crossed behind his back in that way that Annie knew meant he was watching the scene carefully. She stepped out on the porch.

"What's going on?" she asked.

Rufus looked up the stairs at her. "An *English* man came by to see Ruth."

"Here?"

Rufus nodded.

"You don't approve," Annie said.

"It is not for me to approve or disapprove."

"But you don't approve."

"I don't think he knew any better," Rufus said.

"Ruth would not have invited him here."

"No, I don't believe so."

"Then what is there to disapprove of?"

"You are the one who insists I disapprove."

Annie watched Ruth for a few seconds. "It looks to me that she is being polite, just as she would have learned from your parents."

"I have no doubt."

Abruptly Annie realized that whatever troubled Rufus had nothing to do with his sister. "What's wrong, Rufus?"

He shook his head. "It's nothing."

Annie knew she would get nothing else out of him tonight. But she hated the way that truth twisted her stomach.

Nine

May 1892

Joseph lay on his side, eyes closed. "Zeke?"

No response came, and Joseph wrestled with the moment when he might have sunk back into a deep sleep. He sensed the vague presence of sunlight beyond his eyelids. "Zeke."

Joseph pushed up on one elbow. He had been more than agreeable to a night in a hotel, despite the stares that came with it, but Zeke had insisted on having their own room rather than conserve cash by sharing with two *English* men. Joseph raked fingers through his bowl-cut hair and wondered how long ago Zeke had left the room. Swinging his feet to the floor forced Joseph upright and gave him a view straight out the window. The sun blazed halfway up the sky. Joseph had not slept so late since he was a boy. He slapped the thick hotel mattress in blame.

With the heels of his hands, Joseph wiped sleep from his eyes, and then he reached for his clothes. No telling what Zeke would be up to by now.

Joseph dressed, combed his hair, donned his hat, and ignored his hunger. The clerk in the lobby reported that Mr. Berkey had been down for breakfast more than two hours ago and then left the building without indicating his intentions.

Unfortunately for Joseph, the hotel's small kitchen was now closed for breakfast and at least two hours from opening for a midday meal.

He wandered into the sunlight, considering whether it was more urgent to check to see that their horses had been well cared for at the stables or to track Zeke. He opted for Zeke. The stablemen were more likely to look after the horses adequately than Zeke was to stay out of trouble.

Self-conscious, Joseph made his way down Gassville's main street looking through plate glass windows and open shop doors. Finding one Amish man among all these *English* could not prove too difficult a task. Joseph paused outside John Twigg's Mercantile, remembering Zeke's remark the day before about the man's anger and deciding not to enter. He continued a methodical yet subtle search for his friend. Eventually his walk took him back to the Denton Emporium. Instinct told Joseph to push the door open.

A number of people milled around the shop, some with lists, others inspecting the textiles. Zeke stood near the counter at the back of the store.

With the *English* woman.

"Oh, there you are." Zeke gestured for Joseph to step to the counter.

Joseph shifted his eyes from Zeke to Miss Woodley and back again, nodding at them both noncommittally.

"I came in to inquire what sorts of supplies the Dentons can order," Zeke said. "Miss Woodley overheard and has been kind enough to tell me how resourceful the owners are at procuring whatever one might want."

"I see," Joseph said. "Our needs would be simple, of course. *Guder mariye*, Miss Woodley." Good morning.

"I trust you rested well."

The pleasantry in Miss Woodley's eyes seemed sincere. Perhaps with some reflection overnight she decided that Zeke and Joseph were no threat to the fragile peace of Gassville.

A ruckus in front of the store drew Zeke and a few others to the window.

"It's Twigg!" someone called out.

"That does not look like a man with all his wits," Zeke said.

Joseph glanced at Miss Woodley, who gripped the edge of the counter with hands covered in white gloves.

"Does he have a gun?" The question came from Lee Denton, behind the counter.

Zeke shook his head. "I don't see one."

Joseph would have preferred Zeke to stay out of whatever was about to happen. There would be no explaining this to the bishop.

"He's standing in the middle of the street with his arms crossed," Zeke reported.

"He could be hiding a gun," Lee Denton said.

When the voice boomed from the street, Joseph startled.

"Denton, you fool!" hollered John Twigg. "You are hiring people to steal from my store so you can sell those goods yourself. You idiots! Did you think I would not figure it out?"

Joseph moved toward Zeke, wanting to pull him back. In the process, he glimpsed John Twigg, bareheaded and—as far as Joseph could see—unarmed. His face flamed with fury.

Maura heard voices outside yelling back at John Twigg, but she could not tell whose. If she got her hands on whoever was inciting John, she would throttle the culprit. A person would have to be half-insane to take up with John.

The man had lost all sense of reason. He was not always like this. Belle had been enamored of John for so long that she refused to acknowledge the turn in him. Maura worried what might become of Belle if she really did marry John Twigg.

"What happened to Walter?" someone asked.

Maura's stomach lurched, and she released her grip on the counter to turn and face the commotion. "He was sweeping the sidewalk out there a few minutes ago."

"Well, I don't see him now."

Before she could move to the front of the store to look out the window for herself, a *click* behind the counter made her gasp.

The sound of a shooter readying a pistol.

Lee and Ing Denton both stood behind the counter of their emporium with pistols in their hands.

"What are you doing?" she demanded. "That will not solve anything."

"If he has a gun, we have to be ready," Lee said.

"You already asked if he had a gun," Maura said. "Mr. Berkey informs us he does not."

Lee shook his head. "He said he did not see one. That's not the same."

Another *click*. Another pistol cocked.

"Ing, no." Maura slapped the counter. "This is not the way."

"He's the crazy man." Ing Denton nudged his brother out from behind the counter. Lee cocked a third pistol and led the way with a gun in each hand. Ing followed with his. Customers stepped back to clear their path to the front of the store.

Maura swallowed hard and followed them. "Has anyone spotted Walter?" She stumbled on the hem of her skirt and looked down at her shoes.

In that moment, the shots rang out.

"It's Walter!" a woman cried. "They've shot Walter in the heart."

Joseph pushed past Lee and Ing and Zeke and even Miss Woodley, oblivious to danger now, and saw Walter run past the front of the store with his hand over his chest. The boy reminded him of his younger brother, Little Jake, both gangly and fair haired, and his protective instinct kicked in.

He grabbed Walter, who was bellowing now. If the boy was screaming and running, Joseph wondered, how badly could he be hurt? Yet blood spurted between the fingers clasped over his chest.

"Make him lie down." The instruction came from Miss Woodley, but Joseph agreed. The gunshots had stopped, and even if they had not, Joseph would not abandon Miss Woodley and Walter at a time of need. Being a person of peace did not mean withholding compassion.

It was easy enough to lay Walter on the sidewalk he had been sweeping only moments ago. Maura Woodley knelt beside the boy on the other side.

"We must move his hand and see the damage." Maura's face crunched in on itself.

Walter was still thrashing his legs, but he offered no resistance when Joseph moved to pry the boy's fingers apart. Beneath them, he found no wound.

Then Maura held the fingers of Walter's left hand. "Why, he's been hit in the knuckles."

Joseph wiped the boy's knuckles with his shirtsleeve then leaned back on his heels and expelled his pent-up breath. "It looks a lot worse than it is."

"Thank you. You risked your life for my cousin."

Joseph drank in her dark eyes for the first time. All he could think of was that he hoped someone would have done the same for Little Jake. He grabbed his shirt at the shoulder seam and yanked. The sleeve came loose, and he wrapped it around Walter's bleeding hand.

"He should see the doctor," Maura said, her hands helping to wrap her cousin's fingers.

"Of course." Joseph looked up and down the street. "Which way?"

Zeke was suddenly behind him. "I know the way."

Ezekiel Berkey had not been in Gassville any longer than Joseph Beiler, but at the moment Joseph was glad for Zeke's propensity to snoop wherever he went. Joseph's eyes settled on John Twigg, and he pointed. "Someone should help him, too."

John Twigg lay in the street, bleeding from his head like a stuck pig.

"I'll go for the doctor." Zeke scooped up Walter and put him on his feet. "Follow me, Joseph."

"Why did they shoot me?" Walter asked. "And I know where the doctor is better than strangers."

"Just go, Walter," Maura said. "Let them look after you. Don't worry about John Twigg right now."

"I've seen enough hog butcherings," Walter said, "to know that a mad animal takes a long time to die. John Twigg is gonna be like that, I just know."

"Hush, Walter." Maura turned to Joseph. "If Doc Denton is not in his office, try Dr. Lindsay. He's farther away, though."

"I saw his shingle," Mr. Berkey said.

"Hurry!"

Two strangers, whom she had suspected of ill will only yesterday, had custody of Walter. The boy would be fine. For John Twigg's sake, though, Maura hoped Mr. Berkey knew the town as well as he claimed. Around the angry shopkeeper, a few people had realized the severity of his wound and stood and pointed. No one stepped forward to help him, and neither did Maura. No human being, not even John Twigg, deserved Walter's comparison to a hog butchering. But no one could help him—perhaps not even one of the doctors—and nothing Maura did would change that.

The street fell silent as the crowd realized that the Denton-Twigg feud had taken a fatal twist.

It was Belle Mooney that worried Maura now.

Ten

"Are you sure?" Outside his hardware store on Main Street on Tuesday morning, Tom Reynolds crossed his arms, puzzled.

Annie answered without hesitation. "I'll pay you twice your usual rate for taxi service."

Tom waved the offer away. "That's not necessary. If you've made up your mind, I'll take you."

"I promise not to tie up your time for a minute longer than necessary." Annie straightened the bib of her black apron. "Do you know where the Deitwaller farm is?"

"I have a vague idea."

"Good enough for me."

"I'll pull my truck around."

They found the farm thirty minutes later. Annie scanned for signs that someone was home. The land was farther out and more isolated than the Beilers', reminding Annie that most of the Amish in Custer County were farther from town. The day called for no scheduled sewing or quilting gatherings among the women, so unless Eva Deitwaller was making a visit, she would be home. As Tom eased his red pickup to a stop outside the home, Annie saw the family's buggy parked at the edge of the yard.

"You can still change your mind," Tom said.

Annie shook her head. "Wait here, please. I won't be long."

She approached the front door, set her jaw, and knocked.

Mrs. Deitwaller came to the screen door.

"Hello," Annie said. "I wonder if I might come in and talk to you." Amish hospitality would make it difficult for Eva to send her away. For extra assurance, Annie raised a hand to the door handle. Eva complied by unlatching the hook and eye.

Annie tried not to glance around the front room in too curious a manner. The invitation to sit that she hoped for did not come, so she held her hands together calmly and determined not to sound aggressive.

"I wondered if Leah is home," Annie said. "I thought I might invite her to visit the Beilers with me. They have daughters around her age."

"We know who the Beilers are." Mrs. Deitwaller pulled a dish towel off her shoulder and wiped her hands.

"Yes, of course. Sophie and Lydia are lovely girls. I thought Leah might enjoy spending more time with them."

"Well, she's not here."

"Oh?" Annie's fingers twitched. "Perhaps I could leave a note."

Mrs. Deitwaller shrugged. "If you're fishing to know whether Leah has come home, you can stop right there. She hasn't."

Annie tried to look sympathetic. "You must be concerned about her."

"She's a headstrong child. Always has been."

"But. . .where is she staying? You must be wondering if she is safe."

"No need to tell me what I must be wondering."

Annie's right forefinger began to tap. "I'm sure if the two of you sat down and talked about your differences, you could find a way through them."

"Just what do you know of our differences?"

Annie moistened her lips. "I know Leah was. . .unenthusiastic about the move to Colorado."

"We're her parents. We know what's best for her."

Annie's tongue formed sounds faster than she could stop it now. "Leah has been gone more than a week. Isn't it best for her to be somewhere safe, with people who care for her, who will listen to her?"

Even under Eva Deitwaller's long dress, Annie saw her shoes move to shoulder width apart. One hand went to a hip.

"I'll thank you not to come in here with your *English* ways," Mrs. Deitwaller said. "You're barely baptized."

Annie's spine straightened. "I gave a lot of thought and prayer to my baptism."

"What I hear is that you give a lot of thought to Rufus Beiler."

Warmth rose through Annie's face. "I was baptized because I want to be Amish. Because God called me to be Amish."

"You don't have any idea what you are getting into." Eva scoffed.

Balled into fists, Annie's hands moved to her sides, where she hid them in the folds of her skirt. "That's not true. I studied with the bishop. I worship regularly with the congregation."

"Yes, well, time will tell. But when it comes to Leah, you know nothing. She lives in her imagination. You have no idea what kind of trouble she is capable of causing."

"She seems quite sincere to me," Annie said. "She certainly is of an age to fall in love and think about her future."

"She has always made up stories of how she would like things to be rather than how they really are."

"Why would her young man write to her if he did not share her feelings?"

"I can assure you my husband will put a stop to that." Eva waved one hand. "Certainly you can see Leah does not have the maturity for that kind of relationship."

Annie dug her fists into her hips. This was going nowhere. If Leah and her mother would have a reasonable, calm conversation, they might both learn some things about each other. "I only want to help. Everyone deserves to be happy."

"You're as naive as Leah. May God help you both to come to your senses." Mrs. Deitwaller opened the door and tilted her head out toward the yard.

Annie stifled her response and marched, head up, out to Tom's truck. Inside, she slammed the door.

Tom raised a questioning eye.

"In her eyes, I'll always be taken for *English*. But she's wrong."

"Your young man was just here." Mrs. Weichert bent at the waist to rearrange the assortment of Amish jams on the shelf nearest the counter.

Annie tucked her small purse on the shelf under the counter and pushed it to the back. "Did he say what he wanted?"

"No, but he offered to unload my truck."

"I was going to do that."

"I know." Mrs. Weichert gave a slight smile. "He's just waiting for you, dear. Check the alley."

Annie hoped her *kapp* was on straight. She had slouched in Tom's truck all the way back into town, sullen and silent. She crossed the length of the shop and went into the back room. The door to the alley was propped open, and a few seconds later Rufus stepped through with a pair of upholstered dining chairs.

He set them down. "Ah. You're back. Mrs. Weichert was not sure why you were a few minutes late."

"I should have come in earlier instead of wasting my time." She scuffled toward the door. "Is there much more?"

He set the chairs beside a tower of six boxes. "This is the last of it. It's all from an estate sale in Pueblo."

"We almost always find a few things we can use."

"Annalise, why did you say you wasted your time?" He stood with one hand on a chair.

She hesitated.

"I know Leah Deitwaller has been on your mind a lot."

Annie idly stroked the faded fabric and settled her hand next to his. "If she is on her mother's mind, you would never know it. I was just there. I'm worried about Leah, but now I'm starting to wonder if her parents could be charged with neglect."

"Are you thinking of making such an allegation yourself?"

"No." She looked up into his violet-blue eyes. "I'm just grateful that the first Amish woman I met was your mother and not Leah's. We might not be standing here right now if it had been Eva Deitwaller."

"I know you want to help." He covered her fingers with his hand. "And I'm sorry if Leah's mother was harsh with you."

Annie rolled her eyes. "But I should mind my own business."

"There may be more to the Deitwallers' story than we know."

"Or Leah may be a confused young woman who is doing something foolish, even dangerous. Shouldn't somebody care?"

He squeezed her fingers, and she looked again at his face. His lips parted, as if he were about to tell her something. He closed them and moistened them without saying anything.

"Rufus, what's wrong? I'm sorry. I haven't been paying any attention to what might be bothering you."

He shook his head. "I just need to work out some business matters."

"A new project?"

He shrugged one shoulder. "Something a little different. I'm not sure it's right for me."

Rufus tugged on her hand, removing it from the chair and pulling her toward him. He glanced into the shop and then out into the alley before tilting his head to her upturned face and letting his lips linger on hers.

Annie tingled from head to toe. Rufus hardly ever kissed her, certainly not in a place where someone might walk in.

At the moment, though, she did not care. She placed her hands on his broad shoulders and deepened the kiss.

When her shift in the shop was over, Annie walked home and circled her house to the back porch. All afternoon she agitated first over Leah and then over Rufus. Leah was likely to do something rash—probably already had. Rufus likely had never made a rash decision in his life. But there was something he was not saying, something his kiss was meant to tell her.

Before going into the kitchen, Annie checked the small cupboard on the back porch where she kept a basket of garden vegetables. She could make herself a warm supper and have something waiting for Ruth later. And in the meantime, Annie would figure out what to do about Leah.

The basket was empty.

No, the basket was gone.

Ruth must have taken it inside, Annie reasoned. Then she reminded herself that the basket had been there just that morning. Annie had picked green beans before flagging down Tom Reynolds, and Ruth had left for the clinic while Annie was still in the garden.

She turned around and surveyed the yard. Then she descended the three steps and paced over to the vegetable patch. The produce had been thinning for several weeks, but Annie was sure she had bypassed a zucchini plant and one beanpole this morning because she judged she could wait another day or two before picking.

Someone had raided her garden, and Annie was pretty sure she knew who it was.

She smiled. This meant Leah Deitwaller could not be far away.

Rufus pulled open the door of the trailer that housed Kramer Construction and stepped inside the office. Karl Kramer's administrative assistant aimed her thumb toward the inner office, and Rufus stepped past her desk.

In the inner office, the foreman of Kramer Construction rose from behind Karl's desk. "Thanks for coming by."

"It is my privilege." Rufus dipped his hat. "Do you have news from Karl?"

"He has asked me to handle things for a while." The foreman gestured that Rufus should sit in the chair beside the desk.

Rufus widened his eyes. "A while? Is he well?"

"Karl is fine. He just decided to spend more time with his father in Virginia."

"I thought perhaps the fire would bring him home."

"He was angry, but that's a matter for the insurance companies now. The buyers are not sure they want to build again, and their lawyer says that our failure to meet the contract date allows them to change their minds."

"But surely under the circumstances—"

The foreman shook his head. "We're all taking a hit on this, Rufus. I wanted to tell you in person that Karl is not planning to start any new projects over the winter. He wanted to be sure you knew it was nothing personal."

Eleven

Annie straightened the stack of hard-to-find books at the back of the shop, wiping dust from each volume with a cotton rag. Some gems came through the shop, but no one would ever know it unless they stumbled on a volume on a lark of a summer's weekend. Soon the weather would turn cold, and fewer people would be happening on Westcliffe because they were out for a drive.

Once, Annie had mentioned to Mrs. Weichert that it would be an easy thing to set up a website and engage in e-commerce. If they listed with a few trade organizations and invested in some minimal online advertising, people looking for particular rare books could find the shop on the Internet. These books could go to interested buyers rather than get trucked to the Salvation Army in Pueblo, where who knows what happened to them next.

Mrs. Weichert had waved off the idea. She was content with her income and reasoned that dealers in the region knew where she was. If they couldn't be bothered to drive out to her shop, then they must not be all that curious about her inventory in any given month.

Annie had to admit it was probably just as well. Living in

Westcliffe for the last year, well away from her former high-tech life as an innovative software designer, had not completely quelled her entrepreneurial urges. But it was better for her not to be tempted to begin yet another business with computers at its heart.

With one last swipe of the rag, Annie resisted the urge to pick up a book with a faded red binding and open it. If it did not sell soon, though, she would ask for it. Its title promised a wealth of information on nineteenth-century population shifts in western Tennessee and Arkansas. In the last few months, Annie had developed a fascination with stories of people who had taken great risks that changed their lives. All the people she had known in Colorado Springs would have laughed at her curious interest, but she did not care. Wasn't it better to take a risk than just let life happen to you by never wondering what else was out there?

"I'll take those bags of clothes down to the thrift store now," Annie said.

"Thank you." Mrs. Weichert was counting bills at the cash register. "They'll try to pay you, but I don't want their money."

One in each hand, Annie hefted two black plastic garbage bags by the knots tied at the tops.

Mrs. Weichert crossed the store and picked up the red volume Annie had been eyeing. She stuck it under Annie's arm. "You might as well take this. I can tell you want to read it, and it will be next to impossible to sell."

"Thank you." It was not the first book Mrs. Weichert had stuck under Annie's arm after finding her picking it up repeatedly during her shifts.

"You can go on home after that," Mrs. Weichert said. "It looks like rain. No one will be coming in."

"All right. Thanks."

"Don't forget you have tomorrow off. My daughter will be here to help."

Mrs. Weichert held the door open, and Annie stepped out onto the sidewalk. They always took the clothes that turned up in Mrs. Weichert's shop to the thrift store three doors down. Sometimes she bought the odds and ends of an estate sale, and getting the dishes or small furniture she wanted meant she also had to take old clothes.

Vintage clothes, Annie had once corrected her employer. If they just set up one rack in the shop, she was sure they could sell them. Once again her entrepreneurial streak had raised its head, and once again Mrs. Weichert had no interest.

"What delights have you brought us today?" Carlene, perched on a stool behind the counter at the thrift store, raised her eyes and smiled.

Annie liked Carlene's natural warmth. "I'm afraid I didn't even look this time. I hope you find something worth your while."

"I remember how you used to come in here for clothes when you first came to town. You had a good eye for value."

Annie dropped the two bags behind the counter and gestured toward her Amish dress. "Now look at me."

Carlene stood up and hit a button on the cash register. "Let me give you something to take to Mrs. Weichert."

Annie raised both hands. "You know she won't take it."

"I'm not running a charity shop, you know."

"Well, neither is she." Annie scanned the shop. "Maybe I'll have a look around for old time's sake."

"There's some nice bedding in the back if you need any blankets for the winter."

Knowing that Mrs. Weichert did not expect her back, Annie was in no hurry. She ran her hand along a pile of sweaters then opened a blank journal. Farther down the aisle, she picked up a backpack that looked brand new and started checking the zippers and clasps. Voices hissed from the other side of the shelf.

"Why do I have to get a sleeping bag here?" a small boy whined.

The voice sounded like its owner was no older than Jacob Beiler. Annie dipped her head slightly to try to see him through the shelving.

"Because you are the one who lost your old sleeping bag. I'm not paying good money to replace it with something brand new."

"But I didn't!"

"I washed it and hung it on the line myself," the child's mother said. "It would be just like you to drag it off somewhere and get it dirty again. And then you didn't want to tell me the truth because you thought you would get in trouble. One way or another you're going to learn your lesson."

"But Mom," the boy insisted, "I didn't take it off the line. I'm telling you the truth. Why won't you believe me?"

"We're finished talking about this. The only reason I'm buying you another sleeping bag at all is because you were invited on that camping trip."

"I don't want to go if I have to take this dumb little kid's sleeping bag."

"You promised your friend you would go, and you will."

The woman nudged her son's shoulder toward the front of the store. She may not have believed the boy's protests, but Annie did.

"She's not here," Mrs. Weichert said when Ruth ducked her head into the antiques shop looking for Annalise. "I sent her to the thrift store and then told her she didn't need to come back."

"Thank you, Mrs. Weichert."

Ruth paced down the sidewalk to the thrift store, pulled its door open, and nearly tripped over Annalise.

"Ruth, what are you doing here?"

"I'm finished for the day, and I hear you are, too."

Annalise nodded. "I'm still not used to seeing you in scrubs."

Ruth tugged at the hem of her shirt. "I'm not sure I'm used to wearing them, either."

"They look comfortable."

"They are." Ruth grinned. "I'm in the mood for a sandwich from the bakery. Want one?"

"Sure. My stomach has been rumbling for an hour."

They crossed the street and ambled toward the other end of Main Street.

"Ruth," Annalise said, "we didn't get a chance to talk the other day. Why was that man out at the house?"

Ruth's stomach clenched. She knew Annalise was going to ask—and that was one of the reasons Ruth suggested lunch, to get this conversation out of the way.

"I suppose because he wanted my phone number." Ruth steeled herself for Annalise's response.

"An *English* man is interested in you?" Annalise's jaw dropped.

"Is that so hard to believe?" Indignation roiled in Ruth's stomach.

"Well, no, I didn't mean it like that." Annalise hid her hands under her black apron. "I just didn't think. . .well, that you would. . ."

"Be interested in an *English* man? Is that what you can't bring yourself to say?"

"Um. . .yes, actually. I know how you feel about Elijah Capp and how he feels about you."

Ruth kicked a pebble. "And you also know it's an impossible situation."

"I am not ready to concede that point."

Ruth did not want to offend Annalise by suggesting that her friend still thought like an *English* sometimes. "It's complicated, Annalise. Besides, I have done nothing to encourage Bryan Nichols. I don't think he even knows what it would mean to get involved with someone like me, or he would never have shown up at my parents' house."

Annalise nodded. "I have to agree with you there."

"It will blow over in a few days."

"Is that what you want?"

Ruth put one hand in the patch pocket of her scrubs shirt. "It's the best thing. Bryan just doesn't know it yet."

They reached the bakery. Annalise held open the door, and

Ruth moved to one of three small round tables.

"What would you like?" Ruth asked. "My treat. It's the least I can do for free rent this semester."

Annalise set her book on the table and pondered the handwritten menu. "How about roast beef on hearty whole wheat?"

"I'll order." Ruth took her debit card from a pocket. "You sit."

The bakery was empty other than Ruth and Annalise and the two employees behind the counter. Ruth ordered the sandwiches then pointed to two enormous chocolate chip cookies. She sidestepped to the end of the counter and pulled several paper napkins out of a metal dispenser. Behind her the shop's door creaked open.

When Ruth turned around, she was face-to-face with Mrs. Capp.

"Hello, Ruth." Mrs. Capp neither smiled nor scowled.

Ruth cleared her throat, looking for her voice. "Hello. How are you?"

"Fine. We are all fine."

"That's good."

"Elijah tells me you plan to be nearby for a few months."

"Just for the semester. Then I will go back to school."

"Why don't you come for supper one night?"

Ruth nearly choked on the effort it took not to let her jaw go slack. "You're kind to ask."

"I mean it. You and Elijah need some time to talk."

Ruth said nothing, unsure whether Mrs. Capp wanted her to talk to Elijah in hopes they would reunite or so Elijah would let go once and for all.

Two sturdy plates clinked against the counter behind her, and Ruth turned to see the sandwiches and cookies. She picked them up then said, "It was nice to see you."

Annalise's gray eyes were wide with curiosity. "What did she say?"

"She invited me to supper."

"Will you go?"

Ruth moistened her lips before sucking them both in.

"I'm not sure," Rufus said into the cell phone he used only for business conversations. "Might I have one more day to make a decision?"

"I'll ask Jeff if he can wait another day," Tom Reynolds said. "He seems eager to have you. You'll be a reliable worker for a change."

"I appreciate his kindness in considering me." Rufus scratched the back of his head. "But it will mean a very different schedule over the winter, and I must be certain this is God's provision. I do not want to grasp at straws out of lack of faith."

Rufus had kissed Annalise rather than talk to her about the job. It was *hochmut*, he feared, that kept him from being forthright. Pride. He wanted to provide for a woman who was more than capable of providing for herself. The kiss was meant to reassure her, while she waited for words he knew she wanted to hear.

But it might have confused her instead. It certainly confused him.

"I promise to have a decision tomorrow," Rufus said to Tom. "Being away from my family, leaving behind my own work, installing cabinets for an *English*—this is not a change I would make lightly."

"I understand," Tom said. "I'll wait to hear from you tomorrow."

Rufus closed the flip phone and set it on his workbench. When he turned to find his pencil and review his sketches for a new end table design, he saw Joel.

Rufus wiped one hand across his eyes. "I suppose you heard that."

Joel nodded. "The last bit. Enough to know you are thinking of taking a job with an *English*."

"It's not a permanent job," Rufus said. "A few weeks, a few months, perhaps. It's just hanging cabinets."

"Are you serious about it?"

Rufus used his pencil to darken the lines of his drawing. "We both know things are not going as well with the farm as we would like. My cabinetry work has had some disappointments as well."

"And you want to get married."

Rufus was silent.

"You know Annalise won't care about money. Look at everything she has given up."

"I know. But I still have to keep my business afloat."

Joel spread his hands on the workbench and leaned toward Rufus. "If you don't take it, I'd like you to recommend me."

Rufus met his brother's gaze.

"I'm serious. I've helped you hang cabinets enough times to know how to measure and get things straight."

Rufus sank into an Adirondack chair on the front porch later in the afternoon, laid the brown leather accounts book in his lap, and lifted his eyes to the Sangre de Cristo Mountains. Already snow brushed the peaks. In a few weeks, the range would be snowcapped for the duration of the winter.

He relished living in Colorado. Not once had he regretted the decision to move from Pennsylvania and join the new settlement. Though his business faced a setback at the moment, overall work had been steady for the last seven years. God's provision.

Rufus opened the accounts book then picked up the pen laid inside its spine and used it as a marker as he reviewed the small amounts still owed to him. Until now, David had always been sure he could sell whatever pieces Rufus had time to make for the store. Now Rufus faced the question of whether he himself believed the pieces would continue to sell. Could he afford to keep making them, confident he would eventually recoup his investment?

His father appeared at the bottom of the porch stairs. "I hope your business is in better shape than mine."

Rufus closed his accounts book. "Is it so bad, *Daed*?"

Eli Beiler progressed up the steps and sank into a chair beside his son. "You know the harvest from the spring planting was disappointing. The soil is so stubborn out here."

"But you've just planted the winter alfalfa. Joel is learning everything he can about soil nutrients. Things will be better in the spring."

"My faith wavers on that point, Rufus."

Rufus said nothing.

"I let Joel talk me into one more season of alfalfa before rotating the crops. What kind of doddering old man have I become that I take advice from a seventeen-year-old?"

"Farming out here is not like in Pennsylvania. You're both learning."

Eli sighed. "This could be an expensive lesson. The farm needs a few thousand in cash. I can go over my own books night and day, and I still don't see where it is going to come from. I am stretched to my limit with the bank."

"I thought you still had some reserves from the land you sold in Pennsylvania when we decided to come here."

Eli leaned forward, elbows on his knees. "I've been drawing down rapidly of late."

"I didn't realize it was that bad, *Daed*."

"God will provide." Eli lifted his gaze to the mountains. "At the moment, I admit I have trouble imagining how."

Rufus made a decision in that moment. Annalise would just have to understand.

Twelve

Annie did not push against Ruth's hesitancy to answer questions about Bryan Nichols. They finished their sandwiches, and Ruth headed back to work at the clinic while Annie strolled home. She waved at the librarian opening up the narrow storefront branch for afternoon hours and paused to read the sale banners in the dollar store window. When she lived in Colorado Springs, Annie drove everywhere. Now she could work and shop and socialize within a few blocks of her home. She would miss that.

She assumed that when she and Rufus married they would live a few miles from town, as all the Amish families did.

Sometimes, like now, Annie wondered if she were assuming too much. Rufus still had not said a word about getting married. And she was not going to be the one to bring it up.

She turned down the ragged side street that hosted her narrow green century-old house. Outside the house next door, her neighbor stood in the front yard, hands on hips and exasperation flashing across her face.

"What's wrong, Barb?" Annie paused to see if she could help.

"Oh, nothing serious. Just aggravating." Barb flashed her eyes around the yard. "The cat's milk dish is gone."

"The one you leave on the front porch?"

Barb nodded. "If I had a dog, I would understand if it carried the dish off to bury. But cats don't do that."

"I hope it turns up."

"I don't know why I'm looking for it. Obviously someone took it. Who would be desperate enough to take a cat dish?" Barb turned to go inside her home, and Annie—her steps slowed—walked a few more yards to her own driveway. She knew one person desperate enough to take a cat dish.

The same person who would take a lantern, garden vegetables, and a sleeping bag from a clothesline. And perhaps even a cat. Had Leah Deitwaller said where she got the kitten she cradled in her apron that day? Where would she be getting milk?

Annie made up her mind. She had the whole afternoon ahead of her, and a free day tomorrow. She would get on her bicycle and look for Leah even if she had to crank those pedals for a hundred miles crisscrossing the land around Westcliffe.

She paced up the driveway to the back of the house. When she found Leah, Annie wanted to be prepared. The basket on the front of her bicycle would hold some fruit and bread with a couple of water bottles. In the kitchen she made three turkey sandwiches and grabbed an apple and a peach. No telling how hungry Leah would be.

Annie was lifting the garage door to retrieve her white three-speed bike when an old Ford Taurus pulled into the driveway. Julene Weichert got out.

"My grandmother has been taken to the hospital in Pueblo," Julene said. "Mom and I need to head over there right away. Can you watch the store?"

Annie glanced at her bike.

"I know you were supposed to have the time off." Julene dangled keys from one hand. "It might be a couple of days before we come back. Depends what we find out."

Annie gripped the bottom of the garage door and heaved it down.

Annie fidgeted around the store all Tuesday afternoon. For the most part, she simply sorted through items she knew had been on the shelves a long time, separating some to box up and rotating out some new items from the back room.

Two people came into the shop in the space of three hours. Annie chewed on her bottom lip and tapped her toes all afternoon, watching the clock and glancing out the front window every few minutes.

Leah was out there. She was somehow managing to take care of herself and a kitten, but Annie did not like the visions that floated through her head about where Leah might be holed up.

For no good reason. That was the part that burned Annie. Maybe it was unrealistic for Leah to go home to her parents. Maybe their relationship was too damaged to work things out. But was sleeping who knows where and stealing off people's porches really the best option?

Annie groaned in the late afternoon as the sky darkened. Rain. The farms and ranches surrounding Westcliffe needed the water. She had no doubt of that. Even if the rain blew through quickly, as Colorado storms often did, soggy soil would make biking around nearly impossible.

The rain did not blow through. Instead it settled into a steady, drenching rhythm. When Annie closed up the shop, she hung her sweater over her head for the dash home. Over a bowl of soup she sat at her small oval dining room table and stared out the window wondering how Leah was keeping warm. Or *if* Leah was keeping warm.

Why hadn't Mrs. Weichert simply hung the CLOSED sign as so many of the small business owners of Westcliffe did? When Annie first arrived in Westcliffe last year, she was amused by how casually people closed up their shops in the middle of the day and went on errands. And it was not as if it was the busy season for the antiques shop. If someone did not come in on Wednesday and spend a great deal of money, Annie was going to be annoyed at the waste of her day.

Demut, she told herself. Humility. How prideful it was for her to think that her time was worth more than the simple task of honoring her employer's request even if no one came into the shop.

Annie was up at dawn and on her bicycle. She did not have to open the shop until ten. The open land would be too muddy for biking efficiently, especially on the hills, but she could at least try some of the areas accessible by paved roads. The new subdivision beckoned. Several houses were isolated and half-finished. Annie pedaled up Main Street, turned north on the highway, and cruised into the subdivision before the sun was fully up. She had been out there with Rufus several times to see the houses he was working on, so she knew which lots were under construction. Annie had not been there since the fire on her baptism morning, though.

She let a foot drag on the ground as she approached the burned structure. Ten days after the flames, cleanup had already begun. Annie supposed the fire department and the sheriff's office had collected whatever clues they could find, but so far she had not heard a credible account of what might have happened.

Except that someone had set the fire on purpose. According to the Westcliffe rumor mill, the fire chief seemed certain of that much.

She stopped and stared. Surely Leah could not have done this. What motive would she have? Annie shook away the thought.

The fire had burned right through the center of the house, branching off from the hall to scorch Rufus's cabinets in the various rooms. Annie could see their blackened surfaces from the end of the driveway, and grief tightened in her gut—for everyone involved in this pointless loss. At least no one had been in the home at the time.

Annie filled her lungs with fresh energy and put her bicycle in motion once again to move on to the next unoccupied house, knowing she might have only a few more minutes. Construction crews were notorious for getting an early start, and Annie did not want to face interrogation about her presence.

Inspection of three lots yielded nothing suspicious, no sign of a squatter, no residue of an unauthorized visitor. Annie headed back to town, calculating she had time for breakfast at the coffee shop before opening the store.

Between a bite of scrambled egg on a croissant and a sip of plain black coffee—she had given up her indulgence in mocha caramel grande nonfat lattes—out the window Annie saw Brownie trot by pulling the Beilers' cart, with Joel in the driver's seat.

She swallowed the coffee, abandoned her breakfast sandwich, and marched down the sidewalk in pursuit. Finally Joel saw her waving arms and stopped.

"We have to find Leah," Annie said.

Joel turned his head to the left and then to the right. "We tried that already. It didn't work out so well."

"Is that a reason to give up?" Annie widened her eyes and leaned her face toward Joel. "She's confused. That doesn't mean she doesn't need help."

"*Daed* is counting on me for help in the fields. Besides, how do you know she hasn't gone home by now? Or found a bus to. . . somewhere."

"Because my neighbor's cat bowl is missing." Annie listed the items people had reported missing in the last few days, including the food from her own back porch. "She's out there."

"She's seventeen. Almost eighteen."

"You've seen her. She's in no emotional condition to be on her own."

"I'll keep my eyes open," Joel said.

"I don't know when Mrs. Weichert will get back." Annie straightened her *kapp*. "I promised to watch the store."

"I'll try. But I don't expect to be back to town this week."

"You're resourceful. If you see her, find a way to send me a message." Annie tapped Joel's shoulder. "Otherwise I'll see you Friday when I come for supper."

On Friday after supper, Rufus took Annalise's hand and led her out to the front porch.

"I hear you are still looking for Leah Deitwaller," he said.

"Somebody should be."

"It's been twelve days." Rufus leaned against a post, not releasing her hand. "You've seen a few signs that she is around and not injured. It seems, though, that she is quite determined not to be found."

"She is about to meet her match."

Annalise looked up at him with her wide gray eyes. He squeezed her hand without speaking.

"You probably think I'm just being stubborn," Annalise said, "but this is different. I feel something. A tug. A calling. Even if she were already eighteen, I would still want to help her."

He nodded. "Then you should."

"Really? You're not going to talk me out of it? Tell me I'm being *English*?"

"How can you be *English*? You are baptized Amish."

She beamed. "You don't know how great that is to hear you say."

He took both her hands now and faced her. When he heard her intake of air, he knew he was about to disappoint her. "I need to talk to you about something."

"Of course."

"I want you to know I'm thinking of you, of us, and also of my family. I have not made this decision easily."

The light that had flickered in her eyes a moment ago was gone. He told her about the offer of employment to hang premanufactured cabinets over the winter.

"I'll be away for days at a time, even a couple of weeks."

"What about making your own cabinets?" Annalise's face

clouded. "Won't you be setting your own business back even further?"

He nodded. "Possibly. I'll work on them whenever I can be home for a few days."

"It never crossed my mind you would take this sort of job."

"Mine either. But when you pray for God's provision, you cannot spurn the form in which it comes. The income will be more certain than my own business is right now. I want to help *Daed* if I can."

"Is the farm in that much trouble?"

"We'll know more in the spring."

"That's a long way off." Annalise moved her hands and laid them on his forearms. "Won't the church help? Isn't that the Amish way?"

"They will want to, I'm sure," he said. "But everyone is trying to farm. Everyone is stretched thin. It doesn't take much for a settlement to fail."

"Surely that is not going to happen. It's been seven years, and new families arrive every few months."

"I want to do my part, and this is one way I can help."

"You do your part every single day, Rufus. Everybody knows that. I hate to see you give up your craft, the beauty you create that shows the wonder of God."

He glanced into the house, where his siblings were getting ready to play board games. "I know this is not the conversation you were hoping for right now."

She was quiet for too long. "Joel could hang cabinets," she finally said. "It doesn't have to be you."

"Joel would go. But what if he did not come back?"

"Then, God's will. Besides, Joel has told me more than once that he will be baptized when the time is right. He says he is not Ruth, that he is not going to leave."

Rufus put an arm around Annalise's shoulders and turned her to the view of the Sangre de Cristos. "Joel would not plan to leave.

His reasons would not be as noble as Ruth's. There is a difference between leaving and just not coming back."

Her hard swallow was audible, and he leaned in and kissed the top of her head.

Thirteen

May 1892

Belle Mooney charged up the street from the school.

Maura ran toward her, arms spread wide to stop Belle's progress.

"What happened?" Belle pushed against Maura's restraint. "I was at the school cleaning out my desk. I heard gunshots."

Maura closed her arms firmly around her friend. "Belle. . ."

"It's John, isn't it?"

Maura sucked in her top lip. "I'm afraid it is."

Belle thrashed and Maura's hold began to slip.

"I want to know," Belle said. "Tell me."

"It's bad, Belle. Very bad."

Belle broke free. Maura grabbed for her elbow and missed.

"I'm going to him," Belle said. "Don't keep me from him."

Belle broke into a brisk, determined pace, and Maura followed as closely as her tight shoes and long hem would allow. Belle screamed at the sight before her.

"We've sent for the doctor." Maura bunched up the fabric of her navy skirt in one hand to permit a longer stride. Bile rose within her, and she swallowed it down. John Twigg continued to bleed in the street.

Beside John, Belle fell to her knees. "John, darling, I'm here. I'm here." She pulled up the hem of her white dress and dabbed at the bleeding and then gently lifted his head into her lap.

Maura's breath caught at the tenderness before her. Belle cradled John's head, stroked his face, bent to kiss him, spoke of her love. No man had ever made Maura feel this way. No man had made her see past his flaws to what he could be. What did she know of love? Perhaps nothing. Whatever Maura thought of John Twigg, her friend loved him and would love him to the end. In Maura's mind, Belle's capacity for loyalty clanked against John's undeserving. But whatever John's faults, he did not deserve to lie in the street this way. The events of the morning did not resemble justice, Maura was sure of that much.

She glanced up the street for any sight of one of the doctors. Would those Amish men really be able to look after Walter and find a doctor? Walter would be fine, she reminded herself. He was barely hit.

John was running out of time.

Squeezing her head between her hands, Maura tried to count the minutes that had passed since the shots. She did not even know who had fired—Lee or Ing. And did it matter?

"The sheriff," Maura cried out. "Has anyone gone for Sheriff Byler?"

Maura knelt next to Belle, stretching her arms against Belle's shoulders and leaning her cheek into Belle's face. "I'm here, too."

"I'm still bleeding," Walter said.

Joseph looked again at Walter's knuckles. "It's almost stopped."

Zeke bounded ahead of them and took the steps up to Doc Denton's porch two at a time. After a quick rap on the door, he turned the knob and stepped through the opening.

Joseph raised his eyebrows in expectation. "Is this doctor related to the store owners?" he asked Walter.

Walter still cradled his injured fingers with his other hand. "Cousin or something, I think. There are so many Dentons and Twiggs around here I can't keep 'em straight."

Zeke appeared on the porch. "He's not here. Nobody is."

Joseph turned his head toward the blocks they had traversed.

"Pray for that man Twigg." Zeke thudded down the steps. "Get the boy comfortable on the porch."

Joseph swallowed as Zeke disappeared around the corner. He found a wide bench with a floral-patterned cushion on the covered porch. "This looks like a good place to wait. Do you want to lie down?"

Walter sat on the bench, and Joseph helped him swing his legs up and stretch out.

"Do you pray, Walter?"

"Sure. I guess. Doesn't everybody pray when something bad happens?"

"Shall we pray, then?"

"For John Twigg?"

"For you, of course, but yes, Mr. Twigg as well."

"No thanks." Walter popped his head up to scowl. "I'll take my chances. I'm not hurt so bad that I have to do that."

"Have you no compassion?"

"He might have my daddy snookered with his egg prices, but I don't trust him. I'd rather work for the Denton brothers any day."

Joseph leaned against the house with one shoulder. "Do you think you can protect yourself by refusing to pray?"

"I've been minding my own business. Look what it got me." Walter held up his wounded hand. "It's not fair. It's fine by me if Crazy Man Twigg gets what he deserves."

Joseph held his tongue. He had enough discussions with Little Jake while throwing hay down in the barn, away from the ears of their parents, to know that boys this age were stubborn. Even the Amish. Life was not fair. That was not God's purpose in creating. But Walter would not hear it any more than Little Jake did.

"I suppose your friend will tell Dr. Lindsay to take care of John Twigg first."

Joseph nodded slowly.

Walter grunted. "Nobody will care that I got shot, too. Even Maura didn't come with me."

Joseph cleared his throat. "Mr. Twigg's situation is quite serious, Walter."

"I know. I'm just sayin'."

They fell silent.

"What can you see?" Walter asked after a few minutes.

"Not much," Joseph said. "It is too far down the street. And there's a crowd now."

"I'll be all right here, you know. If you want to go."

Did he want to go? Joseph's people only used guns to shoot what they would eat. A gunfight in the street was beyond his understanding. But he understood that he should not leave a boy alone.

"Let me look at your hand," Joseph said. "Perhaps it needs fresh bandaging."

"Well, don't rip off your other sleeve." Walter said. "You can go inside and get bandages. Doc keeps them in the back room on the long shelf."

Joseph suddenly felt exposed and ran his hand up and down his bare arm. He sometimes rolled up his sleeves if he was working in the field with other men, but never in his life had he walked down a street with his arms bare. He unwrapped his dismembered sleeve from Walter's hand and examined the knuckles. The bleeding had stopped. Joseph pressed gently on the spot that seemed the worst.

"Hey!" Walter retracted his hand.

"Sorry." The knuckle likely was broken. "Perhaps I will have a look around for those bandages." *And some kind of splint,* Joseph thought.

"Hurry up, then." Little Jake's tone haunted Walter's voice.

Belle's shoulders trembled under Maura's touch. John Twigg's blood spilled over them both.

"Belle," Maura whispered. "I know how much you care for John."

"John, my dearest love," Belle murmured. She gently mopped the persistent wound.

"I'm sure the doctor is coming." With no such certainty, Maura forced stability into her voice. "Just a few more minutes."

Belle had held steady so far, but Maura felt the tremble morph into wracking sobs.

"We're going to get married, John," Belle managed between gasps. "You promised me. I'm holding you to it."

With one hand on the middle of Belle's back, Maura took in the scene around them. Movement had halted, as if players took their marks on a stage. No one else was within ten feet of John Twigg, but every person from every shop or office seemed to have come out and lined the streets. It was not hard to spot Zeke Berkey trotting back toward the wounded man.

He shook his head.

Maura's heart lurched as she stood to meet him.

"The doctors were both out on calls," Zeke said, his voice low. "Dr. Lindsay's son went for him."

Maura allowed herself a deep breath. "Mr. Twigg is not long for this world."

"No, I think not. *Gottes wille.*"

"What is that?"

"God's will," Zeke said.

Maura put her hands on her hips. "Pardon me, Mr. Berkey, but I am not at all persuaded that is the case."

She turned toward Belle's moan.

"I will get justice for John." Belle's voice had turned to iron. "I will find out who did this and he will hang."

"Belle, no." Maura knelt beside Belle again.

"It's what John would want. *Will* want. I will do everything I can."

"Right now, let's just worry about John." Maura gestured toward Zeke. "Mr. Berkey said the doctor is coming."

With heavy breath, Maura looked again at the gathered townspeople. Ing and Lee Denton stood outside their store, pistols raised, cocked, and pointed, though John Twigg was no threat now.

But he came from a large family. His father owned one of the largest ranches in Baxter County, and John would not be the only Twigg in the family's store.

"We have to do something," she whispered to Zeke.

"The doctor is—"

"Not for John. We'll have a riot on our hands any minute now. The Twiggs will do exactly what Belle is talking about—find justice on their own terms."

"You know your own town."

"Stay with Belle." Maura took charge. She stood and faced the Denton brothers. "Put those guns away."

"No, ma'am," Lee Denton said.

"Can't you see what you've already done?" Maura marched toward them. "We don't need any more bloodshed."

"That's up to the Twiggs," Ing Denton said. "But we'll be ready when they come."

Joseph hustled down the street. Walter's father had heard about the shooting and turned up looking for his son. Joseph left them both sitting on the bench outside the doctor's office, Walter's hand freshly if awkwardly bandaged. He heard Miss Woodley's voice.

"All of you," she shouted, "form a line around the emporium!"

"You want us to be target practice for the Twiggs?" one man objected.

"You're already standing in the street gawking at John," Maura said. "You might as well be useful. Line up. Lee and Ing, you stand behind the line."

"Now, Maura—"

"Do it!" she snapped, and the crowd turned itself into a human barricade.

Mesmerized by her authority, Joseph stepped into place between two men in *English* suits.

"Here they come," one of the men muttered.

From the far end of town, dust rose in robust clouds as horses' hooves churned up the road.

"Who are they?" Joseph whispered.

"John's kin. Those two in front are his brothers, Billy and Jimmy."

"Do they always ride with rifles across their saddles?" Joseph asked.

Maura took her place in the barricade, which now stretched all the way around the Denton Emporium. Joseph inched toward her.

"Your cousin," he said, "is going to be all right. His father is there now."

Maura nodded. "Thank you. Now if we can just keep anyone else from getting shot today."

Joseph watched the Twiggs circle around John. Billy slid off his horse and lowered himself into the stain of blood soaking into the street and put an arm around Belle.

"What time is it?" Maura asked.

"I do not wear a watch," Joseph answered.

"How many minutes?" she said. "How long has he been lying out there like that?"

Joseph swallowed hard. "Nigh to thirty minutes, I would say."

"That's a long time to lie in the street like a half-butchered hog."

"Does he yet live?" Joseph had supposed John was dead already.

"Honestly, I don't know. The blood stopped spurting, but there is a lot of it."

The Twigg gang circled again, staring into the line of townspeople with hard, unbending expressions.

Another horse galloped in and broke through the Twigg huddle.

"It's Dr. Lindsay," someone said.

The doctor knelt with his black bag. Belle's face wrenched with hope. In only a moment, though, Dr. Lindsay looked up and shook his head. On his horse, Jimmy Twigg raised his rifle to his shoulder.

"No, Jimmy, no!" Maura screamed.

Twigg held his pose as Billy and Belle stood and stared at the crowd. "Sheriff Byler had better show up soon."

"You will *not* shoot into an innocent crowd," Maura shouted. "If Sheriff Byler catches you, he'll have reason to shoot you in the back."

Billy Twigg sauntered toward his horse and pulled his own rifle down from the mount. "He's not a shootin' sheriff, and you know it."

Fourteen

Ruth squinted at the tiny print on the form. She supposed no one actually read the stack of forms patients routinely signed when they received care in the clinic, but she was curious how the government's health care regulations over privacy and insurance translated into plain English. Even after nearly three years away from the Amish community, she was still getting used to the prevalence—even the necessity—for insurance in order to receive care. Was it not enough to be sick? It seemed to her that the *English* system left out a lot of people. She had begun to think of someday practicing her nursing skills in a setting that served people who worked hard yet still feared what it would cost to see a health care professional.

With a gasp she looked up to see the face of Bryan Nichols only inches from hers. With his arms anchored on the counter, he leaned heavily forward.

"Hello, Ruth Beiler."

Ruth pushed her rolling chair back a few inches. "Hello. Do you have an appointment?"

"No, but I'd like to make one." He grinned.

Ruth hit the space bar to wake up her computer monitor and

opened the scheduling program. "We don't have any openings today, but a doctor could see you on Thursday."

"But I don't want to see a doctor. I want to see you."

She blinked twice and met his eyes. "I'm a nursing student doing an internship. I can't see patients."

Now he laughed. "I'm not a patient. I'm just a man who would like to get to know you better. Would you have breakfast with me tomorrow?"

Ruth's belly warmed. At the university in Colorado Springs, she fell indisputably in the category of nerd—a serious student who made a solid contribution to a study group before an exam but otherwise did not socialize with many people. And certainly not men.

"Tomorrow's a church Sunday," Ruth said. "I like to go to church with my family when I'm home."

"Lunch, then."

"I'm afraid. . .well, it's the Sabbath. A family day." She was dodging him. The real question was not when she would go out with him, but whether.

"Well, you didn't seem so hot on the idea of my dropping by the house the first time I tried it, so I suppose I won't do that again." He winked. "Not yet anyway."

She blushed. Ruth could feel it. And she could not will it away. For his own good, Ruth had repeatedly told Elijah Capp that he had to let her go, but she had never done so because she imagined herself with anyone else.

"Let me cut to the chase," Bryan said. "Just tell me that you will go out with me, and then we can work on figuring out when."

Ruth shuffled some papers and glanced at the monitor, which had reverted to its screen saver of nature scenes.

Bryan caught her eye in an expectant invitation.

Ruth clicked the point of her ballpoint pen out and then in. "I'm not all that interesting."

"Let me be the judge of that. Okay?"

Ruth reached for her coffee mug, which was empty. She stared into it. "Okay."

Annie's steps slowed as she walked past the newspaper box on Main Street. It was one of those old locked boxes that took quarters and released custody of the day's news. In this case it was the week's news at stake. The Westcliffe paper, read by residents all over Custer County, only came out once a week.

Rufus did not read *English* newspapers. None of the Beilers did. As far as Annie knew, none of the Amish in Custer County or anywhere in southwestern Colorado did. They regarded the contents as *English* business that had nothing to do with them.

But that headline. How could she walk past it and not be curious?

ARSONIST PROFILED.

She was sorely tempted, and she was pretty sure she had a quarter. But when she looked down at the small bag hanging from her shoulder, she saw her green Amish dress. If someone—even an *English*—saw her dropping a coin in the slot and extracting a paper, word was certain to get back to the bishop.

Annie rolled her eyes at her own weakness and picked up speed again. It should not matter whether anyone saw her buy a paper. It did not even matter what she thought of the Amish practice of reading only their own newspapers. She had vowed to obey the leaders of the church. Her baptism was not yet two weeks old and she was already straining against its restrictions.

She reached Mrs. Weichert's shop and put the key in the lock, deciding at the same time that it was time to change the window display. Mrs. Weichert wouldn't mind. Generally the store owner gladly left that task to Annie anyway.

Annie was about to step inside when a touch on her elbow made her turn to see Trey, the newspaper editor.

"I've got some flyers here that the town council wants

distributed." Trey gripped a stack of papers in one hand. "I put them in with all the newspapers, but they'd like them in shop windows, too."

Annie held the door open. "I guess that would be all right." Mrs. Weichert could always take it down if she objected.

"Good. If you'd like, I'll put it up for you."

Annie gestured toward the front window. "What's it about?"

"The fire department is doing a controlled training burn." Trey produced a small roll of tape from a pocket. "After what happened a couple of weeks ago, they want to be sure everyone knows not to freak out when they see smoke this time."

"That sounds wise. Where will they be burning?"

"There's an old house that is a hundred years old if it's a day. You can see straight through the slats. I'm surprised a good wind didn't take it down years ago."

"Where is that?"

"At the edge of the ranch land Karl Kramer owns."

"Is he still out of town?"

"Believe so. I hear his foreman is on the phone with him practically all day every day, but Karl seems in no hurry to come back. But don't worry. They have his permission. He's been wanting to take it down anyway."

"Then I guess it's just as well." Annie tried to picture the failing structure. Gradually an image came into her mind.

"It's amazing what they can tell from investigating the scene of a fire. We've had a lot of interest in our profile of an arsonist."

Annie perked up. "I'm afraid I haven't read the article. Do they really know who did it?"

Trey pulled of a piece of tape and stuck it to the end of one finger before reaching across the display shelf to place the poster in the window.

" 'Fraid not. The article is more general."

Annie wondered if it would be against *Ordnung* to encourage him to keep talking.

"They start with establishing a motive even before they have a suspect," Trey said. "Half the time it's revenge. I never knew that."

"Me neither."

"Then of course there's simple vandalism or monetary gain. And some people do it just for the excitement."

"But how do they know the motive before they have a suspect?" Annie couldn't help asking.

"Certain patterns. A revenge burning rarely uses an ignitable liquid, for instance, because it's not well mapped out. Usually that's a firebomb."

"And the others?" Annie was simply gathering information. What could be wrong with that?

"Vandalism will often have graffiti accompanying it. If the motive is monetary gain, valuables will be missing from the scene. Fires set by someone seeking excitement will eventually develop a pattern. Someone wants attention."

"But that means there would have to be several. I hate to think of that happening around here."

"I don't suppose anyone wants to see that except the person setting the fires."

Annie shuddered at the thought. "So they don't have any theories about the fire?"

Trey pressed on one last piece of tape. "I imagine they do. Once they sort out the kind of fire it was, that will narrow down the list of suspects. But they wouldn't be saying yet, now would they?"

"I suppose not."

The door opened and Mrs. Weichert came in. "What have we got here?"

Trey set a couple of extra flyers on the counter. "It's all here. I'd better move on."

Annie watched him leave and turned to her employer. "I didn't know you would be back. How is your mother?"

"She had a heart attack, but given what it could have been, it's not too bad. They released her last night. Julene offered to stay a few more days to make sure her feisty grandmother behaves herself and to arrange some help to come in."

"I'm glad it wasn't worse."

"Thanks. Now you skedaddle. You've held down the fort long enough."

Annie did not argue. It was barely ten thirty. She could spend the whole day looking for Leah if she had to. Annie picked up an extra flyer and left before Mrs. Weichert could change her mind.

Oblivious to further distraction, she dashed home, put on her most comfortable sneakers, and filled the thrift store backpack. In the days since she had first thought to take sandwiches to Leah, Annie had set aside a box of crackers, a jar of peanut butter, a loaf of wheat bread, and juice boxes she kept in the house for a treat when Jacob Beiler visited. If she could not persuade Leah to go home, she could at least take her some nourishment. At the last minute, she pulled a quart-size canning jar from the cupboard and filled it with milk.

With the backpack strapped to her shoulders, Annie set out. While her previous attempts to find Leah had been random guesses about which direction to head, this time Annie had a destination in mind. The old house Trey had described on the edge of Karl Kramer's ranch sounded just like the sort of place a lonely girl could take refuge. For years it had been abandoned and off anyone's radar.

Now it was on the radar, though. Surely firefighters would double-check to be sure no one was in the building before beginning the training burn, but Annie did not want to take any chances. Fresh adrenaline at the thought of finding Leah speeded the revolution of her pedals, even with the extra weight on her back. Still, it took her most of an hour to reach the ranch, and she was relieved to finally put one foot on the ground to steady her balance.

From the outside, Annie saw no sign the building was occupied. It looked downright unsafe to her—which was probably why it was targeted for destruction.

"Leah?" she called out. But no answer came. Annie got off the bike and laid it on the ground. The weight of the backpack had shifted, and she readjusted it as she walked closer to the old house. There was no door, only a gaping opening where one had once hung. Window frames had long ago lost their glass. Gray, brittle, weather-worn planks held a precarious balance that a large cardboard box could have rivaled.

"Leah!"

Silence.

Under any other circumstance, Annie would not have entered the house, but she had come too far not to determine whether there might be any possibility Leah was squatting here.

The room at what must have been the front of the house at one time was empty. Far from fearless for her own safety, Annie proceeded deeper into the house. At the end of a narrow hall, she found two small rooms. The one on the right was empty.

When she stepped inside the room on the left, Annie tripped on something—and immediately recognized the cat dish. Her pulse pounded as she inspected the rest of the room. A sleeping bag. A lantern. Empty mason jars. A sweater. Four apple cores.

Annie held herself still, breathless, listening for any sound of movement in the house.

Nothing.

She inventoried her options. One: go find Leah's parents and insist they come with her to this desolate, dangerous place their child had chosen. Two: report evidence of trespassing and try to force the authorities to get involved. Three: wait for Leah and insist she go home with Annie. Four: leave the backpack and go home.

Why would the Deitwallers be more likely to track their daughter just because Annie had found her? They wouldn't. Why would the authorities be interested in someone trespassing in a building scheduled for destruction in a few days and whose owner had made no complaint? They wouldn't. And why would Leah be any more likely to accept Annie's offer to help than she had been on previous attempts? She wouldn't.

Reluctantly, Annie admitted she had only one choice that made any sense. She reached into the front pocket of the backpack, where she knew she would find a small notepad and a pen.

Fifteen

June 1892

"The grand jury is back."

At A.G. Byler's solemn announcement a few weeks later, the assembled residents of Gassville ceased their whispered speculations outside the Mountain Home courthouse and entered the building. By the time the jury was seated, the gallery was filled. Abraham took his seat in the inside aisle toward the back. In front of him, he saw Maura Woodley clasping hands with Belle Mooney. Nearly everyone who had been in the street on the day of the shooting was in the courtroom. He did not see the black hats of the Amish men, though they had stood outside earlier. A.G. supposed that entering a courthouse exceeded the sensibilities of their beliefs. He did not know much about them, except that one of them was named Beiler and they were looking for a possible location for an Amish settlement. They were not efficient scouts, A.G. decided, or they would have moved on by now.

The bailiff announced the judge, and silence draped the rows of spectators. The jury foreman handed a slip of paper to the bailiff, who handed it to the judge to read. All eyes were on that slip of paper as it made its way back to the jury box.

Lee and Ing Denton stood and the foreman read the verdict.

No.

The verdict was no. The grand jury did not find sufficient evidence of wrongdoing to bind over for trial.

Belle burst into sobs, and Maura held her tightly. Gasps erupted around the gallery as the judge thanked the grand jury for their service and the stoic jurymen filed out.

"The Denton brothers are going free!" Belle spoke through gritted teeth, but loud enough for her growl to turn heads. "This will not be the end."

Maura rose, lifting Belle in a firm embrace.

A.G. was not sure he wanted to meet their eyes. As a man of the law, he understood the verdict. Both men admitted shooting their pistols multiple times. With three guns firing too rapidly for witnesses to be sure, no one could prove which bullet killed John Twigg. The Dentons were on their own property, and half a dozen witnesses attested that Twigg had approached them in a menacing manner, and not for the first time. Despite John Twigg's death, A.G. believed the grand jury had made the right decision.

But the Twiggs were a vengeful family. As a man of the law, A.G. also knew Belle spoke rightly. This would not be the end.

As A.G. had supposed she would, Maura approached him. Belle still leaned heavily on her friend. Behind them, Billy and Jimmy Twigg huddled in a conspiring tangle with other Twigg men.

Deputy Combs escorted Lee and Ing out of the court as free men.

Belle's slight weight against Maura slowed her, but the sheriff was only a few feet away.

"Good morning, Sheriff," Maura said.

"Morning, ladies."

"It is not good at all," Belle said, "and I won't pretend it is."

"Now, Miss Mooney, this is an upsetting time for you," Sheriff

Byler said. "We all appreciate your loss. You have your good friend to lean on while you get through this."

Behind Maura, Jimmy Twigg took Belle's elbow. "Come with us," he said. "We think of you as part of our family."

Maura winced as Belle shifted her weight from Maura to Jimmy's arm and he escorted her away.

"I'm worried about her," Maura said to the sheriff.

"You're a loyal friend." Sheriff Byler took the end of his beard between two fingers in thought.

"Belle has always been so sensible. We always saw eye-to-eye until this. I tried to warn her away from John Twigg, but she wouldn't hear of it."

"Love is a powerful force," Sheriff said.

"But if the Twiggs use this as a reason to carry their guns a little closer. . .well, I hate to see Belle in the middle of it."

"We'll have to help her get on with her life," Sheriff said. "She still has her work as a teacher, and her father cares for her."

"But he never liked John Twigg. He has no sympathy for John's death." Maura dipped her hat in the direction Belle had gone. "You saw Jimmy. He's trying to claim Belle as one of theirs. She could lose her own family because of this."

"I hope it does not come to that." Sheriff put both hands in his trouser pockets.

"Sheriff, isn't there anything you can do?"

"What result would you be looking for, Miss Woodley? Did you want to see the Dentons bound over to trial and hanged in a public spectacle?"

"No, of course not." Maura's answer was swift. "But I wish we could do something to prevent this from going further."

"I am the sheriff," he said. "I cannot take legal action because a man's attitude strikes me as cocky. I must have at least the suspicion of a crime."

Maura expelled her breath heavily. "I fear there will be no time between suspicion and more tragedy."

They walked together to the doors and exited the building. Joseph and Zeke were waiting at the bottom of the courthouse steps.

"Thank you both for what you did on that fateful day," Maura said, "and for being here now, even though you did not feel you could come in."

Both men nodded, their black hats bobbing in counterpoint.

"The Amish do not use weapons this way," Zeke said, "but we do not turn our hearts from those who do when harm results."

Maura opened her purse and pulled out her mother's white gloves. She would not put them on. She only wanted to hold them, to having something to grip in her fist.

Joseph lifted his chin in the direction of the Denton brothers. "I would have thought they would go home immediately."

Lee and Ing approached.

"You two have been here for several weeks," Lee said. "We figure you might be looking for work."

Joseph and Zeke looked at each other; then Zeke said, "We are on a mission for our church."

"Even a mission needs money," Ing said. "We want you to work for us."

"I don't think our bishop would approve of us working in an *English* store," Joseph said.

"No, not the store," Lee said. "Clearing land on the bluff along the river."

"First thing tomorrow," Ing said. "At Denton's Ferry on the White River." He glanced at Maura. "Miss Woodley can tell you where to find it."

Maura looked at Zeke and then settled her gaze on Joseph. Every time she saw him, his violet-blue eyes pierced her concentration. Behind them, she knew, was a man of kindness and patience. She had no doubt the Amish men carried the ethic of hard work, but did they understand what the Dentons were asking? They would be taking up sides.

Joseph and Zeke had left the hotel after two nights to conserve funds. Instead, they negotiated with the livery owner in Gassville to sleep on the ground outside the stables in exchange for mucking stalls and watering horses. They were free to cook in the open air, and if it rained, they could move inside. For the extra effort of exercising horses whose owners did not call for them, Joseph and Zeke's animals would be well fed.

At daybreak the morning after the grand jury's verdict, Joseph woke and nudged Zeke. "Time to get up. We have work to do today."

Zeke turned over and punched the small pillow under his head. "I am not sure we should go. We did not promise."

"They offered a good wage," Joseph said. "Better than good. And they will pay in cash."

"You know I love an adventure," Zeke said, "but we've been here more than two weeks. We've seen all there is to see of Gassville, Mountain Home, and the land in between."

"We haven't seen everything. We haven't been out to the bluffs over the river."

Zeke sat up. "The landscape is beautiful. But there is no place to start a peaceful Amish settlement around here. Danger hangs in the air."

"What is the harm of a few more days?" Joseph tidied his bedding into a tight roll. "We cannot project our expenses if we continue west or south."

"So you believe we should continue scouting?" Zeke folded his bedroll haphazardly.

"We have not yet completed the task the bishop charged us with." Joseph put his bedroll against the wall of the stable, under the eave.

Zeke paused to lift his eyes and hands to the brightening sky. "This is the day the Lord has made."

"Let us rejoice and be glad," Joseph responded.

"Okay. We will go to Denton's Ferry and see what this work is. But we should send a letter to the bishop."

"Then we will have to wait for his response," Joseph pointed out.

"Yes, I suppose so."

Joseph nodded. They would stay in Gassville for at least a week, maybe several weeks. He wondered how Miss Maura Woodley spent her days and whether she ever used Denton's Ferry.

Zeke rummaged in their foodstuffs and produced some dry biscuits. Joseph lit a fire in the ring of stones they cooked over and prepared the coffeepot.

By seven o'clock, Zeke and Joseph sat on their horses on the thickly wooded bluff overlooking Denton's Ferry.

"It is a shame to think of clearing this land," Zeke said. "They have a thriving ranch, a popular store in town, and a prosperous ferry business on the river. What need do they have for so much wood?"

"None," Joseph answered softly. "We are stepping into the middle of their fear."

Zeke looked at Joseph full on. "You were the one who wanted to accept this work."

"I still do." Joseph dismounted and let his eyes soak up the panoramic view of the gushing foam of the White River and the lush land on the other side. "In the days of our ancestors, the men would have cleared the land along the river so that the Indians could not surprise them with their presence."

"That is what you think this is?" Zeke's horse whinnied, and he patted the animal's neck.

Joseph gripped the bridle on his mount. "If you were one of the Dentons, would you not fear ambush?"

Maura rinsed the rag then wiped down the counter one more time. The kitchen was clean. A roast was in the oven with potatoes, onions, and carrots. She had dusted every crevice of the parlor before lunch and beaten clean the rugs in the hallway. After making sure the home she shared with her father was clean and comfortable, what was left of the afternoon belonged to her. She had a few errands on Main Street.

Maura offered up a brief prayer for a peaceful, uneventful excursion and picked up her purse and a flour sack in which to carry home a few small purchases.

Walter was there with his broom in front of Denton's Emporium.

"How are your fingers?" Maura asked.

"I just saw Doc Denton this morning," Walter said. "My knuckle may be a little knobby, but I'll be good as new."

"Are the Denton brothers here today?" Maura tilted her head toward the store.

"Lee was for a while. Ing is out on the bluff with the crew they hired."

A crew that included Joseph Beiler and Zeke Berkey.

"They come and go by the back of the store and always try to have somebody with them," Walter added.

"They must be so fearful after the verdict yesterday."

Walter pointed down the street. "Wouldn't you be? Look at the Twiggs' store."

Maura peered down the street. Jimmy Twigg sat on a bench in front of the store, his rifle on his shoulder.

"He's been like that all day," Walter said. "The Dentons don't dare walk down Main Street."

"They can't live like that," Maura said.

Walter shrugged. "What else can they do?"

"There must be some other way than waiting to be shot."

Walter pointed with his chin. "Here comes one of those Amish men."

Joseph Beiler rode up the street and dismounted in front of the emporium.

"Good afternoon, Miss Woodley. Walter."

"Good afternoon, Mr. Beiler."

He looked bedraggled, weary with the evidence that he had accepted the Dentons' offer of work. Perspiration soaked his shirt—his only shirt, she knew, since he sacrificed the other to Walter's wound.

"My friend and I are low on our foodstuffs," Joseph said. "I thought I would get a few things from the emporium. Mr. Denton offered us an account as long as we are in their employ."

"Do you cook outside?" Walter wondered aloud.

Joseph laughed softly. "Cook and sleep and everything. The livery owner is generous with his water, though, so at least we can clean up."

"Mr. Beiler," Maura said, "how would you and Mr. Berkey like to have a home-cooked meal with all the trimmings?"

The widening of his eyes made her smile. "I have a roast in the oven that is far larger than my father and I require. You would make me happy if you would agree to be my guests tonight."

Joseph had done his best to rinse out his shirt and hang it in the late afternoon sun to dry. When he donned it, lingering dampness stuck to his skin in places, but he was confident that once he put on his suit jacket the moisture would not be visible. He brushed dust out of his trousers as vigorously as he could manage.

"So you insist on going?" Zeke gulped cool water from a tin cup.

"Miss Woodley offered the invitation in kindness. We should go." Joseph had already made up his mind he would go whether or not Zeke came with him.

"I do not question her motive." Zeke splashed the rest of the water on his face. "Yours concerns me."

Joseph slapped at the dust in his pants one last time. "Miss Woodley will be disappointed you did not come."

"Quite possibly she will be happy to have you to herself."

Joseph met Zeke's eye. "Then for the sake of propriety, you ought to come."

Zeke stood. "Yes, perhaps I should."

Joseph brushed his horse while he waited for Zeke to clean up and put on the shirt he had washed and left to dry the night before. They arrived at the Woodley home promptly at the appointed hour. Smiling, Maura opened the front door to welcome them.

Her scent filled the rooms. Joseph inhaled her allure above even the fragrance of the roast ready for the table. End tables held lamps but also bowls and figurines. Fabric with lively floral prints adorned the furniture. A painting hung over the fireplace. Joseph recognized the bend of the White River and the grove of trees he had helped to cut down that day.

"My mother painted that," Maura said.

"It's breathtaking." Joseph wondered if Lee and Ing Denton might someday appreciate this visual preservation of the land they were so eager to alter. His own mother would have told him that a painting was a graven image and producing one a sinful waste of time. He turned to Maura, wondering if her mother had painted Maura. "Thank you again for your kind invitation."

"It is my pleasure. Give me a moment to bring out the rest of the food and we will be ready to eat."

A man entered the front room. "Hello. I'm Woody Woodley." He extended a hand, which both Joseph and Zeke shook. "Funny name, I know. It's a childhood nickname that stuck, and I suppose I like it better than Francis."

"Thank you for welcoming us to your home," Joseph said. "I am Joseph Beiler, and this is my friend, Ezekiel Berkey."

Maura reappeared with a platter of sliced meat and a basket of rolls. "Daddy, why don't you come ask the blessing for the food?"

They stood behind their chairs, heads bowed, as Woody Woodley spoke aloud a prayer of gratitude. Joseph had never heard an *English* meal blessing before. His people prayed privately, a moment of silence before a meal rather than a rush of words. Joseph rather liked the poetic lilt of Woody's prayer. Just before the *Amen*, he lifted his eyes and found Maura smiling at him.

His lips turned up in response.

Sixteen

Annie rode in the blue Prius with Ruth to the Stutzman farm for church on Sunday morning. She had only a thin sleep Saturday night. Instead she wondered about Leah, prayed for Leah, hoped on Leah's behalf. And she crafted a speech for Leah's mother. Whatever Mrs. Deitwaller said, Annie would proceed with the next sentence of her speech. Her words would not castigate or blame or accuse. Rather, though outwardly Mrs. Deitwaller might not seem receptive, Annie believed that deep down any mother would want to know about the well-being of her child. Annie's words would reassure as much as possible.

"Leah is safe for now."

"I've made sure she has food."

"She can come and stay with me if she wants to."

"I'll let you know if I hear from her."

If Mrs. Deitwaller threw barbs about Annie's intentions, Annie would take a breath and keep going until she said it all. Then she would pray that something penetrated Mrs. Deitwaller's veneer.

The women of the congregation mingled in the Stutzman kitchen for a few minutes. Annie added her own spinach coleslaw to the broad refrigerator and helped with wiping the dishes the congregation would eat off of when the worship service was over. She chatted, still accepting congratulations on her baptism, and was mindful of each woman who entered the room.

None of them was Eva Deitwaller.

In a few minutes, it would be time for the women to take their seats on the benches on one side of the Stutzman barn, while the men prepared to process in and sit on the other side. Women and little girls and the smallest boys began drifting toward the barn. Outside the house, Annie paused to look around. A few children ceased their playing and dutifully answered their mothers' summons. The men were already informally arranging themselves in the order in which they would march in.

No Deitwallers anywhere.

Annie caught Franey Beiler's eye and said, "I notice the Deitwallers are not here. I hope they are well."

Franey scanned the assembly for herself. "I have not heard any news, but perhaps there is illness in the house."

Annie supposed that was possible. She lagged behind, though, still looking for one last buggy to come down the lane.

Rufus smiled at Annalise over the spinach coleslaw on his plate, and she returned the expression. Like most Sundays, they managed to sit at nearly adjoining tables, he with a group of men and she with women. He did not speak directly to her, but her eyes told him she heard what he would say if he could address her.

When the meal began to break up, he lost sight of her for a few minutes and supposed she had gone into the house to help wash dishes. He dutifully began dismantling the tables and benches so they could be loaded onto the wagon that would take them to the farm of the next family to host worship in two weeks.

Wherever he was headed to hang cabinets, Rufus hoped the next church service would find him seated in his usual spot for worship. By then the weather might be too cool to eat outside.

Finally the work was done. Teenagers organized a game of softball between two teams with not quite enough players and irregularly spaced bases. Younger children asked to go feed apples to the horses. Rufus's brother Jacob led the expedition to the meadow where the horses were grazing for the day.

Rufus lingered in the Stutzman front yard, speaking politely with anyone who wanted his attention but gradually moving farther from the house. He knew Annalise would be tracking his movements and arranging hers to intersect his path.

When she did, he smiled at the prayer *kapp* that was not quite straight.

"It's crooked again, isn't it?" Annalise reached up with both hands to rearrange her *kapp*. "I'm beginning to think my head is lopsided. Why else would I have such trouble pinning my *kapp* on straight?"

"You look lovely, just as you are." Rufus hoped that becoming Amish would not snuff out the quirks that drew him to her in the first place.

They walked together, staying in sight of the softball game and the horses chomping apples but carving out a private space around them.

"When do you have to go?" Annalise asked.

"Tonight."

"But it's the Sabbath."

Rufus flinched. "I know. But I have to be north of Cañon City ready to work at seven in the morning. Tom is willing to taxi me up there tonight."

She reached for his hand. "It will be so strange not to be able to picture where you are, not to think of you in your workshop humming hymns as you work."

"I can still hum from the *Ausbund*."

"I hope you will. I hope that will keep you close to us." Annalise turned to look him in the face. "Promise me that you'll call me. You can call the shop. Mrs. Weichert won't mind."

"I would need a phone," Rufus said.

"Believe me, the *English* always have phones."

"If it is God's will that I have such an opportunity, then yes, I will try to call you."

She nodded, as if satisfied. Rufus had expected a stronger insistence because she knew he would not use his own cell phone for a nonemergency call. He was not sure he would even take it with him.

Annalise's lips were slowly moving in and out. She was distracted in thought, and it was not his job that bothered her at the moment. He would not press her, though. Annalise needed no prodding to speak her mind when she was ready

As they ambled, he gradually steered her into a grove of pine trees. She may have been distracted, but Rufus had one thought on his mind that afternoon. He took both her hands so she was facing him and leaned down to find her mouth. She responded immediately, her lips surrendering their perplexed in-and-out motion to eagerly receive the press of his mouth on hers.

Rufus was on his way by now, sitting in the passenger seat of Tom Reynolds's red pickup. The grief Annie felt was not so much about his absence from her. Because she lived in town and he worked on the Beiler land or in outlying construction settings, they only saw each other once or twice a week as it was. No, her grief was that he should feel it necessary to take the job, to be isolated from his people, to be out of the rhythm of work and worship that sustained his spirit.

Would he create a new rhythm, she wondered, surrounded by *English* workers? Would he draw away to the quietness that fed his soul?

She prayed he would, and that it would be possible.

Annie sat at her dining room table, nudged up against the window, nursing a cup of tea and flipping through the red book about Tennessee and Arkansas history before going to bed. It was already late, but her thoughts had not yet fallen into the organized slots in her mind that would allow her to receive sleep. More than twenty-four hours had passed since she left the backpack for Leah—with a note. Was it remotely possible that the Deitwallers were not in church because Leah had gone home? Had Leah even opened the backpack? Did she see the flyer about the training burn? Had she already moved to a new spot without leaving a trail? Yesterday's relief at discovering where Leah was staying blackened now with the realization that, once again, Leah could be anywhere.

The small oil lamp threw a bubble of light across the table in an otherwise dark room. On the shelf above the table, where genealogy books commemorated the connection to Amish ancestors that Annie had discovered in her own family history, sat plain note cards and envelopes. Annie used them to write to her mother once a week or so. She reached for one now, but the name she wrote on the outside of the envelope was Matthew Beiler. The Beilers had left two married sons in Pennsylvania when they moved to Colorado, and Annie had seen enough letters arrive at the Beiler house from both Matthew and Daniel to know the addresses. She wrote now in a firm hand.

Then she turned to the note itself and had far less confidence about what to write. She did not even know the name of Leah Deitwaller's young man, so how could she ask Matthew about him? Franey mentioned a time or two writing to her sons about the family's new friend, Annalise Friesen, but Annie had to admit she and Matthew Beiler were strangers. She could not even be certain he would help.

All Annie wanted to know was whether this young man with whom Leah was desperate to reunite shared the girl's feelings. That information could be meaningful for knowing how to help Leah.

"*Dear Matthew,*" Annie wrote, "*My name is Annalise Friesen, and I am a friend of your family here in Colorado."*

She paused and sipped her now cold tea.

"I've met so many wonderful families during my journey into the Amish faith, and I so admire how they band together to help one another."

"Get to the point," Annie said aloud.

A shadow blurred past her outside the window, and Annie shivered involuntarily. Someone was in her driveway, moving toward the back.

Annie let the pen drop from her hand and moved into the kitchen where she kept a flashlight in a drawer. She turned on no other lights as she crept through the kitchen to the back door. Turning the knob and pulling at a snail's pace, Annie opened the solid door and now had only a flimsy screen door between herself and whoever was in her backyard. She pushed the screen door open just far enough to aim the flashlight.

"I got your note." Over her dress, Leah Deitwaller wore an oversized black hoodie with a pocket across the front.

No doubt stolen, Annie thought as she stepped out on the back porch. Leah stood at the bottom of the three short steps.

"Will you come in?" Annie said. "I want you to. I'll heat some soup."

Leah did not move. The bulge in her hoodie pocket rolled and then two green cat eyes appeared.

"I just came to say thanks." Leah stroked the kitten's head, now fully emerged from the pocket. "Especially for the milk."

"I want to help you." Annie took a cautious step toward the girl.

"I know. You don't give up easily."

"Neither do you."

"So anyway. Thanks. That's all."

"It's going to be a cold night."

"My sleeping bag is rated for twenty degrees below zero. I read the tag." Leah looked away. "I saw the flyer, too. I'll find a new place soon. You don't have to worry about me."

But Annie did worry about the girl, and she could not imagine that she would stop.

"You could stay here. I meant it when I offered. We can go back and get your things in the morning."

It had taken Annie an hour to pedal out to the dilapidated house. How long had it taken Leah to walk into town in the dark? She would be walking half the night to get back. Annie considered telling Leah about the half-written letter on the dining room table. But it would only have been to lure her inside. It was premature to imply that the letter represented any sort of promise that Leah would get what she wanted.

"Good night." Leah walked with the stretchy stealth of a cat.

Annie scampered down the steps now and around the side of the house. Leah was already halfway down the driveway, her form absorbed into the darkness.

Annie stopped chasing her and sighed. How hard could it be to get through to one teenage girl? After all, Annie had been a teenage girl once. She was not completely unfamiliar with the sensation that parents don't always understand their daughters.

A faint meow wafted across night air.

Seventeen

"What would you like?" Bryan asked on Tuesday morning.

Ruth stood next to him in the coffee shop on Main Street. She stared at the menu written in colored chalk behind the counter, but it was a jumbled mess to her nervous eyes.

"Just coffee," she said.

"Latte? Cappuccino?"

She shook her head. "Just coffee. The coffee of the day."

"Still a simple Amish girl, eh?"

Ruth was not sure how to take that remark. The coffee of the day was an Ecuadorian deep roast, and even that sounded exotic. And if she was still a simple Amish girl, what was she doing in a coffee shop with an *English* firefighter?

"I'll get us a couple of sausage-and-egg sandwiches." Bryan pointed toward the list of breakfast foods on the left side of the menu. "How does that sound?"

"That would be great." Ruth's stomach flip-flopped relentlessly, leaving her unsure whether she could actually swallow any food. But she had said yes to a breakfast date, so it was reasonable that Bryan wanted to buy her breakfast.

He ordered, paid, and lifted some napkins from the basket

on the counter. "Where would you like to sit? Comfy chairs or a table?"

Ruth knew she ought to be able to make this simple decision. "A table, please."

Bryan led the way to a table about midway through the shop and pulled out a chair for her.

Ruth managed a smile as she sat down.

"Thank you for saying yes." Bryan took his seat across from her.

"You were kind to invite me."

He chuckled. "Stubborn more than kind, I'm afraid."

His laugh warmed her.

"Now what shall we talk about?" he said. "I promise not to say something stupid like, 'Have you always been Amish?'"

Ruth looked into his green eyes and saw the dance there. But he was not teasing her. It was a dance of curiosity.

"I'll spare you the awkwardness of asking," she said, "and just tell you that I left the Amish community almost three years ago. Our. . .that is, their education system only goes through eighth grade, and I believe God is preparing me to be a nurse. So I got my GED and enrolled at the university in Colorado Springs. I'm on a semester break while I sort out what kind of nurse."

"Really? You've been living in Colorado Springs? And to think I could have just run into you at Target or Starbucks."

Ruth sipped her still scalding coffee. "Colorado Springs is a big place."

A shop employee brought their coffee and breakfast sandwiches.

"I'll say a quick blessing for the food, if you don't mind," Bryan said.

Mind? Ruth's pulse quickened. Was Bryan an *English* with sincere faith? His words were simple but heartfelt, and at his "Amen," she heard her own voice echo the word.

"Now you," Ruth said. "Why have you come to Westcliffe?"

He took a swig of coffee and grinned. "Most people ask me why I went to Westcliffe 'of all places.'"

Ruth bit into her sandwich.

"My friend Alan and I studied firefighting in Colorado Springs, but there are no firefighting jobs available up there. Not even in Denver. We may have to go out of state, but we thought we might have better luck getting jobs if we had something to put on our resumes, so we came down here to be volunteer firefighters. Fortunately the grocery store took us both on, so we can pay the rent and eat all the almost-bad produce and cracked eggs we want."

"My friend Annalise grew up in Colorado Springs. You should talk to her sometime."

"Maybe you can introduce us."

"Perhaps. I'm staying with her while I'm figuring out my next move."

"Not with your family?"

"I went through a tough time with my family." Ruth picked at her sandwich with her fingers. "I'm not shunned or anything, because I was never baptized, but my *mamm* and I—well, it was hard. I have a driver's license and a car now, and I wear scrubs a lot of the time. So I like to go for dinner and church, but it's better if I'm not there all the time."

Abruptly someone slumped into the chair next to Bryan.

"Speak of the devil," Bryan said. "Ruth, you remember my friend Alan Wellner."

"Of course. How are you, Alan? Bryan was just telling me a bit about how you ended up in Westcliffe."

"Because we're a couple of losers who can't get grown-up jobs?" Alan took a strap off his shoulder and set a water bottle on the table before reaching for Bryan's coffee. Bryan slapped his hand away.

"It's a hard time to get a job." Ruth picked up her own coffee protectively. "It sounds like you're doing something smart with your in-between time."

"We already got to help with one fire," Alan said. "And tomorrow there's a controlled burn, so we'll get some hands-on time again."

"I saw the flyer," Ruth said. "Actually, I'm going to be there as well."

Bryan's eyebrows arched. "The fire chief is hoping there won't be too many lookey-loos."

"My supervisor thought it might be good for me to see the scene of a fire. It would just be some background for understanding what burn victims might have been through when they arrive for care."

"She probably cleared it with the chief, then."

"I'm sure she did. We'll stay out of the way. But this is big news in Westcliffe. I'm not sure how they'll keep people away if they really want to be there."

"We should see some good action." Alan tilted his chair back on two legs, hanging on to the table by his thumbs. "Did Bryan tell you he's also certified to drive the ambulance?"

Ruth caught Bryan's eye. "No, he didn't mention that."

"Only because we did not get that far before we were so rudely interrupted." Bryan glared at Alan.

"Don't give me that." Alan's chair smacked the floor, and he reached again for Bryan's coffee, this time successfully. "If you wanted privacy you would not have brought her to a coffee shop."

Bryan pasted a smile on his face. "Alan, would you like me to get you some coffee?"

"Thanks, buddy. As a matter of fact, I could use a warm-up."

"Ruth," Bryan said, "how about you?"

"I'm fine, thank you." Ruth glanced at the oversized decorative clock on the coffee shop wall. "I'll have to leave for the clinic before too much longer."

Bryan stood up. "Behave yourself, Wellner. I'll be right back."

Bryan had no sooner left the table than Alan snapped to his feet. "Dad! What are you doing here?"

Annie stood in her living room and considered the options. With Ruth staying until after Christmas, she did not have a spare bedroom, but she was determined that if Leah would agree to come and stay with her, Annie would do everything in her power to make the girl welcome. The living room was the best option.

The sofa had been new just a year ago, purchased when Annie thought of the house as a weekend getaway and before she stripped herself of her considerable financial resources. It was well constructed with comfortably deep sitting space. If she removed the loose cushions from the back, the remaining cushions were nearly as wide as a twin bed. Annie had no doubt it would be a comfortable place to sleep. But Leah would need some privacy. Annie did not know how long she might be there, and she did not want Leah to feel like she was staying in some sort of way station but in a safe, welcoming home.

Annie felt in her gut that Leah would come. It was just a matter of time.

The room was more wide than deep, stretching across the front of the house. It would be simple enough to section off one-half of the room for a small bedroom. In fact, a trifold privacy screen had just come into Mrs. Weichert's shop. It was old but not old enough for antique status, even if the meaning of the term were blurred. Mrs. Weichert was not going to want to put it out in the shop to sell. The screen had a sturdy frame, making it functional, not merely decorative.

Annie started shoving furniture around. Hardwood floors made the task reasonably simple. The front door would still open into the living room with a couple of chairs, between them an end table that Rufus had made housing a propane tank for the lamp above. The other half of the room would be screened off with the couch prepared for sleeping and another end table beside it. Annie scratched her chin as she pondered bringing down a small shelving unit from her own bedroom for Leah's use.

Upstairs, Annie cleared the shelves. From the hall closet she took a set of sheets and two blankets. They weren't the Amish quilts Leah was probably used to—Annie was still working on her first quilt—but the blankets would keep the girl warm. Remembering a pillow at the last minute, Annie carried the bedding downstairs and set the neat stack on one end of the couch before going back upstairs for the empty shelving unit.

Then she moved to the dining room table and picked up the letter she had addressed to Matthew Beiler. If she hurried, she could still catch the daily pickup time at the small post office at the end of Main Street.

"God," she said aloud, "may Your will be done. If You want me to help Leah, that's what I want to do."

A shudder shot through Ruth. Alan's countenance changed in an instant. In a fraction of a second, he went from playful and cocky to defensive and brooding. Her eyes moved from Alan to his father, then to Bryan on his way to fetch another cup of coffee, oblivious to the interruption.

This was not the way Ruth had imagined a simple breakfast date with an *English*.

"What are you doing here, Dad?"

"I had to see for myself this forsaken hole-in-the-ground of a town you chose to live in."

Alan looked at his shoes. Ruth picked up her coffee, wondering if were possible to just slip out of her chair without a fuss. The moment between father and son seemed far too intimate for onlookers. She scooted her chair back a few inches.

"Please don't go, Ruth." Alan's eyes dimmed. "Dad, this is Ruth Beiler, another resident who *chose* this town. Ruth, this is my father, Jason Wellner."

Ruth felt obliged to say something. "It's nice to—"

"We're not here to discuss anyone's choices but yours."

Jason Wellner did not even look at Ruth, who was relieved to see Bryan making his way back to the table.

"Then there's not much to say." Alan scratched the back of

his neck. "I have a job and a place to live. I'm not asking anything from you."

"This is not what your mother and I had in mind for you. It's bad enough you chose to study firefighting instead of getting a sensible business degree, but to come here? And bag groceries?"

"Look, here's Bryan." Alan pointed weakly.

"This was all his idea, wasn't it? You always did let him lead you around like a whipped puppy."

"Dad."

Ruth's belly twisted in indignation.

"Hello, Mr. Wellner." Bryan offered the fresh coffee, but Jason Wellner brushed it away.

"You're an insurance adjuster, Dad," Alan said. "You know buildings burn all the time. What's so bad about my wanting to help people when that happens?"

"There's no money in helping people." Wellner stroked his gray mustache.

"Maybe life is not about money," Bryan said.

Ruth held her breath.

"This conversation does not concern you, Bryan," Wellner said.

"Then perhaps you should have this conversation in another place." Bryan met the older man's glare.

"You're absolutely right. Alan, let's go outside."

"No." Alan sat in his chair and scooted it in. "I can get some good experience as a volunteer firefighter."

"Very well," Wellner said. "You have thirty days to come to your senses and find your room at home waiting for you. I'll use my contacts to find you a real job. After thirty days, you're on your own."

"He's already on his own." Bryan took his seat again.

A knot rose from Ruth's stomach to her throat.

Jason Wellner pivoted and strode across the coffee shop and out the door.

The trio left at the table let out a collective breath.

Eighteen

June 1892

"Why don't you let me pick it up for you?" A.G. stood at the bedroom door with his hand on the knob.

"You don't even know what I ordered." Bess Byler cast the gray hat onto the bed and picked up the blue one.

"I'm sure the clerk at Denton's Emporium will have a record of the order." A.G. stepped to the mirror and stood beside his wife. "The blue one, dear."

"Aren't you even curious what I want to pick up?"

A.G. tilted his head. "Something useful. Something we must have."

Bess slapped his forearm. "Don't tease me. I want to send some blankets to Malinda."

"For the children."

Bess donned the blue hat. "Of course for the children. It's cold in Colorado."

A.G. chuckled. "Well, it will be, I suppose." Not in the middle of June, but if he knew Bess, she was planning to add some embroidery or a new border to the blankets she was buying.

"I haven't been to Gassville since. . ." Bess fiddled with her handbag.

"Since John Twigg was shot." A.G. stilled Bess's hand then lifted her fingers to his lips. "Are you sure you want to go?"

She took her hand back and snapped the latch on her bag. "I refuse to live in fear. If I gave in to that, I would never want you to go to work."

A.G. knew Bess sometimes scrubbed the kitchen floor when he rode out to break up a fight, but she would never admit the spit shine had anything to do with his job as sheriff of Baxter County.

"The wagon is out front," he said. "I think I'll take an apple out to bribe that stubborn horse."

"I'll be right there."

He kissed her cheek. "Don't dawdle. I need to go over a few things with Deputy Combs over there, but I want to be back for one of your home-cooked dinners."

Outside, A.G. opened his palm and revealed the apple. The horse chomped into it immediately. He glanced at the trim white house with the green shutters, wishing Bess would stay home. Gassville was still jumpy. He did not want his wife in the middle of things.

Bess pulled the front door closed behind her, and A.G. gave her a one-sided smile. At sixty-three, the sight of her touched a spot inside him softer than ever.

As he tied up the mare in front of the emporium, A.G. scanned the street. The talk he had with Jimmy Twigg had successfully deterred him from sitting outside his store with a rifle aimed at the emporium, but that did not mean hostilities were calmed. If A.G. could give Bess an uneventful afternoon, though, he would take some pleasure in the day. He held the door open for her.

Inside the store, A.G. removed his hat and nodded at a few customers as he followed Bess to the counter. "Good afternoon, Leon."

Belle Mooney's father stood in the center of the main aisle

with a claw hammer in one hand.

"How is Belle?" A.G. asked the question softly, deliberately.

Leon shook his head. "How she could let herself fall into the clutches of the Twiggs, I will never understand. She hardly talks to me, even though we're living in the same house."

A.G. put both hands in his trouser pockets. He kept forgetting to mention to Bess that the left pocket had a hole in the seam. "Give Belle some time. Her loss is still fresh."

"It shouldn't be a loss at all." Leon gripped the hammer by the claw.

"Well now, that's for Belle to decide, isn't it?"

"For a man of the law, you don't have much sense of justice."

"For Belle it's a matter of the heart, Leon."

Leon grunted. A.G. patted his shoulder and moved up the aisle to where Bess was running her fingers along a bolt of pink-and-green calico.

"Why don't I go see Deputy Combs and come back for you?" A.G. said.

She looked at him out of the corner of her eye. "Yes, I suppose I might be a while."

The emporium's front door swung open before A.G. reached it, and a stranger swaggered in. A.G. slowed his pace to size him up. About six feet tall, he commanded an even larger presence. His brown suit was a recent cut. A.G. did not need his fashion-conscious wife to tell him that. Glancing at Leon, A.G. decided a welcome was in order. He extended a hand.

"I don't recall that I've had the pleasure. I'm Abraham Byler."

The man, not yet twenty-five, tilted his head and raised an eyebrow before accepting the handshake. "Jesse Roper."

A.G. heard Leon shuffle behind him, and deep in the store, Lee Denton moved behind the counter. A.G. hoped Lee was not trigger-happy enough to pull a gun on a stranger with the sheriff present.

"Leon, have you met Mr. Roper?"

"Don't you know who he is?" Leon snarled. "What kind of sheriff are you?"

"Sheriff, eh?" Jesse Roper said. "You didn't mention that."

A.G. turned his empty hands palms up. "I only meant to offer a friendly welcome."

Roper laughed and moved up the aisle, pausing here and there to inspect unlikely items. What did a young man like Roper want to do with drawers of buttons and threads? A.G. turned to follow his movements.

"He's a Twigg, you know." Leon made no effort to control his volume. "He's a grandson of Old Man Twigg. Probably a criminal."

Lee Denton stiffened. Abraham Byler winced.

"Now, Leon, nobody is looking for trouble," A.G. said. His gaze moved to Lee and held steady.

Between Roper and Denton stood Bess Byler. She had barely lifted her head at the commotion, but A.G. knew she would have absorbed every detail of the exchange.

"Mr. Denton," Bess said brightly, moving toward the counter, "I do believe I would like to look at your special-order book."

Lee mocked. "Sheriff Byler, have you considered it might save you some money if you just took your wife to New York to shop?"

"Lee, are you going to let me see that book or not?" Bess caught her husband's eye, as if to assure him she did not intend to place an order but only to dissipate tension.

Leon stared at Roper, who said, "I believe my business here is concluded. Y'all don't have the items my grandma asked for. Good day, gentlemen." He tipped his tall black hat at the Bylers and rammed a shoulder into Leon's on the way out.

For a moment no one in the shop spoke.

"Leon, are you okay?" A.G. said.

Leon grunted.

"How about you, Lee?"

Lee nodded.

"Promise me you'll keep your pistols out of this if it should turn into anything."

"You do your job, Sheriff Byler, and there will be no need for my pistols."

"The grand jury might see things differently if there is another incident."

Bess set her handbag on the counter with audible firmness. "Mr. Denton, I will thank you not to put my husband in needless danger."

Lee's shoulders sagged. "Aw, Bess, you know how I feel about you two. But I can't control everyone." He jabbed a finger toward Leon Mooney. "Him, for instance."

A.G. moved toward Leon, who was rubbing his shoulder. "Leon."

"Sheriff."

"No trouble."

"There's a town dance tonight, you know," Lee Denton said. "What if this character shows up?"

A.G. pivoted with deliberation. "Mrs. Byler, what do you say we have a night out? Dinner at the hotel and then dancing."

Bess put her fingers to her mouth in feigned shyness. "Why, Sheriff Byler."

Maura wore her mother's gloves, even though she would not last more than twenty minutes with them on.

She had tried to persuade Belle to come to the dance at the town hall. Weeks ago they had planned to attend and sewed new dresses and purchased hats from Maura's uncle Edwin's milliner shop. Belle had confessed her love for John Twigg and hoped they might announce their engagement soon—perhaps even the night of the dance.

Now Belle barely left the house and wore only dark colors. Maura had spent most of the afternoon cajoling and prodding.

She even resorted to heating Belle's iron to give her new dress a fresh press. But Belle would only shake her head.

No. No dance. Not with John Twigg in his grave and his killers unaccountable.

Maura herself did not have a date. She had one, but she broke it the previous week. If she could persuade Belle to go, it would be better to be free to be a companion to Belle, even if neither of them danced. Now Maura was on her own for the evening.

As soon as she entered the hall, Maura saw that Leon Mooney was supplementing the refreshments with a flask of his own. She licked her lips, removed her gloves, and marched toward the small round table where he sat against the wall, leaning his chair back on two legs.

He raised his flask and gave an unpersuasive grin. "So, you could not convince my daughter that she ought to come to the town dance and enjoy herself."

Maura shook her head and sat down. "I tried."

"Thank you for that, anyway."

Leon put his flask in the pocket of his suit jacket. Maura wondered how much he had consumed.

"Who are you going to dance with?" he asked.

She pressed her lips together and swallowed. "No one, I expect."

"A pretty woman like you?"

"In fact, I don't think I'll stay long. I felt obliged to come for some reason, but I wonder if I shouldn't be with Belle tonight."

"She won't have you," Leon said. "She would tell you to go home."

Maura had to agree. Still, the evening held no attraction for her now.

Leon let his chair legs down, throwing his weight on the table. "What's he doing here?"

"Who?" Maura looked around.

"Roper. Jesse Roper. I've been asking around about him. He

is Old Man Twigg's grandson, or the grandson of his brother, or something like that."

"Oh." Maura glanced at Leon's pocket. He did not disappoint. He tipped the flask all the way up this time and his head back, telling her he had emptied it.

He scraped his chair back and stood up.

"Leon." Maura put a hand on his forearm.

He shook it off. "Roper!"

The tall stranger strode slowly across the hall and halted in front of Leon, feet shoulder width apart. "Watch your mouth, Mooney."

Leon jabbed a finger in Roper's chest. "You people destroyed my daughter."

Roper knocked away Leon's arm.

"All the Twiggs are the same way," Leon said.

"My name's Roper."

"Makes no difference. You have their blood." Leon's eyes widened in fire.

Maura stood. "Leon, why don't we go get something to eat?"

"I'm not hungry." Leon stared at Jesse Roper.

Maura put on the too-small gloves just for something to do. Helpless was not her favorite feeling.

"Isn't that the sheriff?" Joseph tilted his head down the street. "Must be his wife. I don't believe I've seen them together before."

Zeke narrowed his eyes and shifted the dry goods package under his arm. "Joseph Beiler, you are giving in to distraction."

"I'm just curious. Beiler. Byler. Wouldn't you be curious if you met someone named Berkley or Buerkli?" He followed the progress of the sheriff and his wife and started walking in the same direction.

"Joseph, are you doubting your faith?"

Joseph's head snapped around. "What would make you say such a thing?"

"When the bishop chose you for this mission, you did not want to come. You came in *demut*, submission. But now I don't recognize what is in your mind."

"Have you heard from the bishop?"

Zeke stopped walking. "No."

"Then I am doing nothing wrong. I am still in submission, awaiting the bishop's will."

"We have the beans we came into town to buy," Zeke said. "We should go back to the livery and start the pot boiling."

"And now I don't recognize what is in your mind," Joseph said. "You have always been the friend to show me that God might smile once in a while."

"I still believe that." Zeke pressed his lips closed and breathed out through his nose. "All right, then. But I am hungry. I will go start the beans."

"I won't be long. I would simply like to meet my distant cousin."

Zeke laughed. "You're making up stories."

The Bylers were well down the street by now, and Joseph lengthened his stride to catch them. Everyone said his family held their heads in a distinctive way. Was it his imagination that Abraham Byler also shared this trait? Or that he seemed gentle and affectionate with his wife the way Joseph's father was with his mother?

The sheriff paused in front of the town hall and leaned his head in toward his wife, saying something that made her laugh. He held the door open for her, and the building swallowed them up.

The forbidden building. Or was it? It was just a hall. The sign tacked to the door said, MUSIC AND DANCE. Perhaps it was not so different than a Sunday night singing at home. An *English* singing.

Joseph pulled the door open.

Maura nearly lost her balance scuttling away as Jesse Roper raised one giant fist, threw Leon against the wall, and held him there by the front of his shirt.

Maura gasped, and conversation around them halted. Few heads turned when the hall's door opened, but Maura felt the draft and allowed herself a glance.

"Sheriff Byler!" she called out.

Jesse Roper leaned his face within inches of Leon's and glared. "You keep your mouth shut, you brainless bigot."

"If I don't?" Leon glowered.

A stone sank in Maura's stomach. Had Leon no sense at all?

Roper responded by shaking his fist, shuddering Leon against the wall. "I'll blow your head off the next time we meet."

"The sheriff is coming." Even Maura's loud announcement did nothing to deter Roper. She tracked the sheriff's direct progress across the hall.

Sheriff Byler approached with his usual calm. "Mr. Roper, I suggest you put Mr. Mooney down now. We'll chalk this up to too much drink, shall we?"

With a downward thrust, Roper put Mooney back in his chair and turned on his heel to march out of the hall.

Mooney shook his fist. "You haven't heard the end of this."

Nineteen

Annie had hardly swallowed her breakfast on Wednesday morning before she was on her bicycle. She had no reason to go watch the training burn—other than the smoldering sensation in her stomach that Leah Deitwaller had not removed her sparse belongings after all. The pedals spun hard and fast as Annie leaned into them with all her weight to keep her speed up even on inclines. She had the day off from working at the shop and figured it was better to be sure Leah did not need further prodding than to later regret not going.

As early as Annie was, the fire department was earlier. Four water trucks circled the old house. Firefighters in full garb milled around, some still with morning coffee in their hands. Annie laid her bike down in the browning fall meadow floor well away from the house and proceeded on foot. All she wanted was to be sure, absolutely sure, that Leah was out of the house and not sleeping through the bright dawn. It would only take a minute to slip in through the front opening and look in the back rooms. If the cat bowl was gone, Annie would be certain Leah had cleared out just as she promised she would. Annie had her eye on the empty door frame now. She needed another few moments and she would clear out of the way herself.

"I'm sorry, but you can't go in there." A yellow-suited arm of a firefighter fell like a gate in front of Annie.

"I'll just be a minute," Annie said.

The helmet atop his head swung from left to right. "No, you won't. No one is going in at this point."

"You don't understand." Annie rubbed her palms together. "A young woman was squatting here. I saw her things the other night. I just want to be sure she got out."

"We walked through the house last night and again this morning. No one is in there."

"And no sign of a cat? Just a kitten? Black and white."

"No cat. No woman. No anything. It's just an abandoned structure that the owner is happy to have removed."

Annie peered at what she could see of the young man's face behind his gear. "Aren't you the man who came to see Ruth Beiler out at her family's farm?"

He snapped his head up. "I might be. Who are you?"

"Annie Friesen. Ruth and I are friends."

"Then, yes, I am the man who came to see Ruth. Bryan Nichols. She told me about you."

Annie pulled her skirt away from her hips on both sides. "I guess my story is pretty obvious. I up and joined the Amish."

"She said you're from Colorado Springs. Me, too." Bryan relaxed his posture but maintained his position between Annie and the house. "Where did you go to high school?"

"Doherty."

"Me, too. We'll have to form an alumni chapter. My friend Alan can join us."

A vague image floated through Annie's mind of what her own classmates' faces would look like if they knew she had joined the Amish church. A few of them did know, in fact, and all of them had chosen not to remain in touch. When Annie closed her Facebook and Twitter accounts, she had cut herself off from those years.

"I just want to be absolutely certain my young friend is out of the house," she said.

In the passenger seat of her supervisor's vehicle, Ruth approached the abandoned house. Already spectators were gathering in clumps, many of them sitting on the hoods of their vehicles or on blankets on the ground to await the excitement. Ruth had mixed feelings. Witnessing the burn might well impress on her the urgency of treating burn victims, but she was fairly certain she already understood that principle. In her lap was a textbook on treating burns and a checklist of standard protocol for making a patient stable enough to transport to a burn center as far away as Denver.

"Looks like we have a few minutes if you want to take a look around." Her supervisor set the emergency brake. "Let's meet back here in half an hour."

Ruth nodded and opened the passenger door, uncertain how close she wanted to go. This place was a good fifteen miles from the Beiler farm. She had had a vague notion of where Karl Kramer's ranch was, but she had no idea any structures this old remained on it. Slowly, she ambled closer and wondered where Bryan was and what his role in this event would be. In full gear, all the firefighters looked alike.

She looped around one of the water trucks and saw a ladder truck roll in and take its position. While Westcliffe and neighboring Silver Cliff together amounted to a pin dot on a map, the fire protection service based in Westcliffe served all of Custer County. Ruth knew they worked hard to keep their equipment plentiful and up to date.

It was not Bryan whom she spotted but Annalise gesturing past a firefighter. Annalise had not said anything about coming out to watch, so what was she doing here with that characteristic look of determination on her face? A few seconds passed before

Ruth realized that the firefighter staring down Annalise was Bryan Nichols.

Ruth approached.

"Here's Ruth now," Bryan said, grinning.

"Should my ears be burning?" She put her hands to her mouth at her own bad joke. "Sorry. What's going on?"

"Leah was staying here," Annalise said. "I just wanted to make sure she got out."

"And I have assured your friend that the fire department has made absolutely certain that no humans or kittens are inside this building, whether voluntarily or involuntarily."

"Then I'm sure she's out," Ruth said.

"The chief had firefighters out here all day yesterday setting up for today. No one is in this structure."

Annalise blew out her breath. "Okay, then. I won't worry anymore that you didn't let me double-check."

Another yellow-uniformed figure approached them, the pieces of his headgear in place. A deep voice boomed. "I'm afraid unauthorized personnel must vacate this area immediately."

"Of course." Ruth stepped back, pulling Annalise's elbow with her.

Bryan, however, moved toward the man and flipped up his mask. "Wellner, where have you been? The chief is about to strike your name from the training manifest."

Ruth rolled her eyes. It was Alan.

"I couldn't get away from work any sooner. I just spoke to our fearless leader." Alan tugged at his gloves. "Not only is my name on the manifest, but the chief is bouncing with joy at my mere presence. Words do not express the abounding gladness."

Ruth held her textbook against her chest with both arms. Alan showed none of the tension she had observed in the presence of his father the day before.

Alan smacked his hands together. "Are we going to burn something today or not?"

Annie looked from Ruth to Bryan to the stranger. "Hello. I'm Annie Friesen."

"Alan Wellner, future fire chief of Custer County. Pleased to meet you."

Annie couldn't help but laugh at this young man's exuberant self-confidence.

Bryan elbowed Alan. "As you can see, my friend does not lack belief in his own ability. But he's right. You ought to move farther away from the house, or the present fire chief of Custer County will be breathing down our necks."

"He's a dragon, he is," Alan said.

The foursome began slow but direct progress away from the house and past the line of fire engines.

"Isn't that your friend Capp?" Bryan asked.

Annie raised her eyes to see Elijah Capp standing behind a water truck, his feet planted shoulder width apart and his arms crossed behind his back. His brown hair fluttered in the breeze.

"I wonder what happened to his hat," Annie said.

"Hello, Elijah," Ruth said softly.

Elijah nodded.

"Looks like we have quite a turnout to watch the spectacle," Bryan said. "We'd better make it a good show."

Annie glanced at the growing crowd. She came because she was worried about Leah. It had not occurred to her that half the town would want to see this old building in flames.

"You all had better get behind the safety line now." Bryan guided the elbows of both Ruth and Annie.

"Actually, I am supposed to meet my supervisor," Ruth said. "I'll see you all later."

Ruth barely looked at Elijah, Annie noticed. But neither did she meet Bryan's eyes. She simply turned and walked around the water truck toward the area where most of the cars were parked.

"We'd better take our positions, too." Bryan nudged Alan. "We'll catch up with you guys after the drama is over."

"Nice to meet you both," Annie said. A moment later, she was left standing alone with Elijah Capp. "I came looking for Leah Deitwaller. As long as I'm here, though, I suppose I should stay and watch."

"Let's find a better vantage point," Elijah said. "We won't be able to see anything from behind these trucks once the fire starts."

"Okay." Annie followed Elijah's lead. "Should we look for your hat first?"

"My hat?"

She pointed to his bare head, uncharacteristic for an Amish man.

"My hat is not lost. I did not put it on this morning."

"Oh."

They walked together for a few yards.

"Franey Beiler tells me that your mother has repainted her kitchen cabinets. How do they look?"

"They were only half-finished the last time I saw them. I hope she is pleased, though."

Annie reached for Elijah's arm to stop his pace. "How can you not have seen your family's kitchen cabinets?"

He sighed and looked away. "I moved out."

Annie's eyes widened. "Where to?"

"An apartment. A large room and bath in an *English* house."

"When did you do this?" Annie could not make sense of what she heard. Elijah had moved out of his Amish home and had deliberately come today without his black felt hat.

"Last week, days ago." Elijah resumed walking. "I'm thinking of becoming a volunteer firefighter. What do you think?"

"Wait. Let's go back to the part about how you moved out of your family's home."

"It's better this way." Elijah kicked a rock and sent it skittering. "They will have a hard time with my decision and will have to shun me. And I don't want to be a hypocrite under their roof."

"What decision are you talking about?" Elijah Capp was one of the most devout, respectful men Annie had met in the Amish church. "What do you mean about being a hypocrite?"

He met her gaze, silent.

"Elijah—"

"It would dishonor my parents to stay where my heart no longer lies."

They had turned their backs on the old house while they walked. The sudden roar of fire startled them both, and they pivoted in tandem. Bright orange flames poured out from the center of the house and shot up billowing black smoke.

None of the firefighters moved.

"What are they waiting for?" Annie asked.

"A fire always has a head start, does it not? Perhaps they are waiting for the response time it normally takes for the engines to arrive."

"This house is a pile of dry sticks. Nothing will be left of it."

As she spoke this time, the teams went into action, each one unrolling hose and positioning themselves. Ladders appeared and rose in height.

"That house won't hold any weight," Annie insisted. "They shouldn't try to climb."

Elijah smiled. "Mainly they are trying out different hoses to see how they perform. That's why the water trucks are spaced as they are. The ladders are an extra drill to improve their time."

Annie drew her head back and stared at Elijah. "And you know this how?"

He tilted his head then straightened it. "You are not the only one who knows how to use the resources of the public library."

"Elijah Capp, have you been on the Internet?"

Twenty

If Elijah heard Annie's question, he refused to acknowledge it. He spread his feet and crossed his wrists in front of him, eyes forward focused on the fire. Annie stood beside him, mesmerized by both the enormity and the proximity of the inferno. Teams of firefighters rolled into action now, raising nozzles, supporting hoses, controlling the flow of water from the massive tanks.

"Did you know my parents' barn burned down when I was young?" Elijah tapped one booted foot.

"No, I never heard that." Annie watched him out of the side of her eye. "What happened?"

"Well, it wasn't an electrical fire. They were sure of that much."

Annie snorted.

"The investigators said it was a gasoline fire, but I'm not sure if they figured out where the spark came from to light it."

"It's amazing what they can determine when you think all the evidence would have burned up."

Before them, the feeble front wall of the house gave way. Annie flinched.

"I was a little boy," Elijah said. "My parents always shooed me from the room whenever anyone talked about what happened.

I've always wanted to know."

"You're grown now. Why don't you ask?"

He shrugged. "It was fifteen years ago. No one was hurt, not even any of the animals. As soon as the rubble was cleared away, the church came for a barn raising."

"Still. If you want to know. . ."

"We are not that sort of family. My family carried on. We moved out here. What's the point?"

They watched the flames. Around them, people in huddles shaded their eyes and pointed at shooting flames. Annie peered at the hurried movements of people in bulky yellow jackets and helmets, trying to pick out Bryan and Alan, the only two firefighters she knew by name and only because she had met them an hour ago. She suspected four of the figures she saw were women who did not miss a beat keeping up with the men.

"So you want to be a firefighter because of what happened to your family?" she asked.

Elijah leaned one direction and then the other without lifting his feet. "It seems a worthy cause, even as a volunteer. Perhaps especially as a volunteer."

"It takes a lot of guts. I'm not sure I could do it."

"You underestimate yourself, Annalise. Look at what you have already accomplished in your life. How can you think there is anything you could not do?"

"It's risky. Scary."

"And necessary, don't you think?"

"Well, yes," Annie admitted. "The rest of us depend on it."

"I would like to be able to do what I am willing to ask of others in this one area."

Annie waited, biding her time and rolling possible words over in her mind.

"Do Amish men become firefighters?" she finally asked. "I mean, the technology. . ."

Elijah turned his head and looked down at her from his height, nearly as tall as Rufus.

"No, I don't suppose they do," he said.

"So, you've made some decisions that are. . .permanent?"

He nodded. "I believe they will be."

"And Ruth?"

"I don't give up as easily as she hopes I will."

Ruth had long ago lost the thread of what her supervisor was explaining to her. She had, however, observed the fact that the woman's husband was one of the volunteer firefighters training on the back side of the structure, which explained more convincingly her belief that being present at the fire had learning value for Ruth.

The remains of a second wall surrendered, and one end of a beam that ran through the house thundered to the ground, shifting the primary direction of the blaze. Unlike the charred half-built house containing Rufus's cabinetry, nothing would be left of this one. The fire department would intentionally let the structure collapse and smolder, instead concerning themselves with ensuring flames did not spread into the meadow around the house.

Ruth cleared her throat and consulted her clipboard, trying to find her place in the oral review of procedures that her supervisor was in the midst of.

Staging area.

Triage.

Chain of command.

Safe transport.

Ruth glanced across the scene to watch Bryan Nichols in action. He was focused, attentive, on task. A few feet away and sharing Bryan's hose, Alan Wellner divided his gaze between the burning house and a clump of spectators. Ruth followed his line of sight and saw the sheriff, no doubt present to be sure the assembly on the gentle meadow slope abided by all safety precautions of the event.

The pen in her hand reminded Ruth to focus again on her list. Her supervisor had stopped speaking, though. Eyes all around the perimeter of the burn focused on the galloping flames and the disappearing structure. Slats of wood that had once been a wall popped and crumbled. Ruth covered her mouth to cough even as smoke infiltrated her nostrils. The movement of lifting her elbow transferred her gaze once again.

Annalise and Elijah stood out of earshot but close enough for Ruth to see they were conversing regularly. Annalise's hair was neatly coiled and tucked under her *kapp*. Well, perhaps not neatly. No matter how long Annalise let her blond hair grow or how many pins she used, strands always seemed to escape her efforts.

Ruth's own brown hair was pulled back and fastened simply at the back of her neck with an oversized plain brown barrette she would never have owned growing up. By Amish standards, it was ornate and might tempt the wearer to vanity. One hand went up now to check the clasp.

Standing across from them and twisting her lips in thought, Ruth's first instinct was to wonder what Annalise and Elijah would be talking about with such concentration. Were they discussing her?

She scribbled at the bottom of her checklist. So what if they were? Annalise had joined the church, after all. Soon enough Rufus would propose and they would marry. Why should she not talk to another member of the church in a public setting? They were the only two Amish people present. Annalise was probably just being friendly.

Tom Reynolds's red pickup roared into the meadow with the horn blaring as if someone had strapped a rock to it. Adrenaline surged through Ruth's midsection as Tom nudged his way past a couple of onlooking families and got as close to the security line as he could. He then jumped out of his truck and marched along the line, waving his hands at the fire chief. A moment later, the chief began pointing and shouting orders. The water supply to Bryan and Alan's hose abruptly shut off, and they began rolling the hose rapidly. Two ladders came down while a second water truck also stowed gear.

Back in his truck, Tom gunned the engine and began backing up. Ruth ran straight toward him, slapping her hands on the hood.

"What's going on, Tom?"

"A fire." Tom turned the steering wheel.

Ruth moved out of the way of the turning front left tire but would not release her grip on Tom's lowered window. "What are you talking about? The fire is right here. They have it all under control."

"Another one."

"Where?" Her heart thudded.

"An old outbuilding on the other side of the highway, about three miles out. I think it's on county land. At first I thought it was the training burn, but I realized it was the wrong side of the road."

Behind Ruth, the engine of a water truck howled. She was glued to Tom's pickup.

"Get out of the way, Ruth." Tom slapped at her fingers on his window and let his foot off the brakes. The truck rolled, and Ruth jumped back.

A moment later Bryan was behind the wheel of his water truck and rumbling through the meadow. His focus was strictly on navigating out of one fire scene and toward another. Beside him in the cab, Alan lifted three fingers in a wave. Ruth gaped at three vehicles being redeployed to the new fire even as she heard the shriek of the siren beckoning volunteers from around the county.

Ruth turned back to the fire behind her just as the final wall tumbled and remaining firefighters rushed in to fill the gaps left by the departing trucks. The glory of the construction burn was nearly extinguished, outblazed by the potential of an unattended fire in open grassland. Spectators were already jumping into their cars and turning them around toward the road.

Gripping her clipboard, Ruth ran toward her supervisor's car, where the older woman already had the ignition fired up. The clinic would need to be ready if someone were hurt.

Word of the second fire advanced through the crowd. Annie saw nothing to be gained by dashing off to watch another fire. Suddenly, though, she wondered how Elijah had gotten to this destination. She had not seen a buggy all morning, and anybody with half a brain would have kept away animals that might bolt. She turned to ask him.

He was gone, already lost from her sight.

Annie turned back to the training burn, which was fast becoming a haphazard pile of glowing half boards. Water still flowed from two trucks but with less fury. When the traffic thinned a bit more, Annie decided, she would fetch her bicycle and head back to town.

A flash of blue caught the corner of her eye, and Annie snapped her head around. Amish blue. The more she handled Amish fabrics, the more distinctive that shade became in Annie's mental palette. It was not the mass-dyed hue of a commercial manufacturer that clung to the surface of an inexpensive material, but the rich saturation that emanated from the core of tight-woven cloth.

Annie realized she was holding her breath and blew it out. Forgetting her bicycle—it was in the wrong direction—she ran after the flash of blue. At least where she thought she had seen it.

Leah had been there. Annie was sure of it. She must have left home with only the dress on her back, because every time Annie saw her, Leah wore the same hue, sometimes with a purple apron and sometimes without. But always the same blue.

At the edge of the dissipating crowd, Annie systematically scanned from left to right. When she finally spotted the girl, she was looking at her back. With her skirts gathered in her fists, Leah ran with surprising dexterity, and Annie did not think she could catch her.

Three miles. That was the rumor. The new fire was only three miles.

Annie looked again at the speed with which Leah moved and thought about the miles she knew the girl had been crisscrossing in the last two weeks. When Annie ran track in high school and was constantly training, three miles was nothing.

Would Leah set fire to another building because she had been forced out of this one? Surely not.

Rufus's words from just after the first fire rankled. *"You talked to her over a crowded, lengthy meal. Can you be certain she was there during the service?"*

Annie was just going to have to find Leah again. To be sure.

Twenty-One

June 1892

"We're shutting down for the day." The Dentons' foreman wiped a handkerchief across his perspiring brow.

Joseph and Zeke gripped the ends of a felled tree sheared of its branches, sharing its weight with Dayton Brown and Oscar Board.

"What he means," Dayton said, "is that he's too old and tired and can't stand the heat another minute."

Oscar snorted.

"We're all hot." Joseph glanced at Zeke. "I'm sure he has in mind the best interest of the entire crew."

"No doubt." Zeke's agreement came quickly.

"You Amish seem nice enough," Dayton said, "but even you can't think a half day off has anything to do with us. It's not even lunchtime. They won't pay us for the afternoon, you know."

"I do know," Joseph said.

They lugged the tree away from the edge of the bluff. Joseph had no idea what the Denton brothers planned to do with the heaps of logs cleared from their land and accumulating farther and farther from the shore. He could now stand well back from their ferry dock and see the curve of the White River. The Dentons would be able to sit on their front porches and see a horseman coming. The work would not last much longer, but Joseph and Zeke had been frugal with their pay. Whatever their journeys did not consume, they would take home to their families.

Joseph put his thumbs through his suspender straps. There was the matter of Hannah waiting for him. Perhaps in his absence someone else had sparked her interest.

She was not the flighty type.

He felt the poke in the middle of his back, Zeke's test of his nerves, and refused to flinch.

"Let's ride the crew's wagon into town," Zeke said. "We can ask at the post office for a letter."

"You go ahead." Joseph still surveyed the river. "I would like to walk and think."

"In the heat?"

"It is not so hot as the *English* believe."

"Surely there will be a letter," Zeke said. "We posed a simple question about the bishop's wishes. I am beginning to fear something has gone wrong at home that would delay his response."

"What does it matter?" Joseph murmured.

Hands on his hips, Zeke moved to stand between Joseph and the view of the river. "My friend, we can continue our scouting mission or we can go home to Tennessee. When the letter comes, we will do one or the other, but we will not linger in Gassville."

"I did not suggest we should." Joseph raised both hands to straighten his hat. When his hands came down away from his face, he imagined flinging his black felt Amish hat into the White River's current. He shook the devilish image out of his mind. "I'll see you back at the livery."

Joseph did not hurry. Eventually he would end up in town, behind the livery. He would go inside to help with the few simple chores they exchanged for the privilege of spreading their bedrolls under the night sky. But for now, he walked without specific destination. Sweat trickled between his shoulder blades.

At the crack of a pistol, Joseph dropped to the ground. Laughter followed the shot. Joseph did not find it amusing to be the target of an *English* gun. Another shot blasted a tin can. Joseph knew that sound. Even Amish boys learning to hunt for food had to practice on something. He crawled toward the shots. Making himself seen was his best hope for avoiding a stray bullet.

"Hello!" he called.

Boots shuffled against the ground.

"I'd just like to get through," Joseph shouted. He looked past the underbrush toward rows of toes reorienting toward him. Black *English* boots. "Is it safe?"

"Who's there?" a voice demanded.

Joseph stood and kept a tree between himself and the clearing ahead. "Joseph Beiler."

"Oh, the Amish man."

That was Walter's voice, Joseph was sure. What was he doing out pistol shooting?

A moment later, Walter tugged on Joseph's sleeve. "You can come out."

Joseph stepped from behind the tree in Walter's protection. Several young men stood with pistols in their hands, the tallest of them Jesse Roper. Joseph had followed Sheriff Byler into the town hall the night of the dance in time to see what Roper was capable of.

"It's just a friendly shooting match." Roper grinned. "Do you shoot?"

After John Twigg's death, Joseph had heard enough *English* talk to know that a shooting match in the woods was against the law in Baxter County.

"Well, do you shoot?" Roper asked again.

Joseph shook his head. "Only rifles, and only for food."

"So you've never fired a pistol?"

Again Joseph shook his head.

"You can use mine." Roper offered the heel of his weapon with a faint smirk.

"No thank you." Joseph scanned the group of shooters. Roper clearly was the oldest and Walter the youngest, with three in between. Joseph did not see a pistol in Walter's hand, a fact that brought some relief.

Jesse Roper fired another shot at another can. "One bullet left. It's yours if you want it."

"Try it," Walter urged. "Maybe you have a knack."

"I don't believe I will." Joseph touched his hat. As good as Roper was, Joseph was certain he was a better shot. He needed no target practice and would not fire for sport. But watching would cause no harm as long as he was behind the shooting line.

"I'll try," Walter said.

Roper laughed. "Some say I'm stupid, but I'm not that stupid."

"I'm a good shot," Walter insisted.

"Well, we're not going to find out today." Roper nodded toward one of the other men. "Your turn."

The shooter missed, which Roper found riotously amusing. In the middle of his laugher, he raised his own gun, aimed, and fired a bullet against the innocent can.

"That's it, boys. I'm hungry. Somebody owes me lunch." Roper pointed at Digger Dawson. "I believe it was you who wagered your mama's cooking."

Digger kicked up a flurry of dirt. "Yes, sir, I reckon I did."

"Let's go, then."

"Oh good," Walter said. "I'm hungry, too."

Jesse Roper shook his head. "Not you."

"Why not?"

"I don't aim to get between a boy and his daddy. You skedaddle on home. And not a word about this, you hear?"

Walter started to protest further, but Joseph caught his eye and gave the look he generally aimed at Little Jake when his brother seemed inclined to foolishness on the family farm. The boy picked up a rock and heaved it into the woods, but he left.

Jesse Roper laughed, and Joseph could not help liking the

sound. Jesse seemed to do just what he wanted at any moment. The voice of Joseph's father jumped the miles and the years to speak to Joseph words of caution, words of warning, words of the scripture about what happened to fools. Joseph had no doubt that all of the Amish and many of the *English* would cast Roper in that category. Still, watching the carelessness of Jesse's face, Joseph wondered what such abandon would feel like. Obviously Jesse could saunter into a strange town and attract a following. What did these young men see in him? A daring spirit? Fearlessness they did not dare explore themselves?

Joseph reached up and tugged his hat.

"You do that a lot, you know." Roper pointed a finger at Joseph then reached for his own hat, high and broad and black with a deep crease in the crown.

Joseph ran his hands down the front of his trousers. "I don't notice when I do it."

"It'll ruin your hat."

"It is not much of a hat to begin with." Nothing like Roper's.

Jesse threw his head back and laughed again. "You got that right. You comin' to lunch with us?"

Joseph shook his head immediately. "Thank you, but my friend will be expecting me soon."

"By all means, we don't want to make your friend jealous that you had a warm, home-cooked meal and he did not."

Joseph swallowed. He had the good sense to decline the lunch invitation because he suspected the rumor that Roper was related to the Twiggs was true.

Roper leaned over and tucked his pistol into the wide cuff of his trouser leg and fastened it in with a snap. "Put your guns away, boys. And get those cans. Your daddies won't be happy if they think I led you to the den of wickedness."

If someone in Joseph's family spoke of a den of wickedness, it would be with all seriousness. Roper found amusement in his defiance. Despite the grand jury clearing the Denton brothers, after John Twigg died, Sheriff Byler made it clear that further illegal pistol shooting would not be tolerated. Even if Jesse Roper's recent arrival meant he did not know this, the others certainly did.

Joseph watched Roper carefully pick up the jacket that matched his trousers from the bush where he had laid it. As reckless as he was toward authority, Roper was a stickler for his clothes and appearance. The young men collected pieces of the cans they had blasted and tossed them in a burlap sack, which one of them slung over his shoulder as the group ambled toward the path that would take them out of the woods and toward the ranch where Roper presumed lunch would be waiting.

None of them looked back to see that Joseph had not moved.

Joseph gave them a head start, while he briefly considered his options, and then followed. His father had taught him well to track prey through thick woods without giving himself away, and Joseph had no trouble following without causing any of the foursome to suspect their surroundings. Curiosity compelled his soundless steps. He and Zeke worked long hours on the Denton cattle ranch, but other than one dinner with Maura Woodley and her father, he had scant experience with *English* households.

It was surprisingly easy to climb a maple tree and lean comfortably into the cradle of its thick branches. From above the sight line of the home's inhabitants, Joseph had a clear view of the front porch, into the front parlor, and through to the dining room. Digger Dawson's mother scowled, but she served lunch. Fried chicken, mashed potatoes, beets, chocolate cake. The table was laid with a light blue tablecloth and adorned with a vase of daisies. The curtains were yellow with white eyelet trim and hung against pale green painted walls. Knickknack shelves and formal photographs reminded Joseph he was looking into a world not his own.

Even with the windows open to catch the breeze, Joseph heard little of the conversation, but periodically Jesse Roper erupted in laughter and the others followed in nervous imitation. Joseph was glad he had not gone in with them.

A horse trotted toward the house pulling a wagon driven by a man Joseph did not recognize. At the porch, the man climbed down and rapped on the front door.

"I've come about the pistol shooting," Joseph heard the man say when a weary-looking Mrs. Dawson opened the door.

She turned and glared toward the dining room. "It's Deputy Combs for y'all."

A moment later, Jesse Roper filled the open door frame.

"You're under arrest," Deputy Combs said, "for shooting pistols. We've had a report from an eyewitness."

Joseph's heart sank. Surely not Walter.

"All of you," Deputy Combs demanded, "come with me."

Roper spread his feet and crossed his arms. Behind him, the other shooters assembled.

Deputy Combs pointed at each one in turn. "I brought the wagon. You get on out there and let me take you into town and do this properly."

One young man came forward. "I only shot once."

"Once is against the law," Combs said. "In the wagon. If you resist, you'll only make more trouble for yourself."

One by one, Digger and his two friends slipped past Roper and straggled toward the wagon.

From his branch, Joseph watched *English* justice in process—and was once again glad he did not take hold of the pistol Roper offered.

"I do believe I will finish my lunch," Roper said.

"You're resisting arrest," Combs said. "You must come with me."

Roper whipped out his pistol and laughed. "You don't say!" He aimed the pistol, his thumb ready to cock it.

Combs turned on his heel and ran to the wagon.

Roper roared in laughter.

Twenty-Two

On Thursday, Annie and Ruth both had afternoon shifts, a coincidence that allowed them a leisurely late breakfast together. Annie laid out bacon strips on a tray to put in the oven while Ruth pulled eggs and cheddar cheese from the refrigerator and whole-wheat bread from the bread box Rufus had made for Annie.

"I'm so relieved no one was hurt in the fires yesterday." With thumb and forefinger, Annie nudged a slice of bacon to the edge of the pan to make room for one more.

"Bryan says there's definitely an arsonist." Ruth positioned two eggs between the fingers of one hand and cracked them simultaneously on the edge of a mixing bowl before reaching for two more.

"I have to learn how to do that," Annie said.

"I'll teach you sometime."

"When did you see Bryan again?"

Ruth cracked two more eggs and picked up a whisk. "Last night. He came by."

Annie pinched her eyebrows together. "How did he know where to find you?"

"I told him I was staying with you."

"He does have a habit of just showing up, doesn't he? Where was I?"

"Upstairs reading in bed already."

"That late?"

Ruth rolled her head toward Annie. "Annalise, it was eight thirty."

Annie slid the tray of bacon into the warm oven. She had to admit it was not unusual for her to be upstairs with a book by that hour. Lately it was the volume on Arkansas history. She was surprised to discover a Sheriff Abraham Byler of Baxter County, who seemed a gentle, well-loved soul.

"So what did Bryan say about the fires?" Annie asked.

"There was nothing in that shed on county land that could have sparked a fire. And it was locked. They found the padlock, and it had not been opened."

"So it caught fire from the outside."

"Except nothing around it burned." Ruth lit the burner under a frying pan. "Somebody started that fire at the back of the shed."

Annie leaned against a counter. "Is Bryan compromising the investigation by telling you this stuff?"

Ruth paled. "It's just his theory. It's nothing formal. It's not like he's the official investigator or anything."

While Ruth shredded cheese, Annie poured orange juice.

"What did you and Elijah find to talk about?" Ruth asked. "Did he mention why he was even there?"

Annie kept her back turned as she returned the orange juice pitcher to the refrigerator. "It turns out he is interested in fires. I suppose he's curious, like a lot of people. He and Bryan might actually have something in common."

"Oh." Ruth shredded with more vigor.

Annie carried the juice glasses to the table in the dining room, where she had laid out two place mats a few minutes earlier. Ruth had given her a perfect opening to say that Elijah had moved off his parents' farm and into town. In fact, the room he rented was not more than half a mile from Annie's home. She wanted Ruth to know. It might change things between Ruth and Elijah before things went further with Bryan. But shouldn't Elijah be the one to tell Ruth? Annie returned to the kitchen and took two plates from the cabinet.

"So do you really think you are going to get Leah to come and stay here?" Ruth dumped the eggs into the sizzling pan.

"I'm going to try. I hope you don't mind that I cut the living room in half to make space for her."

"Would you rather I stay somewhere else while she's here?"

"No! Of course not."

"If I weren't here, you'd have room for her."

"I *do* have room for her." Annie put a hand on her friend's shoulder while Ruth gently stirred the eggs. "And I hope that she'll soon be ready to go home."

Ruth pointed at the oven. "Don't burn my bacon."

When Annie walked through Mrs. Weichert's shop door a few hours later, the older woman was putting the telephone in its cradle. Annie smiled at the gesture. That phone had to be thirty years old, but Mrs. Weichert had no interest in updating. It was an antiques shop, after all.

"You just missed him," Mrs. Weichert said.

"Who?"

"Rufus."

Annie's stomach sank. He was not likely to call again. "What did he say?"

"He'll see you on Sunday. He'll be home all day."

Annie suppressed a grin and walked around the counter to stow her purse on the shelf underneath. A moment later, Mrs. Weichert gave her a short list of tasks for the afternoon and Annie settled into routine.

But the fire still blazed in her mind, and over and over she saw the flash of Amish blue escaping her sight. As she wiped a dust rag over the porcelain pieces and straightened up the Amish jam jars, Annie prayed for peace to come to Leah Deitwaller's heart. And she wondered if it did any good in God's eyes to pray after the fact that Leah please not be the one who was starting fires.

On Sunday afternoon Rufus put his thumbs through his suspenders and leaned a shoulder against the partial wall that divided the dining room from the living room. From this perspective, he had a clear view of Annalise, but she was not likely to see him from her seat on the sofa. For this moment—and he knew it would not last long in the busy Beiler household—she was alone. Her quilt nearly swallowed her up as she bent over her stitches. He had seen her in this pose often enough in the last few months to know that her tongue peeked out of the left corner of her lips when she was concentrating. His mother had been the one to offer to teach Annalise to quilt. A few weeks ago, typical of Annalise's independent streak, she had declared that she would finish on her own. Now she was working on the binding of a traditional Amish nine-patch quilt made from solid-colored fabrics that had once belonged to her mother. She found sentimental pleasure in bringing memories of her *English* childhood into her new life in the Amish church.

With quiet steps Rufus crossed the room and moved enough of the quilt off one end of the sofa to allow him to sit beside her. Her smile melted something at his core every time.

"The quilt is beautiful," he said.

"Well, it's not perfect, but for my first attempt, I think it's pretty good!" She laughed. "That sounds like pride. Forgive me."

"I admire what you have done and the qualities that have allowed you to do it." What he wanted to say was that he was proud of her. "It's a nice afternoon."

"Yes, it is." Annalise pulled the thread taut in preparation for another stitch.

"How would you like to take a driving lesson?"

Her fingers immediately released the quilt. "Really?"

"I'll get Dolly ready."

"I'll put this away and find my sweater."

By the time Rufus pulled the buggy to the front of the house ten minutes later, Annalise was standing on the front porch in the blue sweater his mother had knit for her last winter. While he scooted over on the bench, she clamored down the steps and around the back of the buggy, appearing on the driver's side.

When she grinned, he could not help but grin back. Most Amish women Annalise's age had been driving buggies half their lives.

Annalise straightened herself on the bench and picked up the reins. "Giddyup."

Dolly responded with gentle forward motion. Annalise tugged the reins to the left, and the horse circled the Beiler front yard. Once they traversed the long driveway and approached the main highway, Rufus felt his own foot pressing against the floor as if to slow the buggy. On her side, Annalise pulled on the reins and pushed the brake slightly too hard, and they lurched forward. Rufus only allowed himself to watch her in his peripheral vision lest the turn of his head imply any lack of confidence. Annalise managed to stop Dolly right at the edge of the road and took her time looking in both directions.

"Is it all right if we go toward town?" Annalise asked.

"Wherever you wish. You're the driver."

She giggled. "You don't know how long it's been since anyone said that to me."

"It's probably a good idea to stay on a familiar stretch of road."

"I'm a little nervous about being on the main highway."

"You can do it. You ride with me all the time."

"I won't go fast."

"Dolly will appreciate that. Sometimes I think she likes to have a Sabbath, too."

Annalise pulled the reins to the right and entered the shoulder of the highway. They traveled in silence for a few minutes.

"You're doing very well," Rufus said. And she was.

"You probably remember what happened the last time you took me out. I practically ran over Leah Deitwaller."

"But you didn't. She is the one who ran in front of you without looking. You are the one who stopped without anybody getting hurt."

"You certainly have a knack for seeing the upside of things."

"Mmm." He was not so sure. Seeing the upside of his financial bind was not what made him take a job he was beginning to think was a mistake. Hours of prayer did not give him the peace his soul sought, and being with *English* men all day made him lonely. But he had only been gone six days. Perhaps the next stretch would be better or go faster.

"I suppose you heard all about the fires." Annalise's eyes remained fixed straight ahead.

"Cars can come up faster than you think. Don't forget to check the mirrors," Rufus said. "Yes, Tom filled me in when he picked me up last night."

"Do you really think it's possible Leah set that first fire?"

He glimpsed the lovely slope of her neck as she turned her head to glance in the mirror and then over her shoulder. "Are you concerned she might have started the fire that burned the shed?"

"I don't want to think that." Annalise adjusted her grip on the reins. "But now there's more talk than ever about arson, and no one knows where Leah is most of the time."

A car whizzed by them. Annalise startled. "I see what you mean."

"Maybe we should talk about the fires another time," Rufus said.

She glanced at him. "You're probably right. Tell me about the job."

He let a few yards go by in silence.

"Rufus?"

"I may have made a mistake."

"Why?" She turned her head toward him.

"Eyes on the road."

She complied immediately but said, "Talk to me, Rufus."

"I don't want to make too much of it," he said. "It's a difficult adjustment, that's all."

"You can quit, can't you?" she said. "I mean, if you do decide it's not the right thing."

He reached up to scratch the left side of his face. "One step at a time. Tom will drive me back tonight. The next job is in the hospital in Cañon City. They are renovating a wing of offices."

"My lifetime of habit wants to tell you to do what's right for you. But I know you will always think of your family first."

He wanted to think of her first. He wanted her to be his family. But he could not speak those words while he reserved the possibility that he would choose to save his family's farm with the money meant for beginning his married life.

Ruth grinned when she looked up and saw Annalise leading Dolly into the barn. "How was the drive?"

Annalise paused next to the tack rack and moved to remove Dolly's harness.

"Let me help you with that," Ruth said.

Annalise shook her head. "No. I want to do it. I've watched you all a thousand times."

Sophie stepped out from behind Ruth. "It's easy to tangle yourself up. It's okay to accept help."

"I know," Annalise said, "but I'll learn better if I figure it out by doing."

Lydia nudged Ruth aside. "Don't you know our Annalise well enough by now to know how stubborn she is?"

"I prefer to call it determined," Annalise said. She looked up at the three sisters. "What are you all doing out in the barn, anyway?"

"Milking and mucking don't wait for the Sabbath," Ruth said.

"We're waiting for you!" Sophie said. "We want to hear all about it the minute Rufus proposes."

Annalise hefted the harness up onto its hook. "Not today, I'm afraid."

Sophie groaned. "What is wrong with that man?"

Ruth shot her sister a look. "This is between Rufus and Annalise. It's not our business."

"It's all right," Annalise said. "I know that we're going to be together. It's just a matter of time."

Sophie picked up an empty milk bucket. "We all know that. But I don't see any reason for the two of you to miss this year's wedding season."

"*Gottes wille.*" Annalise straightened the dangling reins.

"Have you started making your dress yet?" Sophie swung the bucket back and forth. "I'm sure *Mamm* will help you."

"And I'm sure I'm going to need her help!" Annalise picked up a brush and began pulling it through Dolly's tangled mane.

"She wants to give you a beautiful wedding day."

Ruth took the bucket from Sophie's hands. "I'll milk. Your mind is not on it."

Sophie offered no objection, and she and Lydia closed in on Annalise while Ruth moved down to the stall where the family's only cow waited. Her jealousy shamed her. She had walked away from the Amish church and a man who loved her—and the beautiful wedding her mother would have planned for her. She had no right to envy Annalise's imminent happiness.

Twenty-Three

Ten days had passed since Annie mailed her letter to Matthew Beiler, plenty of time for him to receive Annie's letter and sit down to answer it. On Monday morning when she stopped at the Westcliffe post office to check her mail, she could not keep from imagining Matthew opening the letter, reading, and picking up a pen to respond—immediately. Annie opened her box, reached in, and extracted the pile of ads. She had not purchased with a credit card over the Internet for more than a year, and she had written to a number of vendors to have her name removed from their lists. Still, the onslaught of ads persisted. Annie fished through them for the letter she knew would be there, her mother's weekly newsy roundup, and slid it into a small outer pocket of her modest handbag. She would wait until she returned to her house to read it, and then she would take a card from the same stack she had used to write to Matthew and promptly answer her mother. Before dropping the stack in the recycling box, she shuffled through the ads one more time to make sure there was nothing from Matthew.

Out on the sidewalk, Annie could smell the yeasty fragrance of the bakery across the street and wondered if giving in to the urge to go buy a scone constituted falling into temptation. After all, she had left the house without breakfast that morning.

When she saw Elijah Capp's horse and buggy, she forgot about both her hunger and the scone. Elijah worked for a business that catered to providing and repairing Amish appliances. He had converted Annie's house, taking it off the *English* electrical grid and instead making sure the lights, furnace, stove, refrigerator, and washing machine ran on energy sources approved by the Amish district.

"Hello, Elijah." Annie stroked the neck of his horse, a habit that had grown on her since she moved to Westcliffe the previous year. "What brings you to town?"

He lifted the bakery's plain Styrofoam cup. "I have not yet gotten very good at making coffee in my new place."

"I suppose it all takes some adjusting." Annie tried to imagine what it must be like for Elijah to be living in a rented *English* room. "Where did you disappear to yesterday? I turned my head and you were gone."

"Everybody was trying to leave at once. I wanted to get my rig out of the way."

Annie nodded. That made sense. "Did you hear anything about the surprise fire?"

"I did not go over there to investigate. My landlady says it is probably a teenage pyromaniac, but I do not think that fits the pattern."

"Pattern? There's a pattern?"

"Two fires in empty structures only a few weeks apart." Elijah set his coffee on the floor of the buggy. "There might be something there."

"Do you really think so?"

"I'm sure your friend Bryan Nichols is more knowledgeable of these things."

"I only just met him that day, Elijah. He's no more my friend than he is yours."

"That's right." He hefted himself up into the buggy. "He's Ruth's friend."

Annie ran her tongue over her top lip. Whatever she knew about Ruth and Bryan—which was next to nothing—she was not going to tell Elijah.

"Where are you headed?" she asked.

"I have to drive out to the Stutzmans'. Edna claims the washing machine is not working properly."

Annie laughed. "Claims?"

Elijah tilted his head. "They have three daughters, you know."

"Can I come with you?"

"Why would you want to go to the Stutzmans'?"

Annie was not so much interested in the destination as the route Elijah might take. "I thought the ride might be nice."

"And?"

Annie kicked a rock. "And it might give me a chance to look for signs of Leah Deitwaller. She was staying in that house they burned down. Now I don't know where she went."

Elijah chortled. "I do talk to Joel, you know. I heard what happened when the two of you tracked down Leah. You could hardly walk for two days."

"We probably won't find her," Annie said. "Besides, if I'm with you, Edna won't encourage one of the girls to cook for you."

"True enough. Get in."

They were almost to the edge of the Stutzman farm and had nearly exhausted their supply of small talk. Annie was not sure how much longer they could avoid talking about Ruth, but she knew she was not going to be the one to introduce Ruth into the conversation. Her eyes soaked up the vista, the gorgeous mountains, the rolling meadows, the brilliant sunshine.

Where would a homeless, confused, Amish teenager go on a perfect fall day?

A ball of black and white flashed across the road. If Annie had not turned her head at just that moment, she would have missed it.

"Stop!"

Elijah pulled on the reins. "What's the matter?"

"The cat. I saw the cat."

"So what?"

Annie was already out of the buggy. "Did you see where it went?"

"Annalise, I am not about to chase a stray cat through open countryside."

"It's not a stray cat." Annie marched a few steps in the direction the cat had gone. "It's Leah's kitten. If the kitten is here, Leah is nearby."

"Maybe the cat got away."

"That kitten is the only living thing in Colorado that matters to her." Annie lengthened her stride. "Are you coming? We'll find her twice as fast with two sets of eyes."

"The Stutzmans are expecting me."

"You know good and well Edna probably loosened a bolt so she would have a reason to ask you to come."

"What am I supposed to do with my rig?"

"Bring it. We might need it."

Annie ignored the sigh that Elijah made no effort to disguise.

"The cat could be anywhere by now, you know," he said.

"It's a kitten. Leah dotes on it. Cats know to go where the food is."

"Amish cats are barn cats. They feed themselves or we don't keep them."

Annie glared. "Elijah Capp, stop arguing with me and turn that buggy around."

Even a fleet-footed kitten left a trace of tracks in the dust. Annie fixed on a spot where she was sure she had seen the kitten pause to circumvent a large rock and discerned the small prints.

"This way. Follow me."

Behind her, Annie heard the scuffling of the horse turning and the creak of the buggy wheels. She did not dare take her eyes off the tracks, though. They were too faint to discover again.

The kitten reappeared, poised on the first of a series of boulders. As the feline leaped from one to the other, Annie followed the probable path.

Leah Deitwaller sat atop a load of gravel in the bed of an unattended dump truck.

Annie stopped and glanced over her shoulder at Elijah, who reined in his horse.

"Whoa. What is she doing up there?" he asked.

Annie rolled her eyes. "I don't read her mind. But we have to get her to come down. It's not safe."

The kitten leaped onto a massive rear tire and splayed as if he might lose his grip. Annie sprang forward to close the yards and nabbed the kitten. The animal wriggled, but Annie held firm.

"Leah?" Annie inched along the side of the vehicle, uncertain that she had ever been this close to a dump truck.

Leah flailed her arms. "It's you again. Wherever I go, you find me."

"I care what happens to you." Annie wrapped her apron around the cat the way she had seen Leah do.

Elijah stood beside her now, speaking softly. "That has to be twelve, maybe fifteen tons of gravel. Must be a transfer truck for a major landscaping project."

"How do you know this stuff?" Annie made sure the kitten could breathe but kept it contained. "We have to get her down."

Leah shifted her position, and a spray of gravel shot off the side of the truck. "I figure that eventually this truck will go someplace where they have buses or trains."

"It will probably dump its load and go back to the quarry it came from." Elijah spoke into Annie's ear.

"It doesn't matter where it's going, because she's not going to be on it." Annie lifted her head and raised her voice. "Leah, I have your kitten. Wouldn't you like to come down and see him?"

"You keep him. I probably can't take him on the train anyway."

Annie blew her breath out, clueless what to say next. She only knew she must remain calm.

"I'll go around the other side and climb up." Elijah was already moving. "Just keep her talking."

"I've never had a cat," Annie said. "It might be fun to have a kitten, but this one is yours. I know he wants to be with you. He was trying to get back to you when I found him."

"He's the best kitten anyone could hope to have." Leah leaned a few inches in the direction of Annie and the cat.

"I know," Annie quickly agreed. "You deserve to have him."

"You know that I'm going to find a way to leave this wilderness."

"I just want you to be safe." Annie could not see Elijah. "I don't think you ever told me your kitten's name."

"I just call him Kitten."

"That's cute."

"You can give him another name after I'm gone."

Behind Leah, Elijah's head slowly rose above the level of the gravel. He began to crawl toward the girl.

"That doesn't look very comfortable up there," Annie said. "And I wonder if you're hungry."

Leah flinched and turned toward Elijah. "You've been trying to trick me!" She swung a foot at him and caught him in the chest.

Elijah fell out of Annie's sight.

Twenty-Four

Annie flew around the truck. Elijah lay flat on his back, moaning.

"Don't try to get up!"

"You don't have to worry about that." Elijah gasped at the effort of speaking. "My chest. She really clobbered me."

"How about your back? Can you feel everything you're supposed to feel?"

"It all hurts, so I guess so. Is she still up there?"

Annie spun around and looked to the top of the gravel heap. Leah was on all fours looking down.

"Leah Deitwaller, you do the grown-up thing and get down here right this minute!"

To Annie's shock and relief, Leah began a cautious climb down.

"Is he all right?" Leah asked. "I didn't mean to hurt anyone."

"We're going to need help. An ambulance." Constraining the kitten with one hand, Annie dug with the other in the bag still hanging from her shoulder and extracted her cell phone. She flipped it open and turned it on. A dark screen glared back at her. "Battery's dead. Elijah, did you bring a cell phone?"

He grunted. "Nope."

Leah was on the ground now and knelt beside Elijah. "I'm sorry."

Elijah closed his eyes. Annie's heart lurched.

"No! You stay conscious!"

"The sun's in my eyes, that's all."

Annie positioned herself between the sun and Elijah. "Leah, one of us has to go for help."

"You should be the one to go."

Annie was not sure which she dreaded more, the thought that if she left, Leah would bolt and abandon Elijah, or the thought that Leah might bolt with the buggy and abandon her along with Elijah.

"Annalise," Elijah said, "can I ask a question?"

"Sure."

"How many times have you handled a horse and buggy?"

"Twice."

"By yourself?"

She cleared her throat. "Never."

"Then Leah has to go."

Annie met the girl's eyes.

"Okay," Leah said, "but you have to let me take the kitten."

"Do you think she'll actually get help?" Annie sat in the dirt beside Elijah as Leah turned the buggy around and headed toward town.

"Do you think she will actually bring my horse and buggy back?"

"I'm sorry, Elijah." Annie wriggled out of her sweater and spread it across his chest. "I dragged you into this, and now you're hurt and worried about your rig."

"I'm not worried about my buggy. *Gottes wille.*"

Annie pulled her knees up, wrapped her arms around them, and propped her chin on top of the mountain they made. "I haven't quite learned to say that as freely as I ought to."

"First you have to believe it." Elijah started to lift an arm.

"Don't do that!" Annie put a hand on his wrist.

"I really think I'm fine. I'll be sore and I have a headache, but that doesn't seem so terrible. Considering."

"Considering you were kicked in the chest, fell off a gravel truck, and landed flat on your back?"

"*Ya*, that. But I landed on earth, not concrete."

"You could have a concussion. Broken ribs. Or your spinal cord—"

"I'm grateful to have such cheerful, optimistic company."

Annie clamped her lips shut.

"If you'll scratch the left side of my nose, I promise I won't try to get up."

"That bargain is more than fair." Annie used two fingers to thoroughly scratch the side of his long, narrow nose then pushed his brown hair away from his eyes.

"Thank you. That's better."

"Does your chest hurt? It looked like she kicked you right in the heart." Annie noticed that his chest did not lift high with his breaths.

Annalise reached for his wrist and put two fingers down in search of his pulse.

"Don't worry. It's still beating."

"You're taking this whole thing too lightly."

"I would shrug if you would let me."

"You will do nothing of the sort."

"Mrs. Stutzman will be in a tizzy by now."

"Oh yes, Mrs. Stutzman. The beautiful coffee cake the girls were going to serve you straight out of the oven—coincidentally—will be ruined."

"They're not so bad. You're just sensitive because Beth had her eye on Rufus. He set her straight weeks ago. You know that."

Annie picked up a pebble and tossed it several yards. "I know. But they don't seem your type, either."

"You know there's only one woman I want."

She did know. "Are you really going to leave?"

"Yes, I believe so. I cannot stay and be a hypocrite for the next sixty years."

"What if leaving doesn't change anything with Ruth?"

"I hope it will, but either way I have to go."

"Don't you believe? In what I just promised to believe and obey?"

"Are you trying to talk me into staying because you chose to join the church?"

"Of course not." She crossed her arms atop her knees. "I know you would never make this kind of decision for someone else."

"I tried that three years ago and it hasn't worked out too well." Elijah squinted at the sun. "I wish I had my hat right now, though. I left it in the buggy."

Annie readjusted her position once again to shade his face.

"If I get my horse and buggy back, I'm going to sell it."

"Really?"

"I'm going to buy a van. Tom has been teaching me to drive. He'll take me for my test."

"He's going to want you to be quite sure."

"I'm sure. You and Rufus are going to need a buggy once you're married. You won't always live on the Beiler farm."

"One step at a time." Annie raised a hand to shade her eyes and stare down the road. "Why hasn't someone at least come about this truck?"

Ruth stepped outside the grocery store and gratefully turned her face up to the sun. Late September at an elevation of eight thousand feet brought days gently sloping off the peaks of summer temperatures, but the sun comforted her nevertheless. She had walked down Main Street to the store, careful not to buy more items than she could comfortably carry the blocks back to Annalise's house. Growing up in the Amish community in Pennsylvania, Ruth rarely stepped inside a grocery store. Her family had their own milk, eggs, and vegetables, and the large church district included families of all trades. Anyone who wanted to avoid the *English* completely could do so for months at a time. Now here she was carrying two canvas bags of groceries so she could feel she was making some contribution while she stayed with Annalise.

Just as she was about to turn off onto the narrow street where Annalise's house occupied the middle of the block, a horse trotted toward her on Main Street—at a speed that lacked caution.

Elijah's horse pulled his buggy—Ruth had spent enough time in that buggy to recognize it anywhere, as much as it looked like so many others—but Elijah was not on the bench.

The driver reined in the horse and stared down at Ruth.

"Leah?"

"I remember you from the day I went to church." The girl on the bench pointed. "You're Ruth Beiler. You were the only one there not wearing the clothes of our people."

Remembering what Annie had told her about Leah Deitwaller, Ruth took care with her tone. "It's good to run into you, Leah. I see you have Elijah's buggy."

"He needs help. Is it true you're a nurse?"

Ruth's heart pushed against her chest. "I'm training to be a nurse. What happened?"

Leah licked her lips and swallowed hard.

"Leah, I want to help if I can. I need to know what happened."

"Do you have a cell phone?"

"Yes."

"Call 911."

Ruth set down the groceries on the sidewalk and yanked her phone out of the pocket of her blue scrubs shirt. "They'll want to know what happened, Leah."

"Elijah fell. Annalise says he needs an ambulance."

"Where is he?" Ruth did her best to focus while Leah described the location of the gravel truck.

As soon as she called 911 with the scant information she had, Ruth picked up her groceries and set them on the floor of the buggy.

"Do you know where Annalise's house is?"

Leah nodded.

"I'm going to run there and get my car. I would appreciate it if you could take these groceries. And you could wait there if you like. The back door is open."

Ruth spun and ran. Her car was in the driveway, unlocked, and she was in it and backing onto the street before Leah had fully negotiated the turn onto Annalise's street. Ruth had no idea whether Leah would take the groceries to the house, or whether she would stay there if she did. It might please Annalise to find her there, but if this thoughtless, headstrong girl had anything to do with how Elijah got hurt, Ruth was not as certain of her own grace. She accelerated past Elijah's buggy onto Main Street and barreled toward the main highway.

At least Annalise was with Elijah. Ruth forced herself to slow the car's speed in order to look for the old county road the Stutzmans routinely used to reach their farm. A twelve-ton gravel truck could not be that hard to find, and if Leah was telling the truth, Elijah would be sprawled on his back beside it.

Ruth saw Annalise spring to her feet before she discerned Elijah's black-and-white-clad form on the ground. She swung the car off the road and screeched to a halt.

"How did you know to come?" Annalise moved out of the way as Ruth knelt and put her ear to Elijah's chest.

Ruth put two fingers on his neck, looking for his pulse. This would be the last time she ever traveled without at least a stethoscope in her car.

"Leah found me walking home with groceries. I called for an ambulance. They should be here any minute."

"I keep telling Annalise I don't need an ambulance."

Elijah weakly nudged Ruth's hand away from his neck.

Annalise's protest was swift. "You promised not to move."

A siren wailed. "Too late," Ruth said. "It's just about here."

Annalise scrambled closer to the road and began to wave her arms.

"I'm glad you came first," Elijah whispered.

"Did Leah do this to you?" Ruth hated the tone in her own voice, but she could not help it.

"Maybe we'll talk about that later."

Ruth put the back of her hand against his cheek, telling herself it was to judge his temperature but knowing that something more than fledgling professional instincts guided her movement.

"I hate the thought that you might be seriously hurt," she said.

He gave her an impish smile. "I love that you hate it. I love *you*."

She was so relieved he was conscious, talking, smiling, trying to move. "The paramedics will be able to give you a thorough going-over, but I can almost guarantee they will take you in. Protocol. They are not going to come all the way out here and then leave because you say you don't need them."

"I do admit to having the wind knocked out of me."

A fire engine and an ambulance rolled into the meadow. Bryan Nichols stepped out of the ambulance.

Annie stood back out of the way and watched. She noticed that Ruth had moved only a few inches, crouching next to Elijah's head and leaving a hand on his shoulder while she spoke softly with Bryan as he examined Elijah. Two other responders pulled a gurney out of the back of the vehicle, rolled it across the ragged ground, and lowered it on the other side of Elijah. Ruth and the EMTs formed a wall around Elijah, and Annie could see next to nothing of what they were doing.

When Ruth pointed to her and Bryan looked over his shoulder, Annie knew she was going to have to give some account of what happened. There could only be one account. Elijah was trying to get Leah Deitwaller down off the heap of gravel, she kicked him in the chest, and he landed on his back. That was what she told Bryan a few seconds later.

"You did the right thing to keep him still and talking." Bryan jotted notes on a form on his clipboard. "He said essentially the same thing you did, so there doesn't seem to be any cognitive alteration. We'll immobilize him for transport."

"Will you take him to the clinic in town?"

Bryan shook his head. "Cañon City. The ortho doc on call at the hospital there will make sure his spine did not suffer any trauma and decide about treatment."

Ruth approached them. "I'm going with him. He needs somebody with him."

Bryan wriggled his fingers in a neutral gesture. "There's room in the back."

"What about your car?" Annie asked.

"I'll come back for it. Would you lock it for me, please?"

Annie walked over to the blue Prius that had belonged to her until a few months ago, opened the driver's door, and snapped the master lock button.

"The other rig is going back to town if you want a ride." Bryan pointed with a thumb.

"Thanks. I'll see if someone knows how to get hold of his parents."

"Good idea."

Annie paced back to Ruth and drew her into a hug. "He's going to be okay."

Ruth nodded against Annie's shoulder. "It's just the thought that maybe he won't be. I can't leave him."

"You shouldn't." Beneath her hands on Ruth's back, Annie felt her friend tremble.

They stood side by side while the EMTs slid the gurney into the ambulance. Bryan waited for Ruth with his hand on the open door.

Twenty-Five

June 1892

Sheriff Abraham Byler stood up from behind his desk in the Mountain Home jailhouse at the trampling sound of a horse's hooves overlaid with the creak and rattle of the wagon the beast pulled. He was outside the small structure by the time Deputy Combs reined in the animal. Three young men hung their sheepish heads. A.G. knew them all by name—and their daddies, too.

The deputy slung down from the wagon bench. "These are the boys who were out shooting—except Jesse Roper. He threatened me with a pistol." He jabbed his finger at the men in the wagon. "They're all witnesses. You can get their statements."

A.G. sighed. Jesse Roper had hardly been in town four days and already was a steady aggravation.

"Boys, you tell the sheriff," Combs said.

"What will happen to us if we do?" Digger asked. "All we did is a little friendly can shooting."

"Which you know good and well you were not supposed to do," A.G. said.

"Let's arrest these boys." Combs signaled that they should get out of the wagon.

"I think Roper is our real trouble," A.G. said.

"That's right!" Digger heaved himself over the side of the wagon on one arm. "He's the troublemaker."

A.G. shook his head. "I reckon he is. But that does not take you off the hook. One at a time, you tell me what you saw when Deputy Combs went to collect you." He pointed at Digger.

He listened carefully to three rapid accounts and then turned to his deputy. "What else do you want to add, Thomas?"

Deputy Combs held up his hand and opened his thumb and forefinger about three inches. "That pistol was this far from my face. It's a clear violation of the law to threaten an officer with a weapon."

"I know the law," A.G. said. He was not going to make it home while Bess's chicken was still hot tonight. "We're going to have to go talk to him."

"We weren't the only witnesses," Digger said. "One of those Amish men was there."

A.G. pressed his lips to one side. "Mmm."

"I didn't see him." Deputy Combs put both hands on his hips. "You have a lot of gall to involve an innocent man in this."

Digger pointed up. "In the maple tree outside my family's house. Must have followed from the clearing. He was there, too."

A.G. looked at the other two men. "Did either of you see him at the house?"

They shook their heads.

"I saw him!" Digger insisted. "He just about fell out of that tree when Jesse Roper waved that pistol in the deputy's face. Wish he had. Then y'all would believe me."

A.G. raised a thumb to the small jail behind him. "You three go in there and behave yourselves. I'd better find you sitting right where I left you when I get back."

"Yes, sir," they all muttered as they filed in.

A.G. pulled the door shut after them and turned to the deputy. "I'll look for the Amish man and get his story. My gut tells me we're going to need a posse to take out to the Twigg ranch. You see who is available. Try to keep Mooney out of it. And none of these boys' daddies."

They tossed some names back and forth, and Combs unhitched his horse from the wagon and saddled it.

A.G. took a deep breath and exhaled. "I will see you in one hour on the road off the Twigg ranch. Stay off their property until I get there."

Joseph splashed water from the barrel inside the stables on his face and neck and rubbed. Then he used a dipper to pour some over the top of his bare head.

"No letter?" he said, when he opened his eyes and saw Zeke's boots in the hay next to him.

"No letter."

"So we wait." Joseph toweled his face dry and ran his hands through his hair. He opened a small leather bag and considered his razor with one hand, while running the other over his three-day beard. If he did not shave soon, people would start to think he had married.

He corrected himself. The *English* would draw no such conclusion. In Gassville a man's beard meant nothing about his marital status.

"We still have to muck," Zeke said. "You'll only have to clean up again."

Joseph did not want to explain the tree sap stuck to his face and hair on the side of his head. "I was hot."

"We could go into town to eat tonight." Zeke grabbed the handles of a cart and parked it at the opening of an empty stall. "It might be cooler. We have not splurged lately."

Joseph took a pitchfork into the stall. "Maybe." He tossed soiled straw into the cart. Once. Twice. Three times, with vigor.

"Joseph, what's wrong?"

Joseph leaned on the fork. "If I tell you, you will tell me to stay out of it."

"Then perhaps you already have your answer."

Joseph raked the fork through straw with less gusto.

"*English* trouble?" Zeke prodded.

Joseph nodded. He gave Zeke the bare facts of the morning. Voices in the stable yard drew them outside. The livery owner stood talking with Sheriff Byler. One man pointed to the stables, and the other stroked his white beard as he raised his eyes toward Joseph and Zeke.

Joseph stepped forward. Zeke grabbed his arm.

"Stay out of it," Zeke said.

"He is here for me. Can you not see that?"

The sheriff approached. "Joseph Beiler?"

"I am Joseph Beiler."

"The owner tells me you are from Tennessee," Sheriff Byler said. "Perhaps we are long-lost kin."

Joseph glanced at Zeke. "I would be pleased if we were."

"Let's chew that fat another day. Right now I need to know what happened this afternoon."

Joseph repeated his account, watching the sheriff nod at intervals.

"That squares with what the others reported," Sheriff Byler said. "It seems that even Thomas Combs did not exaggerate this time."

The sheriff strode back to his horse and mounted swiftly. "We're organizing a posse to go out to the Twigg ranch," he said to the livery owner. "You are welcome to come."

"Twigg?" The owner waved his arms. "No thank you."

The sheriff looked at Zeke and Joseph. "You, too."

Zeke shook his head. "Our people do not ride in posses."

Joseph turned to the stall where his mount awaited.

Maura saw the dust cloud and heard the clatter of hooves before she discerned the individual men.

At least fifteen men on horses. It could only be a posse.

When they paused in front of her uncle's milliner's shop, Maura put a hand on Walter's shoulder.

Thomas Combs looked down from his horse. "Is your father here, Walter?"

"What is this about?" Maura held her grip on Walter's resisting shoulder.

"Just a posse, Miss Woodley. Men's work. Is Edwin here?"

"He was feelin' poorly," Walter said. "He went on down to Doc Denton's."

Thomas scowled. "Sheriff said no Dentons. Not in this business."

Walter wriggled out from under Maura's hand. "Shall I tell my daddy where to find you?"

"Hush, Walter," Maura said.

"I'll come," Walter said.

"You will do no such thing." Even as Maura chastised her cousin, she was planning her own escape from the shop. If the sheriff did not want the Dentons involved, the trouble was sure to involve the Twiggs. "Deputy Combs, I hope you resolve the matter peaceably."

"I'll settle for justice." Thomas tugged on his reins, and the blur of restless men picked up speed once again.

"Your daddy will be back soon," Maura said to Walter, grabbing his shoulder again. "Can you be on your own for ten minutes without getting into trouble?"

"I'm near full grown."

"Yes, you are." Maura's horse and cart were hitched around the corner. "So act like it."

"If you're going, I'm going." Walter shook off her hold.

"No, you are not. Your daddy will look for you right here. Promise me you'll be here."

Unarmed, Joseph Beiler was among the twenty men who thundered with Sheriff Abraham Byler into the ranch yard of Old Man Twigg. Lurking at the back edge of the posse, Joseph coughed and then covered his face with the back of his hand against the rising swirl of dirt. Around the edges of the clearing were the main house, a smokehouse, stables, and a couple of other small outbuildings.

Sheriff Byler lifted one hand as the horses responded to reins and came to a stop, their front legs thudding to the ground in final steps. He slid off his mount and scanned the posse from left to right.

"You men stay in your saddles and put those rifles away," the sheriff said, warning in his tone. "You are here in the event of a sour turn that I sincerely hope to avoid."

Shifting postures of most of the men told Joseph not everyone agreed with the sheriff's judgment, but they would comply with his instructions.

Sheriff Byler crossed the yard and approached the house, hollering in a friendly tone. "Hallo! Hallo! Anybody home?" He did not even brandish a weapon as he turned his head first toward one building and then another. Silence made him slow his steps, peering carefully. He reached the front porch of the house, put his hand on a supporting post, and looked around again. "Hallo?"

Joseph slowly moved around one side of the posse, anxious for the sheriff. He saw the rifle's end poking out through the fissure in the log smokehouse too late. The crack of the weapon swallowed up his cry of caution. Sheriff Byler lurched.

Men in the front of the posse immediately urged their horses forward into the yard and drew their weapons.

"Get the sheriff out of there!" Thomas Combs ordered.

Sheriff Byler stumbled only a few yards from the house when the rifle cracked again. This time the sheriff dropped and did not move.

Joseph responded with the rest of the men, moving into formation that would enclose the yard. Weaponless, Joseph took his horse toward the smokehouse. Two riders slung their legs out of their saddles and crouched over Byler.

"Shot twice!" one of them called out.

Jesse Roper burst from the smokehouse, dropped to his knees, and fired into the posse, first to the right, then to the left. Joseph yanked on his reins to pull his horse to the side, but the fearful animal went up on hind legs. Joseph could see a few men fumbling with their weapons, but the reflexive movement of most of the horses prevented straight shots. Bullets flew across the yard without purpose. When a cartridge lodged in the barrel of his Winchester, Roper worked the lever back and forth with cool aplomb until he cleared it.

Loge Hoppe yelped when a bullet hit his leg. Struck in the chest, Dr. Lindsay's horse crumpled beneath him. The posse fell back, out of range. With the formation broken, Roper grasped his rifle in one thick hand and loped across the yard. He climbed a split-rail fence, turned to remove his imposing black hat, grinned, and waved a final farewell as he jumped down on the other side and pumped his long legs.

Some of the posse men pressed their knees into their horses and urged them into chase.

"Let him go!" Jimmy Twigg emerged from the smokehouse, his face an angry red and his rifle seated against his shoulder. "I will blow the head off of anyone who chases him. You know I mean it."

The posse riders drew their horses to a halt. Roper disappeared into the thick woods of the Twigg property.

Joseph was afraid he would be sick. Was this *English* justice? Off his horse now, he tied the animal to a tree and turned to the throb of attention around Sheriff Byler.

Old Man Twigg's wife ran from her house to kneel over the dying sheriff. "You poor man. You poor old man."

Dr. Lindsay limped from his wounded horse to do what he could for the sheriff.

The clatter of a cart made Joseph look up. Joseph ran and

grabbed the bridle of Maura Woodley's horse, dragging against the animal's movement.

"Miss Woodley—" He did not know what to say next.

"The sheriff?" Maura said as she climbed out of her cart.

He nodded. Maura ran to the huddle and pushed aside Mrs. Twigg and several men. Joseph had seen enough of Maura Woodley before this to know she would have her way even in this situation. She took Sheriff Byler's head into her own skirt, trying to stanch the blood from his chest alongside Dr. Lindsay.

"Joseph!" she called out.

He was at her side immediately, looking into her wrenched face.

"He will not survive," she muttered. She held out her hand to him. "This should not be. This should not be."

He gripped her hand.

Twenty-Six

Elijah was strapped into the gurney. Ruth was glad that if he had an inclination to move, he would not be able to. The fact that he remained as still as he had for as long as he had was telling enough. She reached from her own seat to hold his hand. They had been circumspect around other people when they were younger. When they were alone, though, two teenagers in love held hands and stole kisses.

He was the first to confess love.

She was the first to confess doubt.

Not about whether she loved Elijah Capp. In fact, she knew she loved him months before he ever spoke the word to her. But by then, two years after finishing the eighth grade and facing the church's regulation against further schooling, she doubted that her spiritual calling was to become an adult baptized member of the Amish congregation.

She squeezed his hand and he squeezed back, a gesture that gave her some reassurance of his condition. If he were not wearing the sturdy work boot of an Amish tradesman, she might have been tempted to pinch his big toe to see if he would react. Instead, she swallowed her worst-case-scenario imaginings and smiled at him.

"I'm glad you're here." Elijah's wide eyes fixed on her face.

"I wouldn't want to be anywhere else."

A wispy recollection that she was supposed to work at the clinic that afternoon wafted through her mind. She would need to call or text someone as soon as the ambulance arrived in Cañon City, but for now she did not intend to let go of Elijah's hand.

"The orthopedist should be waiting for you as soon as we get there," she said.

"I'm sure he has actual injured people he ought to be looking after."

"And where did you get your medical degree, Dr. Capp?"

"You forget that my grandmother was a midwife."

"That should come in handy when you're ready to deliver a baby."

"I want to be there when you have our baby," he said.

The EMT sitting on the other side of Elijah perked up.

"Shh," Ruth said. "What kind of talk is that for an ambulance?"

"I have to take advantage of every opportunity to tell you how I feel." Elijah ignored the EMT. "I never know when I'll get another chance."

"I know how you feel, Elijah," Ruth whispered and avoided the EMT's eyes.

"It's going to work out for us."

His eyes shimmered till she almost could not look at them anymore. Neither could she shift her gaze. She swallowed. "You must be starting to feel sore."

"I only care what I feel for you."

The EMT shuffled his feet. "We'll be there soon," he said.

Ruth could not see Bryan from the back of the ambulance. When she looked toward the front, she saw only a wall of medications and equipment. Bryan would be concentrating on doing his job. She already knew him well enough to recognize and admire his ability to ignore distraction. Still, when the urgency wore off, what would he think about what he had witnessed between her and Elijah—or the account his partner would no doubt give him of the conversation occurring in the back while Bryan focused on safe transport?

Ruth waited alone in a small curtained area. The space seemed much larger with Elijah's patient bed missing. She had helped the triage nurse with his basic information, also providing what little she knew about the accident itself. Explaining that the Amish church, rather than insurance or a government program, would cover his medical expenses was more challenging. The *English* forms never seemed to have the right spaces for these answers.

The wait for the doctor was reasonably short, though he did what Ruth had expected him to do after conducting a basic neurological check that revealed Elijah could wiggle his fingers and toes and tell the difference between a pinch and a poke. In a clipped cadence, the doctor ticked off a list of tests for the nurse to arrange. Ruth recognized the abbreviations and knew the instructions were aimed at ruling out spinal damage before Elijah would be allowed to move more freely. While they waited for an orderly to arrive and wheel him off, Elijah had at last dozed. He roused long enough to smile at her before his gurney turned the corner and took him out of sight.

Now Ruth sat and watched the hands of the clock in the hallway of the emergency room tick. Elijah had been gone almost ninety minutes already. She would not have him come back and find the exam area empty, though, so the most she did was pace the small room a few minutes at a time. If she had to wait halfway through the night, she would.

When the curtain finally swished another thirty minutes later, it was a nurse.

"Ah. I wondered if you were still here."

"Yes. I'm waiting for my friend to come back from tests. Do you know how much longer it will be?"

"I'll try to see if I can find out where he is in the process." The nurse dragged a second chair in from the hall. "Some people are here claiming to be his parents. Judging from the way they are dressed, I believe them. They said you are not family."

"Well, no, technically not. But Elijah and I are close."

The nurse waved a hand. "You all can sort that out among yourselves. But it's against hospital policy to have three nonpatients in an ER exam area. Maybe you could use a break."

"I want to know what happens."

"I think that will be up to his parents now to decide what they want to tell you." The nurse stepped into the hall and beckoned with one hand. "You can wait out in the main waiting area if you like. No one is going to kick you out of there."

Reluctant, Ruth stood up. Already she recognized the approaching dull, heavy step of Amish boots and swish of skirts. Elijah's *daed* wore his usual somber expression with an extra furrow in his brow, and his *mamm*'s cheeks lacked their usual blush. Ruth did her best to greet them with encouragement.

"He's just away while they do some tests," she said, reaching for Mrs. Capp's hand. "I'm sorry they won't let me stay with you while you wait for him."

"We don't need you to stay with us." Mrs. Capp withdrew her hand.

"I don't think it should be too much longer."

"Thank you, Ruth, but you can go now."

"I'll just be out in the main waiting room."

"It's not necessary for you to wait. I'm sure you have other things to do."

"Of course I'll wait." Elijah's mother had never spoken to her before with such a clipped tone. "If he asks for me, will someone come and get me?"

"I think it's best if you go back to Westcliffe," Mr. Capp said. "If you want to help, you can ask the church to pray for Elijah."

Ruth looked back and forth between Elijah's parents. Close to three years had passed since she ran out on her baptism and left Elijah behind to make his vows alone. While the Capps had been confused at her choice, they never expressed anger toward her. What mattered to them was that Elijah had joined the church. Only two weeks ago, Mrs. Capp had urged Ruth to come to dinner. She understood they were concerned about their son's condition now, but that worry was underlaid with anger. They stepped into the exam area, their back to her, and pulled the curtain.

"You'll have to go to the waiting room," the nurse repeated. "His family is here now."

The words stung.

When she pushed through the door to the waiting room, Tom Reynolds stood up.

"Hello, Ruth."

"Tom, I'm glad you're here. Did you taxi the Capps?"

"Yes. I said I would wait at least until they know whether Elijah has to stay."

"I guess that depends on the test results."

"You look wiped out. How about if I see if I can find a coffee machine or something?"

She nodded. Coffee might help clear her mind, though she doubted it would fix whatever had just broken between her and the Capps.

Rufus slapped his measuring tape up against the wall, made a pinpoint dot with his pencil, and turned the tape in the other direction to make another mark. His coworkers drew two-inch-wide lines before hanging a cabinet. If they did not, they could not find their own marks. Rufus needed far less assurance that he was doing the job right. This was the first day of a two-week project renovating administrative offices in a Cañon City hospital that seemed to Rufus to require little creativity. The crew would make its way down the hallway and then back up on the other side installing identical manufactured cabinetry into identical offices painted in identical color schemes.

Rufus began to hum, hoping the hymn tune would lead him into prayer for Annalise, for his family, for the decisions he needed to make. Whatever doubts he had about his choice to take this job even on a temporary basis, he would hang every cabinet as if it were one of his custom creations. The same care and precision that expressed his gratitude in his workshop at home would do so here in the hospital and in whatever building he was sent to next. Satisfied with the accuracy of his marks, even if no one else could discern them, Rufus pulled a box cutter out of the carpenter's apron fastened around his waist and sliced through the cardboard box housing the assembly for this office, his second for the day. After inspecting the contents of the carton and satisfying himself that all the pieces were accounted for, Rufus picked up a power screwdriver and began with the hardware for the first cabinet.

His mind turned over the sign he had seen that morning across the street from the hospital in the paved-over front yard of an old house. The business within was a Realtor that claimed to specialize in commercial properties. It might be just what Rufus needed.

"Hey, Rufus!"

He looked up to welcome his assigned partner back into the room. Marcus had a habit of disappearing for curiously long periods of time, but Rufus had to admit that when he was present he was a valuable helper. He was cheerful, did not mind Rufus's humming, and did what Rufus asked him to do without looking for shortcuts.

And Marcus always returned with large Styrofoam cups of steaming coffee.

"You're going to like this one," Marcus said. "Dark. Robust. Rich."

"You found that kind of coffee in a hospital?" Rufus gratefully took hold of a cup and sipped before setting it down.

"You just have to know where to look." Marcus took a generous draft. "Ah! Smooth, eh?"

"Yes, smooth. Now let's do a smooth job of getting these cabinets up."

"Smooth transition." Marcus found a secure place to set his coffee down. "I heard another Amish dude came in through the ER a couple hours ago. Came all the way from Westcliffe in an ambulance."

Rufus dropped the bracket dangling from his fingers.

Twenty-Seven

Rufus took the stairs two at a time until he was sure he was on the ground floor and then darted through the unfamiliar hospital hallways. Stripes in the flooring and signs overhead guided his path without providing visual reassurance that he would, in fact, reach the emergency department. This was his first day working at this location, and he had not yet made sense of the building's layout. He trusted the signs until he came to a registration counter under a hanging sign announcing the ER.

"I understand you had an Amish man come in this afternoon." Rufus managed a calm tone. "I'm concerned it might be a family member."

"Your last name?" A clerk flipped over a pile of papers and looked up from behind her computer.

"Beiler." He spelled it.

"And does the family member you're looking for share your last name?"

"Yes." Joel. Or *Daed*. Had there been an accident that he would have known about if he were home on his family's farm?

The clerk clicked a few keys. "No, I don't see anyone by that name."

"Are you sure? Maybe the name was misspelled? How many Amish men would you have?"

"Sir, I cannot give you any patient information. All I can tell you is we have no one under the name you gave me."

"Thank you." Rufus wiped a hand across his forehead. When he turned away from the counter in relief, he saw Ruth huddled across the waiting room.

"Rufus!" Relief rattled her voice when she saw him. She wiped tears with the heels of both hands.

"What happened?" He sat beside her on the row of interlocking gray armless chairs and enfolded her.

"It's Elijah," she said.

Intent on understanding, Rufus listened to Ruth's account.

"What are you doing here?" she asked. "How did you get here?"

"I'm putting cabinets in offices on one of the upper floors."

"I can't believe you're here on this day of all days."

"*Gottes wille*. Is Elijah going to be all right?"

"I think so. Of course I'm concerned, but why were the Capps so cold to me? It was as if they dismissed me. Why would they tell me to go home like that?"

"He still has your heart, doesn't he?" Rufus leaned forward, elbows on his knees.

"If they think I'm trying to lure their son away, I would assure them that I have gone out of my way not to do that." Ruth ground a fist into her thigh. "That doesn't mean I stopped caring about him. He's a person, after all. Someone I've known well for many years."

"Of course you care about him. When the Capps have the reassurance that Elijah is well, they will look at things differently."

Ruth shook her head. "No, I don't think so. It's as if they are blaming me for something. I had nothing to do with what happened today. Annalise is the one who was there with Elijah, not me."

"If you have done nothing wrong, then you have nothing to fear."

"I'm not afraid. I'm hurt. And I want someone to tell me what is happening with Elijah!"

Rufus absorbed the contortions of his sister's face and wished he knew the words that would smooth them. How thick her heart must be with the burden of loving a man who belonged to a people she called her own less and less.

"Hey, dude!" Marcus dropped into a chair on the other side of Rufus. "The boss is looking for you."

Annie stared at her open back door. While she had taken to leaving it unlocked, it was not her habit to leave it standing wide open.

By the time she got back into town after the morning's drama, she had to go straight to the shop without stopping at home. In the back room, she had done her best to wash up in the old sink and brush dirt off her dress. With a sigh, she realized she had lost yet another prayer *kapp*. It could be in the meadow, snagged on a bush and billowed by wind, or it could be in the rig she had returned to town in, smashed against a floor mat. It made no difference. She would not get it back. Annie resisted the urge to inspect her face and hair in the mirror and settled for pinning her straggly braids back into place by touch alone.

By the end of the afternoon, she was ready for a hot bath and a hot meal.

And word from Ruth about Elijah's condition. Making a series of phone calls from the shop, it had taken Annie most of two hours to track down Elijah's parents and then find Tom to see if he would taxi. Mrs. Weichert, working on the month-end books, looked up periodically with concern. Annie was careful to say only that Elijah had an accident and had been taken to the hospital. For as long as possible, she hoped to leave Leah's name out of the rumors that were sure to fly around town. The truth would come out about Leah's part in the accident, but for now, just for today, Annie did not want to raise questions she could not answer.

And now her back door was standing wide open.

Annie entered her home and laid her purse on the counter inside the back door.

"Annalise?" A faint voice came from the front of the house.

"Who's there?" Still unsettled, Annie decided she would not take a makeshift kitchen weapon to greet someone who knew her name.

"It's me."

Annie progressed into the dining room. "Leah?"

The kitten shot past just then, brushing Annie's skirt on his way to the kitchen. Annie took a moment to light the small oil lamp on the dining room table. Leah came into focus scrunched into the far chair in the adjoining living room.

"Are you all right, Leah?"

The response came slowly, with deliberation. "I guess if I were, I would not have done that to Elijah."

Annie closed her eyes and offered a prayer of thanks before proceeding to sit in the other chair. "You did a great job getting help, Leah. Ruth got there even before the ambulance, and Elijah was so glad to see her."

"Is he paralyzed?"

"No," Annie answered quickly and then thought she should qualify her response. "I don't think so. They took him to a hospital just to be sure."

"Everybody is going to find out." Leah's face was suddenly slick with tears. "His family will want the church to pay his medical expenses, and everybody will know that I was the one doing something stupid, not Elijah."

Annie had no answer. What Leah said might well be true.

"My mother is right. I mess things up all the time. I can't control myself."

Annie pulled a tissue from a box on the end table between the chairs and handed it to Leah.

"But I'm not going to hurt Aaron. If I can just get to

Pennsylvania, I can change. He makes me believe in myself. No one else does that for me."

"I want to help you, too." Annie pointed across the room. "Have you looked on the other side of that screen?"

Leah shook her head. "I've just been sitting here all day. I put away the groceries Ruth bought because they needed to be in the refrigerator, but I didn't want you to think I was touching all your things."

"I would like to show you what is over there. Would you like to see?"

"It's a nice screen. Useful but pretty in a plain way."

"I'll turn on a couple of lamps so you can see better." Annie turned the switch on the propane lamp rising out of the end table. "Come over here."

Annie took Leah's hand and led her the few steps across the room. "The other lamp is over here, behind the screen. Why don't you turn it on?"

Leah gently moved the end of the screen and stepped into the bedroom-like space Annie had created.

"I told you before that you were welcome to stay with me," Annie said, "and I meant it. I've made up the couch like a bed. Your bed."

Leah's eyes widened. "How did you know I would come?"

"I prayed that you would, and I felt a peace about making up the bed. That's a kind of knowing, isn't it?"

Leah exhaled heavily. "But after today you should change your mind."

"I don't think so. God answered my prayer. You're here."

"I don't know why you want me here."

"For the same reason I wanted you to come down from the gravel. I want you to be safe."

"I can't sleep there." Leah stepped back. "I've been wearing the same dress for three weeks. I don't deserve it. I'm filthy."

"You're lovely," Annie said quickly. "As for the rest, I have plenty of hot water and a purple dress that should suit you well."

"An Amish dress?"

"Yes."

"Is that all you have now?"

"Yes. I gave away my *English* clothes months ago." Annie raised a tender hand to Leah's head. "Look, you've still got your prayer *kapp*."

"Of course. I ran away from my parents, not from God."

Annie chuckled. "You wouldn't believe how many prayer *kapps* I have lost trying to run toward God."

"I don't want to be some kind of prisoner." Leah stepped out of Annie's reach. "I could do that at my parents' house."

"I'm not trying to be a jailer. I'm trying to be a friend."

"I don't have any friends here."

"You have me."

"You can't ask me a lot of questions about where I go or what I'm doing all day. I'm not going to tell you."

Annie pressed her lips together. She had questions she did not dare ask in this tremulous moment. Was she willing to take on a distraught teenager without any boundaries? She took a slow breath of prayer.

"I'm not going to hound you," Annie said.

"You have to trust me." Leah's tone dared Annie.

"And I hope you can trust me," Annie said. "Let's start with tonight and see where we go, all right? How about a hot bath?"

Leah nodded.

Ruth accepted the coffee that Tom brought her a few minutes after Rufus returned to work. "Thank you."

"No news yet?"

She shook her head. Surely by now Elijah was back from his scans.

"Pardon me, then," Tom said. "I am going to force the issue by asking to speak to the Capps. I don't want to abandon them, but I need to know what to tell my wife about when I'll be home."

Taking his own coffee with him, Tom sauntered toward the ER desk.

The automatic doors from the outside slid open, sending a draft of cool outside air into the waiting area. Alan Wellner stepped in and immediately spied Ruth.

"I heard about your friend," he said. "I came to see if there was anything I could do to help."

She shrugged. "I'm just waiting. There should be some news soon."

"I could give you a ride back to Westcliffe."

"Thanks, but I'll be all right." Ruth was stranded, and even if Tom Reynolds had room in his truck, the Capps might not want her to ride with them. But Alan unsettled her.

"I know it was weird with my dad the other day." He took the seat Rufus had been in just moments ago and stretched out his long form, arms across the chairs on either side of him. "Stuff like that happens all the time, but it doesn't mean anything. So don't be freaked out by it."

"I'm not." Ruth sipped her coffee and moved her eyes to where Tom stood at the ER desk. "Every family is different."

"My dad is in la-la land sometimes. He'll call me next week like nothing happened."

"I hope you can work things out."

"I let it roll off my back. People sometimes do things just to make a point." Alan's fingers drummed against the back of Ruth's chair, and she stood up.

"So how long have you and Bryan known each other?" she asked.

"Long time. Best friends."

"That's great for both of you."

Mr. Capp had appeared at the desk and leaned in to speak with Tom. Ruth watched for clues about what they might be saying.

"Bryan likes you a lot." Alan grinned up at her. "He tells me these things. He thinks the whole Amish thing is fascinating, and that you're a strong woman."

"He said all that?" Ruth had only seen Bryan a couple of times and thought he understood very little about the Amish.

"He's a man who knows what he wants."

Ruth was relieved to see Tom crossing the room toward her. "Good news?"

"Yep." Tom rubbed his palms together. "They are doing the paperwork to release him now."

"He can go home?"

"Nothing's broken, everything works. And Elijah doesn't want to stay."

Relief swamped Ruth.

"I wish I could take you home, too," Tom said, "but the truck will be crowded as it is. We're going to make Elijah comfortable in the backseat and his parents will both ride in front."

"Don't worry about me." Ruth felt the absence of the car she had owned for the last few months and the independence it provided her. "I'll figure something out."

As Tom walked away, Ruth took her phone out of her pocket and dialed Mrs. Weichert's shop. No one answered. Ruth scrolled through her contact list. Most of the listings were people she knew in Colorado Springs, not Westcliffe.

"Looks like you're going to need a ride home after all." Alan stood behind her. "Good thing I'm here."

Twenty-Eight

"No need, Alan. I can take Ruth home." Bryan took Ruth by the hand and tugged her away from Alan.

"What are you still doing here?" Ruth was grateful for Bryan's presence at that moment. "I thought you would have taken the ambulance back hours ago."

"I did. I had to finish out my volunteer shift, in case there were any more calls."

"And you came all the way back here?"

Bryan squeezed her hand. "I don't like to leave a damsel in distress."

"How did you even know she would need a ride?" Alan slid his hands into his pockets. "She could have been gone already."

"Then why are you here, buddy?" Bryan jabbed his friend's shoulder playfully. "At least I can claim some responsibility since I brought her here in the first place."

He still held her hand, and Ruth relaxed into his grip. It was an odd sensation. Elijah was the only man who had taken her hand this way before, covering her slender fingers in a grasp both affectionate and protective, and only when they were alone. Yet Ruth trusted Bryan's hold.

Alan circled them. “I was only trying to be helpful.”

“Thank you for thinking of me.” Ruth craned her neck to follow Alan’s pacing path.

“Yeah, thanks, buddy, but I’ve got this one covered.” Bryan released Ruth’s hand and put an arm around her shoulder. “How is your friend doing?”

“His parents are here to take him home. No serious damage.”

“I’m glad to hear that. His back is going to be one big bruise.”

“It could have been so much worse.”

“You would know. You’re an almost nurse.” Bryan guided her toward the door.

“I still have a ways to go with my education.” Ruth looked over her shoulder at Alan. “Is your friend going to be okay?”

“Alan? He’ll be fine. He goes into these moods sometimes, usually after he sees his dad.”

“He drove all the way over here because he thought I might need a ride.”

“He likes attention. Being a hero. But he tries too hard and it puts people off.”

“So you’re used to just ignoring him?”

“I learned my lesson years ago.” Bryan pressed his key fob and the lights of the gray Mitsubishi came on.

“You two have a. . .curious relationship.”

“Are you hungry?” Bryan opened the passenger door. “We could get something to eat while we’re in a town with some actual options.”

“I haven’t had anything since breakfast.” Ruth sized up Bryan’s car. It was a few years old, but it was clean inside and out.

“Then we’ll find a place, and I’ll treat you to an early dinner.”

What can you tell about a man based on his car? Ruth wondered. She hardly knew Bryan any better than she knew Alan. So far they had met in public places within blocks of where she lived and worked.

“How about there?” Ruth pointed across the street from the

parking lot to a casual dining establishment. If she decided she was uncomfortable for any reason, she would not get back in his car.

"You got it. Food coming right up." Bryan closed the car door and walked around to the driver's side.

Ruth sat facing the emergency entrance of the building. As Bryan turned the key in the ignition, the hospital doors swooshed open and an orderly pushed Elijah outside in a wheelchair. Behind, his parents carried their worried looks and studied discharge papers.

Tom pulled his vehicle to the curb, blocking Ruth's view of the Capps. While Bryan backed out of his parking space and headed out of the lot, pressure burned in Ruth's chest. Shock. Grief. Confusion. Love. Whatever it was, she ached for relief.

Rufus separated the tools that belonged to him from those his employer supplied. The end of the workday ushered in a swath of moments he dreaded.

The moment when he would decide whether to remain in the motel room he shared with an *English* man who spent his time flipping channels on the television or to seek quiet solitude elsewhere.

The moment when he would not sit down to dinner with his family.

The moment when he would not lie down in his own bed.

The moment when he would wonder what had become of Elijah Capp and have no way to find out.

The moment he would want to take his little brother to the barn to feed apples to the horses.

The moment he would wish for a glimpse of Annalise's smile, the turn of her head.

Rufus double-checked that all his own tools were accounted for in the wooden toolbox he had made himself a decade ago, then did a final visual sweep of the room. The afternoon's labor yielded a satisfactory rank of cabinets. Tomorrow a pair of young hospital publicists would move back into their remodeled work space, while Rufus and the rest of the team began on the next vacated space.

"We're getting together a group for dinner. Wanna come?" Marcus closed and latched a red metal toolbox.

"Thank you for thinking to include me, but I have an errand," Rufus said.

Marcus collected four empty Styrofoam cups to carry out of the office. "A man's got to eat. You might as well use your per diem account."

"I'm not all that hungry." Rufus picked up his toolbox. "I'll walk back to the motel later. It's not that far."

Before he left the hospital, Rufus made his way back to the emergency department, just to be sure Ruth was not still waiting for word on Elijah. A harried woman with three droopy-eyed children now occupied the seats where Rufus and Ruth had sat earlier in the afternoon. Rufus approached the desk.

"Excuse me, you had a patient named Elijah Capp today. Was he admitted to the hospital?"

A new clerk had begun a new shift, and she typed some letters into the computer. "We don't have anybody under that name."

Rufus puffed his cheeks and let out his breath. "That's good. Thank you."

He stepped on the mat that parted the sliding doors and leaned into the outside air sweetened with a flock of blue hydrangea. After a pause to get his bearings, Rufus calculated that the sign he had seen that morning must have been on the other side of the hospital and began to walk around.

Realtors worked primarily in certain geographic areas, he supposed. But southwestern Colorado was spread out, and a Realtor representing commercial property would surely have a larger region. Cañon City was not so far from Westcliffe that he could not find someone to help him.

Rufus rounded two corners of the blockish hospital and found himself where he wanted to be. The old house still had lights on inside.

Ruth ate with nearly embarrassing velocity. The potato soup was hearty, the black bread warm, the meatloaf baked to saucy perfection. Even the roasted broccoli, never Ruth's favorite vegetable, settled into her taste buds pleasantly. All day long she had thought herself too nervous to think about food

"How about some pie?" Bryan reached for the dessert menu against the wall of their booth.

"I can't eat another bite." Ruth protested with two raised hands. "But thank you for all this. The whole day is a blur. I didn't realize how much better I would feel if I ate."

"They have peach pie." Bryan wiggled his brow.

"It can't possibly be as good as my *mamm*'s."

"You'll never know if you don't taste it."

Ruth laughed. "Yes I will. Even I can't make a peach pie that tastes as good as hers. The pies here probably come out of a box in the freezer."

"Somebody had to make them and put them in a box."

She shook her head. "I'm not budging."

"I hope someday I get to taste your mother's pie."

Ruth dabbed her lips with a napkin. "Sometimes she sells them."

"That's not what I was thinking."

She knew that. She just did not know how to respond to what Bryan was hinting at.

The waitress appeared and offered coffee, which Bryan accepted. Ruth had had her fill of coffee for one day. If she had nurtured hope of sleeping that night, she should decline.

"Last chance for dessert," he said.

Ruth shook her head. The waitress poured Bryan's coffee.

"Your family seems really great." Bryan added cream to his

coffee. "I mean, from what you've said about them."

"We're not perfect."

"No family is. But it seems like they accept that you're making your own decisions without freaking out the way Alan's dad does."

"I've disappointed them, but they love me."

"How could you disappoint them by being a nurse?" Bryan clinked his spoon against the side of his mug.

"It means I can't join the church." Ruth pulled apart the remaining dark roll in the basket and nibbled one half.

"You still believe in God, don't you?"

"Very much."

"And you're trying to do something good in the world."

"Yes. But the Amish live apart. We. . .they are not concerned with the *English* world."

"Can't you be a nurse for Amish people?" Bryan held his mug by the rim, ready to raise it to his lips.

"I would very much like to serve the Amish or other groups that do not always have someone to trust when they need medical help. But I still need an *English* education."

Bryan shrugged both shoulders. "So you join another church. You keep praying. You keep serving."

Ruth gave a half smile. If he thought it was that simple, Bryan Nichols did not understand a single rudimentary fact about the Amish. "How's the coffee?"

He took a long drag on the dark liquid and set the mug down. "This Elijah guy means something to you, doesn't he?"

"A great deal." The roll was nearly crumbling between Ruth's fingers now.

"Like, you're dating him?"

"No." Definitely no.

"But you used to."

"Sort of. Yes. I guess the *English* would say so."

"My paramedic partner said he was about ready to tell you two to get a room."

Ruth looked at him blankly. "That sounds like an *English* expression."

"It is. Haven't you heard it? You know. . .when two people want to be close, they get a room."

The blush rose through her face immediately.

"I'm sorry." Bryan set his cup down abruptly and sloshed coffee onto the table. "I didn't mean. . . I would never. . . It's just what he said. He thought there was something more than friendship. Some kind of electricity."

"It's complicated."

Bryan smiled. "Now there's an *English* expression."

"One that I understand."

"I'm not doing this very well." He took the napkin from his lap and sopped up spilled coffee. "I'm trying to say that what you did for Elijah today was awesome. It tells me a lot about the kind of person you are."

Ruth's chest pressed in on her lungs. "Thank you."

"I know I'm being an idiot. But I hope I haven't blown my chance."

"Your chance?"

"To get to know you better. To become friends. To maybe, I don't know, see where things might go."

His words stunned her. "We hardly know each other, Bryan."

"Haven't you ever heard of love at first sight?" He wadded up his soggy napkin. "Okay, this is not that, exactly. It's more like first cousins once removed. . . . Or maybe perfect strangers. . . I just want a chance."

Twenty-Nine

June 1892

Maura looked at herself in the mirror while Belle Mooney fastened the stubborn buttons down the back of Maura's black dress. The buttons on the broad cuffs would be the next challenge. She had first worn the dress for her mother's funeral and only a few weeks ago for John Twigg's.

"You ought to cut the buttonholes longer and stitch them again," Belle said. "Or buy smaller buttons. Mr. Twigg carries a nice selection in his shop now."

"My mother bought these buttons at Denton's Emporium." Maura smoothed her skirt. "She had a different use in mind. I only decided to put them on this dress for her funeral."

"I wish you wouldn't trade at Denton's." Belle picked up her hat from Maura's quilted bedspread. "You know how I feel about them."

"We've both shopped there for years." Maura sat on the bed, lifted a handkerchief from the nightstand, and brushed dust off the black shoes tied around her ankles.

"That was before," Belle said. "You saw what they did to John. Vicious beasts."

Maura sucked in her lips to keep herself from speaking aloud the thought racing through her mind. John Twigg had been far from innocent in the feud between the Dentons and the Twiggs. Instead, she tried another approach.

"The feud is going on too long," Maura said. "You lost John, and now the whole county has lost our sheriff."

"Because of the Twiggs. That's what you mean." Belle fingered the comb holding her hair in place, adjusting. "It's not all their fault."

Maura reached across the bed for her own hat. "Let's focus on Sheriff Byler's funeral. Half of Baxter County will be there to pay respects."

"I'm not sure I should go."

"Why on earth not?"

"None of the Twiggs are going."

"Understandably," Maura said. "They harbored the man who did this."

"Jesse Roper's mother is dead." Belle balled her fists at her sides. "Old Man Twigg is his mama's daddy. He's kin."

Maura stood slowly. "Not to you, Belle. He's not kin to you."

"Nearly. If the Dentons had not stolen my chance to marry, he would be."

Maura did not wish death for anyone, especially not the way John died. But if Belle did not open her eyes soon and see that the Twiggs were instigating harm, her own heart would freeze over in its bitterness.

"Even if he were your kin," Maura said, "he still shot the sheriff."

"Don't you think I know that?" Belle's pitch rose as her face reddened.

Maura moistened her lips. "I'm sorry, Belle. I should not have upset you. Forgive me."

"I believe I've changed my mind." Belle picked up her soft gray handbag. "I believe I will ride to Mountain Home for the service with my daddy."

"I thought we were all going together."

"You have upset me, Maura. You upset me when you try to tell me John was not the man for me. You upset me when you defend the Dentons. I will go to the funeral out of respect to Sheriff and Mrs. Byler because they have been kind to me in the past, but I will ride with Daddy."

"Even your daddy hates the Twiggs." Maura regretted the words as soon as she blurted them out.

This was Joseph's first *English* funeral and his first time in an *English* church. He did not go to the viewing the day before, but even Zeke offered no objection when Joseph said he intended to pay respects. At the church in Mountain Home, he sat at the end of a pew in the back. His black suit matched the garb of mourners, and Joseph even removed his hat and held it in his lap during a lengthy eulogy of the beloved sheriff. Joseph learned Abraham Byler had been sheriff for a long stretch then served in the state legislature before deciding he preferred to be sheriff. The county's citizens had been glad to receive him back to office.

Prayers and a homily followed, before the pews emptied to somber organ music and most of the grieved congregation trailed the carriage carrying the pine casket to the graveyard. Once again Joseph held himself to the edge of the gathering, this time his hat on his head. The brevity of the graveside service surprised him. In his community, the entire congregation would have stood for two hours of sermons and prayers. Here, the minister read from a black book, pronounced "dust to dust, ashes to ashes," and spoke words of hope and resurrection.

Bess Byler stepped forward to throw the first handful of dirt on her husband's casket as it was lowered into the gaping fresh ground wound. Two young men, whom Joseph supposed to be her sons who lived nearby, hovered at her elbows. Bess's face wrenched and paled, but she did not cry aloud.

Walter stood between his parents in a black suit he had outgrown. The ill-fitting clothes were not what captured Joseph's attention, but rather the ill-fitting expression on the boy's face as he watched the sheriff's widow release her husband to God. Walter's expression overflowed with remorse. Joseph wondered if he had even told his parents what he had done.

The assembly slowly turned and staggered back toward the church, where members of the ladies guild had stayed behind to arrange food and refreshment.

Joseph watched Maura Woodley stifle her sobs and put a gloved hand on her father's arm to gesture that he should go ahead. She remained at the grave, on her knees in the grass now. Walter stood stiff as his parents moved with the congregation.

Putting an arm around Walter's shoulders, Joseph nudged him toward Maura. "I think Walter has something he would like to say to you."

She lifted a tear-streaked face, questioning.

Walter shook his head, but Joseph kept the boy pointed toward his cousin.

"Walter?" Maura stood up.

"Jesse Roper made fun of me," Walter blurted. "He treated me like a child."

"What are you talking about?" Maura's eyes moved from Walter's to Joseph's.

"I was there when the boys were shooting cans. I'm the one who told Deputy Combs they would all be at Digger Dawson's."

Maura's breath caught. "Did you shoot?"

"No. He wouldn't let me."

"You should not have been running around with Jesse Roper, but they were breaking the law. You did nothing wrong in reporting them."

"I just wanted to get back at him."

"I grant that your motive was questionable." Maura put a hand to the side of her face.

"If I hadn't said anything, the sheriff would not have gone looking for Roper."

From Joseph's close-up viewpoint, Walter's face looked as though it might crumble into sand.

Maura glanced at the still open grave at her feet. "This is not your fault, Walter. You have some growing up to do, but you did not cause this."

Relief oozed out of Joseph. He turned Walter toward the church. "Go on. Find your parents. Let them take you home."

The boy stumbled then found his gait.

Joseph turned to Maura. "I am sorry for your loss. I did not know Sheriff Byler personally, but he seemed a kind man who only wanted peace for your people."

She nodded, and he saw her struggle to swallow. Wordless, they walked side by side toward the church but at an ever-slowing pace.

"They did not catch him, you know," Maura finally said.

"Roper?"

"Several posses went out that same day and in the days since, but he got away. How can one man escape twenty or more?"

"Perhaps he had help."

Maura ceased forward progress altogether. "Do you truly believe that?"

"It would be an explanation."

"Yes, I suppose it would. A friend of the Twiggs, a change of clothing, a borrowed horse. He could be anywhere."

"And if they do not find him?" Joseph asked. "Is it the way of your people to hunt this man down?"

Maura blew out her breath slowly. "It is our way to bring justice whenever it is possible."

"Is justice not in God's hands?"

"You ask complicated questions, Mr. Beiler."

"Do I?" Joseph meant only to understand the *English* ways.

"If he crossed Bald Dave Mountain into Missouri, he could

go into Indian Territory. Change his name. Change his whole life. Just never come back here." Maura resumed slow steps. "What must you think of this feuding? It makes little sense to me. I can only imagine what your impressions are."

"My people do not always get along," Joseph said, "but we do not shoot at each other."

"And justice when there has been a wrong?"

"Our tradition teaches forgiveness. Justice is for God to decide. Whatever happens is *Gottes wille*. God's will."

"That it is God's will for Jesse Roper to get off scot-free is a hard pill to swallow."

" 'Vengeance is mine; I will repay, saith the Lord.' "

"I can see you are quite persistent, Mr. Beiler."

"My people are persistent in peace."

Maura looked toward the church. "We should at least go in and have a cup of coffee."

"*Kaffi*," Joseph said. "I wonder if people of all churches soothe their difficult moments with a black bitter drink."

A smile escaped her lips even on this somber day. "The truth is, I do not care for coffee. I drink it to be polite."

"Perhaps they will have tea," he said.

"Or church ladies' punch."

"Lemonade with too much sugar."

She laughed, for one second, then sobered.

"I am sorry," Joseph said. "I do not make light of the occasion."

"No. Of course not." She had no doubt of his sincerity.

"Please forgive me."

"I am guilty as well. I laughed." Maura's forward motion did not display her reluctance. "Sheriff Byler was a man of good humor. He would have agreed with you about the lemonade."

"I wish I had had the opportunity to know him better."

"Even though he was an *English* lawman?"

"Even so."

"I'm so worried about Belle." Maura put one hand over her eyes for a few seconds. "I've offended her. She would not even ride to the funeral with me."

"This is a difficult day for many people," Joseph said. "You will speak again on another day."

"I am not so sure. She has always been the more sensitive one, but she has turned a new corner in refusing my company. I cannot seem to say anything right."

"Time heals many wounds."

Maura stopped again and turned fully toward Joseph. "Suppose they have been looking in the wrong places."

"For Roper?"

"Yes. I have seen an entire posse swayed by one man's assumption or conclusion. What if that one man is wrong?"

Joseph tilted his head and met her gaze. "I do not know much about posses, but would not another man speak up?"

She shook her head. "That's the point. They get something stuck in their heads and can't see past it."

"Miss Woodley, are you trying to tell me that you have an idea where the outlaw might be?"

"I might have an idea who would help a man like Roper," she said. "That's all."

"Then perhaps you should speak to Deputy Combs. I would be happy to accompany you. He's probably drinking coffee right now."

With one hand, she unpinned her hat, removed it, flipped it over in her hands, and fleetingly wondered why the Amish men never took their hats off. "I don't want to cause a stir on the day of the funeral if it turns out to be nothing. There is no point in disturbing Bess Byler on a day like today with talk of posses and criminals."

"I suppose not. It is a day to remember the sheriff."

"Besides, Thomas Combs has proven himself a coward. Nevertheless, he will insist that I should leave such thoughts to the menfolk."

"Then another day?"

"No. Today." She set her jaw and made up her mind. "We won't talk to the deputy just yet. I'm going to take my cart and make some inquiries. I would very much like it if you would come with me."

"Are you sure that would not be unseemly?"

"That I am going to investigate on my own, or that I invite an Amish man to be my companion in the endeavor?"

"Both. And I am quite sure it would be unseemly for an Amish man to involve himself in this manner."

"Do as you wish. I am going with or without you."

"Miss Woodley, I admire your spirit of independence, but—"

"Time is a-wastin', Mr. Beiler. Are you coming?"

"Where is your cart?" Joseph asked. He could not bring himself to let her drive off alone without even knowing where she intended to go.

In the field across from the church, the small, light cart Joseph had seen Maura use around town was still hitched to the dark mare that pulled it. They sat beside each other on the narrow bench, and Maura picked up the reins. Joseph's stomach tied itself into a tight knot as he wondered about the number of people who saw them leave together and how he would explain this to Zeke Berkey later. Maura urged the horse out of its malaise and turned the cart down a road Joseph and Zeke had not explored. Joseph's eyes scanned for landmarks to remember. A fallen log. A small clearing. A shed.

Maura Woodley was as competent a driver as any man Joseph had ever met. A single animal pulled her cart, but he could easily imagine her handling a team of four horses. She was small beside him, well sized to her diminutive cart but eight feet tall in her determination.

"Would I be rude to ask a question?" Joseph held the edge of the bench with one hand.

"Depends on whether it is a rude question." Maura turned, and her brown eyes danced.

He cleared his throat. "Are you certain that the deputy has not already spoken to the person you intend to interrogate?"

"*Interrogate* is a strong word, Mr. Beiler."

The road narrowed before them, yet she let the horse maintain pace with unwavering confidence.

Abruptly she pulled on the reins. "Did you see that?" She jumped out of the cart before the horse had come to a stop.

Joseph did not dare let her get out of sight. He lurched out of the cart and followed her stomping pace.

"There!" She pointed.

Joseph saw nothing.

"There! You must see it." She kept walking.

Jesse Roper's tall, broad, black hat sat on a fence post.

Thirty

No more coffee.

Ruth was not sure she could ever drink coffee again without thinking about Elijah on the gurney, his mother on the rampage, and Bryan on the make.

The whole day would not have happened if Leah Deitwaller would just grow up. Coming home to find her asleep in the living room next to a low-glowing lamp and Annalise looking overly content with a cup of tea at the dining room table rattled Ruth. She went upstairs to bed as quickly and with as little conversation as possible.

In the morning Ruth waited until she was sure Annalise had left the house before she emerged from her bedroom. In the kitchen, she mixed up a pan of cinnamon rolls—Elijah's favorite. She had first made them for him when they were sixteen years old. While they were in the oven, she dressed in a simple skirt and top of plain colors and sturdy fabric. When the rolls were done, she wrapped them between cotton dish towels and whispered thanks that she had a car. Steam would still be rising from the rolls when her tires crunched the gravel in the Capp driveway.

Ruth knew Elijah might not be awake, or not able to get out

of bed to greet her without pain, but she refused to believe that his mother would be so inhospitable as to turn away the rolls she knew her son loved.

Steeling herself to be polite no matter what, Ruth pulled up to the Capp house and turned off the engine.

I just want to leave these for Elijah, she would say.

Or better, *I made these for all of you to enjoy.*

Ruth was a good cook. She knew it, and Mrs. Capp knew it. Warm rolls could help thaw whatever had frozen between the two women, and even if they did not, Ruth would be amicable to the end.

And then she would send Joel over to see how Elijah was.

Mrs. Capp was in the yard hanging sheets on the line. Ruth picked up the tray of rolls in one hand and opened the car door with the other.

"Good morning," she said. "I brought some rolls. They're still warm."

Mrs. Capp took a clothespin from between her lips. "We had breakfast hours ago."

"Of course you did." Ruth walked toward her. "A midmorning treat, perhaps?"

The older woman pulled a pillowcase from her laundry basket and snapped it on the line.

"Yesterday was a hard day for all of us," Ruth said. "But we can all give thanks that Elijah was not hurt worse."

"If you're hoping to ply him with warm rolls, you've come to the wrong place."

Ply him? "I only meant to cheer him up. I can just leave the rolls if he's sleeping."

"He's not here. He insisted we take him to that. . .place where he is staying."

Ruth's breath caught. "What do you mean, Mrs. Capp?"

"He would not even let me take care of him for one night. *One night.* Was that so much to ask?"

Ruth moved closer. She saw that Mrs. Capp had hung the last of the bedding. At the bottom of the basket were four jars of canned green beans, perhaps to weight the basket if a wind kicked up through the valley.

"Where is Elijah?" Ruth asked.

"Renting a room. In an *English* house. He has decided that is better than living with his own parents."

Ruth felt the blood drain from her face. "I didn't know anything about his moving. When did this happen?"

"Last week." Mrs. Capp stooped and picked up a jar of beans. "He saw an ad tacked up on the board in the grocery store. Some woman was looking for boarders."

Ruth knew the ad. She had looked at it herself before deciding to stay with Annalise.

"It's your influence, with all your *English* ways. Like that awful car." Mrs. Capp hurled the jar, and it smashed against the hood of Ruth's car.

Once again Ruth turned off the engine in front of a house. This time the rolls were cold and she had lost interest in them.

Mrs. Capp had muttered an apology as soon as the jar smashed, but Ruth had hustled to her car and pulled away. Elijah left his family home and moved into an *English* house. And never said a word to her. Ruth was not sure which fact stunned her more.

She sat in the car and stared at the house, trying to picture what it must be like for him to live inside, in a room, by himself.

After nearly ten minutes, during which Ruth's heart rate returned to a normal range, she got out of the car and approached the front door to ring the bell.

She rang again about a minute later. The thought that no one was inside except bruised and weary Elijah made her lean far to the right to peer between the curtains in the front room. He was in no condition to be left alone all day, but his landlady had no obligation to care for him. Ruth buzzed her lips in agreement with Mrs. Capp. Elijah should have gone where someone could look after him. Perhaps she could still persuade him to go home.

Tentatively, she rang the bell a final time and at last heard movement.

"Coming!"

It was Elijah's voice. Remorse for causing him to get out of bed scratched at her conscience.

He opened the door. "Hello, Ruth."

"May I come in?"

He took two steps back, and she entered a plain living room with furniture that looked outdated and uncomfortable. After sweeping her eyes around the room once, Ruth focused on Elijah. His hair was tousled, but he was in fresh clothes and stood fairly erect. She had pictured him more bent over.

"First of all," she said, "how are you?"

"Well enough, considering. The doctor said I could go back to work when I felt up to it."

"Take a few days. Old Amos will understand."

"I'm not very good at sitting around doing nothing."

"You should sit now." Ruth gestured toward a faded mauve sofa.

"I'm not supposed to use this room," Elijah said. "I have kitchen and laundry privileges, but otherwise just the one room and bath."

"Oh." She gained his gaze and held it. "Why didn't you tell me?"

"You try too hard to talk me out of things." He waved a hand to the hall. "You might as well come and see the room. I don't suppose we're breaking *Ordnung* now."

Ruth had never been alone in a house with Elijah. They always found each other on top of the flat rock behind the Beiler land, now part of a town park. It made her nervous to see Elijah standing up, though, so she followed his shuffling gait toward a rear bedroom.

"The room came furnished," he said.

A full-size bed, a desk, a dresser, an upholstered side chair, a rickety stand for a small television, which was turned on with the volume dialed low. On the desk Ruth saw a cell phone plugged into the wall.

"Oh, Elijah, what have you done?" Her voice was barely a whisper.

Elijah gingerly lowered himself into the side chair. "I'm not going back."

"But your family—"

"I'm not going back."

"So you're leaving the church?" Guilt swept through her, though she had done nothing to encourage this choice.

"You and I talked about this years ago. It has just taken me longer to be brave than it took you."

Ruth gulped the tide of emotion. "I think you have been very brave to keep your baptismal vows all this time."

"I did not make them lightly," he said, "and I do not break them lightly. But I am not going back."

She believed him. And she resolved to say nothing more that would suggest he should return.

"Have you spoken to the bishop?"

"Not yet. But I will."

"Your mother will hate having to shun you."

Elijah gave a careful shrug. "I don't think our district will be overly strict in their interpretation. It is not the end of the world to eat at a separate table. They can still see me if they want to."

"Do you think they will want to see you?"

"I hope so. I will want to see them."

Ruth blew out her breath.

"Do you think Rufus would like to buy my horse and buggy?" Elijah asked.

"Maybe. If he ever gets around to proposing." Ruth sat on the edge of Elijah's bed a few feet from him.

"I'll have to find a new job, of course. It probably shouldn't be in Westcliffe. I thought I would move to Colorado Springs after Christmas."

Ruth was due to return to the university in January.

"You don't have to decide that now." She ran her hands along her thighs, suddenly aware of how much she was perspiring, and looked around the room.

"Ruth."

She looked up at him.

"You can choose me or not choose me, but this I have chosen for myself."

Annie wiped her lunch plate dry and set it in the cabinet. She had looked in the living room four times already for clues about where Leah might have gone. Annie stayed up late and got up early, and still Leah slipped through her grasp.

Not that she could have stopped her.

Leah's one condition for staying last night was that Annie not ask about where she spent her days. For instance, around old sheds or gasoline cans? Annie could not ask directly, but she needed to know.

The back door opened and Annie glanced over her shoulder, hoping.

Not Leah. Ruth.

"Hey, Ruth."

"Hey, Annalise."

"I made tuna salad. Would you like some?" Annie reached for the plate she had just washed and put away.

"No thanks. I'm not hungry right now." Ruth laid her purse on the kitchen counter, next to where Annie habitually left hers.

"I feel like we should talk about yesterday," Annie said. "It all happened so fast, and then we didn't see each other all day."

"Maybe I'll just have some water." Ruth went to the refrigerator for the pitcher of chilled liquid.

Annie handed Ruth a glass.

Ruth poured and then drank. "I wasn't expecting Leah to be here last night."

"I know. I wasn't either. She was here when I came home."

"And you were ready for her."

"You knew I had set up the space. Ruth, she needs help."

"I know. I'm sorry. It's just hard to be gracious after what she did to Elijah." Ruth drained her glass.

"I understand." Annie took Ruth's empty glass and set it in the sink. "But I have to ask you one question."

"What is it?" Ruth pushed up the sleeves of her top and scratched an elbow.

"Leah doesn't just need a safe place to stay. She needs someone to help her sort things out. To sort herself out."

"Isn't that what you're trying to do?"

"I'm not qualified. She needs a mental health professional."

"So what are you asking me? I'm not a counselor, either."

"I need to know how the church feels about mental health. Am I supposed to just pray for her, or can I find someone who will see her?"

"This might be a question for the bishop."

"I don't want to ask him if it's way out of line." Annie picked up an apple from the fruit bowl on the counter and began to polish it on her sleeve. "Have you ever known anyone who saw a therapist?"

Ruth let out a long, slow breath. "Well, I've heard of people trying herbs and vitamins, along with prayer and hard work."

"But not a professional?"

"I didn't say that. Actually, I think most people—the women, at least—would agree that the mind or spirit can be ill, just the way the body can be."

"So then it's all right to see someone?"

"I said *most* people would agree. I'm pretty sure Mrs. Deitwaller is not one of them."

Annie nodded. "Leah is almost eighteen."

"But she's not. The *English* will have laws about this."

"The bishop's wife might intervene. Maybe she could talk to Mrs. Deitwaller."

Ruth rubbed her temples. "Annalise, can we talk about this another time? It's hard for me to talk about Leah. I know she needs help, but she hurt Elijah. I need some time to see past that."

"I'm sorry." Annie set the apple back in the basket. "You were amazing yesterday. I didn't get a chance to tell you that."

"You were the one who kept Elijah still while you waited for the ambulance."

"But it was you Elijah wanted to see. I could tell it meant the world to him that you rode along to the hospital."

"Did you know he moved out?" Ruth locked eyes with Annie.

Annie cleared her throat.

"Annalise."

"He told me the day of the training burn. I thought he'd forgotten his hat, but he said he left it behind on purpose."

"I wish you had told me."

"Was it really mine to tell?"

Thirty-One

June 1892

Joseph and Maura clattered back to Mountain Home in the cart. He held Jesse Roper's hat on his lap, feeling its height and breadth, the broad brim, the crown creased deeply and precisely, the starched, proud shape. If Joseph's own soft black hat had ever had a distinctive shape, it had long ago dissipated into everyday practical use. It exuded nothing but simplicity and humility. He felt no affinity for what Roper had done—which Joseph had seen with his own eyes—but the confidence of the man intrigued him. His people would say it was *hochmut*, pride, that got Jesse Roper into trouble. Joseph supposed it was. But still, what might it feel like to be that sure of himself?

Maura seemed to have lost her reluctance to disturb the postburial gathering. By the time they reached the church, the crowd in the church hall had thinned. Ladies were stacking dishes and carrying them out of sight. Deputy Combs sat with Bess Byler and her two sons.

"It is too bad Malinda could not come from Colorado," Maura said. "I suppose the journey would take too much planning with twin babies and a three-year-old."

"By God's grace, her sons are with her." Carrying Roper's hat,

Joseph followed Maura's march across the hall.

Combs shot out of his chair at the sight of the hat. "Where did you get that?"

"We found it," Maura said.

Combs snapped toward Joseph. "Were you hiding evidence, Mr. Beiler?"

Joseph hardly knew how to answer the accusation and said nothing.

"Don't be ridiculous, Deputy Combs." Maura took the hat from Joseph. "I just told you we found the hat. It was sitting on a post at the edge of White Ledge Ranch, clear as day. I will not insult you by suggesting any of your men would have missed it had it been there two days ago."

Bess Byler shrugged off her sons and stood up. "Then you think somebody was sheltering Roper?"

Maura nodded. "At the very least, he was hiding out on the property."

"Looks that way, Bess," Thomas said. "I'll go out and ask some questions of the owners and any hands working the ranch."

"That was our intention." Maura gestured to Joseph. "But once we found the hat, we felt we should come right back."

Joseph was uncomfortable with Maura's use of plural pronouns. The intention had been hers and the choice to return hers.

"Maura, you should not have gone out there alone," Thomas said.

"I was not alone," she snapped back. "Mr. Beiler was with me."

"And unarmed. What good would he be?"

Joseph's spine straightened. "With all due respect, Deputy, twenty men with guns did not save your sheriff."

Bess reached out and touched Joseph's forearm. "My husband would have liked you. Even though he was a man of the law, he was not quick to resort to guns."

"Obviously Roper left his hat on purpose," Maura said. "He wanted someone to find it. Even though he was not here long, everybody knew how he flaunted that hat. He is not a man who makes mindless mistakes."

"Well, he made a mistake in shooting our sheriff." Thomas looked at the widow. "Sorry, Bess. I will get some men on this right away. We have a new starting point."

"We won't give up, Bess," Maura said. "We will bring Jesse Roper to justice."

Joseph stepped back from the group, away from the enticement of Maura Woodley's *we*.

In Gassville on the following Monday, Maura lingered outside her uncle's shop. The day was stifling. She could not decide whether she was more miserable indoors or outdoors. The task of checking her uncle's accounts for the previous month was unfinished, so she would have to return to the stuffy back room at some point. For the moment she would have welcomed the slightest hope of a breeze.

Old Man Twigg stomped down the street toward Maura, bearded and bareheaded. Maura considered retreating into the shop, but clearly he was aiming for her and would only follow.

"I heard you had my grandson's hat." Gruff hostility shot through his words.

Maura took one step back toward the shop's doorway. "I found it, if that's what you mean."

"I want it."

"I don't have it," Maura said. "You'll have to speak to Deputy Combs. It's evidence."

"It's a hat, that's all," Twigg said. "It's all I have left of my grandson, and he was all I had left of my daughter. I want it."

"As I said, you'll have to speak to Deputy Combs." Even as she spoke, Maura wondered how well Combs would stand up to Twigg. He spoke with determination about finding Sheriff Byler's killer, but Jesse Roper had not been the first person on the other side of the law to intimidate Thomas Combs.

"They sent another posse out after him, didn't they?" Twigg glared at Maura. "He's just a boy."

Maura returned the glare. A posse had ridden out Saturday night and not yet returned. "He shot the sheriff, and the way I hear it, you were there making sure he got clean away."

He harrumphed. "They won't find him."

Finally he moved on, stomping his way toward the post office.

Maura leaned against the door frame and let herself exhale heavily. Roper's mother must have been John Twigg's sister. The old man had lost two grown children in recent months. While she was sorry for the deaths, Maura refused to let that sway her feelings toward Twigg's part in the murder of a man she considered her friend as well as her sheriff.

Perspiration trickled into one eye, and she delicately wiped it clear. When she opened her eyes again, blinking three times rapidly, she started to call to Joseph across the street.

Before the sound left her mouth, she realized it was not Joseph. The man was dressed identically to Joseph and Zeke and was about Joseph's height with a similar build. But his hair was dark and trimmed shorter than Joseph's. He could be nothing other than a third Amish man in Gassville, standing in the street holding the reins of his horse.

She crossed the street to greet him. "Welcome to Gassville, Mr.—"

"Bender," the man replied. "Stephen Bender."

"Mr. Bender." Maura double-checked the cut of his black suit. "May I be so forward as to inquire whether you are seeking Mr. Beiler and Mr. Berkey?"

"*Ya*," Bender said. "The bishop sent me. Do you know where they are lodging?"

Maura nodded. "Behind the livery. I will take you there." With one hand, Maura indicated the way.

He led his horse, and they walked the blocks to the stables at the end of Main Street. Mr. Bender was not given to conversation, Maura decided. Her attempts at offering openings for him to say more about himself were met with brief replies. She remembered Joseph's nervousness when she first approached him and how long it had taken him to find his words. She supposed that this young man was equally unaccustomed to conversing with an *English* woman. At least this time, Maura had the advantage of knowing something of the Amish people.

Joseph and Zeke sat in the shade of the livery's front overhang with tin cups of cool water. Their work helping to clear the Dentons' land was complete. While Joseph had wanted to accept the offer of work, the more trees the crew ripped out, the more he grieved the ravage of the land. Before much longer, Zeke would insist they should leave Gassville. Joseph would have to face a decision he had avoided for the last several weeks.

"Here comes your *English* friend." Zeke lifted his cup toward the street then stood up. "I believe that is our Stephen Bender with her."

Joseph set his cup down beside the bench and stood as well. There could be no doubt it was Stephen. Joseph had sold Stephen that charcoal mare himself.

"I believe you know Mr. Bender," Maura said.

"Hello, Stephen," Zeke said. "We are pleased to see you. Aren't we, Joseph?"

Joseph nodded. "Hello, Stephen. *Guder mariye*, Miss Woodley." Good morning.

Curiosity pooled in her dark eyes, and he could not resist meeting her gaze.

Stephen was already opening his saddlebag. "I brought letters from both your families. And the bishop. And Hannah sent a special letter for you, Joseph."

Stephen sorted the letters, handing Joseph a letter from his parents and the one from Hannah. To Zeke he gave news from the Berkey family and the bishop's letter.

Joseph broke the seal on the letter, written in his mother's hand, and scanned the news of the new foal and the fence line his brothers had repaired. One of her best layers had stopped producing eggs. Although the news was trivial, Joseph felt his mother's warmth. He folded the letter closed. Zeke had chosen to read the bishop's letter first.

"He is not calling us home yet," Zeke muttered.

Relief coursed through Joseph as he raised his eyes to Maura again.

"He asks for an estimate of our available resources," Zeke reported, "and has sent a little money from the church for us to continue to look for a location for a new settlement."

"Stephen, are you to carry the answer back?" Joseph asked.

"Not immediately." Stephen fastened his saddlebag closed. "The bishop felt there might be benefit in my joining you for a time."

Joseph felt Stephen's eyes on him and shifted his weight, wondering what range of topics Zeke had written about in his letter to the bishop.

"What is the news from Hannah?" Zeke nudged Joseph in the elbow. "Aren't you going to answer the letter?"

"Is Hannah your sister?" Maura asked, smiling. "Is Zeke sweet on her?"

Zeke and Stephen laughed. Joseph watched the blush in Maura's face.

"Hannah is *my* sister," Zeke explained, "and she is *en lieb* with Joseph. They are practically engaged."

"Oh. I see."

Joseph's stomach lurched. Maura's face paled in an instant, the smile gone from both eyes and lips as she looked at him.

"We are *not* practically engaged." Joseph eyes widened toward Zeke. He wished Hannah's letter would disappear from his hand.

Maura had already stepped back. "My uncle will be waiting for me to finish the accounts. I'm sure you all have much to catch up on." She nodded toward Stephen. "It was a pleasure to meet you, Mr. Bender."

Joseph moved a step toward her, but she had already turned away.

Joseph straightened his hat with both hands and turned toward Stephen. "You must have other news for us as well."

But Stephen was watching Maura. "Joseph, why did that woman look at you that way?"

"I do not know what you are talking about." Joseph stepped back to the bench in the shade and picked up his empty water cup.

"You are my friend, Joseph," Zeke said, "but I cannot encourage you in this deceit."

"What deceit?" Stephen demanded.

Zeke and Joseph stared at each other.

"What deceit?" Stephen repeated. "Does it have to do with the *English* woman?"

"Joseph has feelings for her," Zeke said.

Indignation welled in Joseph. "You speak freely of my private matters."

"We are three now," Zeke said. "We are far from our people. We must remind each other of our ways and the reasons for them."

"The bishop will not be pleased to hear this," Stephen said.

"It is not your business to tell him," Joseph said. "I have done nothing and said nothing to Miss Woodley."

"But you feel something," Zeke said.

Joseph swatted at the bishop's letter still in Zeke's hands. "You said he wants us to continue to look for land to settle on. Does he give specific instructions?"

Zeke unfolded the letter again. "He asks us to take one last trip farther west, beyond Mountain Home. Then we are to return home to give a report and recommendation. He is concerned that we have been gone from the community for too long."

The stable doors burst open behind them, and the owner emerged with two horses. "Lee Denton is organizing a fresh posse. He will be here soon for his horses."

Zeke took the horses' reins. "We will be sure he gets them."

"If you men want to ride, I can do without you for a few days."

"Thank you, but no," Zeke said.

"When are they leaving?" Joseph asked.

"As soon as they have a dozen men," the stable owner said.

Joseph looked from Zeke to Stephen. "Our work on the Dentons' ranch is finished. I will ride with the posse."

Thirty-Two

Ruth clicked open the interoffice e-mail and read the doctor's instructions:

> *Please make sure Mrs. Webb gets on the schedule with Jerusha on Friday for an initial visit. Call patient to confirm time.*

Jerusha was the counselor who came from Pueblo once a week to see patients through the clinic. She would see patients there three or four times. After that, if she thought they needed a more indefinite therapeutic relationship, she encouraged them to arrange visits to her regular practice, where open appointments would be more available.

This was already Wednesday. Friday might be full. Ruth clicked through to Jerusha's schedule and found one opening, so she located Mrs. Webb's phone number and called to offer the appointment before returning to her e-mails to look for further follow-up notes from practitioners. Before her shift ended, she also needed to confirm all the appointments for the following day.

Elijah was supposed to check in with a local doctor after a

week, but Ruth doubted he would follow that advice. She had stopped in to see him again that morning, and he was already talking about at least going into the office at the back of Old Amos's house to help with paperwork if Amos would not let him go out on calls to the Amish homes needing appliance repairs.

Leah had left Elijah's horse and buggy on the Capp farm for his parents to find. She had not known any more than Ruth did that Elijah had moved and was boarding his horse at the edge of town. Ruth's instinct was to offer to drive him out to get his buggy, but she did not want any more jars of beans broken over her hood.

As frazzled as she was, Leah had done the sensible thing with the rig. Ruth paused with her fingers over the keyboard to pray for forgiveness and compassion to rise up, because she could not muster it in her own strength.

She could at least suggest to Annalise that Jerusha might be able to help Leah. Ruth prayed again, this time for Annalise to forgive the heartless spirit of their conversation the evening before.

Ruth closed out of Jerusha's schedule and checked the sticky note of tasks she had written for herself at the beginning of her shift, scribbling out several accomplished items.

Jerusha was an *English* counselor. Would she understand enough of the Amish ways to be helpful without being offensive?

Alan Wellner. Now that was someone who should see an *English* counselor, Ruth thought. Something was not right in his soul.

"I've made some initial inquiries," Larry, the Realtor, said to Rufus on Thursday afternoon, "but I have to be honest. It's going to take some work to sell this property, if that's what you decide to do."

Rufus leaned back in the wooden chair across from the Realtor. The coffee the receptionist had offered sat untouched on the desk between them.

"What obstacles would we have to overcome?" Rufus asked.

"To begin with, the whole market is slow. I've been handling commercial properties in southwestern Colorado for twenty years, and this is about the worst I've seen."

Rufus inhaled through the sigh he wanted to let out and considered the balding, fiftyish man before him. "What else?"

"You're talking about land that may have to be rezoned to attract a commercial buyer who could invest in reasonable access. Were you planning to run a business from that location when you purchased it?"

Rufus nodded. "Also to live there." The notebook in the small desk in his bedroom on the Beiler farm held sketches of the house he wanted to build for Annalise and the new workshop where he would build cabinets and chests.

The Realtor clicked his tongue. "There's no livable structure on the land. I didn't see anything at all when I drove out there."

"I was planning to build a home." He hoped to use plans similar to the Beiler home but on a smaller scale.

"Tell me again how much you paid for it." Larry picked up a pen and pulled a yellow pad closer.

Rufus gave the figure. "Two years ago it seemed like a good value compared to what some of my people have paid for their land."

"I'm sure it was—at the time. The market is different now."

Rufus could not deny that even construction of new homes in the area had dropped off, which was part of the dilemma that brought him to this conversation. It did not surprise him to hear that properties with commercial potential also suffered. He simply never expected to face the choice before him now.

"I'm happy to take on the listing." Larry's laptop emitted a sound announcing an e-mail, and he glanced at it. "I just always like to help my clients have realistic expectations for both the process and the outcome."

"I understand."

"You haven't said why you're considering selling. But it seems to me the question is whether you want to sell so you can be out from your financial obligations as the purchaser—I assume there's a mortgage—or if you were expecting to see a profit on undeveloped land after only two years."

"I do have a mortgage, but the payments are manageable." Knowing from experience that his business could have lean times, Rufus had been careful not to overextend himself. The debatable point was whether he could afford to build a house to live in with Annalise.

"What is your equity level?"

Rufus told Larry how much he had put down on the land, combined with advance payments he made when business was strong.

"If it were a larger plot, we could look at selling off pieces, but I don't advise that."

The land was big enough for a house, a barn, a workshop, pasture for horses and a milk cow, and a vegetable garden. But Rufus had never intended to farm, so he had not looked for the expansive acres most Amish families sought.

"You have my card," Larry said. "Call me if you decide to proceed. In the meantime I will unofficially keep my ears open for anyone looking for land out that way."

"Thank you."

Larry scratched the top of his head. "Maybe you should hang on to it for another year. The market might settle as the economy improves. You could come out well."

Another year could be too late for his *daed* if Joel's land did not have a good yield.

On Friday afternoon, Annie closed up Mrs. Weichert's shop and strolled the few blocks home. She compelled herself not to rush but to walk slowly and breathe in deeply and out fully every several strides. She rolled her shoulders and moved her neck. For good or for bad, the week had brought more than its share of stress.

Elijah's injury. If she had not dragged him into the hunt for Leah, he would not have been hurt. She did not force him to climb that gravel truck, but she had not stopped him. When Annie thought about it logically, Elijah's plans to leave the church should not have come as a shock. As teenagers, Elijah and Ruth had both questioned whether they ought to be baptized. Annie knew their story. Yet she found herself conflicted about understanding his choice and being disappointed that someone she cared for was setting aside the very vows she had taken.

Ruth's frustration. On top of her ongoing emotional turmoil about her feelings for Elijah, Ruth was frustrated with Elijah's mother, with Annie, with Leah. The air in Annie's small home had become tenser than she imagined possible. These weeks of being roomies with her dear friend and future sister-in-law were supposed to be full of joy and companionship. But they weren't now.

Leah's behavior was erratic. Leah made her bed and straightened her end of the living room before she disappeared every day, but she was still gone before Annie came downstairs. Enough food was finding its way out of Annie's cupboards for her to know that Leah was eating. As the days shortened and grew cooler, Annie wanted to suggest Leah should come home before dark for her own good. But to suggest any kind of rule would shake the fragile trust that kept Leah sleeping in a safe place at night.

That afternoon Annie had dropped a vase that shattered on the shop floor. The symbolism did not escape her. When she turned off Main Street onto her street, Annie breathed prayers for insight and peace in the hearts of all around her.

And she missed Rufus.

P.S., God, she thought, *let Rufus come for a visit.*

Ruth had only four items to take through the checkout line on Friday evening. She suspected that Leah was the one absconding with Ruth's food contributions to the household, but so far she had not seen Leah awake all week, so she was not going to press the point. She was living rent-free and had enough money saved to cover her minimal expenses until Christmas, even if she had to buy the same food twice a few times.

She spotted Bryan working a cash register and debated getting in another line, but in the moment she spent wavering, the other cashier plunked an orange CLOSED sign on the conveyor belt and turned off her light. Ruth smiled as she set her items on Bryan's belt. What else could she do?

"I wondered how long it would be before you came in during my shift." Bryan slowly waved a container of yogurt over the scanner.

"I don't know what your schedule is."

"I find out every Thursday." He set the yogurt down and picked up the bag of four apples to weigh.

Ruth had never seen a checker punch in a fruit code more slowly. She glanced to make sure a line was not forming behind her.

"I'm off tomorrow night." Bryan picked up the half gallon of milk and waited for the scanner's beep. "Maybe you would let me take you to a movie."

Ruth nudged her last item, a carton of orange juice, forward. She had never been to a movie, and she did not think this was the time or place to explain that reality to Bryan. He might never understand her, she realized, but he was consistently kind.

"How about it?" Bryan finally got the juice to beep.

"How about what?" Alan Wellner swooped in and scooped up Ruth's four items, rapidly dropping them in a bag.

"None of your business, buddy." Bryan hit the TOTAL button and reported the sum to Ruth. She scanned her debit card and watched the cash drawer pop open.

"Nuts." Bryan pushed a button above the cash register, and a light blinked. "I'm out of quarters."

"You don't eat much," Alan observed.

"I don't like to buy more than I need, and I like fresh food," Ruth said.

"Frugal and healthy. I like that." Bryan grinned.

The shift manager shuffled over with a new cash drawer. "You keep running out of everything. Let's just fill you up."

"Great idea." Bryan stepped aside for the manager to swap the drawers.

"Alan," the manager said, "remember you owe me half a shift for Wednesday morning last week."

"Right." Alan tapped the side of his head.

"The next time you need to leave early, just say something instead of disappearing before we're finished with the overnight stocking."

"Yes, sir."

Last Wednesday. Something stuck in Ruth's brain, and she tilted her head as if to shake it loose.

Last Wednesday morning was the day of the planned training burn.

And the unexplained outbuilding burn.

"I couldn't get away from work." Ruth was sure she had heard those words from Alan's mouth on the day of the burn. If he was not at the store, and he was not on time for the training, then where was he?

Could he have been three miles away?

Thirty-Three

Annie came down the stairs on Saturday morning and instantly knew something was different. Ruth was gone, but Annie knew she had a morning shift at the clinic. At first she thought the whimpering she heard was the kitten, but he brushed by with the casual arrogance of most cats Annie had ever known and scratched at the back door to be let out. Annie ignored the kitten's plea, uncertain whether Leah would approve and not willing to disturb the fragile peace of the household over a cat's wanderlust.

Rustling in the living room confirmed the source of the whimper. It was after eight in the morning, and Leah was still home.

Annie sucked in a deep, uncertain breath and closed the yards between the staircase in the middle of the house and the sectioned-off half of the living room. Careful to respect Leah's privacy, Annie remained on her side of the screen.

"Leah?"

The girl blew her nose but did not respond.

"Did you sleep?" Annie heard Leah come in around eleven, so she knew she was in the house all night.

Sniffles.

"Are you hungry?"

"No."

At least it was an answer.

"I could make you a cup of tea."

"Okay."

Progress.

Annie withdrew to the kitchen and started the kettle. Hopeful that Leah would accept some morning company, even without conversation, Annie took two mugs down from the shelf. She checked the kettle to make sure the water was warming and then stood in a classic impatient, foot-tapping pose, all the while listening to the noises coming from the other end of the house. The cat abandoned the quest for the outdoors and slinked back through the rooms.

At the first hint of a whistle, Annie grabbed the kettle and poured boiling water over green tea bags. She gripped one handle in each fist and followed the cat.

Leah had emerged from her bed and now sat in one of the chairs, her eyes red but dry. Annie handed her a mug and sat in the coordinating chair.

"I suppose you want to know what's going on." Leah blew on the hot tea.

"We have a deal." Annie leaned back in her chair, hoping to appear far more nonchalant than she felt. "No questions."

"So you don't want to know?"

"I'm here to listen to whatever you want to tell me." Annie's heart raced.

"It's been over a month! No letter in over a month. What if he doesn't love me anymore?"

There it was.

On top of Leah's heartbreak over being separated from her young man, she was in a panic over his lack of response. Thirteen days had passed since Annie's letter to Matthew, and she had heard nothing, either.

"I'm sorry you're hurting so much." Leah's anxiety was palpable, but Annie would not promise everything would be all right.

"Aren't you going to say *Gottes wille*? That's what everybody says to me when I'm unhappy."

"I don't think God means for us to be unhappy."

"Then why doesn't He fix things? He could make Aaron write a letter. He could make my parents understand that I love Aaron. He could give me a job so I can earn train fare to Pennsylvania. God could do lots of things, but He doesn't."

Annie moistened her lips and then hid them behind the mug of steaming tea. She hoped this disappointment would not put Leah over an edge Annie could not predict.

"So you going home for the weekend?" Marcus sliced through the bottom of a carton and stepped on it to flatten it.

"My friend should be here soon to drive me." Rufus wiped sweat off his forehead then dropped the rag in his toolbox. His small bag of personal items, removed from the motel that morning, waited for him next to the door.

"I live up toward Cripple Creek or I would have been glad to drive you home," Marcus said.

"That's kind of you. Tom doesn't mind coming."

"Who would have thought we'd finish with this place in a week? You're a speed demon when it comes to this stuff." Marcus tossed the flat box on a stack in the corner.

Rufus gave a half smile. "I've had a lot of experience with cabinets."

The door opened, and Jeff, their employer, came in. He nodded with approval. "Nice work, guys."

"Thank you," Rufus said.

"Look, this job went a lot faster than what I scheduled. I don't have things firmed up for the next job yet. I've let everybody know to plan on a few days off, and I'll call you next week and let you know where we're going to be working."

"Give a hint where?" Marcus said.

"Alamosa, probably," Jeff answered.

Marcus groaned. "That's a long drive. You have to go around half the world to get to Alamosa from here."

"We have to follow the money, my friend." Jeff gave a playful salute. "When you're finished cleaning up, you can go. Talk to you next week."

Rufus tugged on the brim of his hat in thought. Alamosa was on the other side of the Sangre de Cristo Mountains. None of the highways were a direct route on the map. On the other hand, Amish settlers were increasingly numerous in Alamosa and Monte Verde, far more than in Westcliffe. He might find a family to extend him hospitality.

His mind turned to Annalise and the land she did not know he owned. She did not know he was coming home, and now he could stay longer than just for the Sabbath.

The land meant to be home to Rufus and Annalise might keep his parents in their home. And Joel and Lydia and Sophie and Jacob. Before Annalise sold her thriving software business and gave away most of her money, she would have seen the funds the Beilers needed now as loose change. She could have solved their problems with a phone call and an electronic funds transfer.

Rufus decided to drive Annalise out to see the land. She deserved that much.

Annie put on a warm jacket and took her bike out of the garage. It was late in the afternoon, but she believed she had enough light for a long bike ride. This time she would not even mind the hills, instead anticipating a good workout to burn off the week's stress.

Leah had finally agreed to a proper hot bacon and eggs breakfast that morning, but as soon as she finished eating, she picked up the kitten and went out the back door. Annie was left with a stack of dirty dishes and a sense of dread that Leah would not return.

Garden chores called. Annie pulled in the last of the squash and stacked it in the kitchen. She cleaned the house from top to bottom, except for Ruth's room. With a broom, she thrashed at the leaves piling up on the front walkway, then found a rake in the garage and attacked the leaves on the browning grass. During and in between her efforts to find something she could control, she remembered to pray and pray again for a quiet, humble, discerning heart.

Still, she feared she would not sleep if she did not first exhaust herself. She would ride, take a hot bath, pray some more, and go to bed early before a fresh wind of discontent blew through her. Ruth had plans for the evening, though she had not said what they were, and Leah would do what Leah decided to do.

What did it mean to seek God's will? What did it mean to accept God's will? And what did it mean to do God's will? Questions tumbled without answers.

Whenever Annie went for a bike ride without a predetermined destination, her feet seemed to automatically pedal toward the Beiler home. She would be welcome, she knew, if she stopped in. But if Annie stayed too long and darkness fell, someone would have to drive her home in a buggy, and she did not want to presume on any of them. She made up her mind to ride as far as the rise in the road that would allow her to see the farm and then turn back.

She came to the rise and stopped at the highest point, prepared to look with heartfelt yearning on the scene before her.

Instead she saw smoke.

She pedaled hard down the sloping highway.

Ruth was not at all sure she had done the right thing in accepting a date with Bryan. But standing in the grocery store yesterday, she had agreed to a meal rather than a movie. Bryan said he knew a place in Walsenburg he would love to take her.

"Nothing fancy," she had insisted. "I wouldn't have anything to wear."

"You'll look great whatever you wear," he had said.

"And home early," she said.

"Right," he said. "The next day's the Sabbath."

So here she was, in the passenger seat of his Mitsubishi while he challenged the speed limit just enough to display his anticipation of the evening. In another hundred yards, they would pass her family's home.

"I don't like the way the sky looks up ahead," Bryan said.

Ruth leaned forward as they went over the rise in the road.

Flames.

"Is that on your land?" Bryan accelerated.

Ruth gasped. "I think so. It looks like Joel's field."

"Is there anything in the field that could catch fire?"

"His whole crop!"

"I mean a building, an electrical wire, a can of gasoline too close to a match."

"There's an old shed. It was there when we bought the land. Joel might keep a few tools in it but nothing of value."

"We're only five miles from town. It won't take long to have an engine here."

Bryan had his phone out now and spoke calmly into it reporting the details of the fire.

Rufus was relieved to be almost home. He enjoyed talking with Tom, who had come to understand the Amish ways well during his years of taxiing for them and doing business with them through his hardware store. But Rufus was anxious to surprise his family. He probably had not even missed supper yet.

A siren wailed behind them, and Tom pulled to the shoulder of the highway. A water truck and a ladder truck whizzed past.

Tom's pickup shuddered in their wake.

Rufus put a hand on the dashboard and leaned forward. "What could be burning out here?"

"Maybe nothing," Tom said calmly. "It might just be a medical call."

The trucks were out of sight now. Tom drove past one acre of trees after another. Rufus scanned the horizon from left to right and back again.

Finally he sank back in his seat and muttered, "Joel's field."

He could hardly breathe.

Thirty-Four

Annie held Rufus's hand, not caring who might be watching, and the two of them huddled with Ruth.

"Bryan is trying to find a way to help." Ruth folded her arms across her chest, gripping her elbows. "But he's not suited up. They won't let him do much."

Annie put a hand on Ruth's back. "He knows how to be safe."

The trio stood well back from the fire, which had demolished the shed and unfurled to low-growing crop around the field. Firefighters aimed hoses and pumped water. A layer of foam quickly covered the ground, stifling the efforts of windblown embers to find fuel and burst.

"It's just about out," Rufus said.

"This is going to ruin Joel's crop, isn't it?" Annie looked a few yards to her right, where she saw Joel sitting on the ground with his knees raised and his hands hanging between them. Behind him Eli knelt with a hand on his son's shoulder. Lydia and Sophie on either side.

"The chemicals they're spraying will change the soil," Rufus said quietly. "I'm not sure what it will mean."

"It's not good." Ruth spoke sharply. "This was supposed to

be Joel's first crop. Now look. What isn't burned or ruined with chemicals has been trampled or rutted by the trucks."

"He's been working so hard." Annie's throat thickened.

"He persuaded *Daed* he could get one more crop before they let the field go fallow." Rufus scratched his cheek. "It was going to be the start of a financial stake for him."

"At least it didn't spread to the other fields," Annie said. "They'll be all right, won't they?"

"This was not an accident." Ruth took a few steps forward. "Somebody started the fire that burned your cabinets, Rufus, and somebody started the fire in that county building along the highway. Now this."

"But why would anyone come after your family?" Annie asked.

"I haven't worked that out yet. Bryan says there's always a pattern, and when this scene cools down, they'll figure out what it has in common with the others."

"The fire on the highway and this one both started in sheds," Annie mused, "but the first one was a half-built house."

"But it was empty," Ruth countered, "and the fire started in the back. At least that's what Bryan thinks. The highway shed burned from the back, too."

Annie could not keep herself from scanning the horizon, this time for a flash of purple. Leah had left the house that morning wearing the dress that had once been Ruth's and then became Annie's first Amish dress.

"Let's not get ahead of things," Rufus said. "Since this fire happened on Beiler land, surely *Daed* will receive some information about it."

"I hope they will investigate." Ruth swung her arms down to her sides, her hands still fists. "Tell *Daed* to insist."

"But what started the fire?" Jacob wanted to know. He kicked one heel softly against the leg of his chair.

Rufus was glad his mother had kept his little brother away from the fire scene, but conversation and speculation swirled around the Beiler home as Franey put a delayed supper on the table. It would be impossible for an inquisitive little boy like Jacob to understand the event that had cast a pall on the evening.

Annalise and Ruth stayed to eat, with the promise that someone would drive them home. Ruth had seemed relieved that Bryan Nichols declined Franey's invitation to stay as well. Bryan said he wanted to go to the fire station and see for himself what evidence might have been collected from the scene. Ruth, Rufus thought, was simply not ready to mix her family with an *English* young man. And perhaps to his credit, Bryan understood that now.

"We don't know how the fire started," Rufus said in answer to his brother's question. "Sometimes an event happens and we never know why."

"*Gottes wille*?" Jacob asked.

"I suppose so."

"There was nothing in that shed but a rake and a hoe," Joel insisted. "Maybe a couple of muddy rags. There was no lightning, there was no anything. Do you believe it was God's will for someone to set a fire?"

"But if it happens, then it's God's will, right?" Jacob said.

"Not this time," Joel muttered.

"Joel." Eli's calm demeanor nevertheless intoned severe caution.

Joel slumped back and pressed his lips together.

Not until the dishes had been cleared and Jacob tucked in bed did the family gather in one room again, this time in the comfort of the living room. Annalise sat on the floor between Lydia and Sophie with her knees neatly tucked to one side. She looked tired to Rufus, but he supposed all of them appeared beleaguered under the circumstances.

"I'm so glad to be home," Rufus said.

"If only you could stay more than a day this time." Seated on the couch, Franey put her tired feet on a cushion on the floor.

"As God would have it, I can," Rufus said. "We have an unexpected break in the schedule."

"That's good news." Franey reached over to an end table and picked up an envelope. "You got a letter from David's shop in Colorado Springs. Perhaps he has some orders for you."

Rufus slit the envelope and glanced through the letter. "Several customers have been in asking about my pieces. He may have some special orders after all."

"That's great news," Annalise said from across the room.

"I don't know if the time is right," Rufus said.

Joel cleared his throat. "You took the job with the *English* because you were concerned your business was dropping off. Why would you not jump at the opportunity to go back to your craft?"

Rufus glanced at Annalise, seeing the same question in her eyes.

"I've made a commitment to Jeff. He is expecting me to be available all winter."

Joel waved a hand. "Things change. For instance, today I lost my livelihood for the season. You could send me to fulfill your obligation."

"It is more difficult to live away from our people than you might realize." Rufus looked again at Annalise. Her eyes pleaded with him to stay home.

Franey shuffled her feet on the cushion. "Joel, I don't think that it is wise for you to think this way. As Rufus said, it would be difficult."

"Do you think I do not have the strength of faith that Rufus has?"

"I did not say that."

"Joel," Eli said, "are you sure you would want to do this?"

"I am probably more sure than Rufus was when he left the first time."

"And Rufus," Eli said, "do you believe it would be possible to offer a substitute for your labor?"

Rufus met his brother's eyes and let out his breath. "If I assure Jeff that Joel is capable, then, yes. I believe it is possible."

"Then I think you should stay home and Joel should go."

❧

On Sunday morning, Ruth drove Annalise to church in the car. This time, though, she let Annalise sit forward in the congregation with the Beiler women, and Ruth dawdled in the back, near the door, and finally took a seat when she could see the men were lining up outside to process in. *Daed* was shoulder to shoulder with Ike Stutzman among the bearded married men, while Rufus and Joel marched farther back with the smooth-shaven unmarried men. Walking with the men, Jacob grinned from ear to ear. Rufus leaned over and whispered to Jacob, and the boy straightened his shoulders but maintained his exuberance.

Ruth smiled. Rufus was old enough to be Jacob's father, and it seemed to please him to act in fatherly ways. If he did not propose to Annalise of his own accord soon, Ruth might just take it upon herself to prod her eldest brother into action. Rufus and Annalise could have their own *kinner* soon enough. *Mamm* would love having *boppli* in Colorado when she was so far from the grandchildren in Pennsylvania.

Ruth lost her place in the first hymn, stabbed with wondering how *Mamm* might receive Ruth's children someday. They would not be Amish *boppli*.

She shook off the thought. She had no aspiration to marry anytime soon, and why should she borrow worry from the future?

As the congregation assembled that morning, news of Joel's fire, as it was already deemed, dispersed through one conversation after another. Now, during the sermons, the ministers chosen to preach both focused on forgiveness and God's will. Ruth tried to concentrate and fleetingly wondered if Annalise's German had improved enough that she understood sermons without Sophie leaning in to whisper translation.

Forgiveness.

An easy enough idea to talk about, especially when it was not your friend who was kicked in the chest and not your brother whose field had burned.

Ruth could forgive. Just not yet.

During the final low, slow hymn, she slipped out of the barn housing the congregation that morning. Rufus would look after Annalise, and Ruth did not feel like facing a boisterous potluck meal or answering a barrage of questions or hearing anyone say *Gottes wille*. Instead, she walked to her car and started it, grateful for its quiet engine.

She drove to the place she always wanted to be when she was most confused, to the trail the community had created in the summer and to the monument of a rock just beyond the boundary of Beiler land. Ruth took her purse with her because it contained an item that was the main reason for her lack of concentration this morning.

It niggled at her.

Thinking that she might never get used to approaching the rock from a parking lot rather than cutting through her family's land, Ruth found the old familiar footholds. At the top, with her legs stretched out in front of her beneath her long skirt, she pulled the strap of her purse off her shoulder and opened the thrift store imitation leather brown bag.

And from its shallows she pulled a black strap to run through her fingers again.

As her stunned family made their way from the field to the house the previous evening, Ruth had idly picked up the strap. She supposed it had belonged to one of the firefighters, though what it had secured she could not surmise. It did not strike her as particularly heavy duty.

The strap was less than an inch wide, with a thin blue stripe zigzagging down the center. At one end was a broken carabiner latch.

"Ruth!"

She looked over the edge of the rock to see Elijah standing below her.

"Elijah! Are you all right?" Ruth scrambled to her feet.

"I'm fine. I'm coming up."

"No sir, you most definitely are not climbing up here today."

Confident that even six days after his fall she could move more quickly than Elijah, Ruth snatched up her purse. In a matter of seconds, she had descended and circled the rock and stood on the ground facing Elijah.

"I didn't know if you would come to church," she said.

"I thought you might be there. But if I had gone, it would give my *mamm* false hope, and I do not want to hurt her any more than I have."

Ruth looked toward the parking lot. "I see you got your buggy back. Are you sure you ought to be out by yourself yet?"

"I'm not by myself. I'm with you."

She smiled. "Technically. But you didn't know that when you came."

"I never give up hoping to find you here, in our place."

His sentimentality sluiced through her. "Elijah, I'm not sure what you want me to say."

"Yes you are."

She met his eyes then looked away. He was right. She knew what he wanted to hear, but she could not say it.

"What do you have there?" Elijah asked.

Ruth spread the strap between her hands. "I suppose you heard about the fire yesterday."

He nodded. "These days the whole town gets jumpy when we hear a siren."

"I found this."

He shrugged. "It's just a water bottle strap. The *English* use them all the time."

Ruth inhaled and took a long time to exhale.

"Ruth? What's the matter?"

"I've seen this strap before. And it doesn't belong to anyone who was at the fire yesterday."

Thirty-Five

June 1892

Joseph removed his hat long enough to drag a sleeve across his forehead and down one side of his face. A streak of gray resulted on his shirt, new dirt, as opposed to the sweat and dust of the last two days that may have permanently discolored the soft white cotton garment.

For the third time in ten days, he had ridden out with a posse chasing a fresh rumor. He doubted Deputy Combs would organize another ride. The claims people made to have seen Roper lacked substance. Some even insisted they had seen his hat, which Combs still kept locked up in the sheriff's office and for which Old Man Twigg harangued the officer on a daily basis.

Combs would surrender the hat soon. The men riding in posses would decide they could no longer afford to be away from their own shops and ranches. And the citizens of Baxter County would choose a new sheriff. Finding Jesse Roper was likely the deputy's last hope of being elected sheriff.

Joseph hung back from the posse riders who would disburse to their properties. He tugged the reins to take his horse to the edge of town. To the livery. To Zeke and Stephen and their concerned scowls and news of their own scouting jaunt. When he reached the stables, he stilled his mount and assessed the scene. The small building closest to the road looked as tidy as it always did. The owner's wife made sure the business presented well. Set back from the road, the stable's doors were open wide and Joseph could see straight through the building. Two stable boys were mucking and another was bringing fresh hay. In the yard beyond the far end, two men brushed burrs from their horses' manes. Joseph slid off his horse and led the animal around the structures.

In the rear yard, Zeke stopped brushing. "Joseph. You've come back."

"I never said I would not." Joseph straightened his hat with both hands. "And your journey? When did you return?"

"Yesterday."

"And have you found God's will for the new settlement?"

"We're going home," Stephen said. "We will give our report there."

"You must come with us," Zeke urged.

"I pray you are taking a favorable report." Joseph ignored Zeke's admonition. "The land of Baxter County has much to commend itself. Wide open acres for farming. The river nearby. A town on the railroad route."

Zeke shook his head. "You speak rightly of the virtues of the county. But this is a place of strife. Even beyond Mountain Home and Gassville, the feud between the Dentons and the Twiggs is a subject of conversation and speculation. Other families are quarreling as well. I cannot recommend to the bishop that we bring our people of peace to this region."

"Perhaps we can be an influence of peace," Joseph said.

"We seek a place to live apart," Zeke said, "not to resolve the *English* mistreatment of their own."

"The horses are nearly fully rested," Stephen said. "We will leave at first light."

Joseph held silent.

Belle Mooney covered her eyes with her hands and leaned her back on the door. On the other side, Maura Woodley pounded.

Belle breathed in and out with deliberation, lodging her weight against the door lest Maura should manage to turn the feeble lock and try to enter.

"Belle, I miss you!" Maura pleaded. "We have been friends too long for this to stand between us."

Belle moved her hands to cover her ears and began to hum the tune of "What a Friend We Have in Jesus." Never in their entire lives had she gone ten days without sharing at least a few minutes with Maura. Their mothers had been friends before their daughters were born, and it was a daily ritual for one of them to walk to the other's home on any pretense or none at all, children in tow. Maura and Belle had sustained the tradition after they came of age and after their mothers passed on.

But that was over. Maura had never understood about John. She had taken the Dentons' side.

She would leave town, Belle decided. Her mother had passed on years ago. John was gone. Her father hated the family of the man she loved. Her best friend refused to understand. She would go somewhere else, another county, even another state. Schools were everywhere. She would find a position and leave Gassville. It did not matter that she would be an old maid schoolteacher. In a new place, she could remember John in peace.

"Belle, please," Maura said, loudly now since Belle had begun to sing the hymn with full voice. "Can't we talk?"

"No!"

"I do not accept that circumstances have come to this."

"You don't accept a lot of things." Belle turned and faced the door, her open palms pressed against it now. "That's what gets you into so much trouble. I'm finished with that. I'm finished with you."

"You cannot mean that."

"Don't tell me what I mean. All my life you've been doing that."

"Belle! What has gotten into you?"

"Go away, Maura Woodley. Leave me be."

Belle exhaled at the silence that came from the outside. She heard the rustle of Maura's skirt and knew she was wearing the new petticoat they had worked on together.

"Belle Agnes Mooney," Maura said. "I will be your friend forever. That is all there is to it. I am leaving your porch, but I am not leaving you."

Silence.

"You know where to find me when you're ready."

"I will never be ready!" Belle pounded the inside of the door with one fist.

Finally she heard Maura's shoes hitting the porch steps one at a time in careful rhythm. Belle moved to a front window, stood to the side where she could not be seen from the outside, and watched the truest friend she had ever known—other than John—walk away. When Maura turned for a moment to glance at the house, Belle glided into the interior hall without looking back.

Maura did not for one minute believe what Belle said. Joseph was right. Belle needed time. She would come to her senses once her heart began to mend.

Still, Belle's words stung. Instead of turning toward home, or even toward Main Street, she let her feet carry her out of town. She walked so far she began to wonder if she should have brought the cart. No, it was better to be alone, unencumbered even by a horse that never hesitated to serve her well. At least she was wearing practical shoes, and pinched toes would not distract her from what weighed on her mind. Miles passed beneath determined steps. The closer she got to the White River, the more strongly she felt she wanted to sit on its bluff and let her heart soak in its beauty while the wind whipped cool dampness and deposited it on her clothing. Across the open ranch land, an occasional darting rabbit, cattle with fly-swatting tails, and the swarming flies of summer were the only moving beings she saw.

She cut through the woods along the inland edge of the Denton ranch, staying under the canopy of shade as much as she could. Humidity weighed down with its outrageous magnification of the heat to the point that Maura wondered if anyone would care if she meandered down the sloped side of the bluff and waded away from the river's edge. Despite her anticipation of standing in awe of the river, her heart collapsed in on itself as she moved through the Denton land and the woods thinned until she could hardly find a tree for a passing moment of shade. With horror, she realized that Ing and Lee had ravaged their own land beyond recognition. In the name of honest work, men like Ezekiel Berkey and Joseph Beiler and a dozen others from Gassville had labored to deprive the land of its enchantment.

Finally she reached the crown of the bluff and felt the movement of air swirling up from the path the river carved. Northeastern Arkansas was hardly the frontier. It had not been for some time. Trim little towns like Gassville dotted the landscape, and travelers could begin journeys in any direction in the relative comfort of a railroad car—even sleeping Pullman compartments.

Maura heard footsteps crunching behind her and spun around. "Joseph."

"It's a beautiful spot, is it not?" He tilted his hat toward the rushing water.

Maura spread her arms. "It was more beautiful before. . .how could Lee and Ing take out so many trees?"

"At first it was just going to be a few, so they could see the river from the house." Joseph moved to stand beside Maura. "Then it was a few more, and a few more."

"It's awful." She shook her head. "It's just awful. There's nothing else to say. But why should the riverfront be pretty when the county is one big gunslinging pile of hate?"

He had no response.

"I'm sorry. I don't mean to accuse you. If you hadn't wanted the work, they would have found someone else."

"True enough. But now that I see what it must look like through the eyes of someone who grew up here, perhaps I was overeager."

She sucked in her bottom lip and let it out. "I'm sure if the posse had turned up something I would have heard the news."

"Nothing," he said. "I don't believe they will ride again."

"If anyone can talk sense into them, it would be you."

"You flatter me. But my people are not given to pride, so I will only humbly respond that the men want to get back to their own businesses. Catching Mr. Roper will be up to whatever system you *English* have for such matters once a man has disappeared as undeniably as he has."

"Yet the feud continues." Maura put both hands on her hips and surveyed the water. "Old Man Twigg and Leon Mooney go after each other with hateful words practically every day in the middle of the street. It's only a matter of time before one of them carries a gun again. Why cannot we live in peace? Surely there is enough prosperity for everyone."

With her lips pressed closed, she inhaled deeply the scent of Joseph Beiler mingled with stumps and river spray. This spot would never again smell as it had before the trees were removed, but now it would at least remind her of Joseph Beiler, the most unlikely visitor she had ever welcomed to Gassville.

"Zeke is going to tell the bishop the county is too violent for a settlement of our people," Joseph said quietly.

"We should have welcomed you all with open arms. But it would seem that even the death of a man as noble and well loved as Abraham Byler cannot force people to treat each other like human beings."

"Surely the present sentiment will not last forever."

"I'm not sure I want to be around to find out." Maura surprised herself with her words. "Maybe I should just get away. Go back east. Go south. Go north. Just go someplace where people are more civilized.

"Would you really leave?" Joseph's eyes widened, and Maura's spirit stumbled under the import of what she had voiced.

If Maura Woodley would consider leaving Gassville, perhaps she would consider leaving with him. Joseph dried his clammy palms on his trousers and straightened his hat with both hands.

"Are your people truly peaceful?" she asked, her voice full of quiver.

Joseph wished he could give an unequivocal answer but settled for the truth. "We have our quarrels. We are sinners, too."

"But you stick together somehow."

"Somehow, yes. By God's grace."

"I cannot imagine God is very pleased with the likes of Gassville right now."

"God is love."

Maura paced away then returned. "You talk about the closeness of your families. The Dentons and Twiggs might say the same thing, but look what they are doing."

Joseph cleared his throat. "That is because they are motivated by pride, not submission. That changes everything."

"So why are you here, Joseph? Why are you riding with the posses?"

Joseph had asked himself the same questions a hundred times. "A man has to test his convictions. To be sure they are his own."

"And are they?"

Her brown eyes begged him for an answer that made sense. If only he had one.

"Halt or I'll shoot!" The anger in the man's voice jolted them both, and they startled. A second later they stared at the end of a pistol.

"Ing Denton, what are you doing?" Maura roused and reached out to slap the pistol away.

"What are you doing on my land?" Ing demanded.

"I've been strolling through your land since I was a little girl."

"And what about him?" Ing thrust a finger toward Joseph.

"I suppose working on your land made me come to admire it," Joseph said.

"Well, I'm not taking any chances with those crazy Twiggs around. Get off my land. Both of you. Now."

Thirty-Six

"Yes, it's Alan's."

Bryan ran his finger along the blue zigzag as Ruth held the strap.

"But he wasn't at the fire last night." Ruth felt a tremble take hold in her knees. "Why would his water bottle strap be in our field?"

"He was definitely working at the grocery store last night."

"How can you be sure?" Elijah spoke for the first time. "Ruth says she was with you before you discovered the fire."

Ruth's stomach crunched. She had hated having to reveal that fact to Elijah. The words sounded even worse coming from his mouth.

Elijah pressed the issue. "If you weren't working, how can you be sure Alan was?"

"Alan was on the schedule," Bryan said. "The store manager was leaning on him pretty hard not to blow it off."

"Pardon me if I am being rude," Elijah said, "but that does not sound the same as being certain."

"I saw him go into the store at the start of his shift, about an hour before Ruth and I left town."

Ruth looked from Elijah to Bryan. Neither man's eyes budged from the other.

"The carabiner is broken." Ruth wound the strap around one hand. "Wouldn't his water bottle have fallen off?"

"That's hard to say," Bryan said. "Maybe he left the strap in one of the engines and it happened to fall out last night in the field."

Ruth shook her head. "The spot where I found it was not anywhere near where the engines were parked. At first I thought it might belong to one of the firefighters, but the more I thought about it, the less sense that made."

Bryan shrugged. "Then maybe I'm wrong and it's not Alan's."

"No one in my family has anything like this. Besides, it's decorative."

"So?"

"So the Amish would not so much as put a ribbon in their hair or on the band of a hat," Elijah said. "They certainly would not carry a strap like this."

"Let's not jump all over each other." Bryan put up both hands, palms out. "I want to help. But if this is Alan's strap, and you're implying that he had something to do with the fire, well, that's serious."

"I don't mean to imply anything," Ruth said. "I'm asking questions, that's all. Trying to make sense of things."

"Why don't you let me talk to Alan?" Bryan reached out with an open hand. "Let me take the strap. I could say I found it."

"I don't want you to lie," Ruth said.

"I think Ruth should hang on to it in case it turns out to be important." Elijah glared at Bryan.

"Hey, Alan is my friend. I care what happens to him. If he has something to do with the fire, I want to get to the bottom of things as much as you do."

"It's all right." Ruth put a hand on Elijah's arm. "Alan trusts Bryan, and so do I."

On Monday Ruth checked her cell phone at a frequency she would have been embarrassed to confess. It was fully charged. It was turned on. Even in the pocket of her scrubs, it would vibrate enough to alert her of activity, and even at work at the clinic she would be able to step away and at least listen to a message.

She was not sure what she expected. Bryan had said he would get to the bottom of things, but he had not promised immediate results. Only a day had passed since she let the strap drop into his hand over Elijah's objection. Although they were roommates, Bryan and Alan did not always work the same shifts at the grocery store or volunteer together at the fire station. Those schedules were in the hands of other people. In reality, they probably saw less of each other than she and Annalise did.

Ruth's clinic schedule on Monday was all day. She worked the morning at the front desk then spent the afternoon shadowing a physician's assistant. Normally she looked forward to opportunities to at least observe the medical staff rather than be buried in files and phone messages, but on Monday, her concentration had been no better than during church on Sunday. Halfway through the shadowing shift, she snagged a notepad from the front desk and forced herself to write notes in an effort to pay closer attention.

When her day ended at four o'clock, her phone had not rung all day. She took her jacket off the hook in the staff room and slid her arms into the sleeves while she weighed the pros and cons of trying to track down Bryan in person. He had never said where he lived, just that he lived with Alan, but the town was small enough that she could cruise the streets and look for his car. Or she could casually stop by the grocery store for some shampoo or something else she did not need.

No. She would not go looking for trouble. She trusted Bryan. He would find her when he knew something.

Ruth draped her purse strap over one shoulder and went out the back door of the clinic.

When a form moved out of the shadows, Ruth sucked in her breath and stepped aside.

"What's the matter, Ruth?"

Alan.

"May I walk you home?" He produced a genial smile.

Ruth might have felt better if she could see his hands. They remained plunged into the pockets of his gray fleece-lined jacket. She glanced toward Main Street.

"A lot of people would drive to work." Alan touched her elbow now. "I suppose you people like your exercise."

You people?

"Sometimes I drive. It depends on my mood or whether I'm running late. It's only a few blocks, after all."

"You must have been on time this morning. I didn't see your car."

"I didn't know you knew my car." Ruth wished he would take his hand off her elbow as they walked.

"You could have asked me about that strap, you know."

The pit of her stomach hardened.

"I'll bet Bryan didn't tell you that we got identical straps and water bottles about two years ago."

"No, he didn't."

"They were a perk from the gym where we worked out in Colorado Springs."

"Oh. Well, that sounds healthy."

"Perhaps you miss my point."

Ruth held her tongue, grateful to be progressing toward a well-populated block.

"My point," Alan said in his easygoing tone, "is that you can't be sure that strap is mine. It could be Bryan's."

"Why would it be Bryan's? He would have just said so."

"Would he?"

She said nothing.

"I've known Bryan a long time. I would hate for you to get hurt because things are not what you think they are." An alarm sounded on Alan's phone. "Oh, I gotta go."

He tapped her shoulder and began to sprint down Main Street.

Rufus read David's letter again before turning on the cell phone he used for business and calling the shop in Colorado Springs.

David could guarantee one hope chest larger than the ones on the store floor and was waiting to hear from another customer about a set of matching bookcases.

He set the phone down and began mental calculations. While Rufus was grateful that David carried his furniture, he needed more work. He would not miss hanging manufactured cabinets, though he would have said a proper good-bye to Marcus if he had known he would not be returning.

The workshop door was propped open. Rufus looked up when a shadow fell across his workbench and Joel was standing in the doorway.

"I just wondered if you were able to get hold of your boss." Joel's gangly arms hung from his sharp shoulders. "About the job."

Rufus lowered himself onto a stool. "You've had a day to think. Are you as sure as you were last night?"

Joel nodded. "More. I'll try again in the spring, but in the meantime I need to feel that I'm contributing something to the family."

"*Daed* is grateful for your help in all the fields, not just the one that burned."

"I'll be eighteen soon, Rufus. I need a start at something. I thought it would be farming, but now I'm not sure."

"You have better instincts for the farm than all the other Beiler sons together."

"Matthew and Daniel seem to be making a go of it. And you have your woodworking. Everything is so different here than it was in Pennsylvania. Maybe I shouldn't assume I'll farm."

"Beilers have always farmed."

"You don't. Elijah doesn't, either. I see other Amish families starting businesses. If I earned some money to get started, I could do something, too."

Rufus picked up a pencil and parked it behind his ear. "The job is yours if you want it. Jeff will call when he has the details arranged."

The cell phone on the workbench rang, and both brothers leaned toward it.

"This is another matter," Rufus said. "I'll see you at dinner."

The phone rang a second time, and a third. Rufus waited until Joel was out of earshot before picking up the call right before it went to voice mail.

"I might have a deal for you." Larry sounded upbeat.

"You said the market was slow," Rufus said.

"It is. I just stumbled onto this. My cousin in Denver mentioned a friend of his was thinking about taking up a simpler, rural life. Working from home, growing their own food, animals, the great outdoors, that sort of thing."

Rufus smiled to himself at the description that matched his life. But the smile faded in uncertainty. "What if I'm not sure I've decided to sell?"

"I'm not sure they've decided they want to buy. This is just an opportunity to strike while the iron is hot."

"I'd like some time to think."

"Of course. I'll check back with you in a couple of days."

Rufus shut the phone off, not wishing another interruption to his thoughts. He had saved for years for a solid down payment on land, and he was confident the land was a good choice for the future. Jacob was only eight. His parents were probably a dozen or more years away from having an empty nest, as the *English* liked to say. Although he and Annalise might start married life under his parents' roof, they needed a nest of their own.

It was time to take Annalise to see his dream of the future.

Thirty-Seven

Rufus tied Dolly to the tree bulging the sidewalk in front of Mrs. Weichert's shop on Wednesday afternoon. If he remembered correctly, Annalise would finish working in a few minutes. The bell jangled as he pushed through the door.

Mrs. Weichert looked up from the stack of papers she was studying behind the counter. "She's using the telephone in the storeroom. You can go on back if you like."

Rufus nodded his thanks and crossed the store. The door to the storeroom stood open, and he could see Annalise hunched over the small desk in the corner, a computer in front of her and a notepad under her hand. She looked up at him.

"Hello. I can't believe they put me on hold again."

"I thought you might like to take a drive."

"Mmm. Sounds nice. Depends on how long this takes."

"Trying to get a price on something?"

Annalise held up a finger and turned her attention back to the screen, where the image of a picture frame filled the shape.

"We think it's from the 1940s," she said into the phone. She paused to listen. "Okay, we'll wait for your call. Thank you."

Rufus crossed his arms at the wrists.

Annalise scraped the wooden chair back and stood. "A drive, you said?"

"I would even let you do the driving, if you'd like. Aren't you off soon?"

"I am." She pushed her bottom lip out. "But I have a couple of personal calls to make. Mrs. Weichert doesn't mind if I use the phone here, and it seems like the easiest thing to do."

"I'll wait."

"I'm trying to line up some appointments for Leah. I have to call Ruth at the clinic and see if she was able to get Leah into the counselor's schedule on Friday."

"After that, then."

"I'm afraid I'd only have about half an hour." Annalise stacked papers and tapped them against the desk to straighten them. "Leah sometimes comes home in the late afternoon, and I want to catch her before she decides to leave again."

This excursion was not one Rufus cared to rush. "What does your morning look like?"

"Oh! That's much better." Annalise brightened. "Would you mind so much? I could bike out to the farm so you don't have to fetch me."

"I'll come for you." They would have more time together that way. "I want to show you something. Then I'll bring you back into town."

Annalise wrote a note on a pad of yellow paper. "I'm sorry to be inattentive. I can't get my mind off Leah."

"Tomorrow is soon enough." Rufus glanced over his shoulder and saw that Mrs. Weichert was consumed with her own stack of papers. He stepped over to Annalise for a quick kiss. It deepened unexpectedly. He did not want to leave her. But if they were going to spend their lives together he had to recognize her independence for the blessing that it was.

She smiled shyly. "I didn't deserve that after turning down your delicious offer."

He dipped his head. "Tomorrow."

"I do not think it is a good idea." Elijah pressed his palms flat on the coffee shop table.

"I would be careful." Ruth countered by calmly sipping her tea.

"You already don't trust Alan. He makes you uncomfortable." With the heels of his hands on the tabletop, Elijah thumped his fingers. "Why would you want to try to attract his attention?"

Ruth looked a way for a few seconds then met Elijah's gaze. "Because I think he knows something. Or did something. And what if what I suspect is true and I did nothing?"

"The *English* have their sheriff for these things," Elijah said. "Shouldn't you report Alan?"

"And say what? That he has a suspicious strap on his water bottle?"

"You found it in the field where the fire was."

"That doesn't prove anything. Alan could say I was the one who put it there."

"Why would you have his strap?"

"The reason is not the point. Or he could say it was Bryan's strap and that Bryan is trying to frame him."

"The *English* have a strange concept of friendship." Elijah picked up his coffee at last. "And what if Alan is right about Bryan?"

"Do you mean that?" Ruth could believe that Elijah might be jealous of her friendship with Bryan, but casting accusations at Bryan was going too far.

"Bryan and Alan have been friends a long time. You've chosen to trust one and distrust the other. What if things are not what they seem?"

"If you spent any time with the two of them, you would see the difference for yourself." Ruth pushed her tea away.

Elijah reached across the table and grabbed her hand. "I'm on your side. I just want you to be safe."

Bryan was consistently calm and carried a ready smile everywhere he went. Alan was the unpredictable one, congenial one moment and elusive the next.

"No. I'm not wrong. I'm not the naive Amish girl who left the valley three years ago."

"But your *English* friends are all women," Elijah pointed out.

"I attend a large university. They have workshops about being safe." Ruth withdrew her hand from Elijah's grasp. "I have to get Alan to talk to me, and to do that I have to be friendly."

"Then let me go with you."

She shook her head. "If he suspected anything, he would be gone before he would say anything."

"I'll stay out of sight." Elijah leaned forward, elbows on the table. "I can't just turn my head and let you arrange something that might be risky. You mean too much to me."

Ruth wanted to bend across the table and touch her forehead to his, to feel his breath on her face. Instead she glanced nervously around the shop and pressed her spine against the back of her chair. "It has to be somewhere private enough to talk."

"It has to be somewhere public enough to be safe," he said. "I don't have to be able to hear what he says, but I want to be able to see you."

At last she nodded. "When I figure something out, I'll text you."

"I'll keep my phone on."

Annie tossed her mail on the dining room table and went immediately upstairs. Once again she had let her prayer *kapp* slide off her head, and this time it had landed in a puddle. Chronically seeming to need a spare one, she wanted to rinse it out and lay it to dry immediately.

From the bathroom sink at the top of the stairs, she heard the back door open and cocked her head to try to discern whose footsteps would pad through the house. Ruth moved in quiet, subtle ways, but Leah was a master of stealth. Annie laid her *kapp* flat on a towel to dry, hoping it would hold its shape. She moved into the hall.

When she heard the kitten meow, Annie knew Leah had come home. She went down the stairs immediately.

Leah stood at the table with an envelope in her hands. "Why is Aaron writing to you?"

Annie's heart pounded. "I didn't realize he had."

"He hasn't even written to me in weeks." Leah's face flushed as her pitch rose.

Annie approached Leah carefully. The girl clutched the envelope, a fist on each end, showing a neat, blockish handwriting.

"I trusted you!" Leah sliced the air with the envelope.

"And I don't want to disappoint your trust." Annie put a hand on Leah's shoulder. "I was not expecting a letter from your friend."

"I don't understand. How would he even know you?"

"He doesn't. I wrote to someone else."

"You wrote to someone about me? Who?"

"Matthew Beiler. He's Rufus's brother."

"Have you ever met him?" Leah turned the envelope over to look at the back.

"No. But when I first heard your story, I wanted to see if I could help. I wrote to Matthew to see if he knew your friend."

"I never asked you to do that. I hardly know Matthew Beiler." Annie watched Leah crumple one end of the envelope

"I didn't mean to complicate your situation."

"I didn't ask you for any of this. All I wanted was help to get to Pennsylvania."

"I know." Annie held out one hand. "May I have the letter?"

"Are you going to open it?"

Annie gently took the letter. "I don't know what it might say, Leah." Without any idea why Matthew had not simply answered her letter himself, or why Aaron would take it upon himself to write to her, Annie was reluctant to read the letter in Leah's presence.

"If he tells you why he stopped writing to me, when he didn't tell me, I don't know what I'll do."

All the more reason Annie did not want to open the letter. "Before we talk about that," she said, "I want to tell you about something."

"I need to know what that letter says!"

"I'm not trying to hide anything from you."

"Then open it."

"Leah," Annie said, "I made a call today. The clinic here in Westcliffe has a counselor who comes on Fridays. I thought maybe it would help if you talked to her."

"An *English* counselor? I didn't ask you to do that, either."

"I know."

"I just want to know what is in that letter."

"So do I. I think we should open it together with the counselor."

Leah sank into a chair. "What if I don't want to?"

"The letter is addressed to me."

"But obviously it's about me."

Annie held her gaze steady. "Leah, we've worked hard to trust each other. Let's trust each other with this."

Leah pounded the table. "I want to see the letter with my own eyes."

Annie nodded. "With the counselor."

Leah rolled her eyes. "What time?"

Thirty-Eight

June 1892

Belle stuck a fork in the sizzling slice of ham, which her father expected for breakfast every morning, and turned it.

"Daddy, your breakfast is ready." She snatched the toast off the stovetop metal frame and slathered butter on it. "Daddy?"

Belle stilled her movements to listen for footsteps on the stairs. She glanced at the clock. It was early, but her father had risen with the dawn all her life. He would come down the stairs looking for his breakfast any moment. Whether or not they disagreed about John Twigg, her father expected his meals. She held the skillet above a plate and dumped the meat and then set the toast beside it. The coffee needed a couple of minutes to finish percolating.

Leon Mooney had not yet appeared by the time his breakfast was ready and laid out in tidy fashion on a green-checkered cloth on the kitchen table. Belle wiped her hands on her apron and paced down the hall that ran through the house.

"Daddy? Breakfast!"

"Wrap it up," the gruff reply came. "I'll take it with me."

"It's early. You have plenty of time to eat before going out to the ranch."

"I'll lose the trail."

Belle's stomach clenched. "What trail?" With fists lifting her skirt, Belle took the stairs like a naughty child.

"Word is Old Man Twigg moved over the state line into Missouri. Jimmy is with him. I'm fixin' to fetch them both back to Baxter County, dead or alive."

Belle stood in the doorway of her father's room. Sitting on the bed, he looked down the barrel of his Winchester. Despite the heat of summer, he wore a jacket with pockets bulging with ammunition.

"Daddy, have you lost your mind?" Belle charged into the room and gripped the barrel of the weapon.

He looked straight into her eyes. "No. You lost yours when you fell for the lies John Twigg offered you."

Belle tugged on the rifle. "That's not the way it was, and you know it."

He easily pulled the gun out of her grasp. "Don't stand there and defend his kin. You know they had a hand in shootin' the sheriff."

"Jesse Roper did that."

"And his granddaddy helped him shoot his way past the posse. I may not be able to find Roper, but I can catch Old Man Twigg and Jimmy. They've run scared, but they are not going to get off scot-free if I have anything to say about it."

"Does Deputy Combs know you are doing this?" Belle moved to stand in the doorway, even though she knew she could not physically restrain her father.

"It's none of his business." He stood up and shoved more bullets into his trouser pockets. "Missouri is not his jurisdiction."

"Daddy, please don't do this."

"The mare just got new shoes. I'll take her. I know at least three men who will ride with me if I ask them to."

"Please don't ask them to. You're going to get yourselves killed."

He slapped his hat on his head and gripped his rifle in one fist. "Now how would that be justice, child? Move."

Woody Woodley slept later and later. Maura kept her head cocked for the sound of his steps, though she doubted he would be up and moving for at least half an hour.

Woody had been seventeen years older than his wife. No one expected that he might be the one to wander through the rooms the couple had shared looking half-lost. His wife's sudden and brief illness stunned everyone in Gassville, and almost overnight Woody went from an aging but vibrant man to an elderly gentleman to whom everyone offered deference. He sold his ranch acreage to Leon Mooney. Occasionally he made rounds as a hired hand with another rancher to check on a herd, but for the most part he was content to nap and read the newspaper or one of the books Maura brought home from the small library in Mountain Home.

Maura sat alone at the unadorned kitchen table with a second cup of coffee and an open Bible. The verse her heart focused on that morning, Psalm 34:14, was simple, straightforward. "Depart from evil, and do good; seek peace, and pursue it."

The Bible spoke so simply and beautifully. The people of Gassville could fill two churches, and everyone would nod assent to these words. Why, then, could they not live at peace with each other?

The back door opened and Walter sauntered in. He inspected the empty griddle. "I don't smell any food."

"I haven't started yet."

"Uncle Woody's not up?"

"I like to make his breakfast fresh when he's ready."

"Got any blueberries? Mama just made plain griddle cakes."

"You mean your mama fed you and you're still coming here looking for breakfast?"

"That was an hour ago."

"It's time you learned to make your own pancakes."

"Women's work."

"Well, not this woman, not this time." Maura picked up her coffee cup, now nearly empty. "Pour me some coffee."

"If I do, will you make me some blueberry pancakes?"

Maura eyed him. "You might just have to take your chances on that bargain."

Walter lifted the coffeepot from the stove.

The back door flung open again, and Belle burst through. Maura nearly turned the table over getting to her feet.

"Belle! What in the—"

"Daddy's gone crazy. Just plumb crazy. I can't stop him."

Maura's heart pounded. "Stop him from what?"

"He wants to chase Old Man Twigg over the state line." Belle gasped for breath. "Dead or alive, Daddy said. He's going take other men with him if they'll go."

"What's so crazy about that?" Walter put the coffee back on the stove. "I'll go with him."

Maura flashed disapproval. "Walter, I think it would be best if you held your tongue."

Walter pulled out a chair, dropped into it, and crossed his arms to sulk.

"He's serious," Belle said. "Maura, I take back everything I said yesterday. Every word. You're the only person I can depend on. I don't think I have a friend left in this whole town."

"You have me." Maura stepped across the small kitchen and wrapped her arms around Belle. "You always have me."

"You have to help me." Belle sobbed into Maura's shoulder.

"Of course I'll help you. This madness has to stop." Maura expelled heavy breath. "I'll find Joseph. He's been riding with the men looking for Roper. He'll know where their sentiments lie."

Belle trembled. Maura nudged her toward a chair.

"You stay here," Maura said. "Walter, pour Belle some coffee. When my daddy gets up, you tell him. . .tell him I might be gone for a while."

Outside the house, Maura felt the tremble rise within her.

Joseph left his bedroll open.

"The horses are rested." Stephen pushed his spare shirt into a saddlebag. "There is nothing to keep us from going."

"Except Joseph," Zeke said. "He is not ready."

Joseph swirled the last of his coffee in a tin cup and reached for the pot hanging over the morning fire.

"Joseph," Zeke said, "if you do not come with us now, you will only have more to explain later."

"Maybe I do not have anything to explain." Joseph burned his tongue on the coffee. Zeke would not be happy with his answer.

"The bishop. Your parents. My sister. Your little brother." Zeke ticked off several more names on his fingers. "Are you planning to simply disappear from their lives?"

"Of course not." In time, Hannah would recover and marry someone more deserving of her affections, but Little Jake was a sensitive boy.

"The bishop, Joseph. Are you in submission?" Zeke poured water on the fire and kicked dirt onto the remaining embers.

"Must you ask?"

"You ask Stephen and me to leave you here. Alone. Where is the community that will guard your faith?"

"I am not saying I will never go home. Just not now." Joseph swallowed more coffee.

"This is about Miss Woodley." Stephen hung his tin utensils from a saddle strap. "You have let her cause you to stray."

Joseph's back straightened involuntarily. "If I have strayed at all, Miss Woodley is not the cause. Do not look for someone to blame where there is no one." He was loath to leave without expressing himself to Maura Woodley and awaiting her response, but no, she had not caused him to stray. He bore his own responsibility. She might yet meet the hope in his heart with her own dream of peace.

A stir in the livery yard drew all three black-suited men around to the front of the stables, Joseph first, followed by Zeke, and then Stephen with the horses. Maura Woodley sat on her restless dark mount without pulling the cart. Joseph rushed to hold its bridle.

"You must come, Joseph," she said. "Belle's father is going to get himself killed if somebody doesn't stop him. He's going over the state line after Old Man Twigg."

"What can I do?" Joseph held the horse still and looked into Maura's fiery brown eyes.

"Joseph!" Zeke's tone was as sharp as Joseph had ever heard it. "Stay out of this *English* business. It is nothing to do with you. Get your bedding and we'll go."

"You're leaving?" Maura's brow creased, and her disappointment stabbed him. "You didn't say anything."

"Where is Leon now?" Joseph focused on Maura's need rather than Zeke's indignation.

Maura waved a hand. "Gathering his forces."

Zeke swung up onto his horse. Stephen settled himself in his saddle then handed Joseph the lead to the third horse.

Galloping horses found their rhythm in the street.

"It's Leon," Maura said.

"And three others." Joseph named Leon's co-conspirators.

"Joseph." Zeke's voice carried questions, warnings, and disappointment.

"Please, Joseph," came Maura's soft plea. "They need your message of peace."

Joseph slapped the rump of Zeke's stallion. "You go without me."

On his own horse now, Joseph rode beside Maura, coughing in the swirling dust of the vengeful riders.

Thirty-Nine

"How can I drive if I don't know where I'm going?" Annie took the reins from Rufus on Thursday morning.

"Just go as if you were going to my family's house for supper. And then keep going. I'll tell you the turns."

Knowing she had at least five miles of familiar road, Annie settled in.

"Leah agreed to see a counselor," she said.

"I'm surprised," Rufus said. "But it's probably a good idea."

"And...I wrote to your brother Matthew about the young man Leah says she's in love with."

"Matthew? What were you hoping for?"

"Not what I got." Annie glanced at Rufus out of the side of her eye. "I thought it might help to be sure if she was reading the relationship accurately."

"And?" Rufus nudged his hat off his forehead.

"I'm not sure. Matthew didn't write me back. Leah's young man did."

"Seems like that would be reliable information. Why are you uncertain?"

"Leah found the letter before I could open it. So now we're

going to open it during her counseling session tomorrow."

"I see."

They listened to the horse clop.

Annie reminded herself to hold the reins firmly but lightly. "You think I overstepped, don't you?"

Rufus reached over and covered one of her hands with his. "I have not even spoken to Leah Deitwaller. You are the one who has taken time to try to know her. I am not sure it's up to me to say you overstepped."

She exhaled relief. "Thank you, Rufus. Ever since I was baptized, I feel so much pressure to make the right decisions."

"Have you done anything you know is against *Ordnung*?"

"No, of course not."

"Then follow your heart."

"Do you still think Leah could have started that first fire?"

"Did I sow seeds of doubt in you when I suggested it was at least possible?"

Annie shrugged. "Maybe. I've seen for myself how fast she can move and how well she stays hidden. When I caught a glimpse of her at the training burn, I wondered if she had been out to the highway."

"Have you spoken to the *English* authorities?"

"No. I don't have proof of anything. I don't even have good reason to suspect."

"Was she in Joel's field last week?"

"I didn't see her. But I was busy watching the fire."

"We all were."

"Never mind." Annie shook off the grim thought. "I just thought you should know what's been going on. Maybe you can pray for Leah and me while we open the letter tomorrow."

"Thank you for asking me to. And I'll ask you to pray for Joel."

"So he got off this morning to the new job?"

Rufus drew in a deep breath. "He was eager to go. *Mamm* was not so enthusiastic."

"My heart tells me Joel is going to be all right." Annie dared to take her eyes off the road for a quick glance at Rufus. "Are you sure you don't want to tell me where we are going?"

Rufus smiled. "Just a few more minutes."

He gave directions one turn at a time until Annie took the buggy onto a narrow stretch that was hardly more than a horse path. When even the path petered out, Rufus asked Annie to take the buggy across open meadow.

"Stop here," Rufus said finally.

Annie pulled on the reins, and Dolly slowed to a stop. "Where are we?"

Rufus scooted closer to her on the bench and put an arm around her shoulders. With the other he pointed.

"On that little ridge is where I picture the house—facing the mountains, of course. My workshop would be in back, but not so far from the house that I could not hear you call."

Annie sucked in a gale of air. "This is your land?"

He nodded.

Her eyes widened. The Sangre de Cristos beamed down from their snowcaps. The meadow, a mystery only a moment ago, sprang to life around her. She breathed in the scent of horses to come and listened to the cackling hens she would feed with their children.

He was taking such care to arrange the perfect moment.

"We'd need a barn, of course," he said. "We'll want to keep a cow and chickens."

Annie felt a grin creeping up from her toes. This would be a proposal story they could someday tell their grandchildren.

Ruth systematically—but slowly—pushed a cart up and down every aisle in the grocery store and then started again.

She knew Alan was working. He was not up front bagging, though, so he must be in the storeroom, and it was only a matter of time before he would emerge. Most of the stocking happened in the early hours while Westcliffe's population still slumbered in confidence they could buy fifty kinds of breakfast cereal or seven brands of dog food later in the day. But Ruth had been in the store at the start of the business day enough to know that some tasks remained for stockers to finish up even after carts roamed the aisles.

And Alan was one of those stockers.

Ruth put a box of tissues in her cart and moved to the frozen foods aisle to ponder the vegetables. Eventually she chose a bag of cauliflower and proceeded to the dairy aisle.

Alan was maneuvering a pallet heaped with yogurts to one side of the aisle.

"Hello, Alan." Ruth greeted him with warm eyes.

"Hi, Ruth." Alan leaned one elbow on a stack of boxes and put one hand in the pocket of his blue store apron. "I was afraid you wouldn't speak to me again. You didn't seem pleased to see me the other day."

She waved a hand. "I know you meant well."

Alan pulled a box cutter out of the apron and sliced into a carton of yogurts. "I guess we're all a little jittery about the fires."

"Yes, that's it." She reached for a container of sour cream from beside Alan's pallet. "Are you working all day?"

"I'm off around one o'clock."

"That's nice. You can still enjoy the afternoon." Ruth reached in the other direction and picked up a tub of cottage cheese. "I'm off at two today myself, but I think I'll go to the library. It would be nice to read something other than a textbook."

"I know what you mean." Alan swiftly stacked single-serving yogurt containers on the shelf and sliced open another box. "It's a little strange to be out of school and actually have a choice about what to read."

"That's what I mean!" Ruth chewed one corner of her mouth, mentally repeating cautions to remain casual. "Why don't you meet me at the library? I know it's small, but we might find something to recommend to each other."

Alan eyed her and transferred another batch of yogurt to the shelf. "Yeah. That's a good idea. I'll be there."

Her face beamed, and Rufus allowed himself a moment to bask in it. Perhaps her joy would give him the courage to hang on to the land and the future he imagined would come to be. Their children would learn to gather eggs without disturbing the hens, and Rufus would till Annalise a vegetable garden. He would come in from the workshop at lunchtime and ask how her morning had gone. For decades, they would take their morning coffee out to the front porch and stare at the Sangre de Cristos as they murmured prayers for the day.

"It's perfect, Rufus." Annalise sighed and leaned her head against his shoulder.

He opened his palm to her, and she laid her hand in it. Small, slender, feminine.

"You never even gave a hint you were buying land," Annalise said.

"I did it the summer before you came. I had some savings, and the price was right."

He knew the words she wanted to hear, and he ached to speak them.

The sound of a car engine wedged into his reverie.

Annalise turned her head, puzzled. "Who would that be?"

Rufus's suspicion sank his stomach. The car rumbled toward them and slowed to a stop.

"Rufus." Annalise sat up straight. "The side of that car has a Realtor's logo on it."

"Yes, I see."

The car stopped, and a man emerged from the driver's door while a man and a woman got out of the passenger side. The driver raised a hand to wave.

"Do you know them?" Annalise asked.

"I know Larry," Rufus said. "The driver."

"A Realtor."

"Yes."

The stone in Rufus's gut hardened another layer.

"But this is your land," Annalise said. "You just told me you bought it more than two years ago."

"Hello, Rufus," Larry called. "I didn't know you'd be out here."

If Rufus had known Larry would be coming, he certainly would not have brought Annalise out here.

"I've got some people interested in your land." Hands in his pockets, Larry moved toward the buggy. "The people from Denver. I told you about them."

"Yes, I remember."

Larry was close enough now that an introduction was mandatory.

"This is Annalise Friesen," Rufus said. *My fiancée,* he wanted to say. But he had not gotten that far when he had his opportunity.

"Glad to meet you." Larry extended a cheerful hand, which Annalise accepted. "Rufus has a great piece of land here."

"Yes, it's beautiful."

Rufus saw how hard she was working to cloak her bewilderment in hospitality. He swallowed and descended from the bench.

"Did I misunderstand you when we last spoke?" Rufus said.

"Oh, no, I realize you haven't made a decision." Larry gestured to the couple, who stood and gazed across the meadow. "And neither have they. But they came all the way from Denver. It seemed like a serendipitous opportunity to let them see what they could get if they decided to buy out this way."

"I see." Rufus glanced up at Annalise, who had shifted in the bench to look at the visiting couple.

Husband and wife stood with their arms linked now, pointing and gesturing.

And smiling.

Rufus stifled the urge to exhale his disappointment.

Forty

June 1892

"They can't have gotten too far." Maura trotted her horse beside Joseph's as they left the livery and headed down Main Street.

"It might be wise to pause long enough for you to draw me a map of how they might cross the state line," Joseph said.

"Why? I'll be with you." Eyes forward, Maura braced for his refusal.

"This could be dangerous, Maura."

"I asked for your help, Joseph. I did not ask you to bear the entire load."

"And if we don't find them in time? Or Leon won't listen to reason?"

"Then at least we will have tried. I want to give that much to Belle." Maura hastened the pace of her horse. "Leon has to see that the price of his choice may be his daughter."

"Right now he does not see past his anger."

"I was on the Twigg land in Missouri once, perhaps ten or twelve years ago. My parents used to be quite friendly with Old Man Twigg."

"Then I hope God has blessed you with a good memory."

"We will have no trouble asking where their property is once we start to follow the north fork of the river."

Maura kneed her horse and galloped ahead of Joseph before he could suggest again that she remain behind.

"We're close." Joseph reined in his horse and pointed to the hoofprints in the soggy ground. "Four horses, all well shoed. And not too long ago."

The winding, marshy, sometimes disappearing shoreline had made tracking the vigilantes difficult. More than once Joseph had been tempted to admit to Maura he had lost the trail. Thick woods on both sides of the White River's north fork could disguise a host of men.

Maura had not flagged, even at the hottest part of the day. Three times Joseph passed his water jug to her and insisted she drink deeply. Twice they stopped to refill the container from natural springs that began to appear with frequency. Once, he stopped to gather pine nuts and wild berries, but she wanted none of it. She cared nothing for food as long as Leon Mooney remained beyond their sight.

Finally, Joseph spied him through the trees. Joseph slid off his horse and handed the reins to Maura.

"What are you going to do?" Maura whispered.

"I'm not sure. I don't want startle him into shooting."

"Be careful!"

Joseph took a deep breath and guarded his steps through the woods. He made enough noise to be noticed but not enough to sound threatening. Mooney was alone for the moment, though the others could not be far off. Joseph continued forward, even as he realized Leon was peering into the woods, suspicious. Joseph held his empty hands up to view as he approached a man whose rifle was within reach.

"What are you doing here?" Mooney barked.

"I came to find you." Joseph paced ahead, controlled, patient. "Belle is concerned."

"Belle is blind to the truth." Mooney made no move for his gun.

"Why don't you tell me what you have in mind?" Joseph lowered himself to the ground beside Leon.

"Justice, that's all." Leon reached into a leather bag and pulled out a strip of beef jerky.

Joseph's stomach grumbled. "Our Lord asks us to forgive, Mr. Mooney."

Leon grunted. "I prefer to think I am an instrument of divine justice."

"How can any of us be sure of that?" Joseph kept his voice low.

"An eye for an eye. A Twigg for a Byler. That's the way I see it."

Joseph filled his lungs, exhaled slowly, and swallowed. "And if the response is a Mooney for a Twigg? Will that be justice? Will that bring peace?"

Mooney scoffed. "Peace. We won't have peace in Gassville as long as Old Man Twigg lives."

Joseph gestured up the river. "But he moved out of town. Is that not a sign that he is ready for peace?"

"It's a sign that he's scared, that's all. And he should be." Now Mooney picked up his rifle and tossed it from one hand to the other.

Joseph straightened his hat with both hands as he looked over his shoulder at the sound behind him. The three Gassville citizens who had followed Mooney across the state line stood with a hearty catch of crawfish.

"Looks like we'll have two more for supper," Mooney said. "You can come out, Maura. I know you're there."

Maura picked at the boiled crawfish served to her in a tin plate. It was her first food all day, and she knew she ought to try to eat it if for no other reason than to accept Leon Mooney's gruff hospitality, but the vice in her stomach made her hesitant to swallow anything.

Joseph ate slowly, she observed, but he consumed both fish and bread. He lifted his water jug and leaned toward her. "Come with me to get fresh water."

Maura set her plate aside as casually as she could manage and followed Joseph deeper into the woods. He knelt at a gurgling spring and dipped the jar's open mouth.

"These springs are all over," he said. "Mooney has his eye on one he thinks the Twiggs will use in the morning."

"How can he be sure?" Maura glanced around the woods as she knelt next to Joseph.

"It's farther upriver, at the edge of Twigg's land. They've already been up there and seen where they water the horses."

"I'm sorry, Joseph." Maura pinched her eyes between thumb and fingers. "I dragged you up here for nothing."

"You have a heart for peace, Maura. That's all you want."

"I understand that disputes will happen." Maura sank onto a boulder. "I can even accept war for a righteous cause. But this? I do not understand this burning vengeance."

Her pulse coursed harder when he took her hand in both of his, but she did not withdraw it. She looked into his violet-blue eyes, shimmering in the moonlight, as he gently stroked her palm.

"The question now," Joseph said, "is if you would like to stay the night or leave."

Maura glanced back at the four men eating fish around a dying fire. "What is it like where you live?"

He shrugged. "Not so different from here. Rivers. Woods. The handiwork of God."

"I mean your people," she said. "Your family, your church." *Hannah,* she wanted to say.

"We are people of submission." He held her hand still now. "The good of the family and the community are our greatest concern."

"I always thought Gassville was my community. But it's just a place."

He squeezed her hand. "We face our own decision now. Shall we go or stay?"

Pressure squeezed her chest as he released her hand. Joseph Beiler was like no other man she had known.

"Have we tried everything?" she said. "Is there no hope?"

"I like to believe there is always hope," Joseph said, "but we submit to God's sovereign will, even in this."

Joseph put the stopper in his jug and stood.

"If we cannot avert what Leon Mooney has fixed in his heart," Maura said, "we may be of aid when someone is hurt."

Joseph nodded. "We will stay, then. I only wish I had a bedroll to offer you."

"I will not sleep a wink anyway." Maura pointed to a wide tree. "If you talk to me, perhaps I will not say something foolish to Leon Mooney."

"Then I will be happy to talk to you."

Joseph took the blankets from under their saddles and spread them on the ground at the base of the tree Maura selected. They settled in shoulder to shoulder. Mooney and his men grew quiet, though none slept as far as Maura could see.

"Joseph," Maura said quietly, "will you be in a great deal of trouble for not going home with Zeke?"

He nodded slowly. "Some. My parents will be disappointed, and the bishop will give me a stern speech when I see him."

"And Hannah?" Maura could hardly believe the question escaped her lips.

"Hannah." Joseph took Maura's hand again. "Hannah is a sensible choice. She is eager to marry and would be eager to please her husband. Everyone believed the bishop selected me for this journey because I am sensible as well. But it turns out I am not so sensible after all."

"Because. . ."

"Because of you, Miss Woodley. When I left I was not sure Hannah Berkey was God's will for me. Now I am certain she is not."

Maura's breath caught as she stared into the darkness. "What are you saying, Joseph?"

"You have raised many questions in my heart."

Leon Mooney moved in stealth toward them. Maura stared up at him. Joseph stood.

"I want you two to promise me you will stay out of the way," Mooney said. "There's no reason to see you hurt."

"Why does anyone have to be hurt?" Maura said. "Let's go home, Leon. Home to Belle. She must be frantic with worry."

"She won't have to worry much longer. It will all be settled at daybreak."

Under cover of darkness Leon Mooney moved his entourage upriver.

Before daybreak, four men found protection behind trees at the base of a hill and carefully calculated their clearest shots.

Joseph whispered to Maura that they should stay back. But she saddled her horse and followed Mooney, and Joseph did not want to let her out of his sight.

As a pink dawn broke over the north fork of the White River, Old Man Twigg and his son Jimmy led their horses down the hill to the spring, just as Mooney had anticipated they would.

Joseph opened his arms and enfolded Maura when the rapid spray of bullets began. She put her hands over her ears and her face against his chest. Joseph watched everything.

Old Man Twigg never even had a chance to lift the rifle he carried. He fell dead with the first firing. Joseph pushed Maura to the ground and covered her as Jimmy fired back, although Joseph doubted he could see any target. In only a few more seconds, Jimmy dropped with wounds to his leg and shoulder.

Maura pushed Joseph off and sat up, weeping.

Forty-One

Rufus took the reins. Annalise offered no resistance. He clicked his tongue, and Dolly answered with forward movement directly across the meadow. Rather than turning onto the road that would take them back to the highway, though, Rufus crossed into the old mining property and halted the horse once again on open land.

"I want you to know this is not how I planned the morning." He let go of the reins and turned on the bench to face Annalise.

"What happened back there, Rufus?" Annalise's gray eyes were wide, and the day's light swam through them.

"When I was working in Cañon City," he said, "I found Larry's office. I wanted to ask some questions."

"About selling your land?"

"Possibly. I would use the money to help *Daed*."

"So why did you bring me here?" Annalise's voice dimmed.

"Because I wasn't sure. About the land. I'm sure about you, Annalise. I wanted to see you there on the land at least once. I wanted it to be the place where we choose our future together even if we do not live there."

"Rufus Beiler, are you proposing marriage?" Annalise's face cracked in a grin.

"I seem not to be very good at it—which should assure you that I have no experience with proposals."

She laughed, and Rufus let himself breathe.

"So do it," she said. "We can at least get that settled. Then we'll face the rest."

"You walked away from a fortune. You changed your whole life. I always thought I would offer a good start to married life."

"God provides."

"What if God provides by bringing a buyer for land I had not even decided to sell?"

"We'll figure it out, Rufus." She reached for his hand. "Ask me and kiss me and then we'll talk about all this."

Rufus swallowed and held both her hands now. "Annalise Friesen, I believe God wants me to be your husband. Would you have me?"

"Yes!"

The burst of joy rippled through their intertwined fingers. Rufus leaned toward Annalise's eager face and put one hand behind her neck, his fingers in the hollow of her hairline. On the first day he saw her straw-colored hair hanging loose around her lovely face, he had found her beautiful—even if she was *English*. She was no longer *English*, and the beauty of her spirit far outshone golden sun on her hair. His lips met hers, and something startling passed between them. They had known for months they wanted to be husband and wife, but this moment of deciding, of choosing, of accepting sent a jolt of electricity through their lingering kiss. Annalise put her arms around him and returned every searching softness with her own.

They separated, breathless.

"I will arrange to have the banns read," Rufus said.

"I'm not supposed to tell anyone before that, am I?"

"Traditionally, no."

"I don't know if I can keep this secret!"

"It won't be long now."

"I hope not. I very much want to marry you." Annalise stroked his arm.

"Many things are uncertain still. My land—*our* land. I always imagined we would stay with my parents over the winter and build next spring."

"We still could."

"So you want me to keep the property?"

Annalise shook her head. "I want you to do what you feel is best for us, for our family."

Our family.

She already belonged with the Beilers.

"I own my house free and clear, you know." Annie laced her fingers through his again.

Rufus stilled her moving fingers. "I would not be comfortable living in town. It is not apart."

"Of course not." Annalise was quick to speak. "I didn't mean that. I mean that the value of my house will be *ours* now. We can decide how to use it."

"You would sell your house?"

"Or rent it out for income. If I'm not going to be living there, it shouldn't sit empty."

"I know you used to have a great deal of money in your *English* life. You have already sacrificed so much."

"I have sacrificed nothing but greed and ambition," she said.

"I want you to feel secure and cared for."

"Rufus Beiler, we're going to spend our lives together. Nothing makes me feel more secure than that."

He kissed her again.

"God provides," she whispered, her breath on his neck.

Ruth tugged on the library door. By now Elijah would be seated in a reading cubicle on the other side of the main aisle. The library was a narrow space between two shops on Main Street. The number of books on the shelves at any given time was limited by the space, but Ruth had always found the two part-time librarians accommodating and helpful in placing holds on other books in the wider library system. Anything Ruth had ever requested arrived within four days.

Elijah was wearing *English* jeans and a blue work shirt he had found in the thrift store a couple of blocks down. Ruth caught a glimpse of his back—his Amish hat gone as well—and calculated that an interest in biographies would keep her within his sight. All he had to do was glance up or quietly scoot back his chair.

Ruth glanced around, relieved that Alan had not arrived first, and ambled down the main aisle, running a finger along the shelves and glancing at titles.

A moment later, the front door creaked and Alan entered. Ruth flashed him a welcoming smile then pulled a biography of Thomas Jefferson off the shelf and began to flip through it as her peripheral vision tracked Alan's movement toward her.

"Biographies, eh?"

Alan stood next to her now.

Ruth casually turned another page. "When I left Westcliffe, I had to get a GED before I could enroll at the university. I had a lot to catch up on when it came to American history."

Alan took a book from the shelf. "Alexander Hamilton. Now he was an interesting character. Some people say the whole national debt traces back to his idea to borrow private money to pay for the Revolutionary War debt."

Ruth chuckled softly. "I hope we're not still paying for the Revolutionary War."

"Your people don't believe in wars, do they?"

"Well, we believe they happen. We don't participate. It goes against our peacekeeping ways."

"Do you like to read about science?" Alan pointed with a thumb to the other side of the aisle.

"Nursing is science." Ruth closed the Jefferson book and slid it back into its place. "I suppose fire is a science category all its own."

"It definitely is." Alan pulled a book from the shelf. "No one ever seems to check this one out. I come to look at it, and it's always here."

Ruth looked over his shoulder at the photos of burning fires and shuddered. "Why don't you check it out and read it more leisurely?"

"I can't have it around the apartment. Bryan would never let me hear the end of how he got a better grade than I did when we studied origins of fire in school."

"Considering that you haven't been in Westcliffe all that long," she said, "it seems like you have seen quite a few fires already."

"I missed the last one." Alan replaced the book on the shelf. "I was at the store stacking apples and peaches."

"That's right."

"Bryan was there, though."

She nodded. "We discovered the smoke together."

"You know, it's not that hard to lay a fuse so the fire won't start right away."

Through the stacks, Ruth saw Elijah stand. She caught his brown eyes and looked away.

"You must learn all that stuff in school," she said to Alan.

"And Bryan was at the top of the class. He was a whiz with chemical reactions and retardants and all that jazz."

Ruth took a random book off the shelf. "You know him better than I do."

Alan touched her elbow then, and Ruth heard the step Elijah took. She looked up to meet Alan's gaze.

"Sometimes insiders get involved with fires." He leaned toward her. "Bryan could always calculate how much time would elapse before a certain kind of fire would explode. Exactly."

The librarian stepped into the aisle, stared at them, and put a finger to her lips. Elijah was the only other patron in the building, but the librarian could not know that Ruth wanted him to hear every word.

Ruth lowered her voice. "You're not saying Bryan had anything to do with the fires, are you?"

Alan's eyes danced, which startled Ruth. Elijah moved on the other side of the shelf.

"I think I'll stick to biographies." Ruth again began to run her finger along the spines on the biography shelves.

Alan checked the time on his cell phone. "I have to go."

Where? Ruth wondered. But she did not ask.

Alan gave a look of courteous amusement. "I hope I'll run into you again." He sauntered toward the door.

Elijah came around the stacks. "Satisfied?"

Ruth pulled the fire science book off the shelf again and ran a finger down the table of contents page. "He's been filling in the gaps."

"He wasn't trying to hide it."

She looked up and met Elijah's eyes. "It's a dare."

"I need to ask you some questions, Leah." Jerusha sat in an armchair with a notepad in her lap on Friday afternoon. "We can ask Annie to leave the room if you like."

"She can stay."

Leah looked pale to Annie. Two days of wondering about the contents of the letter had taken their toll. But at least Leah had cleaned up and was on time.

"Have you ever felt like hurting yourself or someone else?" Jerusha asked.

"Sometimes I feel like I just want to blow something up." Leah pressed her palms together. "But anyone would feel that way if they were going through what I'm going through."

"So you might want to hurt some *thing*, but not yourself or another person."

"Right."

Jerusha watched Leah. "If you felt like hurting yourself, would you tell someone?"

Leah glanced at Annie. "I guess I could tell Annalise. But I don't want to hurt myself. I just want to go to Pennsylvania. And I want to know what's in that letter she got."

"I understand. We'll get to that soon." Jerusha picked up the pen that lay on her notepad. "Why don't you tell me in your own words why you think you're here today."

"If I didn't come, Annalise would not let me see the letter."

Annie groaned inwardly and crossed and uncrossed her ankles beneath the hem of her dress.

"Is that the only reason you agreed to come?" Jerusha asked.

Leah tapped her foot steadily for about thirty seconds. "I guess not. I've been behaving strangely, I suppose."

"And why do you think that is?"

Annie calmly raised one hand to pull on a prayer *kapp* string, a habit she had developed at moments when she wanted to pray silently. The letter lay in her lap.

"My parents won't listen to me," Leah said, "and I'm anxious that I'll never get my life back."

"Your Pennsylvania life?" Jerusha wrote a quick notation.

Leah nodded.

"I understand Annie got a letter from someone in Pennsylvania you care deeply about."

Leah kept nodding.

"Perhaps we should talk about what would happen if the letter says something you don't want to hear."

Annie held her breath. This was exactly the reason she wanted Jerusha present when she broke the seal on the envelope.

"Why don't we just find out what it says?" Leah eyed the envelope in Annie's lap. "If it's good news, we don't even have to finish this conversation."

"I only want to help you be prepared either way."

Leah's eye flashed. "You've made up your mind it's bad news. You don't know that."

Jerusha held her calming pose. "No, I don't have any idea what the letter will say. I would want to help you whether or not there was a letter."

"But there *is* a letter." Leah moved her eyes from Jerusha to Annie and back again. "If I answer your questions, do you promise me we'll open the letter?"

Forty-Two

"Why don't you read it to us?" Annie handed the letter to Jerusha after nearly ninety minutes of conversation between Leah and the counselor.

"Is that all right with you, Leah?" Jerusha asked.

The girl nodded.

Annie was relieved that Leah was surprisingly calm now that the moment had arrived. After resisting Jerusha for much of the session, either actively or passively, Leah had made some remarkable and transparent insights about herself. Annie had no doubt that Jerusha would suggest that Leah see her again, but for now, Leah seemed as settled as Annie had ever seen her.

Jerusha pulled at the flap of the envelope, and it gave way easily. Annie knew it would. More than once she had—fleetingly—considered opening that flap for a preview of the letter. But she had given her word to Leah.

"That's his paper!" Leah jumped to her feet. "It's really from him."

The unfolding papers crackled in Jerusha's hands, and she reached for her reading glasses on an end table.

Dear Miss Friesen,

First of all, I wish to extend to you the right hand of fellowship. Brother Matthew Beiler has told me of your baptism and, indeed, how fond his family is of you. My heart warms with yours at your obedience and union with Christ.

I am sure you are surprised to be hearing from me rather than Matthew. I hope you don't mind that he exercised the liberty of sharing your letter with me. Although our farms are some distance apart, he took time to make the drive and seek me out. He felt that you had asked for his opinion on a matter he was not overly familiar with. That being the case, perhaps it was better to provide you with direct, reliable information.

I understand that you have not met Matthew, but I assure you that this approach is quite typical of him. I hope the day comes soon that you and Matthew will be able to meet. He mentioned that his mother's letters suggest that she hopes you will soon be a member of the Beiler family, as well as the congregation.

The most important thing I wish to say to you is that I care for Leah Deitwaller as deeply as any married man I know cares for his wife. I cannot emphasize this point enough.

Jerusha paused, and she and Annie both looked at Leah, who sank back into her chair, smearing tears across her face.

"Are you all right?" Jerusha asked.

Leah gasped a sudden intake of air. "No one believed me because of all my mistakes. But I was telling the truth."

"Do you need some water?" Annie offered her bottle.

Leah shook her head. "Just keep reading, please."

Jerusha looked back at the pages in her hands.

I respect that Leah's parents have the authority to do what they believe is best for her. Her father asked me not to write to Leah again, and I have honored his wishes. Please tell her that my heart has not changed, and I treasure the letters she sends.

Leah and I have both been baptized. I know you understand the seriousness of our commitment, since you have chosen to take the baptismal vows yourself.

I have talked with my parents at great length. After a season of prayer and searching, they have given their blessing to my union with Leah and would welcome her to their home as their daughter even if we are not able to marry immediately. I would be grateful for any assistance you can give to bring Leah to us. I believe our greatest happiness would come from receiving the blessing of Leah's parents as well, and I pray that God will reveal His will in the matter. My daed will write to Mr. Deitwaller, and we will await further word.

My heart aches for Leah and for her happiness. You have been so kind to show an interest in her and search for the truth by writing to Matthew.

Most sincerely,
Aaron Borntreger

Annie stood up and crossed to Leah's chair, kneeling in front of the girl and taking her hands. Leah sobbed.

"I was right! I was right! No one believed me, but I was right!" Leah's chest heaved. "I would never have acted so crazy if someone had believed me."

Annie's throat choked up. She had no words but only gripped Leah's trembling hands.

Jerusha folded the letter and slid it back into the envelope.

"I'll be back here next Friday," the counselor said. "I suggest that we meet again then. I wonder if we might have Leah's parents with us for at least one future session."

Annie squeezed her eyes shut. Jerusha might as well have asked for the mountains to move.

Annie held Leah's hand, which still trembled as she stood at the appointment desk in the clinic and arranged to see Jerusha again. They traversed the blocks through town and to Annie's quiet street with few words. As they made the turn off Main Street, Annie spotted Ruth coming from the other direction. Annie lifted a finger to her lips, and Ruth felt into step with them without a greeting.

Was it only yesterday that Rufus had shown her his vision of their future together? Had it only been a day since they had agreed to marry? Ruth should be the first person to hear the news—and not when the banns were read. Fatigue rolled through Annie as she pushed open the back door and the trio entered a house hushed in the shadows of a fading afternoon.

Leah moved ahead of the other two, walking in her soundless way through the house to her makeshift bedroom in the living room.

"Is she all right?" Ruth whispered.

"It's a long story."

Annie was not sure how much she could share with Ruth. The story was Leah's more than it was hers. Certainly she would not try to recount the afternoon's events while Leah was in the other room. She turned the switch on a propane lamp that sat on the end of the kitchen counter.

"I could make us something to eat," Ruth said quietly.

Annie nodded. "I'd like to freshen up."

"Maybe I'll change first, too."

When she passed through the dining room to the stairs, Annie was surprised to see Leah sitting at the table. Annie stopped so suddenly that Ruth nearly bumped her from behind. Their eyes fixed on Leah. She held a lit match between thumb and forefinger, and the oil lamp was positioned in front of her. Leah stared at the flame as the match burned down, only at the last minute touching it to the waiting oil and watching the mantle burst into brightness.

Annie moistened her lips. "Are you hungry, Leah? Ruth has offered to make some supper."

Leah gazed at the lamp. "I don't think I can eat. It's been a long afternoon."

"We'll save something for you, then. You can have it later."

The kitten grazed past Annie and jumped into Leah's lap.

"I think I'll go out." Leah held the kitten against her cheek and stood up. "I promise not to stay out late."

"All right then." What else could Annie say? "We'll leave a plate in the oven."

Leah left through the back door without speaking again.

Ruth turned to Annie. "Is it my imagination, or was she a little too fascinated with that burning match?"

Annie puffed her cheeks and blew out her breath. "It's not your imagination. She's been so sad, so confused. So angry. So hurt. I have wondered more than once whether she was capable of setting a fire as a way of acting out. I honestly don't know."

Ruth raised both hands to her temples. "You suspect Leah? Of all the fires?"

"*Suspect* is a strong word." Annalise pulled a chair from the dining room table and sat down. "I have nothing to go on except the fact that the fires happened and my extremely nonprofessional assessment of Leah's emotional state."

"I know what you mean." Ruth sat down now, too.

"You've been very patient, Ruth. I appreciate it. I know it's not easy for you to have Leah here."

"That's not what I'm talking about." Ruth pushed the burning lamp toward the middle of the table. "What you just said about the fact of the fires and a person's emotional state—I've been thinking about that, too."

Annalise furrowed her brow. "So you think Leah could really be a suspect."

"I don't know. Maybe. But I'm talking about Alan."

"Bryan's friend?"

Ruth gave in to the shiver that ran through her. "He just seems off. His father came to town one day, and the air between them was as frigid as the North Pole. And he knows a lot about fires."

"There's a big difference between two things happening coincidentally and one causing the other."

"I know." Ruth put her elbows on the table and hung her head in her hands. "We can't go around accusing everybody with emotional issues of criminal action."

"But what if it really is one of them?"

"It can't be both." Ruth raised her head and met Annalise's eyes. "They don't even know each other and have nothing in common."

"We're assuming one person started all the fires," Annalise said. "That may or not be true."

"Alan thinks it could be Bryan." Ruth hated to even speak those words aloud.

Annalise's posture snapped up. "Bryan? Your Bryan?"

"He's not 'my' Bryan. But yes."

"Aren't the two of them friends?"

"They say they are. But they're both pointing fingers at each other."

"Bryan thinks it's Alan?" Annalise asked.

Ruth shrugged. "Not exactly. After the fire in Joel's field, I found something I was sure belonged to Alan. But when Bryan asked him about it, Alan said it wasn't his. It was just a water bottle strap, but Alan made a point to tell me Bryan had one just like it, too."

"Which leaves us nowhere."

"And I don't even have the strap anymore. I gave it to Bryan."

"It sounds like you trust Bryan, and you don't trust Alan."

Ruth pulled pins from her hair and let it hang loose. "That's what my gut tells me. I tried to be friendly with Alan and see if he would talk to me, but he just points out that I don't know Bryan as well as I think I do."

"And now you have doubts?"

Ruth took a moment to think. "No. You know what? I don't."

"So we're back to Alan or Leah."

Ruth stared into the burning lamp. "Or someone we haven't even met."

Forty-Three

June 1892

Joseph hitched his horse in front of the milliner's shop, stroked the slope of the animal's face, and turned to enter the store. Walter was cleaning shelves.

"I'll be glad when school starts again," Walter mumbled. "My daddy doesn't want me to have a moment to myself."

"Being a hard worker is a fine trait." Joseph glanced around. "I wonder if Maura is here."

"You all got back day before yesterday." Walter shuffled toward Joseph and ran a rag across the shelf unconvincingly. "She still won't tell me what happened."

"It is better that way." Joseph and Maura agreed not to fuel Walter's fascination with posses and gunfights. The boy did not need to know that Leon had let Maura try to stanch the blood flow before hefting Jimmy onto a horse and tying him to the saddle for the bumpy ride back to Baxter County and reluctantly surrendering him to the care of Dr. Lindsay.

"Maura," Joseph said. "Is she here?"

Walter gestured with his head. "In the back."

A pair of dark green cloth panels separated the shop from the back room where Maura's Uncle Edwin created women's hats.

Joseph tentatively pushed a hand between the curtains.

"Maura?"

She looked up immediately and laid her pen down on the open accounts book. "What happened?"

Joseph leaned one shoulder against the wall. "Dr. Lindsay took the bullets out of Jimmy's shoulder and leg then patched him up. Deputy Combs made Jimmy promise to leave Baxter County and never show his face here again."

"It's about time the deputy found his spine." Maura puffed her cheek and exhaled. "And did Jimmy agree?"

Joseph nodded.

"What about Leon? And the others?"

"What they did was outside Baxter County," Joseph said. "The deputy can't charge them with anything."

"So it's over?" Maura stood. "Will Jimmy really leave?"

"He seemed sincere to me. Dr. Lindsay offered to take him back to Missouri in a wagon, and Jimmy is in no condition to resist."

Maura smoothed her hair back with both hands. "What Leon did was horrible. I'm not sure if I'd like to see him held accountable, or just let it all be over."

Joseph took two steps toward Maura and tapped his fingers on the edge of the desk. "That decision is not yours to make. You can't take that burden on yourself."

"Shouldn't someone?"

"*Gottes wille.*"

"God's will?"

"Yes," he said. "Can you leave it to God now?"

The muscles twitched in her face as her eyes held steady with his. They had shared an easy way with each other riding to Missouri and back. She was close enough now that he could reach out and take her hand and feel it quiver in his own. He wanted to.

He moistened his lips. "Zeke and Stephen will be nearly home by now."

"Will you be going, then?"

He searched for some sign in her face of the answer she wanted to hear. "Would you go with me?"

She was silent.

"I miss my people," Joseph said, "but the thought of leaving you weighs heavy."

She opened her mouth then closed it without speaking.

"We don't have to stay," Joseph said. "We can find another settlement. We can help to plant a settlement. You can find the life of peace you have been seeking."

Maura dropped back into the wooden chair at the desk. She had wondered if this moment might come. Even hoped it would.

Walter stuck his head through the curtains. "Are you two going to stay back here all afternoon?"

"Walter, you have work to do," Maura said.

"So do you. Daddy wants the books done today. I heard him tell you."

"I'm working on them. Please excuse us for a few more minutes."

"I'm not sure why you can't tell me what's going on."

Maura clamped her mouth closed and glared at her cousin.

"Don't tell me it's none of my business," Walter said. "I'll find out eventually. Leon Mooney will make sure."

"Then you'll just have to wait for Leon's version." The shop door jangled, and Maura heard the familiar thump of her uncle's footsteps. "There's your daddy now, Walter. Joseph and I are going to take a short walk."

With a glance toward Joseph, Maura brushed past Walter and his open mouth.

Outside, she said, "I'm sorry about Walter."

"He reminds me of Little Jake," Joseph said. "Always full of questions. You'll like him, I think."

"I'm sure I would enjoy meeting your brother," Maura said, "but the matter of leaving with you is a serious one."

"I know. I do not suggest it lightly."

Joseph straightened his hat, and Maura knew he was as nervous as she was dancing around this question. He was proposing marriage. He knew it, and she knew it.

"There is the matter of my father." Maura paced a little faster down the sidewalk. "It has been hard for him since my mother died. He depends on me."

"It seems to me a great many people depend on you," Joseph said. "Who do you let yourself depend on?"

Maura had no response. She was supposed to say God. She was supposed to depend on God, but she was not sure she could honestly say she did. And she had come to depend on Joseph, though she hesitated to admit this.

"Come with me," Joseph said, "or let me come back for you after I speak to the bishop."

"What would you tell the bishop?" And what would he tell Hannah Berkey?

"The bishop is a kind man at heart." Joseph touched her arm, causing her to slow her steps and turn toward him. "A simpler life without fearing violence from your own people—do you not want that?"

"Well, yes, I do, but—"

"And a life of faith, where your hope for peace could fill your heart?"

"In your church?" Maura asked. "Is that what you mean?"

"Do you think you could join us? We would follow the Lord together."

Maura nodded, her throat thickening.

"And a husband," he said. "Do you not want that? Do you want me?"

This was indeed a proposal.

"Joseph, I greatly admire you and have become deeply fond

of you." She nearly lost her nerve in his violet-blue eyes. "But my father. . ."

"Even the widowers among our people hire someone to keep house."

"It won't be the same." She broke the gaze and resumed walking. "And Belle. How can I leave Belle right now? She hardly knows her own mind from one day to the next. In a few weeks she is supposed to return to her duties teaching school, and I am afraid she will not be strong enough."

"Can you make her strong?" Joseph asked.

"I suppose not. But I can let her know I care for her while she makes herself strong again." Maura raised her eyes to look down the block then reached to clutch his arm. "There's Belle now. Something's wrong."

Belle hurtled toward them on foot.

"An accident." Belle put one hand on her chest as she gasped for breath. "There's been an accident."

"What happened?" Maura and Joseph spoke in tandem.

Belle looked from one to the other, seeing something between them that she had never seen before.

"A cow went over the side of a bluff." Belle focused on Maura. "My father and your father are there trying to figure out how to get to it and haul it up. But it's a full-grown cow. They need longer ropes and leverage."

"I'll go immediately," Joseph said. "Where are they?"

Belle described the location. She had run for two miles to get back to town, but a horse could close the distance in minutes.

Joseph and Maura pivoted, and the three of them marched back toward the milliner's shop.

"I'll get some rope from the livery," Joseph said.

"I'll take my cart," Maura said. "Belle, you can ride with me."

Joseph mounted his horse in one swift motion and thundered

down Main Street toward the stables. Belle lifted the hem of her skirt to keep pace with Maura as they cut down a side street to the Woodley home, where the cart and the horse occupied a small barn behind the house. Maura went through the familiar motions of hitching cart to horse, and they clattered back through town, meeting Joseph on the way.

At the bluff, Joseph jumped off his horse, a coil of rope over each arm.

"I'm going down," Belle heard her father say as he squatted at the edge of the bluff.

Belle stepped to the edge and peered. The cow lay on its side, moaning in protest. "Can't she stand up?"

"I'm going to find out." Leon Mooney tested his footing on the steep slope.

"Wait for a rope, Daddy." Belle scrambled over to Joseph, who was securing one end of a long thickly braided length to the harness of his horse. As he then tied the horse snug to a tree, Belle ran with the loop at the other end.

When she saw her father disappear from sight, she screamed.

Woody Woodley and Maura were on their knees, reaching down with their arms. Leon was beyond their grasp, caught in the branches of scrub growth.

"Daddy." Belle dangled the rope over the edge. "You should have waited for the rope, you old fool."

"I cannot afford to lose this cow." Leon's gruff reply rankled in Belle's mind. When would her father learn to think things through?

Joseph was beside her now and had taken the rope from Belle's hand. Below them, Leon wrestled with the branches and abruptly fell several feet lower.

"I'm fine," Leon reported.

Belle watched as he gripped a bush and got his feet into secure footholds.

"I'll swing the rope down," Joseph called out.

Belle held her breath as Joseph stood and wound up his arm to throw the rope wide of the bushes on the side of the bluff. As it passed him, her father reached to grab it—and missed.

This time he fell solidly on his back with a leg bent behind him, next to the groaning cow.

Belle leaned over the side precariously herself. "He's not moving."

"Give him a minute," Joseph said. "He's had the wind knocked out of him."

Finally, Leon Mooney pushed himself up on one side and attempted to stand. Instantly he howled and sank back down. Belle saw the bone protruding below his knee.

Joseph sighed. "Looks like we'll have to haul them both up now."

"If he had just waited two more minutes," Belle said, "we could have gotten him down there safely."

"Belle," Joseph said, "we'll get him up. Don't worry."

"What about the cow?"

"Let's worry about your father."

"He won't want to come up without the cow."

Joseph looked over the ledge. "Neither of them is in immediate danger, but your father is going to need a doctor to look after that leg."

"I'll go for Dr. Lindsay," Belle said. "I'll take Maura's horse."

"He's out of town." Joseph decided not to tell Belle that Dr. Lindsay was escorting Jimmy Twigg out of the county. "You'll have to go for Doc Denton."

"Doc Denton! You want me to ask a Denton to look after my father after what they did to my John?"

"It's the best thing for your father." Joseph glanced at Maura, who nodded.

"I'll go with you," Maura said.

"No." Belle looked down at her father again. "I can do it if you'll let me take your horse."

"Of course."

Belle was swiftly astride the horse with knees in its flanks. As she thundered down the road, Woody Woodley stood up. "Get another rope ready. I'll go down."

"Let me," Joseph said. He was a good forty years younger than Woody Woodley and trusted his own reflexes against Leon's rash impulses.

Forty-Four

July 1892

Maura watched her father pick up his newspaper from the sideboard in the dining room and shuffle into the front room to sit in the chair that had been his favorite since before she was born. A few years ago her mother had insisted on sending it out for new stuffing and fresh fabric, and Maura was glad she had. The alternative had been to haul the chair to a trash heap. At least this way Woody Woodley got to enjoy its familiarity.

She saw the stoop in his shoulders, more pronounced since Leon's rash retribution against the Twiggs had drawn her into harm's way and his equally impulsive attempt to single-handedly rescue a fallen cow had raised Woody's heart rate for an entire afternoon. From the doorway between the dining room and the kitchen, Maura watched him settle into the chair, pick up his glasses from the end table that had been a wedding present from her grandparents, and scan once again the same newspaper he had read from start to finish over his breakfast five hours earlier. He was likely to spend the entire afternoon there, and she would never know what thoughts passed through his mind.

He was tired. And alone. He had plenty of longtime friends in Baxter County, but Maura knew they did not fill the void her mother's death had left. She did not pretend that she filled it, either, but she was his daughter. As much as she could not stand the thought of Joseph's departure, neither could she imagine leaving her father. Joseph would have to understand. After all, the ties of family bound his community together.

Maura was not entitled to any hold on Joseph. Already he had stayed several days longer than he should have, hoping for a change of her heart. But there would be none.

She could not leave her father.

She could not leave Belle.

Perhaps Joseph would return to Tennessee and find happiness with Hannah Berkey after all.

Maura pushed the swinging door open and went through to the kitchen. Leon Mooney's leg was broken in two places. Belle had hardly left his bedside in the last four days, refusing several offers of assistance from Gassville residents. Maura could not do much to make Belle's emotional tumult easier, but she could at least spare Belle having to worry about food. She laid a towel in the bottom of a basket and began to arrange small covered dishes in the flat bottom.

She glanced at the clock. In five hours Joseph Beiler would appear at her front door for the meal to which she had invited him.

Outside her father's bedroom, Belle took the sodden handkerchief from her skirt pocket and dabbed at her eyes for at least the twentieth time that day.

How could she have thought that caring for her father while he recovered from his injury would somehow bring them closer? She had been a fool about so many things in the last year.

The bell to the front door rang.

"Whoever that is, tell them to go away," Leon barked.

Belle straightened her shoulders and stuffed her handkerchief back in her pocket. "I will make sure you are not disturbed."

"Take these dishes away. I don't want to eat this rot."

Belle went into the bedroom to retrieve the tray she had only brought up only ten minutes earlier. The bell rang again.

"Didn't I tell you to make them go away?"

"One thing at a time." Belle lifted the tray from the bed.

"Don't give me back talk."

"No sir." Belle left the room as swiftly as possible. In the hall, she set the tray on a table and flew down the stairs to answer the door before the bell could ring again. She opened the door to Maura and another basket of food.

Belle forced a smile. "Hello, Maura." She stepped aside so Maura could enter.

"You must think I'm trying to feed an army." Maura lifted the basket, and Belle took it from her. "I just want to help, and I don't know what else to do."

Belle burst into tears. "You're trying to fix something that can't be fixed."

Maura enfolded Belle in her arms, and Belle did not protest.

"Is he not any better?"

Belle wiped her tears with the back of one hand. "He has only been immobile for four days, and already he has pointed out my every failure in how I care for him."

"He is lucky he has you."

Fearful that their voices would waft up the staircase, Belle led the way to the kitchen. "I thought he would calm down. He hated the thought that I wanted to marry John Twigg, and that's impossible now. Then he made sure I could never have anything to do with Old Man Twigg and chased off John's brothers."

"I'm sorry that he cannot see the tenderness of your heart," Maura whispered. "I'm sorry that *I* could not see the tenderness of your heart."

"Why can't my father ever leave well enough alone?" Belle set the basket on the kitchen counter and began to unpack it. "I have nothing left of the family I thought I would spend my life with, and that's not enough. How long is he going to punish me?"

"This business between the Twiggs and the Dentons—"

"A feud," Belle said. "You can call it what it is."

Maura turned her palms up. "It wasn't always that way. The people of Gassville remember better days."

"But no one will ever forget that it was a Twigg who shot Sheriff Byler." Belle opened the icebox and set a plate of ham slices inside.

Maura fiddled with the edge of the towel lining the basket.

Belle reached for her handkerchief again. "I think maybe you're the only friend I have left in this town."

"I'm sure that's not true," Maura said. "You teach half the children in town. So many families know how lucky they are to have you in the classroom. You'll see. Things will be better once school starts in the fall. Gassville will see better days again."

Belle looked at Maura's face for the first time since she arrived. Maura was saying the right words, but the sentiment was absent from her countenance.

"What about Joseph?" Belle asked. "Are you. . .will you go with him?"

"He wants me to."

"Love is powerful."

"But not simple."

Maura's roast was tender and juicy, just as it should be. Her baking powder biscuits were lofty and fluffy. The green beans had a just-picked flavor that made Joseph homesick. The potatoes were free of lumps and nearly floating in butter, just the way Joseph liked them.

Yet the pall over the meal nearly strangled him.

Maura's eyes followed her father's movements more than anything else. No matter how many times Joseph tried to catch her glance, she had another place to look, something to fetch from the kitchen, a dish to pass. By the time she brought out cherry pie and coffee, the three of them were eating in near silence.

Woody dabbed his lips one last time and scraped back his chair. "I believe I will retire early. You young people enjoy the evening."

"Are you all right, Daddy?" Maura asked.

"I'm fine. Just tired."

Joseph waited until Woody was well on his way up the stairs before speaking.

"Come with me, Maura. Your father would want you to be happy."

"How could I be happy without him?" Maura stacked the dessert dishes.

Joseph stilled her motion with both of his hands. "Can you be happy without me?"

Tears welled in her eyes. "I understand that you can't stay in Gassville," she said. "You've tried our *English* ways. They are not your ways. But my father. . .and Belle."

"You haven't answered the question."

She looked away, refusing to meet his eye. "No. Probably not happy. But I will have a fulfilling life."

Joseph cleared his throat. "In case you should have any uncertainty, I want you to know I feel the same. I know I cannot remain here, but without you. . ."

"Hannah is waiting for you. She loves you, and she knows the ways of your people."

He shook his head. "I will not marry Hannah Berkey."

"You should."

"No, I shouldn't. She deserves better."

"Better than you? She will not find such a man."

"She deserves a better love than I would give her. She would know my heart was elsewhere." Joseph laid his hands in his lap under the generous drop of the tablecloth. "I will set out tomorrow. First thing."

Maura exhaled. "I know you must go."

"But I will come back. Belle's father will get well. They will find their way back to each other. With time she will believe that happiness is possible once again."

"Perhaps. And my father?"

"I pray God makes His will clear."

Forty-Five

A tap on the shoulder made Ruth turn around just as she finished ordering her sandwich at the Main Street bakery on Saturday.

"Bryan! Hi."

"I hope I didn't startle you."

"No. I'm sorry I didn't see you come in." Ruth gestured to the handwritten menu above the counter. "Are you going to have something to eat?"

"I think I will. Let me buy your lunch, too." Bryan asked for a roast beef on rye. "We never got to have the dinner I promised you in Walsenburg."

The clerk took the twenty-dollar bill Bryan offered and counted back change. Ruth and Bryan moved to one of the small tables to wait for their food.

"The bread is so good here," Ruth said. "I confess it's better than anything I make."

"I'm glad I ran into you." Bryan pulled two napkins from the dispenser on the table. "I've been wanting to talk to you about a couple of things."

"Oh?" Ruth hung her purse on the back of the chair.

"I'd still like to take you to dinner—a proper date."

"You just bought my lunch. Thank you, by the way."

"You're welcome. But I'd still like to spend more time getting to know you."

The clerk came around the end of the corner and set their plates in front of them. Ruth rearranged the two halves of her ham sandwich and the dill pickle.

"Maybe it's just as well we didn't go to dinner," she said. The last thing she wanted to do was hurt Bryan Nichols. "My life is. . . well, a little inside out right now."

Bryan bit into his sandwich and chewed, not moving his eyes off Ruth. After he swallowed, he said, "Is this because of what Alan said to you?"

"What do you mean?" Hoping to appear less nervous than she felt, Ruth bit into her own sandwich.

"He flipped out about that water strap. He said he was going to make sure you knew it could just as well be mine. I couldn't talk any sense into him."

"He did make that point rather adamantly."

"You don't believe him, do you?"

She set her sandwich down and put her hands in her lap, where it would be less obvious that she could not hold them still. "No, I don't. I've learned to trust my own impressions about people. And I trust you."

"Good."

"Alan makes me unsettled, though. I think I might talk to the sheriff."

"I'll go with you," Bryan said quickly. "As soon as we finish eating."

Ruth perked up. "Really?"

"That strap is a small thing, but I know it's not mine. I haven't been able to get it out of my head."

"I'd love to have you come with me," Ruth said. "It might mean something coming from a person who actually knows Alan."

"It's the right thing."

She smiled. "You're a good man, Bryan Nichols."

"I am glad to hear you say that. I hope it means you will reschedule dinner." He chomped into his sandwich again.

"I'd better not." Ruth winced inwardly. "It wouldn't be right."

Bryan chewed slowly. "It's Elijah Capp, isn't it?"

"Yes," she answered. "And I don't think it will ever be anyone else."

"Are you sure you don't want to back out?" Elijah asked.

"Why?" was Annie's retort. "Do you want to back out?"

"I didn't say that."

"You're giving up your only mode of transportation."

"Amos has a buggy for the business." Elijah stroked the horse's neck one last time. "I'm not sure how much longer he'll let me work for him since he knows I'm leaving the church, but he'll let me use the buggy until the time comes."

Annie signed the check. The price of a horse and buggy would make a serious dent in her bank account once the check cleared, but it was time. She could not ride her bicycle around the hills all winter.

"Are you sure Rufus is going to understand this?" Elijah folded the check in half without looking at it and tucked it into his shirt pocket.

"Is there something about your horse that you don't want Rufus to know?"

"Of course not."

"Then leave Rufus to me. I want to surprise him."

"Taking care of an animal is a lot of responsibility."

"Save the lecture for your own *kinner* someday." Annie ran her hands along her new pitchfork. "I've mucked enough stalls with the Beiler sisters to have some idea what I'm doing."

Elijah grabbed the strapping around a bale of hay and tossed it onto the floor of the garage. "I wish you'd let me come by and do it for you."

"I don't want to get dependent. You won't be here much longer."

"Until I go, then. I won't leave before Ruth does."

"I'm sure she doesn't want you to." Annie surrendered the pitchfork, and Elijah used it to spread hay.

"Are you sure you're ready to drive on your own?"

"I have to do it sometime, don't I?" Annie kicked at the hay, remembering the first time she stumbled into the Beiler barn accidentally and hardly knew what to make of the horses and cow and buggies she saw there. Whatever Rufus decided about his property, she could at least bring this much to their marriage. It was an old horse and an old buggy. He could not object that she had splurged unnecessarily.

"What have we got here?" Ruth paused at the end of the driveway. "Is this what I think it is?"

"*Ya*." Annie took the horse brush off the hook where Elijah had hung it and began running it through the horse's mane.

"The garage is a barn now?"

"The lot is zoned for horse property. I hope you don't mind parking the car in the driveway."

Ruth grinned. "If Elijah was going to sell to anybody, I'm glad it's you."

Annie looked from Ruth to Elijah. Their eyes locked on each other. If ever two people belonged together, it was Ruth and Elijah.

Ruth's phone rang, and she reached into her bag to find it and look at the caller ID. "It's the sheriff."

"I have Alan Wellner here," the sheriff intoned.

"But I only just spoke to you a few minutes ago." Ruth's chest tightened. "I didn't realize things would move so fast."

"Don't worry," the sheriff said. "We didn't have to make a scene. We found him at home, and he agreed to come in for questioning under his own volition."

"That's good, I guess."

"It's very good."

Ruth took in the puzzled expressions on the faces of Annalise and Elijah. She had not yet told either of them that she had decided to talk to the sheriff.

"What are you charging him with?" Ruth was almost afraid to hear the answer. At least no one had been hurt in any of the fires.

"Nothing yet. We don't know that Wellner did anything. We have only the opinions of you and Mr. Nichols that he might have."

"Yes. Right. Sorry."

"I made it clear this was not an arrest. We'd only like to have Mr. Wellner answer a few simple questions to determine if we consider him a person of interest. The thing is, he said he won't talk to us unless he gets to talk to you first."

"Me?" Panic welled. "I thought you weren't going to tell him where the lead came from."

"We didn't."

Ruth swallowed her anxiety. Alan must have figured it out for himself. If they had asked him about the strap, it would not have been difficult.

"You'll be perfectly safe," the sheriff said. "I'll have an armed officer in the room with you at all times, and I'll watch through the glass."

"I don't want him to get hurt," Ruth said.

"We all hope it won't come to that. He seems calm for now, just adamant that he must speak to you."

"What if I don't come?" The phone trembled in Ruth's hand. What had seemed like the obvious next step a few hours ago at the bakery with Bryan now felt like a personal risk she had failed to calculate.

"If we can't get him to talk, we may have to let him go. Unless we can get a psych hold. That might get us a couple of days."

Ruth had seen enough television shows to know what a psychiatric hold was. She looked up at the befuddled Elijah and Annalise.

"Can I bring my friends with me?"

"Bring anybody you want," the sheriff said, "but he wants to talk to you, nobody else."

Ruth's mouth had gone more completely dry than she had ever experienced.

"I'll be there in a few minutes." She clicked the phone closed.

Elijah stood the pitchfork on end in the hay. "Wherever you are going, I am going."

Ruth let out her pent-up breath. "I wouldn't have it any other way."

Ruth clenched Elijah's hand unabashedly as the two of them and Annalise walked to the sheriff's office.

"Do you have any idea why he is so emphatic about speaking with you?" the sheriff asked when she walked through the door.

"None whatsoever." Unless he was going to threaten her. Or Bryan. Or Elijah.

"What is the nature of your relationship?"

Ruth scrunched up her face. "We don't have a relationship. Alan is a friend of someone I met a few weeks ago—Bryan Nichols. He was here with me earlier. I already told you everything I know."

"An officer is with Mr. Nichols now trying to verify the existence of the water bottle strap."

"Can I just get this over with?" Ruth returned Elijah's squeeze on her hand.

"Your friends can have a seat and wait here."

Reluctantly, Ruth disentangled her fingers from Elijah's. At least he would have Annalise with him and Ruth could be sure he would be there when she emerged. She followed the sheriff into a sparse side room, where she found Alan seated on one side of a metal table. Just as the sheriff had promised, an armed officer stood against one wall.

The sheriff pulled a digital recorder out of his shirt pocket. "Mr. Wellner, would you have an objection if we recorded your conversation with Miss Beiler?"

Alan met Ruth's eyes finally. "Ruth, do you mind?"

She shook her head, not trusting her voice.

"Go ahead," Alan said.

The sheriff put the device on the table and pressed a button. "I'll be just outside," he said to Ruth.

Ruth nodded, still mute, and the sheriff left. She tried not to let her eyes drift to the officer against the wall.

Alan smiled his broad, affable grin. "Am I making you nervous?"

She moistened her lips. "A little."

"I wonder what you must think of me. I don't blame you. If the tables were reversed, my imagination would be running wild."

"I just want the fires to stop," Ruth said. "I hope we can help make that happen."

"When we were kids," Alan said, "Bryan was the one fascinated with matches." His lips turned up. "Surprised? I tried to tell you that you don't know him very well."

"Matches are dangerous," Ruth said, "but even Amish children are sometimes curious."

"Bryan used to start fires in a metal trash can so he could time how long it took him to put them out."

Ruth sat motionless, feet together under the table and hands in her lap. "He told me that he'd always wanted to be a firefighter."

"Sometimes there is a fine line between being a fire starter and a firefighter."

Ruth had no response.

Alan leaned back nonchalantly in his chair, tipping it precariously as Ruth had seen him do before.

"My father was furious when I said I wanted to study fire science rather than business." Alan let his chair legs fall to the floor with a clank. "Well. You saw how he is. Imagine living with that all the time."

"I'm sorry you did not get along with your father."

"Instead of applying to an elitist four-year college, I enrolled at the community college. They have a great program."

"I've heard that."

"It's true." Alan scraped his chair back a few inches.

Ruth was relieved to see that the officer behind Alan had taken note of his movement.

"Maybe I wanted to be found out," Alan said. "Maybe I dropped that water bottle strap on purpose. Did you ever think of that?"

"So it was your strap."

"You are more observant than I gave you credit for. How many people would pay attention to something like that?"

Ruth refused to divert her gaze. "You did drop it when you set the fire in Joel's field."

He slapped the table. "Why, yes, I did. I was supposed to discover that fire, but you and Bryan turned up first."

"And the others?" Ruth hoped she was asking questions that might be useful to the sheriff.

"I made sure no one would get hurt. Only empty structures with space around them."

Ruth waited.

"I tried to vary things just enough to break the patterns we learned about in school."

She waited some more, mindful of the recorder on the table.

"If my father could see that I was doing something important, he would get off my back and let me follow my own career."

"So you were going to solve the arson case." The light went on in Ruth's mind. "You were going to set Bryan up. You wanted to be the hero who put out the fire, and then you wanted to expose Bryan as the one who set the fires. That's why you wanted to make me doubt him."

"I miscalculated you," Alan said. "I did not want to believe you were anything more than a naive Amish girl."

The knot in Ruth's throat was about to choke her.

Forty-Six

Ruth sat at Annalise's dining room table with her chair scooted toward Elijah's and one arm linked through his elbow. She was not sure when she would be able to let go.

"You were so courageous." Annalise carried a pot of coffee in one hand and three mugs by the handles in the other. She set everything in the middle of the table.

"I wish I could do something to help Alan." Ruth used her free hand to pull a mug closer.

Annalise poured coffee. "I think you did."

"I wish he didn't have to go to prison."

Elijah patted her arm. "I understand sometimes the *English* work out a deal of some sort."

"If he cooperates," Annalise said, "the charges might not be as severe as they could be. Either way, I suspect he'll get some mental health help."

"I hope so." Ruth poured cream in her coffee.

"I've been reading a book about Arkansas history," Annalise said. "There was a Sheriff Byler who was killed by an outlaw. Well, I suppose killing the sheriff is what made him an outlaw. They sent out posses, but he got away. From what I read, they would have hanged him on the spot if they'd caught him. I like to think that law enforcement is more humane now, while still keeping people safe. If Alan needs help, that's what he should get."

"And Leah?" Elijah asked. "Do you think she will cooperate with getting help?"

Annalise nodded. "It's her best hope for getting what she wants—to go to Pennsylvania with her parents' blessing."

Ruth took a long swallow of coffee and set her mug down. "We should go out to the house for supper."

Annalise glanced at the clock on the wall. Her eyes lit. "We have time to help set the table. Franey won't mind the extra mouths. I'll drive."

"Oh, no, no, no." Ruth waved her free hand. "It will be dark soon, and you don't have enough experience driving a buggy at night. We'll take the car, and I will drive."

Annalise pouted. Ruth picked up her coffee.

"Word will get around town quickly that the sheriff has detained Alan," Ruth said. "I realize my parents might not have any reason to go into town for quite a while, but I want them to hear about what happened from me."

"I agree," Annalise said. "And I'd love to tell Rufus about how things went with Leah."

Ruth realized she was going to have to let go of Elijah to drive.

"I'll check on the horse." Elijah pushed his chair back. "Perhaps you can drop me at my new place."

Ruth clenched his arm. "You're not coming to supper with us?"

"Would you like me to?"

She lost herself in his eyes, so relieved to have him near.

"They won't approve of the decision I've made." Elijah put his hands in his jeans pockets. "I don't want to cause trouble."

"They're going to have to get used to it." Ruth stood and pulled Elijah to his feet. "I think they will be pleased that we are going to be a package deal after all."

Elijah grinned.

Annalise gasped. "Is it all settled?"

Ruth chuckled. "We haven't even talked about it yet. But I don't think there will be much to discuss."

Elijah cleared his throat. "Now if Rufus would just get it through his head that it is God's will for him to propose to you."

Ruth caught the smile that Annalise tried to obfuscate. "He has, hasn't he?"

Annalise nodded.

Ruth finally let go of Elijah in order to embrace her friend. "Why didn't you say anything?"

"It only happened yesterday. And you can't say anything! He wants to be traditional and wait until the banns are read."

As Ruth backed the car out of the driveway a few minutes later, Leah approached on the sidewalk. Ruth stopped and rolled her window down.

Leah leaned in. "I came home this afternoon and there was a horse in the garage."

"There still is." Annalise leaned forward from the backseat. "He's mine. The buggy, too. You probably recognize it. You drove it."

"Don't remind me." Leah rolled her eyes. "I'm so sorry for all the trouble I caused that day."

Ruth pushed the button for the automatic unlock of the back door. "Why don't you get in? We're going out to my family's farm."

Leah's eyes widened. "Why would you invite me?"

"I think you'll be interested to hear some of the things we're going to talk about." Ruth reached behind her seat and pushed open the door from the inside. "Besides, they are your people, your church. You should get to know them."

"Wait a minute," Annalise said from the backseat. "I have one condition."

Ruth scrunched up her forehead.

Annalise put a finger to her lips. "No one says a word, not one word, about the horse in my garage. I want to surprise Rufus when the time is right."

A week later, Annie felt as if tectonic plates had shifted.

A public defender representing Alan struck a deal with authorities that would assure he got the help he needed. And Alan wrote an article for the local newspaper apologizing to the entire town for the disruption and anxiety he caused. His father refused to see him, but his mother had driven down from Colorado Springs to make sure he knew she had not given up on him.

Leah had eaten breakfast and dinner with Annie every day for the past week. She still wandered during the day, but she accepted a jacket from Annie and came home before dark every day. During Friday's session with Jerusha she nodded agreement to let Ruth drive her to Pueblo to see the counselor in her office once a week and not to try to leave Colorado before they both agreed she was ready for the life waiting for her in Pennsylvania. Annie would make sure the counseling bills were paid.

Just after ten on Saturday morning, Leah brought the horse in from the small pasture behind Annie's house.

"Are you sure you don't want me to drive?" the girl asked.

Annie patted the side of the horse's neck and slipped the bridle over his head. "I admit I'm glad to have an experienced buggy driver with me, but I feel ready."

"It's ten miles—twice as far as the Beilers'."

"I know. You can help me harness the horse to the buggy."

Together they positioned the horse in front of the buggy and double-checked the arrangement of leather straps.

"Let's go." Annie hoisted herself up onto the buggy bench and took the reins in her hands.

Leah climbed up beside her and let out a protracted, well-managed sigh.

"Nervous?" Annie asked.

The girl nodded. "I've been practicing in my head all day what I'm going to say."

Jerusha had encouraged Leah to make an initial overture toward peace with her parents as a first step.

"Did you mail your letter to Aaron?"

"Yesterday." Leah rubbed her trembling hands across the fabric of her lap. "And I'm going to keep on writing even if he doesn't write back."

"He wants to respect your *daed*." Annie signaled the horse to begin the trek.

"I know. And I love him for it. It shows me how much he wants to be a man of respect."

"I do want to make one stop," Annie said.

Leah smiled with one side of her mouth. "Rufus?"

"Yes, Rufus."

An hour later, Annie turned her rig into the long Beiler driveway. Eight-year-old Jacob looked up from where he was scattering chicken feed. He dropped the bucket of food and lit across the clearing to Rufus's workshop. Annie did not try to stop him. By the time Rufus emerged from his work, Annie had parked the buggy and was leaning casually against its frame.

"Good morning." Rufus looked around. "Where has Elijah gone off to so quickly?"

"Elijah is not here," Annie said.

Rufus grinned. "He's a brave man to loan you his horse and buggy."

"He didn't loan it to me. He sold it to me."

Rufus planted his feet and crossed his arms. "Annalise Friesen, what have you done?"

"We're going to need our own rig." She moved toward him. Little Jacob dashed to the house. Annie knew in a matter of moments Franey and the girls would scramble down the porch steps to see for themselves what Jacob was even now describing to them. "No matter where we live, we'll need a buggy."

Rufus's violet-blue eyes, inherited through ten generations, shone in the cerulean of the Colorado sky.

Annie stepped closer. "I trust you to make the right decision about the land and where we live and how we make our livelihood—and even when to marry. If you want to wait, we'll wait." She paused to point at the buggy. "But you don't have to face anything alone. I'm not going anywhere. This is my down payment on our future."

She wished he would kiss her then, and she knew he wanted to, but the screen door snapped open and footsteps tumbled down the wooden steps. Rufus touched his hat and nodded ever so slightly, and she saw the flash of approval roll through his complexion.

When Annalise had gone and the commotion settled, Rufus saddled Dolly. In a leather bag he had carried for years, he packed his sketch pad, two charcoal pencils, and three apples for the horse. After nearly seven years on the farm, he knew its boundaries well. He could recall from memory the surveyor's legal description of the property he and his father had chosen when they pooled their resources to buy land and erect a sprawling house for the eight members of the Beiler family who joined the new settlement.

He rode now around the perimeter of the land and then followed the horse paths that cut through it, dividing fields. His parents always talked about someday building a *dawdi* house where they would retire to enjoy grandchildren by day before sending them back to the main house and their parents—whoever that would be—when they tired of them. Joel would take over the farm, Rufus had always assumed. He had a much richer love of the soil than Rufus did, and it was too early to say what Jacob might like to do.

But the land could sustain a third house. If he situated it at the far corner, it would not interfere with the crop rotations and irrigation rows.

Rufus slid out of the saddle and stood to gaze at the line where the land met the sky. In his pad, he sketched the layout of the farm and drew rectangles for the existing buildings. He marked off where a new house could sit, with its front porch soaking up the vista of the Sangre de Cristos just as the main house did.

For now he and Annalise would be happy living on the farm with his parents. Rufus did not know if Larry's Denver clients would choose to make an offer on his land. He did not know if the land might sit empty for two years or five years. He did not know if the farm would turn the corner toward financial stability. He did not know if he would build a home on the land he had purchased or here on the corner of the farm.

When the time was right, he would build Annalise a house, and wherever it was, it would be the right place because Annalise would be there and their children would be there. Time would reveal *Gottes wille*, and Rufus only wished to stand in that place.

Annie took the buggy over the final ridge and pulled on the reins slightly to slow the horse's gait down the gentle slope onto the Deitwaller farm.

"You're coming with me, aren't you?" Leah asked. "Into the house, I mean."

"If that's what you want." Annie intended all along to be at Leah's side. Unlike her last encounter with Leah's mother, this time Annie was armed with the truth, and she was prepared to step in if Leah's composure diminished.

Leah sat forward on the bench. "There are my brothers. What rascals. I'm sure they are supposed to be doing chores."

The boys, tumbling over each other on an empty wagon bed, had spotted the buggy and now stood still to watch the arrival.

"*Mamm*!" The older one turned toward the house and hollered. "It's Leah!"

Annie slowed the rig and pulled alongside the boys.

"Have you come home?" the younger boy asked.

"I've come to talk," Leah answered calmly. "Do you know where *Daed* is?"

"In the barn."

"Will you please go get him?"

Both boys sprinted toward the barn. The screen door creaked open, and Annie looked up to see Eva Deitwaller standing in front of the house with a mixing bowl in her hands.

"*Daed* will want to finish what he's doing." Leah slowly climbed down from the buggy bench. "He likes to do one thing at a time."

Annie noticed Leah glance toward the barn rather than move closer to her mother. The scene reminded Annie of a standoff in a B-rated cowboy film, the sort of thing she and her sister used to laugh at on Saturday afternoons when they were kids. This time, though, Annie felt the tension, wondering who would make the first move.

Leah's father finally emerged from the barn. In no rush, he paced across the yard, halting only when he was within a few feet of his daughter. As if on cue, his wife now approached. Beside Annie, Leah tensed.

"You look well." Mr. Deitwaller inspected Leah, who wore a freshly laundered dress and crisp prayer *kapp*.

"You're thin." Mrs. Deitwaller examined Leah from head to toe. "I suppose that's what comes from living like a wild animal."

"Leah is not a wild animal." Annie took a half step forward.

Leah stopped her. "I've been staying with Annalise. I'm going to stay there until I'm ready to go to Pennsylvania."

"You've still got that nonsense on your mind?" Mrs. Deitwaller scowled. "I've got work to do, so if you've come to say something then just say it."

"I know you asked Aaron not to write to me, and he has respected your wishes. But he has written to Annalise. His parents have invited me to live in their home."

"I won't have it."

"In three weeks I'll be eighteen." Leah's jaw was set. "I'm going to work hard to make better decisions, and I don't want to hurt anyone. But Aaron wants me, and his parents want me, and I want to go. I have come to ask your blessing."

"You'll do no such thing." Mrs. Deitwaller shook a finger in Leah's face. "You'll not have our blessing."

Leah's features strained against the assault, and her breathing quickened as she clenched her hands behind her back.

Annie spoke softly. "Your daughter is going to go. Wouldn't it be better if she left on peaceable terms? That's all she asks."

"This matter does not concern you." Mrs. Deitwaller glared at Annie.

"Eva." Mr. Deitwaller had only to speak one word in that tone to silence his wife. "I am the head of this household. It is my decision whether to give Leah my blessing. Everyone deserves forgiveness. And love."

Annie intertwined her arm with Leah's. The girl trembled as her father stepped toward her and kissed her cheek.

Forty-Seven

July 1892

The night yawned deep and dark, taunting Joseph with every wakeful shift on top of his bedroll. In the midsummer heat, he lay watching the moon's progression across the sky. He both yearned for the release daybreak would bring him and dreaded the finality.

No. Not finality. Maura would change her mind. The weeks since his arrival in Gassville seemed to him a lifetime away from the ways of his people, but to Maura they would have been brief and muddled with anxiety, frustration, confusion.

Joseph rolled onto his side and tucked a hand under his neck. A brush of pink teased his flittering eye open, and he sat up with a sigh. The moment could not be far off now, but first he would start the day with prayer. For Maura. For Belle. For Woody. Even for Leon Mooney. And for Hannah and Little Jake.

For the light of God's gracious will and hearts ready to see it and accept it. He breathed deeply and began to speak his prayers softly.

When he opened his eyes, dawn had broken with sufficient light for Joseph to gather his belongings and slide the stable door open and lead his horse out. He took the steed to the trough and pumped water. While the animal drank, Joseph slapped the blanket over the horse's back and filled the saddlebags.

"Joseph."

He spun at the sound of her voice, and Maura stepped from the early morning gray.

"I couldn't sleep all night," she said.

He straightened his hat with both hands. "I was awake as well."

"I wanted to see you one more time."

The sun lit her from behind, casting a glow around her that would have been angelic if his heart were not cracking. Joseph was unable to speak.

"I'm worried for you," Maura said. "You're going to face judgment, and it is all my fault."

"No. No." He stepped toward her and held out a hand.

"There's no telling what Zeke will have told everyone by the time you get home."

"Stephen will have the bigger mouth." Maura's hand felt so small in his. Joseph tightened his hold.

"What does it matter? Either way, it's the same in the end."

He shifted his hand to intertwine his fingers with hers. She offered her other hand.

"It is true that some of my people will say I was foolish to get involved with the *English*, that I fell into temptation. They will say God's will brought me back from the brink."

"And you?" Maura searched his face. "What will you say?"

Joseph felt the tremble in her fingers laced through his. "I have no regrets."

He leaned in to kiss her. She offered soft, eager lips, and he owned them until they were both breathless.

"Joseph," she murmured when they stepped apart.

"Shh." He put a finger on her lips. "I will be back. Those are the last words I want you to hear from me."

She kissed his fingertips but said nothing. Joseph swung into the saddle and trotted his horse out of the stable yard. He did not dare look back.

Belle hung her handbag over one arm and a basket over the other.

The cupboards were getting bare. The Twigg store, where she had shopped for months, was closed. No one from the family was left to run it. Driving over to Mountain Home to buy the sugar and eggs she needed immediately would take longer than Belle was willing to leave her father alone. He was liable to be foolish enough to try to get out of bed on his own. Returning home promptly would require that she shop at the Denton Emporium—though she was tempted to discover how long it would take her father to worry about her absence.

Outside the emporium, only moments after it opened for the day, Belle shoved down the knot in her throat. She pushed open the door and stepped inside. Ing Denton eyed her from behind the counter. Ignoring the pressure in her chest, Belle paced slowly up the center aisle toward the basket of eggs she knew from years of experience would be sitting on a small table. She found a mixture of brown and white, glanced at the price, resolved to start keeping laying hens again, and listened idly to the conversation of two women.

"Yes, I'm starting any day now."

"But why would Woody Woodley hire a housekeeper? Maura is more than capable."

"Oh, don't tell me you haven't noticed she has a young man. He's from over in Tennessee. They'll be married before you know it."

Belle's heart nearly stopped. Maura had said nothing to her about leaving with Joseph!

But neither had she said she would not go.

Belle stomped through the store. Her father would have to wait.

She found Maura sitting in the Woodley kitchen. The breakfast dishes were still in the sink. Maura's eyes swelled and reddened with the tears she could not hold back.

"Maura, why didn't you tell me?" Belle demanded.

Maura stared at her. "What haven't I told you?"

"I thought Joseph was leaving."

"He did. I said good-bye this morning."

"I don't understand."

"Belle, what are you talking about?" Maura wiped her nose with a handkerchief.

"You're getting married."

"I'm what?"

"Did you think that because I lost John I could not be happy for you?"

"Belle, I'm not getting married. I told you, Joseph left a few hours ago."

"Then why has your father hired a housekeeper?"

"What?" Maura was on her feet now.

"I heard it with my own ears at Dentons'. Widow Sacks claims that she is going to start working for your father any day now."

The kitchen door opened, and Woody Woodley entered. "What is all the commotion about?"

"Daddy," Maura said slowly, "have you engaged the services of a housekeeper?"

"Why, yes. Mrs. Sacks and I came to an agreement yesterday. She will come in the afternoons to tidy up and make sure I have some dinner. I'm sure I can get my own breakfast. I'm not a doddering old man quite yet."

"You might have said something," Maura said.

Woody pulled out a kitchen chair and sat in it. "Maura, you've done a wonderful job of looking after me since your ma died. I admit I still miss her every day. But when your Joseph came out to rescue Leon Mooney, I saw in your eyes that you feel about him the way I felt about your mother."

"But I never told you I was leaving."

"It's just a matter of time. If it is not Joseph Beiler, it will be someone else—but I think you would be crazy as a loon not to accept a fine man like that."

Belle reached out and gripped Maura's hand. "One of us should be happy. I had my chance at love. You should have yours. Do you want Joseph?"

Joseph's kiss still lingered. Maura had not allowed food or drink to pass her lips for fear of losing his taste.

"Yes," she said. "Yes! I want Joseph Beiler."

"Then let's get you packed."

"Now?"

"Of course now. How much of a head start does he have?"

Maura looked at the clock, her bottom lip trembling. "About three hours."

"That's not so long. You're a good rider."

"I don't know the way."

"He'll follow the train tracks where there is no road. Everyone does."

Maura stared at Belle.

"It's one of the few useful things my father has said to me in the last year." Belle grabbed Maura by the elbow and pushed her out of the kitchen. "I'll get your horse. You get whatever you can stuff in the saddlebags. Wear sensible shoes."

Maura stumbled to her bedroom, unprepared for these rapid choices. She picked up the photo of her mother and slid it out of the frame then snatched up the too-small gloves. Then she gasped at her own thoughtlessness. Joseph's people would accept neither the photo nor the gloves, and she did not intend to cause him any more discomfiture than would already await him when she rode into his community with him.

From a hook in the wardrobe, she took a simple dark calico dress and rolled it into a bundle. Sitting on the bed, she took Belle's advice and changed her shoes. A black shawl was her final selection. She heard her father's steps in the hall and looked up to see him.

"You're fixin' to leave, then."

She nodded. "We'll be back. Joseph won't keep me from you."

"Come back a married woman, and you will make your daddy happy."

Maura smiled. "I can do that." She stepped across the room and kissed her father's cheek.

Joseph had already dawdled too long at the watering hole outside the railroad station in a small eastern Arkansas town. The horse had had its fill of refreshment and so had Joseph. A few other travelers had mounted and trotted away, leaving him alone. He knew he ought to be making better time, but somehow he could not make himself hurry.

He was stroking his horse's neck when he heard the thundering gallop approaching from the west. A shaft of sunlight distorted the view. Joseph thought his eyes were playing tricks, making him see what he hoped to see. The horse and rider emerged from lines of streaming brilliance and settled into a constant form.

Maura.

Her dark hair, with no hat, had lost its pins in the wind. She leaned forward, low and tight in the saddle, her knees unrelenting in the horse's side.

Joseph stepped into the road that paralleled the iron rails, spread his arms wide, tilted his head back so far his hat fell off, and laughed with glee. Moments later, Maura Woodley was in his arms. His heart, his future.

He kissed her and reveled in her eagerness to share his life.

Forty-Eight

"Are you sure you wouldn't like to be at church?" Ruth grinned at Annalise over breakfast on Sunday.

"It does feel odd not to be there." Annalise poured herself a third cup of coffee. "But Rufus wants to do things the traditional Lancaster way, and he says the bride does not come to church on the day the banns are published."

"He's right," Ruth said, "but we're a long way from Lancaster. Each district has its own traditions."

"I want it to be perfect for Rufus. I just want him to be happy."

Elijah helped himself to a second cinnamon roll. "He's marrying you. What else does he need?"

"Is the date set?" Ruth asked. "The first Thursday in November?"

Annalise nodded.

"You have a lot of sewing to do!"

Annalise twisted in a sly smile. "I bought the fabric for the dresses weeks ago."

Ruth grinned. "What color?"

"Purple. To remind me of the first Amish dress I ever wore, your purple dress." Annalise sipped her coffee. "Thank you both for keeping me company this morning."

"You haven't eaten anything." Ruth put a roll on a plate and set it in front of Annalise. "It's nice that Leah went to church—and that you let her take the buggy."

"Leah and I have come to an understanding of the heart. Of course I let her." Annalise stood and picked up her coffee, leaving the roll untouched. "I'm restless. I think I'll go sit on the front steps."

"Rufus will be along soon enough to tell you how it went." Ruth handed the plate to Annalise. "Distract yourself by eating."

Annalise ignored the plate and ambled through the house and out the front door. Ruth looked out the front window at a used seven-passenger minivan parked in front of the house.

"I can't believe you got a license to drive a car and did not tell me."

Elijah shrugged. "You got one. Why shouldn't I?"

"So you'll taxi?"

"At least for the next couple of months." Elijah picked up the roll Annalise had abandoned. "Tom is always saying he has more taxi business than he has time for and still run his hardware store properly. And I'll have room for a family."

Ruth lifted the lid on the coffee carafe to confirm her suspicion that it was empty. "I guess I'll be here alone with Leah after Annalise and Rufus get married."

"When will she go to Pennsylvania?"

"After Christmas, she thinks. She promised Jerusha a few weeks of regular sessions before she makes a major change. Yesterday her father agreed to help her with train fare."

"I suppose she and Aaron will marry soon enough."

"Even if they wait until next fall, at least they'll be together." Ruth picked at the remains of the roll on her own plate. "Elijah?"

"Yes?"

"What will our wedding be like?"

His countenance transformed. "Our wedding?"

"We're going to get married, aren't we?" Ruth dabbed at her mouth with a napkin. "I've turned you down so many times. I hope you're going to ask one more time."

Elijah stood and pulled Ruth to her feet then held both her hands. "Ruth Beiler, our wedding will be anything you want it to be."

She wrapped her arms around his neck and waited, watching his face as he lowered his mouth to her and kissed her with the longest, most delicious kiss they had ever shared.

"I still want to finish my degree," she said when they broke for air.

He kissed her again.

"That means we'll have to be in Colorado Springs."

He sought her lips again.

"It's not going to be easy. It took me a long time to get used to living in the *English* world."

This time he put a finger on her lips before kissing her yet again.

❧

The bench at the base of the Beiler staircase was a tight fit for six people adorned in new wedding clothes. Even if Annie wanted to move her arms freely, she would not have been able to. Crunched between Sophie and Lydia Beiler, her attendants wearing clothing identical to hers, Annie tried to keep her white cape and apron from becoming crumpled before the ceremony. She would have neither photograph nor ring nor pressed flowers to remember this day by. Instead, she breathed in every detail around her, committing as much to memory as her brain would hold.

She could not even get a good look at Rufus at the other end of the bench, where he was flanked by his brother Joel and Levi Staub, one of the young men Rufus employed when he could afford to take on extra help. She would have liked to get a better view of his new black suit and bow tie before the formalities began. Wedding guests had been arriving for most of an hour already. They slowly made their way past the bench where the wedding party were seated, shaking hands and offering congratulations. Annie listened for the lilt in Rufus's voice as he greeted the members of the church district by name, her chest swelling with the assurance that she would hear that voice for the rest of her life and have the joy of calling him husband. After offering their greetings, the men circled around and returned to the outdoors, while the women took their coats and shawls upstairs to the master bedroom set aside for their fellowship before the wedding.

Leah stepped through the front door of the Beiler home. Annie smiled as the girl crossed the room and then stood to kiss her cheek.

"I'm so glad you could come," Annie said.

"You're so kind to invite me. I only wish you could be at my wedding someday."

"These are my new sisters." Annie gestured to Sophie and Lydia. "I hope you will get to know them before you leave for Pennsylvania."

Behind Leah came Ruth and Elijah in unadorned simple *English* clothing. Although the bishop had advised that they should refrain from coming to church in the wake of Elijah's decision to forsake his baptismal vows and leave the congregation, they were welcome as wedding guests. Annie could not think what to say to Ruth in such a moment. When they met each other two summers ago, who could have known they would become such dear friends—and sisters-in-law? Elijah somberly shook her hand, and a wordless peace passed between them. Annie knew Elijah would lay down his life for Ruth. Whatever awaited them in the *English* world, they would face it together.

Annie hardly sat down again before her eyes listed to the next group to enter and filled with tears. She looked past Lydia and Joel to Rufus and saw that his eyes were fixed on the same sight.

"They came." She swallowed her sob. "I wasn't sure if they would."

Rufus smiled, his violet-blue eyes sparkling.

Annie wanted to run to the front door, but she held her dignified position and waited for the guests to come to her.

Her parents. Her sister. The family who had been so confused last summer by her choice to join the Amish church but who had taken Rufus into their hearts. Her parents' acceptance of the man she loved so deeply, evident by their presence on this occasion, made her knees go weak in gratitude. Annie embraced each one in turn, clasping their shoulders and feeling their heartbeats.

Ruth had walked Annie through every detail that would follow, and now she focused as much as she could through tear-brimmed eyes on the procedures.

The arrival of the bishop, who would preside at the ceremony.

The seating of her parents and Rufus's parents, who loved her as their own daughter.

The entry of the young people, some of them looking at each other with yearning before they went their separate ways, the men to sit with the men and the women to sit with the women.

A hymn began, and Annie and Rufus followed the bishop to a room that had been prepared for them to hear his words of encouragement in Christian marriage. By the time they returned to the main rooms, the congregation was singing a second hymn. The wedding party took their seats in six matching chairs. Annie and the Beiler sisters faced Rufus and his side sitters.

A sermon.

A silent prayer.

A reading from the Bible.

And the bishop's words, "What God hath joined together let not man put asunder."

The main sermon.

And the bishop's words, "If any here has objection, he now has opportunity to make it manifest."

Annie smiled at Rufus as no one made manifest any objection, and the bishop said, "If you are still minded the same, you may now come forth in the name of the Lord."

Rufus offered his hand and she took it, walking forward to stand before the bishop.

"Can you confess, brother," the bishop intoned, "that you accept this our sister as your wife, and that you will not leave her until death separates you? And do you believe that this is from the Lord and that you have come thus far by your faith and prayers?"

Rufus left not an instant of hesitation. "Yes."

The bishop turned to Annie and asked the same question. Softly, confidently, she answered, "Yes."

The bishop spoke again to Rufus, and then to Annie with the same question to which Rufus had given a somber answer.

"Because you have confessed, sister, that you want to take this our brother for your husband, do you promise to be loyal to him and care for him if he may have adversity, affliction, sickness, weakness, or faintheartedness—which are many infirmities that are among poor mankind—as is appropriate for a Christian, God-fearing wife?"

Annie's pulse pounded. "Yes."

The bishop took Annie's right hand and placed it in Rufus's right hand. "The God of Abraham, Isaac, and Jacob be with you and give His rich blessing upon you and be merciful to you. May you have the blessing of God for a good beginning, a steadfast middle, and a blessed end, this all in and through Jesus Christ. Amen."

Annie squeezed Rufus's hand, free of doubt and full of certainty that she had indeed come to this moment by faith and prayer.

Author's Note

The Valley of Choice series began with imagining the lives of people who lived three centuries ago and discovering a personal connection to them. This third story in the set comes closer to me generationally. The historical thread is based on what happened to my grandfather's grandfather, the first sheriff of Baxter County, surrounded by some embellished historical characters and a cast of people who never lived but might have. And now I've come to the end of the three stories feeling enriched by this foray into history and reflecting on the themes that follow us through the centuries and into our contemporary lives. Anger. Hurt. Grief. Vengeance. Forgiveness. Love.

I have again taken liberties with the region around Westcliffe, Colorado, in creating this confluence of what might have happened long ago and what might yet be waiting to greet us in our lives as we confront these same themes. May you name these experiences as they occur in the circumstances of your life—as they do for all of us—and find the blessing of stepping into a land of grace.

Olivia Newport's novels twist through time to find where faith and passions meet. Her husband and two twenty-something children provide welcome distraction from the people stomping through her head on their way into her books. She chases joy in stunning Colorado at the foot of the Rockies, where daylilies grow as tall as she is.

Coming soon from Olivia Newport:

Wonderful Lonesome

Amish Turns of Time

Book 1

In a struggling Amish settlement on the harsh Colorado plain, Abbie Weaver refuses to concede defeat to hail, drought, and coyotes even as families begin to give up and return east. When Abbie discovers the root of a spiritual divide that runs through the settlement, she faces her own decisions about what she believes. She must choose between a quiet love in her cherished church, passion with a man determined to leave the church, or learning to imagine her life with neither.

Summer 2014